SHADOWS & DREAMS

KATE KANE, PARANORMAL INVESTIGATOR

ALEXIS HALL

Riptide Publishing
PO Box 1537
Burnsville, NC 28714
www.riptidepublishing.com

This is a work of fiction. Names, characters, places, and incidents are either the product of the author's imagination or are used fictitiously. Any resemblance to actual persons living or dead, business establishments, events, or locales is entirely coincidental. All person(s) depicted on the cover are model(s) used for illustrative purposes only.

Shadows & Dreams (Kate Kane, Paranormal Investigator #2)
Copyright © 2014 by Alexis Hall

Cover art: Kanaxa, http://www.kanaxa.com
Editor: Sarah Lyons
Layout: L.C. Chase, http://lcchase.com/design.htm

All rights reserved. No part of this book may be reproduced or transmitted in any form or by any means, electronic or mechanical, including photocopying, recording, or by any information storage and retrieval system without the written permission of the publisher, and where permitted by law. Reviewers may quote brief passages in a review. To request permission and all other inquiries, contact Riptide Publishing at the mailing address above, at Riptidepublishing.com, or at marketing@riptidepublishing.com.

ISBN: 978-1-62649-101-4

First edition
June, 2014

Also available in ebook:
ISBN: 978-1-62649-100-7

SHADOWS & DREAMS

KATE KANE, PARANORMAL INVESTIGATOR

ALEXIS HALL

To H, again

TABLE OF CONTENTS

Prologue: Lovers & Murders 1
Chapter 1: Brothers & Bureaucrats 3
Chapter 2: Abductions & Arguments 15
Chapter 3: Questions & Cellars 25
Chapter 4: Exes & Apple Juice 33
Chapter 5: Dinner & Wankers 43
Chapter 6: News & Regrets 55
Chapter 7: Fighting & Fucking 65
Chapter 8: Hippos & Heroes 75
Chapter 9: Lockes & Doors 87
Chapter 10: Witches & Warlocks 99
Chapter 11: Friends & Lovers 113
Chapter 12: Rescues & Calls 123
Chapter 13: Dust & Ashes 133
Chapter 14: Vampires & Champagne 147
Chapter 15: Trains & Tupperware 157
Chapter 16: Angels & Demons 171
Chapter 17: Shadows & Dreams 187
Chapter 18: Wolves & Lambs 199
Chapter 19: Kissing & Telling 209
Chapter 20: Breaking & Entering 217
Chapter 21: Blood & Glass 227
Chapter 22: Metal & Feathers 237
Chapter 23: Lions & Wolves 245
Chapter 24: Conflicts & Resolutions 257
Chapter 25: Patrick & Sofia 269
Chapter 26: Serpents & Gifts 283

PROLOGUE
LOVERS & MURDERS

My name's Kane, Kate Kane. I'm a private investigator, operating out of a dingy office just off Bow Street.

Thirty-something years ago, my deranged faery queen of a mother left me on my dad's doorstep wrapped in a wolf skin, in a basket made of briars.

Fifteen years ago, I was deep in the closet, dating a vampire dickhead who hated himself, failing my A-levels, and trying to come to terms with being a faery princess. A faery princess with a bunch of scary hunter powers and a mum who keeps trying to take over her body.

Ten years ago, I'd dumped the vampire, moved to London, done a BTEC in private investigation, and got a job with a bloke named Archer.

Last year, I split up with my long-term girlfriend, slept with a client, and got my partner killed (not entirely in that order).

Three months ago, I was hired by Julian Saint-Germain, one of the four most powerful vampires in England, to investigate a murder at one of her clubs. I saved her from a crazy faery sewer lord, but along the way, I ended up striking a deal with a giant rat gestalt, swearing fealty to the Witch Queen of London, and playing sex chicken with an alpha werewolf. Also, I sort of accidentally killed a thousand-year-old vampire prince.

Oh, and me and Julian are sort of seeing each other.

CHAPTER ONE
BROTHERS & BUREAUCRATS

*S*now *was falling through silver mist on the Dream of a city.*
I edged forwards over the icy bridge, my sword raised to strike. The Sorceress raised her hand to the pearl-grey sky. The clouds cracked open. I threw myself aside, and a lance of green-tinted lightning struck the place where I'd just been standing. I rolled to my feet and charged.

Our blades met in silence.

The snow glistened on the edge of my sword and dusted the dark green coils of the Sorceress's unbound hair.

I wrapped my free hand round her sword arm and pinned it against my body, turning my own blade back to bring the point level with her throat.

She smiled. Her eyes gleamed like absinthe behind her ornate mask. She leaned towards me and ran her fingers gently across my cheek. In the half light, her nails sparkled, bright as emeralds.

I ran my sword through her throat.

She billowed into green smoke and dissipated into the mist.

I awoke to the smell of fresh coffee and the taste of wormwood. I'd been having these dreams since I'd sworn fealty to Nimue. Sometimes it was a lady in green, sometimes it was a giant pig, sometimes it was shadowy armies, and once it had been this weird monster with a snake's head, a lion's body, and rabbit's feet that I'd chased in circles and then lost somewhere in Seven Dials.

To be honest, I wasn't exactly thrilled with my new nighttime adventures, and I missed the days when the dreams I remembered involved three nuns and a set of handcuffs. But Nim had given me her help when I'd asked for it, and it could have been a lot worse.

There was a knock on the door. "It is eight o'clock, Miss Kane."

Speaking of deals with supernatural beings. Elise had been foisted on me by a crazy rat god as the price for some annoyingly vague information. She turned out to be an animated statue, but she doesn't take up much space, she brews a mean cup of coffee, and she fixed my washing machine. So it was working out pretty well.

I pulled on my fluffy dressing gown and went through to the living room. There was a mug of coffee and a banana waiting for me on the dining table. Elise was a big believer in the practical value of the humble banana.

I do not like bananas.

"Did you sleep well?" asked Elise.

She still looked like a supermodel, but since she'd started buying her own clothes, she'd taken to dressing like a librarian. She was currently wearing a long tweed skirt and a silk blouse with a grey woollen cardigan over the top. She told me once that she chose her clothes partly for their texture. I unloaded her laundry a couple of weeks ago and she's got some of the nicest underwear I've ever seen. And I like to think I'm an expert.

"Same old, same old." I slumped down at the table. "Misty London, scary chick in green, faint sexual undertone."

"I am concerned, Miss Kane. Restful sleep is a necessary biological function. I do not believe this can be good for you."

"Elise, I drink, I smoke, I'm dating a vampire." I picked up the banana and waved it under her nose. "Apart from these, I don't think I do anything that's good for me."

"That is poor reasoning. The fact that you undertake many activities that are harmful to you should lead you to minimise risks in other areas of your life. But I am pleased you are still eating your bananas."

I diligently ate my banana, finished my coffee, and got dressed. By the time I got down to the car, Elise was settled in the driver's seat and was programming the TomTom. Since Elise doesn't eat and only pays me a nominal rent, she spends most of her salary on gadgets. My flat is piling up with coffeemakers, sandwich toasters, automatic coin sorters, and hard-core power tools. She also has this remote control helicopter, but after the incident with my drinks cabinet, she's no longer allowed to use it in the flat.

I got in and buckled up. I never used to be comfortable in the passenger seat. It was kind of a control thing. But driving makes Elise so damn happy that I feel like a dick saying she can't. And I've come to appreciate the headspace. Or the extra twenty minutes sleep.

A lilting Welsh woman instructed us to turn left out of the driveway.

I gestured at the TomTom on the dashboard. "You've been driving us to work for three months now. Why do you need a satnav?"

"I thought it would be useful to have a second opinion."

"And I don't count, do I?"

"Your voice is not so pleasant, Miss Kane."

"What's wrong with my voice?"

"I do apologise. I was merely teasing. I assure you, your voice is sweet and melodious."

"Damn straight."

Sometime later, the Welsh woman helpfully informed us that we had arrived at our destination, and we went up to the office. Archer's name was still on the door, but Elise had taken his desk. She'd made a few other changes too, like getting the paperwork off the floor and into the filing cabinet, and I had about half as many unprocessed invoices and unpaid bills as I'd had three months ago.

We were just wrapping up the Fletcher case. Mrs. Fletcher had hired us to find out if her husband was cheating on her. That sort of job is the bread and butter of the detective business, but it's fucking depressing because, basically, everybody loses. Either they're cheating and so your marriage is ruined. Or they're not, in which case you've wasted a tonne of money and destroyed the trust in your relationship. Mr. Fletcher had been cheating, but it had been tough to get evidence because his mistress was a ghost, so she hadn't actually shown up on film, which meant we'd had to shell out for some good, old-fashioned spirit photography.

Wrapping up the job left me officially between cases, and frankly, there wasn't much chance of anything major coming up until after Christmas.

Elise would probably want to use the time productively to get on top of the bookkeeping. I was looking forward to taking a break, spending some quality time with my vampire girlfriend, and heading back up north to visit the folks. I hadn't seen much of Julian since I'd rescued her from the King of the Court of Love, because there'd been some major political fallout since I'd taken the Prince of Swords down a sewer, and he hadn't come out again. The advantage of not seeing someone as much as you'd like is that when you do, the sex is fucking amazing. On the other hand, since Julian is the vampire prince of pleasure that kind of comes as standard. So you're mostly left with the disadvantage, which is, well, that you don't see them as much as you'd like.

I'd known what I was getting into from pretty much the moment I walked into her office, and I'm well past my spend-every-moment-together-I-am-nothing-without-you phase, but I don't like keeping to someone else's schedule. Maybe I'm messed up, but missing her makes me feel needy, and that makes me feel annoyed, and that makes me drink too much, and that makes Elise sad, and that makes me feel guilty, and that makes me more annoyed.

And then I see Julian and it's all wonderful.

I stared moodily out of the window and thought about going outside for a fag break. Since Elise started working for me, I'm legally obliged to provide a smoke-free environment so I don't give her lung cancer, despite the fact that, as far as I know, she doesn't have lungs.

That was when Tash walked into my office.

I'd pulled her at the Candy Bar about three months ago but entirely failed to follow through. She'd given me her number and I'd given her my card, but I'd never called her and I'd never expected to see her again. It was pretty obvious this wasn't a social visit. She still had that quirky pixie look, but it was like someone had stolen all her magic dust.

"Uh, hi," she said. "I know this is weird, but I need your help."

Truth be told, it was a little bit awkward, but my social weirdness threshold has gone way up since my girlfriend tried to murder my ex-girlfriend because her ex-girlfriend tried to murder her.

"Take a seat." I waved across my desk. "Can I get you anything?"

"Perhaps a cup of tea would be appropriate?" offered Elise.

Tash huddled into a chair. "Yes, thank you." She had surprisingly good manners for a girl who'd been up for shagging in the doorway of Pizza Express. Elise disappeared into our tiny kitchenette, and Tash seemed to relax a bit.

I shunted my midmorning whiskey behind a stack of old case notes and tried to look professional. "What's the problem?"

"It's Hugh." The words came out in a rush. "My brother, Hugh, he's disappeared. But he broke his leg. We called the police, and it's been more than two days, and I'm worried. He isn't answering his phone, and nobody's seen him. There's this leaflet, and it says ninety-nine percent of people come back within forty-eight hours, but it's been forty-eight hours and he hasn't come back. And I don't know what to do."

I should probably have said something comforting but I couldn't think of anything. "Who saw him last?"

"I don't know." She picked up one of the Kane and Archer pens Elise had recently ordered for publicity which were now scattered all over the office. "Probably somebody at the hospital."

"Which one?"

"The Whittington. He broke his leg changing a lightbulb. Because he was standing on a swivel chair because he's an idiot."

"Any history of depression?"

She shook her head.

"Any personal problems?"

"No, he was doing really well. He was doing this MA at Brunel, and he'd just got this major internship or something."

"If he was at Brunel," I asked, "why did they take him to the Whittington?"

"He did it at his girlfriend's house in Highgate. He was only supposed to be in overnight but there were complications."

"And he had no enemies or anything like that?"

"What? Hugh?"

"You'd be surprised." I shrugged. "I know he's your brother, but it would be really helpful if you could find out if he gambled, drank, or took drugs or if he had any debts or dangerous friends."

She thought about it for a moment. "He played D&D."

Eve had tried to get me into that. I played a gnome paladin and got killed by a big cube of jelly when I was level 3. After that, I just hung out on the edges of the group and stole their pizza.

At that moment, Elise came in with tea for Tash and a coffee for me. "Would you like me to take notes, Miss Kane?"

"Any objections?"

Tash shook her head.

"Okay. Miss..." I suddenly remembered that Tash's surname was not *the Teetotal Lesbian*.

"Shawcross."

"Okay, Miss Shawcross is looking for her brother, Hugh, who disappeared from the Whittington Hospital in Highgate, between two and three days ago. He was being treated for a broken leg. The police are looking into it, but the family hasn't heard anything yet. The police will probably see him as low risk given his age and circumstances. He was studying for his master's at Brunel, and he'd recently started an internship. The accident happened at his girlfriend's house, which is in Highgate. As far as Miss Shawcross knows, he had no enemies, no mental health issues, and no personal problems."

"Just the broken leg," added Tash. "That's weird isn't it? Disappearing when you can't walk?"

That could have meant he'd been abducted, but the police take things like that very seriously. Since he was still floating around the MPB and hadn't been kicked up to Serious Crimes, it meant it probably wasn't a kidnapping. Or at least didn't look like one to the police. So that left either the plot of an episode of *Miss Marple*, in which a man with a broken leg discharged himself from hospital for no clear reason, or there was something supernatural going on. Right now, the supernatural explanation looked more likely. But, then again, when all you've got is an enchanted hammer, every problem starts to look like a possessed nail.

"It's a little unusual," I said, impressed with my own tact. "I'll need his contact information, current address, a photograph, as recent as you can get, digital is fine. I'll also need details of the internship, his friends, and the name and address of his girlfriend."

Tash pulled out her phone. "I'll email you some photos. It's Kane@kaneandarcher.com, right?"

I nodded. I remember when you had to wander around with a single copy of a crappy Polaroid. It's way easier now everybody puts a tonne of shit online, but you still have to remember that, whatever people say about our media-obsessed age, people don't put their whole lives on Facebook—just the bits of their lives they want their friends to know about. It's not like you ever see so-and-so has updated their status: *Borrowed 20 grand from Jimmy "Machete" Carter to fund my secret crack habit.*

Tash glanced up again. "Done. I've also sent you all his contact details and his girlfriend's address. Her name's Sarah. They met at York when he was in his first year. They've been going out forever, like three years or something."

"And the internship?"

"It was with Locke Enterprises. Hugh wouldn't stop talking about it."

Well, fuck. I was about to be hired by a woman I'd very nearly slept with to find her missing brother who was working for the woman who'd left me for a tech start-up at the tech start-up she left me for.

Not that it's a start-up anymore. I've never quite understood what Eve does, but whatever it is, it's massive. She's the only person I've ever heard of who's been on the front cover of *TIME*, *WIRED*, and *DIVA* in the same month.

There was a slightly uncomfortable silence.

"How much is . . ." began Tash. "I mean, how much do you—"

"Well, it depends on how much work I end up having to do, but it'll probably work out at about three hundred a day."

Tash turned a sort of grey colour. "Do you think you can find him?"

"I can't make any promises."

"I'll get the money. I've got some savings and I can ask my parents if I have to."

I nodded. "Have you still got the same number?"

"Yeah."

"I'll contact you if I need more information. And if you think of something or hear anything, let me know immediately."

"So, what, do I just wait around?"

"Pretty much. But I'll keep you up-to-date."

Tash nodded, put down her almost untouched tea, and made her way to the door. She turned. "Thanks, Kate."

"It's okay; it's my job. I'll do what I can."

"Okay." She left.

"Well, it looks like those accounts are going to have to wait." I tried not to sound inappropriately happy that some guy had gone missing.

"You seem devastated, Miss Kane."

"We'll need background checks on Shawcross, Tash, the girlfriend, and the family as well. There probably won't be anything, but you never know when someone is going to turn out to be a secret member of The Royal Society for the Promotion of Human Sacrifice."

"I will take care of it."

"Thanks. And try to find out a bit more about this internship. What it involved, who else went for it, that kind of thing."

"Of course, Miss Kane."

I could really get used to having Elise around. She dealt with all the things I didn't want to deal with, like paperwork and my ex-girlfriends.

I pushed back my chair and stood up. "I'm going to head to the hospital, see if I can find out why the police don't think this is shady as all hell."

"I will forward any relevant information to you."

I nodded, grabbed my hat and my coat, and jumped on the Tube to Archway. It was a short walk up Highgate Hill to the Whittington, which was one of those shiny hospitals, all yellow brick, revolving doors, and gleaming glass. The reception area looked like something out of a hotel. Or maybe a spaceship. White floor, white tiles, and a circular pine-effect desk.

I took the direct approach.

By which I mean, I lied.

"I'm here to visit Hugh Shawcross. He's in with a broken leg."

The receptionist tapped apathetically at his keyboard. "He was moved to Nightingale ward the morning after he was admitted but"—more tapping—"it looks like he's no longer a patient here."

"You mean you sent him home?"

Tap tap tap. "Mr. Shawcross appears to have informally discharged himself."

I guess that was hospital speak for *just walked out*.

"Thanks anyway."

Nobody was paying attention to what I was doing, and the receptionist was already dealing with another enquiry, so I wandered off down a corridor. Hospitals are a funny mix of high and low security. They'll never tell you anything, but because they're technically public buildings, you can bod around them as much as you like, as long you don't try to walk into intensive care or something.

I followed the signs to Nightingale ward. Once I got away from reception, it was quite busy. There was a lot of running around and people in white coats whispering to each other in the corridors. I got the feeling this was not a happy hospital. Closer to Nightingale, things got even more frenetic, and I arrived just in time to see them rushing a covered body off the ward and into an elevator.

I'm not a doctor, but this wasn't looking good.

Nightingale turned out to be the respiratory unit, which struck me as a strange place to stick a guy with a broken leg. The whole ward was in lockdown. I went to peer through the glass panels in the doors, but then I got pulled out of the way by a man in blue pyjamas who told me I shouldn't be there.

"I heard my friend was transferred."

"The ward is off limits to visitors at the moment."

I faked concern. Probably not very convincingly. I'm fine with lying, but emotions, in general, are outside my comfort zone. "Oh no. Why? What's wrong? Will he be okay?"

"The ward's very crowded, but everything's under control. Why don't you try calling the hospital for an update in a day or two?"

My distraught visitor impression had exhausted my limited acting ability. "Okay." I walked off the way I'd come.

So, Hugh had been admitted with a broken leg and ended up with some unknown contagious disease. This is exactly why I don't like hospitals.

I really, really hoped this wasn't going to be another zombie plague. There'd been an outbreak when I'd taken Eve up to Lake Windermere for our third anniversary, and we'd spent the whole weekend under siege in the hotel, making Molotovs from the minibar and clubbing reanimated tourists to death with souvenir walking sticks.

It sounded like the only thing I was going to pick up hanging round the ward was a horrible illness. It was time for a new approach. I don't know much about hospitals, but I do know if you want information about pretty much anything, you find an administrator. It's easy to be dismissive about pen pushers and bean counters, but there comes a point in your life when you really need to know where your pens are and how many beans you've got.

I followed the signs to the admin block and blustered my way into the hospital administrator's office. She was young, hot, sleek, and irate. But then I had just barged in on her unannounced. The plaque on the desk read Rhona Conway.

"Can I help you?" she asked, in a tone that suggested she intended to do nothing of the sort.

There were two ways to do this. I could be subtle and clever and tease the information out of her with a plausible sequence of well-constructed fictions. Or I could not do that.

"Name's Kane, Kate Kane. I'm a private investigator. I've been hired by the family of Hugh Shawcross to investigate his disappearance."

Rhona raised one perfectly shaped brow into a delicate arch. "Thank you, Miss Kane, but I've already told everything I know to the actual police."

Ooh. Burn.

Was it wrong that I kind of wanted to do her right there?

Okay, Kate. Be professional about this. Also you have a girlfriend. A girlfriend who can juggle cars.

"A man is missing, Ms. Conway. One of your wards is locked down. Mr. Shawcross was admitted with a broken leg, contracted an unknown respiratory infection, and then simply disappeared. This isn't looking good for you."

"I'm under no legal obligation to talk to you. In fact, I'm fully entitled to have you ejected from the building."

"Look," I said, "I don't care how you run your hospital. I don't care what's going on in Nightingale ward. All I want to do is find Mr. Shawcross. I don't want to make your job difficult, but I can."

Rhona's eyebrow went up again. *Ngh.* "Can you?"

"Mr. Shawcross's sister is very upset and very photogenic. And the only thing the newspapers love more than a kidnapping is a health scare."

"He wasn't kidnapped," she snapped.

"You seem pretty certain of that."

She sighed. "Fine, you can see the tapes if it'll get you out my hair. But there's no mystery here. He just got up and walked out."

"With a broken leg?"

"People leave hospitals with injuries and illnesses all the time."

"Why was he transferred to Nightingale?"

"That is none of your business."

"His health will affect his behaviour. Is he dying? Is he delirious? It makes a difference."

"I absolutely can't discuss a patient's confidential medical records with you."

Well, it had been worth a try. "Can you at least tell me who was on duty the night he disappeared?"

"Give me a moment." She keyed a few commands into her computer. "All right. It was Tony Suen. He's on days from Thursday, but if I find you harassing my staff, I won't hesitate to press charges."

"Don't worry, I don't harass people. I just annoy them."

Ten minutes later, I was sitting in a back office, going through security footage with a bloke called Reg. This basically came down to watching empty corridors in real time for about six hours. And it's not like you could kick back with a beer and a bucket of popcorn, although Reg did have a packet of dry-roasted peanuts, which he was happy to share. You can speed the process up very slightly by spinning through the bits where there's blatantly nothing happening, although that can be counterproductive if you're looking for supernatural creatures. Vampires move so quickly they're hard to see even at regular speed, never mind on fast-forward. Sometimes I'd see a flicker and I'd have to go back and watch ten seconds frame by frame. By the end, Reg probably thought I was nuts.

A little bit after midnight on the third of December, the doors to Nightingale ward opened and Hugh Shawcross strolled out. Well, no wonder the police ruled out abduction. He was wearing jeans and a shirt and a knitted tank top, no coat and no cast. For a man with a broken leg and an unknown respiratory ailment, he seemed remarkably healthy. It took a moment to synch up the camera feeds but I managed to track his progress through the hospital. He didn't do anything out of the ordinary, and nobody stopped him, but why would they? The last shot was him walking across reception before he disappeared into the night.

I get quite a few missing persons cases that go this way. I'd been trying not to jump to any conclusions, but from where I was sitting now, it seemed fairly clear-cut. Sudden disappearance. Short respiratory illness. Immediately healed of minor physical injuries.

Sorry, Tash, your brother's a vampire.

CHAPTER TWO
ABDUCTIONS & ARGUMENTS

rang Elise from the front entrance of the hospital.

"Good evening, Miss Kane."

"Hugh's a vampire."

"Are you attempting to convey information, or are you trying to recreate a popular Abbott and Costello routine?"

"What are you talking about?"

"I am sorry. I thought you may have wanted me to reply 'I don't know' so that you could respond with 'No, I don't know's a werewolf.'"

"Elise, you can rest easy in the knowledge that I would never, ever want you to do that."

"That, Miss Kane, is because you have no soul."

I started walking down the hill back towards Archway. "Okay, let me start again. Elise, Miss Shawcross's brother is a vampire."

"Does this mean the case is closed?"

"Well, I still haven't found him. But at least now I know what I'm looking for."

"Do you wish me to continue my current tasks?"

"There's no point shutting anything down at the moment. I don't know why he was turned, or who did it, but it's even more important we find him quickly. He could freak out and nom a bunch of people." I paused. "Actually, prioritise finding the girlfriend because she could be in danger. New vampires tend to go back to what they know, and they can have real self-control problems."

I arrived at the Tube station and started pushing my way through commuters. I'd really timed this badly.

"Very well, Miss Kane," said Elise. "Shall I meet you at home, or does this merit an all-nighter?"

"It's okay for you. Some of us actually sleep. But you're right, this is important. I'll come back to the office."

"Would you like me to compile the takeaway menus?"

"Can we just get pizza this time?"

I looked up and saw Sir Caradoc, the eldest vampire kid of the last Prince of Swords, coming towards me. People were getting out of his way quickly. I'd only met him once before, and I'd been unfortunately naked at the time.

"Give me a minute, Elise." I slipped the phone in my pocket but didn't hang up. You never know when you'll be glad someone was listening.

I glanced over my shoulder. There was another vampire behind me and two more coming in on either side. They wore sharp black suits and crisp white shirts, which made them look like the undead FBI. But, for some reason, they seemed to have the St John Ambulance cross embroidered in red on their ties.

This was also probably not a social visit.

And they also probably weren't going to teach me how to put people in the recovery position.

Sir Caradoc came steadily through the crowd and got right up in my grill. He was a chiselled, blond Hasselhoff-alike. If we hadn't been in a crowded place, and he hadn't been an eight-hundred-year-old vampire who could have ripped my head off without thinking about it, I'd have lamped him one.

"Katharine Kane," he actually fucking intoned, "by the authority of the Council, I arrest you for the murder of Aeglica Thrice-Risen, Prince of Swords."

Well, fuck.

I was dead.

I didn't even bother to think about running. He'd have caught me before I could turn round. And trying to resist arrest would look really bad. Not that I was expecting a fair trial. People who get taken away by vampires don't come back. When all else fails, try bravado.

"I don't think so. First off, I didn't do it. Secondly, if I go with you I'm fucked. If I don't go with you, I'm fucked. If I try and run, I'm fucked. If I try and fight, I'm fucked. I'd rather you just killed me now and got it over with."

"You have no choice. You will come with me, and you will stand trial for your crimes."

He stared at me coldly, and fear came crashing over me. Vampires are creatures of passion, and the half of their power that doesn't come from blood comes from overwhelming the emotions of others. Julian feeds on desire, pleasure, and surrender. My dickhead ex-boyfriend fed on the twisted needy obsession he called love. And Caradoc, like all his bloodline, feeds on fear. Things were way more fun with Julian.

I braced myself and tried to meet his gaze.

It was the primal irrational terror of childhood and phobias. The kind that freezes you and breaks you, even though you know it comes from nowhere.

I was shaking, but I tried not to show it. I dragged my head up and looked him in the eye. "Enough of that. Let's get this over with."

He blinked and it stopped.

His three minions swept in and deprived me of my knives and my phone. I didn't know how much of the conversation Elise had heard or how much use it would be anyway. I wanted to tell her not to worry, but I didn't want to let Caradoc know she might have been listening.

They marched me out of the station and into a black sedan with honest-to-God tinted windows.

I was so dead.

After a miserable stop-and-start drive through rush hour traffic, I was unloaded in front of Aeglica's rundown mansion near Holland Park. They bundled me inside and dragged me downstairs where they locked me in the cellar.

Well, fuck.

It was one of those proper dungeony cellars that TV serial killers always seem to have. Stone walls, stone floor, reinforced doors with little bars on them. I briefly wondered how you got one of these things fitted. Is there some kind of bespoke dungeon outfitter you can call in?

I checked the obvious things. Sadly, none of the flagstones were loose, the door did not conveniently lift off its hinges, and if there were any secret passages, they were too secret for me to find.

I'd been expecting this to come back and bite me in the arse. The only question had been when. Three months ago, Julian had been abducted by a crazy faery lord and I'd formed a rescue posse, which had included Aeglica Thrice-Risen, the Prince of Swords and all-round vampire badass. Things had gone, as we say in the business, tits up, and we'd only got out because Aeglica had held the faery lord down while I ran them both through with a magic sword. I still felt pretty shitty about it. Although I was going to feel a lot worse if I got executed. I had no idea how vampire courts worked, but somehow I didn't think they were big on mitigating circumstances.

There was a slightly grimy mattress in one corner of the room, which put it easily in the top ten nicest places I've ever been locked up. I went and lay down because what else can you do? I get captured a fair bit. It's kind of an occupational hazard. I should probably take up tai chi or something to pass the time while I'm waiting for the villain to come in and explain their master plan to me.

After a while, I heard raised voices outside, and then a stream of smoke and shadows poured through the grill in the door before coalescing into Julian.

She was dressed in the closest thing she ever got to formal wear—knee boots, leather trousers, outrageous cravat, military greatcoat with gold frogging and epaulettes. She looked like the bastard lovechild of Audrey Hepburn and Captain Hook, and for a moment, despite being in prison, all I wanted to do was feed her chocolate and fuck her senseless. Unfortunately it looked like that was the last thing on her mind. She had that pale, cold look that vampires get when they're seriously ticked off.

"Next time you murder one of the four most powerful vampires in England," she snarled, "I suggest you tell me. Otherwise, sweeting, we all end up looking very silly."

"I didn't murder anyone." I rolled off the mattress and got to my feet. "There was a fight. He got killed."

"On the point of your sword. On the point of the sword you were given by the Witch Queen of London."

"He told me to." It sounded pathetic even to me.

"I'm sure he did, sweeting, but you have no way to prove it." Julian paced the length of my cell. "Mercy and Caradoc are out for your blood, and there's nothing I can do about it because you didn't bother to mention this three months ago." She whirled to a halt and glared at me.

It wasn't so much that I hadn't bothered. It's just that it's hard to find a good time to tell your girlfriend that you've stabbed one of her oldest mates. I hadn't exactly been hiding it, just hoping it would never come up. "I didn't expect you to do anything about it. It's not your job to protect me."

"Strange as it may seem, Katharine," she drawled, "this is not about you. How can the Council respect me if I don't even know what my own girlfriend is up to?"

"What, you mean if you can't keep your pet mortal in check?"

"I didn't say that."

"No, but you meant it."

"I did not. But what you do reflects on me. And if you don't trust me enough to tell me the truth about something like this, then you make a mockery of . . . of . . ." She threw her hands illustratively into the air. "Everything."

I scowled. "I'm sorry I reflect badly on you. What do you want me to do? Sit at home in a white dress and bake vampire cookies?"

"Sweeting, I don't think I'm being unreasonable here." She was pacing again. "You didn't embarrass me at the company picnic. You murdered one of my colleagues, and now the rest of my colleagues are annoyed about it and want to kill us both."

There was a long silence broken only by Julian's bootheels striking the stone floor.

"Look," I said, "I'm sorry, okay, but I did what I had to do to save your, y'know, life."

"Yes, yes, you're my hero." She gave a swift, sudden smile. "But where I come from, when you rescue someone, it's bad manners to get them executed afterwards."

"How do they even know?"

Julian sighed. "Kauri."

"He sold me out?" He hadn't seemed the type.

"He didn't have a choice. He's young, and several members of the Council can read minds."

I didn't know whether that made it better or worse. He hadn't betrayed me, but I didn't like the idea of the vampire gestapo fucking around with his brain. "Is he okay?"

"We're not psychopaths." She paused. "Well, most of us. But he probably feels bad for dropping you in it, which by the way, he wouldn't have been in any position to do if I'd known what had happened."

I slumped back down onto the mattress and rested my back against the wall. "Okay, I get it, I fucked up. But what could you even have done about it?"

"In case you've forgotten, sweeting, I'm a motherfucking vampire prince. There's always something I can do."

"What about now?" I asked hopefully.

"That's the thing. It's a little late. I could bust you out of here, and we could flee somewhere beyond the reach of the Council, and we could spend our lives dodging assassins and living in youth hostels." She ran a hand through her hair. "I should just let them have you. I'd be very, very upset for a couple of decades, but I'd get over it. And, rationally, it's clearly the best option for me."

I gave her a look. "Rationally, I should have left you chained up in a sewer."

Julian came over and sat next to me. She snuck a kiss onto my cheek. "Obviously, I'm not going to do that. I have, after all, never been good at being rational."

"That's the nicest thing anyone's said to me all day. Then again, the last thing somebody said to me was 'Get in this cellar.'" There was another silence, and Julian took my hand. "So," I said, "what are we actually going to do?"

"Politics."

That youth hostel was starting to sound really tempting. "That's your plan? You go and cut dodgy deals with a bunch of bloodsucking power brokers."

"No, sweeting, *you* go and cut dodgy deals with a bunch of bloodsucking power brokers. The Council already thinks you're my pocket assassin. There's no way I can protect you and protect myself at the same time. And while I am very, very fond of you, I don't think we're in the *lay down my life* stage of the relationship."

"Why am I going out with you again?"

"Because, my one, my only, I am spectacularly good in bed."

I laughed. "I knew there was something."

Julian lifted her brows. "Many, many things. Many, many times."

I had the feeling we were getting sidetracked. "How is this going to work? And you do remember I hate politics, right?"

"Not nearly as much as politics hates you."

"No, seriously. I haven't got a clue. In case you haven't noticed, you guys are really fucking secretive. I know there are four princes and you do stuff. And there's a Council which does stuff. But, beyond that, my knowledge is pretty vague."

Julian stood up again. "You're worrying me now, Kate. Quick crash course: the princes are the local powers, the Council is a loose association of twenty-two vampires that monitors Europe, the Near East, and about half of America."

"So they're in charge?"

"Not really. They just stop things going too batshit insane. We worked out a long time ago that if too few people have too much power it gets really bad for everyone when they disagree. The Council resolves disputes, recognises princes, and deals with stuff like, well, this."

"Holy shit, are you telling me there are twenty-two super powerful vampires in town? And I have to make them all like me? I'm fucked."

Julian grinned down at me. "The whole Council hasn't gathered for centuries. You only need eight for quorum, including local princes and equivalents."

"This sounds remarkably civilised for people who drag you off the street and throw you in cellars."

"We are civilised creatures, but civilisation is power and control. It does not preclude throwing people into cellars."

"Or—" I glared. "—looming over them, blocking what little light they get in the dungeon you've chucked them in."

She rolled her eyes and hunkered down in a creak of too-tight leather. "Better?"

Well, no, it wasn't really because, to be honest, the dungeon was bothering me more than the looming. But being pissy about it wasn't going to help anyone. "So who's in town?"

"There's me, sweeting, but I won't get a vote on this one because I'm rather obviously compromised. Aeglica would have had a vote, but you sort of killed him, and we haven't chosen his successor yet. Sebastian, the Prince of Wands, has come up from Oxford."

"Ooh, I'm honoured."

"And Thomas Pryce, the Prince of Coins, of course."

"But he hates me. There's no way he can be impartial."

She interlaced her fingers between her knees. "It's not about partiality, it's about power. Besides, Thomas never lets his emotions override his judgement. It's one of his many infuriating qualities."

"I'm so fucked." I put my head in my hands.

"The Regent of the North is technically entitled to a vote as well, and I heard word he'd be in town for this one."

I had no idea how all this stuff fit together, but I'd run into Halfdan the Shaper back when I'd been dating Patrick. There'd been a big territory dispute between him and the local werewolf pack, and I'd been stuck in the middle of it, as usual. I was pretty sure I wasn't really on his radar anymore, which is how I like to keep it when it comes to shady vampire power brokers.

"That just leaves the Council members: the High Priestess, the Emperor, Justice, Temperance, and Death."

I looked up again. "And *Death*?"

"They're just titles and largely symbolic."

"*Death*?"

"I told you, they're just symbolic, but he is a bit of a fucker. His name is Diego de Flores. He was an inquisitor in life and it shows. He's coldhearted and ruthless to the point of sadism, and he doesn't like me very much. But he cares about the truth, and if he genuinely believes you're innocent, he'll say so."

"But I'm not innocent."

"Everyone's innocent of something. The hearing isn't about whether you stabbed Aeglica. It's about whether you *murdered* him. Whether you planned his death with, as they say, malice aforethought, and whether I ordered you to do it." She gave me an odd little half smile. "You know, you're sort of making history here, sweeting. We've never actually put a mortal on trial before."

For some reason, I didn't find that particularly comforting. "What makes me so fucking special?"

"Well, not to put too fine a point on it: me. I have enemies, Kate, and they can use this. In a way, I'm as much on trial as you are."

There was a pause. I wasn't quite sure, but I think I was giving her a look.

She patted my arm consoling. "Don't get me wrong. This is only the second time a Prince of England has been destroyed, so you really have achieved something."

Here lies Kate Kane. She achieved something. Beloved daughter. Sorely missed.

"Okay, so what about the rest of them?" I asked.

Julian eased herself down beside me, tucking her velvets up so they didn't trail in the dust. "The High Priestess goes by Sybil. She was a high priestess of something, back in the day. She's three parts bonkers and, frankly, I don't know why she's here."

"Great."

"The Emperor is Abu Ishaq Jabril al-Rashid. He's a risen vampire, like Aeglica was."

Risen vampires are a whole different deal to turned vampires. Basically they're people who were so pissed off about dying that it just didn't stick. They're insanely hard to kill—though, as I now knew, not impossible—and they were far more likely to have their own weird powers. Obviously, every vampire bloodline ultimately traces back to one of the Risen at some point.

"There's an unconfirmed rumour," added Julian, "that Sir Caradoc killed him at the Siege of Jerusalem back when they were both mortal. So he might be bearing a useful grudge."

That was all very well in theory but I had no idea how it would work in practice. *So, that guy who killed you that one time. Bet you're mad at him, huh? How about letting me off?*

"He's one of the big players in Istanbul, which means he's very, very good at politics."

I slid her a sideways glance. "Why, what's up with Istanbul?"

"It used to be Byzantium. It was also briefly capital of the Roman Empire. Its vampire population is more than a little factionalised."

"Who's next?"

"Justice. That's Kemsit. She's another Risen. She spent her first centuries of unlife buried in the tomb of King Aha. She's a little . . . disconcerting."

That did not sound good. "Disconcerting how?"

Julian shrugged. "She looks about twelve, she's five thousand years old, and she has a creepy obsession with death and judgement."

That sounded even worse. "Next?"

"Temperance is Dr. Acton Knight—"

"Wait. You mean Patrick's dad?"

"Oh, is that what he told you?" She managed not to laugh at me, but she made damn sure I knew she'd managed it.

"Yeah, I used to go to dinner with the family all the time."

"And you never noticed that they looked nothing alike?"

"He had two gay dads. I was pretty sure he was adopted."

"Well, he was in a sense." Julian smirked. "He's one of Acton's waifs and strays. To be honest, you probably know Acton better than I do."

"We haven't spoken in ten years."

Julian blinked at me. "Vampire. Ten years is nothing. I have people I consider to be reasonably good friends who I haven't spoken to since the nineteenth century."

So, to get out of this alive I had to win over two vampires princes, one of whom I'd had thrown out of a window by the guy I'd killed, a bloke I'd met once when I was seventeen, a crazy priestess, a power player from the place that invented plotting, a five-thousand-year-old adolescent, an honest-to-God member of the Spanish Inquisition, and my ex-boyfriend's dad.

I was so very, very fucked.

CHAPTER THREE

QUESTIONS & CELLARS

e sat for a while in silence, contemplating how fucked I was, until we heard footsteps outside and the cellar door opened to reveal a slim, olive-skinned youth with startling green eyes.

"Your Highness." He bowed gracefully. "The Council is in session and requests the attendance of the prisoner."

There was something about his stillness and the way he stood that reminded me of Elise.

"Thank you, Hephaistion," said Julian. "We'll be along directly."

He nodded and withdrew.

"If you want to make a break for it," she added, "it's now or never."

I honestly thought about it. But if I was going to die, I'd rather it wasn't in a youth hostel. "No, I'm good." I climbed to my feet. "Let's get this over with."

She led me upstairs, past the dragon skull and into one of the vast empty rooms that Aeglica had never used. They'd assembled an old oak table and a few chairs into a makeshift courtroom. It didn't seem very stately, but it didn't have to be. I was in a room with eleven vampires who, if you put them all together, were older than monotheism. Julian was eight hundred, and I'd seen her walk through fire and toss motorcycles around like frisbees. And since vampires tend to get more powerful with age, I didn't even like to think about how dangerous some of these people were.

I desperately surveyed the gathering, trying to work out who was who. It was like some kind of dreadful party game or one of those icebreakers where you have to find someone who plays a musical instrument and speaks Portuguese. Except you die if you get it wrong.

I already knew Caradoc, and since Mercy had six-inch talons and was dressed like an Edwardian widow, I would have recognised her anywhere. Acton Knight obviously hadn't changed in the last ten years on account of being immortal, and wore the same look of well-groomed sincerity he'd had when I'd been dating his "son." The Regent of the North probably hadn't changed either, but to be honest, I couldn't remember that much about him. He seemed shorter and slighter than I remembered, but his eyes were just as bright and just as green. He had his feet on the table. Next to him, the Prince of Coins was watching me coldly—Julian had said he wouldn't let his feelings get in the way of things, but that wasn't something I fancied betting my life on. It seemed like all the local vampires were sitting together which meant that the pretty blond with the faraway look in his eyes must have been Sebastian Douglas, the Prince of Wands. The Elise-alike who'd come to summon us was standing beside him, a hand resting lightly on the prince's shoulder.

So far, so good.

That just left the Council. At the risk of making assumptions, the Middle Eastern gentleman in the sharp suit was probably al-Rashid, the guy dressed like a priest was probably Diego de Flores, and the batty hippie in the floaty dress was probably Sybil.

That just left the incredibly creepy girl sitting cross-legged in the middle of the table. She was barefoot and wearing oversized jeans and a faded green T-shirt. This had to be Kemsit. There was a set of brass scales on the table in front of her.

"Katharine Kane, Princess of the Deepwild, Knight of the Witchcourt of London," she said, "you stand accused of the murder of Aeglica Thrice-Risen, Fenwalker, Shadowdweller, Oathbreaker, Kinkiller, Manslayer, Exile, Hero, who in England was called the Prince of Swords."

"Uh," I tried, "not guilty."

The Inquisitor laughed. I've heard some evil laughs in my time, but this guy sounded like he practiced.

Great. I was fucking this up already.

"This is not a mortal court, Katharine Kane." Kemsit's voice was, at once, girlish and ancient. And, it went without saying, creepy as fuck. "We care only for the truth."

"So what am I here for?"

"To give it to us. Now speak."

I looked at Julian, hoping for a clue, but she wouldn't meet my eyes. Thanks a lot, Your Highness. I took a deep breath. "I did not murder Aeglica Thrice-Risen."

"Lies!" cried Caradoc, banging his fist on the table.

Kemsit turned her head slowly and stared at him. I guessed this was some kind of faux pas. Perhaps I'd get really lucky and my enemies would fuck this up worse than I did. Finally, she turned her searchlight gaze back to me. "We have a witness who saw him die on the point of your sword."

This was where it got tricky. I was not at all comfortable standing in front of a vampire court and presenting a defence that basically came down to *well, it depends what you mean by murder*.

"We were fighting a faery lord called the King of the Court of Love. Aeglica was caught in full daylight. The only chance we had was for him to pin the creature down while I ran it through."

There was a moment of silence. Kemsit stared at me, black eyes unblinking.

"If it please the Council." Mercy turned to me. "It seems to me that you knowingly sacrificed the Prince of Swords to save Julian Saint-Germain."

And I was pretty sure *he told me to* wasn't going to cut it either. It had sounded bad enough when I'd said it to Julian. "Aeglica knew what he was doing. None of us would have escaped if it hadn't been for him."

There was another silence. I could feel a prickle of sweat on the back of my neck.

To my surprise, the Prince of Wands spoke up. "It seems to me," he murmured, "that it is manifestly implausible for Miss Kane to have overpowered Aeglica Thrice-Risen. That she was able to hurt him at all is surely evidence that the situation was truly as hopeless as she claims."

I hadn't expected anybody to be on my side. This was either really good or really bad in ways I couldn't work out yet.

Diego de Flores leaned forwards, with his chin on his hand. "You forget there was witchcraft involved."

"We have already spoken to the Witch Queen and the Priestess," said Kemsit. "I am satisfied they were not part of this."

"I am not satisfied." Diego again.

Kemsit stared at him. It was kind of like watching tectonic plates push against each other. "That is your right."

"What of her sword?" asked Halfdan, so casually it had to be a big deal. I just had no idea how.

I squirmed a bit. "It's enchanted. Nim— I mean, the Witch Queen told me there was nothing it couldn't kill. It was the only thing that could stop the King of the Court of Love."

Al-Rashid cast an incredulous glance in the direction of the London vampires. "Is this correct? Have you permitted the sorcerers to unleash a weapon that could kill all of you?"

"Only one at a time," I offered. And immediately regretted it.

Until about twenty seconds ago, they'd all been looking at me like I was some kind of bluebottle, mildly irritating but probably too much effort to swat. And now they were looking at me like I was a deadly Australian spider that had been smuggled in on a pot plant. Potentially highly dangerous and best crushed quickly.

Well, fuck.

Caradoc shot to his feet. "We do not tell you how to run Constantinople. Do not tell us how to run London."

Wow, this guy was worse at politics than I was. Maybe I was imagining it, but I was pretty sure Mercy was smirking behind her veil.

"Forgive me," said al-Rashid calmly, "but I was not aware that you did, in fact, run London. Nor will you, unless the Council recognises your petition."

Thomas Pryce looked up sharply. "Sit down, Caradoc. You're making us look foolish." Caradoc took his seat, glowering, and the Prince of Coins continued. "While this blade does, indeed, sound dangerous, I would remind the Council that we are long past the age in which the sword is the pinnacle of military technology. We will, of course, keep Miss Kane and her mortal instrument under observation, but there are other weapons in this world that pose a far more significant threat to our interests."

"This is a distraction," interrupted Kemsit. "Katharine Kane if you have anything more to set before us, do so now."

I couldn't think of anything, and I thought it was probably best to stay silent, so I shook my head.

"You may return to your cell. The Council will disperse while its members deliberate your fate."

Knowing vampires, that could mean two hours or two years. I had a case to solve and a client potentially in danger. I couldn't afford to sit on my arse in a cellar until a bunch of glorified cadavers decided whether or not to execute me. I needed a Plan B, and I needed one now.

Julian stepped forwards. "With the Council's permission, I would ask that Miss Kane be released into my custody. She has proven useful to our interests in the past."

The Prince of Coins raised a polite hand. "With the Council's permission, the extent to which Miss Kane's behaviour supports the interests of this body is exactly the matter under consideration. And, even if she is to be given the benefit of the doubt, to release her into the custody of someone known to be her lover is—if you will pardon my bluntness—laughable."

Typical. You kill a guy's progeny and you get him thrown out of a window, and he goes and holds it against you.

"Agreed." I was getting the feeling Diego didn't like me.

"It does seem inappropriate." And neither did al-Rashid.

Acton Knight coughed gently. "While I share the Council's concerns, I have known Miss Kane for many years. I can certainly vouch for her. If the Council feels the Prince of Cups is not a suitable guardian, then I will gladly offer myself."

They took a vote, and to my surprise, twenty minutes later I'd been given my shit back and released into Acton's care. I just had time to say a brief good-bye to Julian and call Elise to tell her I was still alive, and then I was being whisked through London in Acton's Mercedes S55 AMG.

Well, this was weird.

"So, um, how've you been?"

He smiled. "Very well, thank you, Katharine."

"How's the family?"

"Thierry's just back from Paris. He's been designing a new park. Shelley and Heather are in New York for the magazine launch. Endymion is still trying to find his path, poor lamb. And Thom has a show opening at the Saatchi Gallery." He paused for a moment. "Oh, and Patrick, of course, is still working for Sebastian. He's undercover in a school in Finchley. I think he's met someone."

"When you say met someone... she's not seventeen again, is she?"

"Patrick's young."

"He's a hundred and fifty."

"As I said, he's still young. It's different for our kind."

I let it go. Nothing good could have come out of telling Acton his son was a dickhead. And maybe this would get Patrick off my back.

"Thanks for letting me crash."

"It's a pleasure to have you, Katharine. You're still family, after all." Oh God. "I'll try to persuade the Council to relax the terms of your release. But I'm afraid until I can, you'll be confined to the house." Oh God. "Of course, you must make yourself at home." Oh God. "Thierry and I are having a small dinner party tomorrow. I hope you'll attend." Oh fuck.

"That'd be great." I gave a rictus grin.

The Knights lived in a converted church hall in the fashionable part of Hackney. It was way less spooky than it sounds. It was all Dutch oak flooring and marble. It had decor. When I was seventeen, it was the kind of place I'd only seen in movies. Nowadays it was the kind of place I only saw if I'd been placed under house arrest by a cabal of ancient, amoral fiends. I guess that's what you call progress. Patrick had the attic room, which he'd decorated in shades of granite, wrought iron, and self-loathing. At the time, I'd thought it was unbelievably cool and edgy.

Endymion was tinkling apathetically on the white grand piano in the open-plan living room, looking bored and beautiful. Thierry was sitting by the fireplace, wearing a turtleneck sweater and reading the sort of book which had a cover that looked like flock wallpaper. As I stomped inside, he looked up with an expression that suggested he was genuinely pleased to me.

"Katharine, *chérie*," he exclaimed. "To what do we owe this pleasure?"

His accent was much less outrageous than I remembered it being.

"On trial for my life," I said cheerfully. "Long story."

"I'm sorry to hear that. Acton, my love, what is this?"

Dr. Knight had come in behind me. "Council business. It seems that Katharine killed Aeglica Thrice-Risen."

Thierry glanced from Acton to me and back again. "I'm sure you had a very good reason. Now, if you'll excuse me, I'll make up the guest room. Perhaps you would like a bath? It must have been a long day."

"Thank you, my love." Acton went over and kissed him lightly on the lips.

The Knights had always walked a fine line between heartwarming and nauseating. Right now they were getting a pass on account of saving me from a cellar.

Endymion had started picking out the *Danse Macabre* on the piano. It was the closest he came to acknowledging my presence.

I followed Thierry upstairs, drew myself a bath in their second bathroom, which was just as vast and marble as the first, and then crawled into an oversized but perfectly made bed and passed out.

CHAPTER FOUR

EXES & APPLE JUICE

I opened my eyes in the unfamiliar Dream of an unfamiliar room. I rose and took up my sword. An unexpected heaviness dragged at my limbs as I stumbled through a greyscale echo of the Knight family home. I could feel them nearby: one a presence like a sea without waves, another twisted round the house like ivy, the third something hard and cold, like a jewel without warmth or light.

Nimue waited for me downstairs in a dress of mist and silver. She held out her hand.

"Come."

I reached out to her and we were standing in a glass and steel chamber high above the city. It was like looking down on a map. No, it was like looking at a hundred maps, pressed one on top of the other. I could see streets and houses, the grey serpent of the Thames, but also the multicoloured ribbons of Tube lines spiralling out from King's Cross, the glittering fragile spiderwebs of wireless networks, the shadowy imprints of the sewer system with its lost rivers, and eight million points of pulsing light, each one a heartbeat and each one tied to countless others by threads of love and hate and loyalty.

"It's beautiful."

"Yes," said Nimue, her hand resting lightly against the small of my back.

I realised the heaviness had gone.

"I felt strange."

"Vampires. They draw strength from the Dream, though only the most dangerous realise it."

"Why have you brought me here?"

"To show you. This is my kingdom. War is coming."

"What about that green chick I'm normally fighting?"

Nimue was silent a moment. "She is something else." The glass around us shattered and she swept her hand over the cityscape below. The mists swirled into new configurations. "Look."

I saw a shadow fall over London like black wings.
Nimue turned her hand palm upwards.
And I saw streets with darkness flooding them like ink.
"What is that?" I asked.
"I do not know. It clouds my vision. It challenges my sovereignty."
Nimue turned to face me, and everything fell away into a silver mist. Snow began to fall in soft, thick flakes. It glistened on the edge of my sword and dusted the dark coils of her unbound hair. "Find it."

"How?" I asked the ceiling in Acton Knight's spare room.

It did not answer.

I scrabbled for my mobile. I'd slept 'til nearly noon. Turns out that the threat of execution really wears you out. I rang Elise, explained the situation, and asked her to drop off a change of clothes, the charger for my phone, and my work laptop.

I lay around on the ridiculously comfortable mattress enjoying the ridiculously soft sheets and then went for a ridiculously lavish shower in the ridiculously lovely bathroom.

It would have been a great place to stay if I'd actually been allowed to leave.

I pulled on the clothes I'd been wearing yesterday and went downstairs to see if there was any hope of coffee in a house whose occupants never drank . . . coffee.

Endymion was lounging on a sofa, one arm draped over his brow. And Thierry was bouncing around the pristine kitchen doing terrifying things to food. Clearly when you're immortal, life is no longer too short to stuff a mushroom.

"What's going on?"

Endymion turned his head almost imperceptibly in my direction. "Father is cooking for mortals," he drawled, "and he's fearfully excited about it."

"Don't be like that, Dimmy," trilled Thierry. "We have this enormous beautiful kitchen, and we never use it."

"Yes, it's amazing how little use you get out of a lemon zester on an all-blood diet."

"Is there any chance of any coffee?" I asked.

"Absolutely, *chérie*." Thierry busied himself with a French press, and soon the smell of cooking was overlaid by the—frankly superior—smell of coffee.

There seemed to be a lot of food happening. Thierry had already prepared three plates of canapés.

"Uh, how many people are you expecting tonight?"

"Seven."

"And how many of them actually eat?"

"Two, but it's all about the presentation."

"Right. Hang on, who's the other one?"

"Patrick's new girlfriend. We're all really looking forward to meeting her."

Well, fuck. I hated big social gatherings, I hated seeing Patrick, and I was about a decade too old to be hanging around with teenagers. I had no idea what seventeen-year-olds were into these days but, unfortunately, in this girl's case, the answer seemed to be Patrick, which would make for some awkward conversations.

Hi, so, One Direction, eh? They're a popular beat combo. Has he started watching you sleep, yet?

If they were at the meeting-the-family stage, that meant they'd probably had about a month of him pretending to hate her, another month of *no, no, stay away from me*, and a month of *I cannot exist without you*. If they kept to schedule, people would be trying to murder her by Christmas.

I drank my coffee and made small talk until the doorbell rang.

"That'll be for me. Do you mind if we use the study?"

"Oh, make yourself at home," said Thierry, with an extravagant gesture. "You're still family as far as we're concerned."

Oh God.

I went and let Elise in. She looked worried.

"Are you well, Miss Kane?"

"Honestly, I'm fine. Obviously I won't be so great if they execute me, but so far, so good."

"What can be done?"

"Nothing really. Anyway, we're on a case."

"Indeed. I brought the files."

I led her into the study and sat down on Acton's huge leather swivel chair. I'd seen these things in catalogues, but they cost more than my car. Though, to be fair, that wasn't difficult. I've probably had takeaways that cost more than my car.

Elise stood like always and de-bagged my laptop. I booted it up and plugged my phone in to charge. That was one crisis avoided, at least.

"I've located the girlfriend, Miss Sarah Katz. She works as a new media consultant and owns a small flat in Highgate."

"Good work. She's not a vampire or anything, is she?"

"Not that I could ascertain, Miss Kane."

"What about his friends?" I couldn't help myself. I started spinning round on the chair.

"My investigations revealed that Mr. Shawcross was not an especially sociable young man. He has a small, closely knit circle of friends with whom he had a weekly *Vampire: The Requiem* game."

I stopped spinning. "What: the What?"

"I spoke to a particularly helpful young gentleman who went by the name of Warlock. He informed me that it was a form of interactive collective storytelling in a modern gothic milieu. He invited me to join their group." Elise paused a moment. "He seemed most insistent that I would find it pleasurable."

I'll bet he did. "I take it this has nothing to do with actual vampires?"

"No, Miss Kane. When I enquired, Mr. Warlock was very keen to explain to me that they understood the game to be a work of fiction, and they would under no account become lost in the steam tunnels under the university, nor would they ritually sacrifice anyone in an attempt to, and I quote, 'take the game to the next level.' I confess, Miss Kane, at this stage I had rather lost track of the conversation."

"No shit." I found the tilt lever on the side of the chair and put it all the way back. A little footstool unfolded underneath. "Is there anything else about Mr. Shawcross?"

"I ran thorough background checks. Student loans aside, he was financially solvent. He was living on campus at Brunel, where he was pursuing a master's degree in computer game design. I believe he was particularly interested in motion capture. I found no evidence of any serious personal problems and nothing that would have brought him into contact with vampires."

I was really comfortable, but I try to avoid talking business when I'm horizontal. I propped myself on my elbows. "What about this internship? It seems like a lot of supernatural power players have Locke Enterprises on their radar. Maybe someone's using him to get to Eve."

"All I know is that the internship itself was entirely aboveboard. I believe he was part of a research group specialising in image analysis." She paused. "You seem disappointed, Miss Kane. Have I done something wrong?"

This was turning into a big pile of dead ends, and I guess my frustration was showing. "You've done fine, Elise. It's just that we're still looking in the wrong places. If Mr. Shawcross has become a vampire, and I'm pretty sure he has, then we probably won't find him, unless we find out who made him one. And how. And why. And we're no closer to that than we were yesterday."

The door opened and Thierry stuck his head round. "Sorry to interrupt. I just wondered if I could get you anything?"

"No, thank you, Thierry."

"I've got that cloudy apple juice you like."

I dimly remembered that when I'd come here fifteen years ago, I'd said that I liked the cloudy apple juice they had in their fridge at the time, and Thierry had dutifully provided it for me at our every meeting since. I gave up. "That would be lovely."

He turned his smile on Elise. "What about you, Miss—"

"Oh, sorry," I said. "Thierry, Elise. Elise, Thierry." Try saying that six times fast.

"If it is not too much trouble, I would like a mug of boiling water and a tray of ice cubes."

There was a brief pause. It looked like Thierry was trying to work out whether this was a completely bizarre request or perfectly normal for a mortal. "Yes, of course. And I'll bring some biscuits as well."

We'd made very little progress by the time Thierry returned with a tray. It was a classic chicken-and-egg problem. We wouldn't know who had turned Hugh into a vampire until we found him, but we couldn't find him until we'd worked out who'd turned him into a vampire, and we couldn't do that until we knew why he'd been chosen. A thought struck me.

"Thierry," I said. "Do you mind if I ask a personal question?"

He perched on the edge of a low bookcase. "Not at all, Katharine."

"Why would you make someone a vampire? I mean, vampires in general, not just you."

"All sorts of reasons—love, jealousy, loneliness, pity, guilt, obsession. Sometimes you think someone will be useful."

"Could it ever be an accident?"

"Thank heavens, no. We are not like humans. Making someone a vampire takes time. It is a delicate process." His eyes went all dreamy. "When I turned Acton, I stayed with him all day and all night for a week."

"So you'd normally stay with the person? You wouldn't, say, just let them wander out of hospital on their own?"

"That would be highly dangerous. Unless you were very old and very powerful, you would have no way of controlling them."

I got that sinking feeling. "Just how old and how powerful are we talking?"

"Older and more than powerful than me." He shrugged. "But it would still not be a good idea. Without care, they may simply die."

"So if, just hypothetically, someone had been turned and left to fend for themselves in a hospital in Highgate, what sort of vampire would have done it?"

He thought about it for a moment. "Someone very cruel or very careless."

"Thanks, Thierry. You've been really helpful."

"Of course, *chérie*. Can I get you anything else?"

"We're good, thanks."

"And the hot water and ice cubes are what you wanted?"

Elise took a sip of the water and then picked up an ice cube. "They are perfect, thank you, Mr. Thierry."

He beamed. "You must join us for dinner, this evening."

She glanced at me uncertainly.

I gave her my best *Oh God, yes please, come to dinner* look.

"Thank you, Mr. Thierry, that would be lovely."

He went to the door and then paused. "I apologise if this question is a little intimate, but are you, in fact, human?"

Elise turned slowly to face him. "That is an interesting philosophical question, Mr. Thierry. I can think of no qualities that humans do not share with me that they do not also share with other entities that are not human. Certainly I am a representation of a human. And I believe, on reflection, that I consider myself to be one."

"I think," I said, "he's asking if you'll be eating the food."

"Oh. I can eat, Mr. Thierry, although I derive no pleasure from it. I can, however, simulate pleasure if you so wish."

"But—" Thierry's forehead creased. "—you like ice and hot water?"

"And," I added, helpfully, "washing machines and helicopters."

"I will see what I can do." He rushed out.

"So," I said, as the door swung closed behind him, "as far as we know, Hugh had no vampires in his life. That means we're looking for someone who would turn a complete stranger in a building full of other people, and then just leave them to wander out on their own. That pretty much narrows it down to a psycho, probably a powerful psycho."

"Where does that leave us, Miss Kane?"

"It sounds callous, but our best chance of finding this guy is to wait until he kills someone."

"That seems suboptimal."

I fiddled with the chair again and managed to get it more or less upright. "It's all we can do. Our best hope of keeping everyone alive is to protect the people who were in his life before his transformation, but unfortunately, fifty percent of our operation is currently under house arrest." I struggled off the chair and started pacing while I gathered my thoughts. "It's most likely he'll go for the girlfriend, assuming he doesn't just randomly start killing people in the middle of Trafalgar Square. Of course, we can't rule out the possibility that it's someone so powerful they're controlling him from a distance. In which case, it was probably targeted, in which case, it was probably about Eve." I sighed. "Which means when I get out of here, I'm going to have to call my ex."

"This thought appears to sadden you, Miss Kane. If you prefer, I could go in your place."

"It'd be better coming from me," I said. "No offence, but sending an employee would look really, really pointed."

Elise was silent a moment, and then, "I am sorry, Miss Kane. I am only eleven months old, and sometimes the subtleties of these things pass me by. My creator imbued me with all his knowledge of conventional social interaction, but I am discovering that this seems to be inadequate."

"It's okay, it's complicated."

"What would you like me to do now?"

"Just dot the Is, cross the Ts. I think we're on the right track, but take another look at Hugh's background in case he had a secret trip to Transylvania we somehow overlooked. Or, y'know, was cheating on his girlfriend with a vampire. And after the dinner party tonight, could you just swing by Sarah's house and make sure she's not being murdered or anything."

"Would it, perhaps, be more prudent to watch Miss Katz's residence all night?"

Walking wasn't helping, so I dropped back into the chair. "That shouldn't be necessary. He's been quiet for the last three days, which means he's either controlling himself or something's controlling him. Most vampire attacks happen around midnight. It's when they're strongest and hungriest."

"That is good news." She smiled happily. "I was so looking forward to tonight's party."

I stared at her. "It's going to be awful. It's going to be me, you, the dickhead ex you helped me stab, his new seventeen-year-old girlfriend, and his crazy vampire family."

"But Mr. Thierry seems very pleasant. And I have never had the opportunity to see so many people interacting in a confined space."

Wow, way to make me feel like a loser, Elise. "Well, at least one of us is going to have a good time."

Elise leaned down and gave me a hug. "Do not be sad, Miss Kane."

I patted her back awkwardly like the way straight dudes do when they hug each other to show they're not gay. "Uh, thanks."

She packed her things and left me alone with my mobile, a laptop, a glass of cloudy apple juice, and the realisation I was going to have to ring the love of my life to ask if any vampires wanted her dead.

I still had Eve's personal number in my address book because I'd never had the bollocks to delete it. It was strange that I could still dial Patrick's number from memory because we dated in the 1990s when mobile phones were these weird luxuries only posh people had. But I couldn't remember any of Eve's contact details because they were all stored under *Eve* in a file somewhere in my phone.

I was going to need more than cloudy apple juice to handle this.

A couple of hours and the key to the Knight family drinks cabinet later, I was just about ready to talk to my ex.

I pressed dial.

She picked up after three rings. "Kate?"

"We need to talk."

"What do we need to talk about? I know I didn't get you pregnant, and you've already broken up with me."

Wow. Harsh. "I broke up with you? You walked out on me."

"Because you told me to."

"Because you were never there anyway."

"What was I supposed to do? Let my company go under to make you feel better?"

This wasn't going the way I'd planned. "I was there for you when you had nothing but a half-built smartphone app."

"And you held that over me for three years."

Okay, change the subject. "Look, Eve, is anyone trying to kill you?"

There was a very long silence.

"Well, that's a new one," she said, finally.

"I'm looking for one of your interns. I think he's been turned into a vampire. I'm worried someone's trying to get to you."

"I'm not a faery princess, Kate, but I'm pretty sure I can handle one neonatal vampire."

"It's not the intern. It's whoever sent him. And you didn't say no one was trying to kill you."

"Not your problem."

The line went dead.

The world was a bit fuzzy, and I wasn't thinking too clearly, but I had a feeling that hadn't gone so well.

CHAPTER FIVE

DINNER & WANKERS

I staggered downstairs and slumped onto a sofa. Thierry was still whirling around the kitchen, and Acton was trying to lend a hand with the bemused sincerity of someone who, never having cooked a meal in their life, nonetheless feels they ought to be helpful. That used to be me with Eve. Endymion was back at the piano, playing something slow and evening-y.

"While staying at the monastery of Valldemossa," he purred, when he saw I was listening, "Frédéric Chopin became convinced all his friends had died in a sudden rainstorm and he himself had drowned in a lake. This prelude is the result of that conviction."

He closed his eyes and continued playing.

"It's, uh, nice," I said.

He didn't reply.

This was going to be a long evening.

There was a rap at the door, and Acton glided across the room to open it.

Oh shit, it was Patrick. I made a determined attempt to hide inside the sofa.

"Good evening, Father. This is Sofia Kyprianides."

"It's a pleasure to meet you." That was Acton. "Please come in."

They came in. I reluctantly sat up.

"Sofia," Acton went on, "this is my husband Thierry—" He waved from the kitchen. "—our son Endymion—" He ignored them and continued playing. "—and this is—"

"Katharine," snarled Patrick.

Patrick's new girlfriend was very seventeen. Long dark hair and big dark eyes. And, from the way she was glaring at me, it seemed like he'd been saying things.

Patrick looked just like he always did: tousled copper-coloured hair, intense copper-coloured eyes, very pale skin, and an expression of deep personal despair.

"Uh, hi," I tried.

"What are you doing here?" he asked, as if he'd found me raiding his underwear drawer. He clutched Sofia's hand protectively.

"Long story, Council business."

His eyes narrowed. "So you say. I must speak with you, Katharine." He paused for effect. "Alone."

I took a moment to relish the memory of ramming a metal spike through his heart. "Whatever, Patrick."

He dragged me into the study and slammed the door. "Why are you really here, Katharine? Don't you know it's over between us?"

I twisted my arm free. "Oh, thank fuck. Yes, Patrick. It's over. It's been over for a decade."

"You must stop following me." He posed dramatically with his hands pressed up against the wall. "Every time I turn around, you're there."

I'd known Patrick for fifteen years, and I really thought I'd seen the full extent of his psychosis, but this was shiny and new. I had a horrible feeling that Patrick getting over me was going to be worse than Patrick refusing to get over me. "I'm not following you. I don't give a fuck what you do."

"How can you say that when you've wormed your way into my family's home to come between me and Sofia?"

"Really, I don't care. You've found another needy seventeen-year-old. I'm happy for you. I feel sorry for her, but that's not my problem."

I realised about three seconds too late that Sofia was standing in the now-open doorway. She was giving me a look that said *I do not know how you became the twisted old woman you are, but I both fear and pity you.*

Patrick bamfed over and took both her hands. "Do not worry, Sofia. I will not let her come between us."

Back when I was seventeen, he'd said exactly the same thing to me when we ran up against Katya, the vampire who'd made him. I remember her as a jealous, obsessive creature trapped in a past she could never reclaim. With hindsight, for all I knew she might have just been trying to buy some milk. Or, y'know, the vampire equivalent.

"I'm okay, Patrick," said Sofia. And then to me: "Why can't you just leave us alone?"

I left them alone.

When I got back to the living room, I was relieved to see that Elise had arrived. Before I had a chance to hide behind her, there was another knock at the door, and Sybil floated into the room. She was wearing a long white dress, her hair was trailing down her back, and an honest-to-God python was draped around her neck like costume jewellery gone wrong.

"Sybil," cried Acton, "what a lovely surprise."

That's not quite how I would have put it. I would have said something more like *holy fuck, you brought a snake to a dinner party.*

Sybil said nothing.

"Of course, you know Katharine already. This is Elise, her assistant."

Sybil said nothing.

"And our son, Endymion, is at the piano."

Sybil said nothing. I was starting to sense a pattern.

"Well, this is nice," I exclaimed. There's a reason people don't ask me to dinner parties.

"Canapés!" trilled Thierry, swooping in with a plate of artistic nibbles.

As the only living mammal in the room, I felt a certain amount of pressure to eat the food. Thierry watched me excitedly. "Delicious," I offered, through a mouthful of thing-wrapped-in-other-thing.

"I do like your snake, Miss Sybil," said Elise.

Sybil said . . . well, you get the idea. But she did smile. I didn't know if that was a good sign.

"I am very much enjoying the music," continued Elise.

Endymion not only said nothing, but showed no signs of even having heard.

"Miss Kane," Elise tried again. "I appear to be the only person speaking. Am I doing something wrong?"

"Not at all, Elise," Acton was quick to reassure her. "Sybil is a woman of few words and Endymion is, frankly, just being a little surly tonight."

"Endymion can hear you, you know," drawled Endymion, without looking up.

"Tell me, Elise," Acton went on, "do you enjoy being a private investigator?"

"Oh, Mr. Knight," she said gleefully, "I am so excited to have this opportunity to practice small talk. I am not precisely a private investigator. I assist Miss Kane in her investigations by doing what she calls 'the shit she can't be bothered with.'"

He flicked up a mischievous brow. "Is that so, Katharine?"

I mumbled something incoherent about Elise being a valued member of the team.

There was another knock at the door. Acton went to answer it, and the Prince of Wands sauntered inside. He was wearing a gleaming cream-coloured linen suit, and a Panama hat. The weirdest thing about this was that he was not the most outlandish-looking person in the room by a long way. Not that Little Miss Dresses-Like-Bogart over here has a right to complain.

"Hephaistion, the gift." He gestured gracefully.

The pretty-boy who'd fetched me from the cellar appeared at his side. He was holding something bottle-shaped and wrapped in tissue paper.

"Oh, you shouldn't have," said Acton, pressing a hand to his heart.

The Prince of Wands smiled wickedly. "Oh, I should, Acton. I refuse to spend all night drinking the hospital surplus you favour. This is from my private reserve. It was siphoned in a moment of desperate hope, and has a subtle but memorable flavour."

"Thank you, Sebastian." Acton took the bottle less reluctantly than I'd expect from a man with his principles.

We endured another round of introductions and long silences. And then Thierry, who had been darting back and forth into the kitchen throughout the ordeal, came back to tell us dinner was served. Patrick and Sofia were retrieved from what I was sure had been an intense, romantic conversation about how terrible Patrick's world was and how he could not bear to bring another person into it. And we all sat down, except Hephaistion, who stood behind his master. I was seated between Elise and Endymion, the two guests least likely to want me dead.

Thierry emerged from the kitchen bearing a vast tureen of what he excitedly proclaimed was a minted pea and watercress soup. He ladled out portions to me and Sofia. I didn't know what he was going to do with the rest. Probably donate it to the homeless or something.

For Elise, he'd prepared a small silver bowl full of ice cubes. And in front of each vampire he set a crystal glass into which he decanted a measure of blood. When I'd first come to one of these events fifteen years ago, it had freaked me the fuck out. It said something about the way my life was going that now it felt just a little bit twee.

"Our aperitif tonight," announced Thierry, "comes courtesy of Sebastian. Now, *bon appétit, mes amis.*"

I tucked in. I like to think of myself as a pie 'n' chips sort of girl, but truthfully, Thierry's an amazing cook, and sometimes it's nice to have a meal that contains more garlic than batter. Although I still sometimes have trouble working out what you're actually supposed to eat and what's just decoration.

"Thank you, Mr. Knight," said Sofia, in that careful voice you use when talking to your boyfriend's parents. I bet when she left she'd say *thank you for having me.* "The soup is lovely."

"Call me Thierry, *chérie*. You're family now."

Run, girl. Run, and don't look back.

She smiled prettily.

Sigh.

Elise was passing an ice cube over her fingertips, frowning slightly. "May I ask," she said, indicating Hephaistion, "why this gentleman is not sitting down with us?"

"He is my servant, Elise," returned the Prince of Wands, with a sardonic smile. "A created being, hewn from stone and animated with stolen fire."

"That is no reason he cannot dine with us."

"He has no need to eat or rest. Indeed, he has no physical desires. What benefit could he possibly derive from a dinner party?"

"Is that not his decision?"

The Prince of Wands tilted his head, still smiling faintly. "Hephaistion, do you wish to join us?"

"I wish only to please you."

There was a horrible silence.

"So, this is nice," I exclaimed.

"Oh, that reminds me," said Acton. "Katharine, with Sebastian's help, I've managed to renegotiate the terms of your release. As long as I accept responsibility for your actions and you remain in London, you may leave the house freely."

Hmmm.

This was basically good news, but I wasn't comfortable owing the Prince of Wands a tenner for pizza, let alone my liberty, and possibly my life. "Uh, thanks."

I couldn't see any reason at all for him to help me. Julian had once told me that the Prince of Wands played a very deep game, and half the things he did were just straight-up misdirection, so it's possible he was just trying to keep people guessing. If it wasn't that, then I was probably fucked, and worse, I was fucked without knowing how or why.

"Don't thank me, Miss Kane," he murmured. "I believe executing you would set a bad precedent."

I had to agree. It would be especially bad for, say, me.

Acton nodded. "My feelings exactly, Sebastian."

"If I may enquire," asked Elise, "what manner of precedent?"

The Prince of Wands glanced at her curiously, and I wished she'd shut up. The last thing we needed was Sebastian Douglas taking an interest.

"The Council has great power," said Acton. "If that power is not tempered with mercy, then we would become little more than petty tyrants."

From where I was sitting, that ship had already kind of sailed.

"Well put, Acton." The Prince of Wands took a sip from his glass. "But my rationale is rather more pragmatic. Mortals are simply outside Council law. The Council would not imprison me for killing a human. Nor should it imprison any human for killing me."

"But it is the Council's responsibility to curb the excesses of our kind. We cannot kill indiscriminately without fear of reprisal."

"Because to do so would risk exposure."

"And," said Acton, with surprising sincerity for a man holding a glass full of human blood, "because it is wrong."

The Prince of Wands smiled. "Morality is a poor basis for policy, particularly for a Council of immortals. While I lived, a slave could be used at the will of his master, for any purpose. He could be made to fight to the death, or be cast into a pit of lampreys, or suffer any other indignity of his master's choosing. A mere handful of centuries ago, in this very city, they hanged eight-year-old children for the most insignificant of crimes. Diego spent most of his mortal life torturing heretics, and Kemsit was poisoned so she could be buried alongside her king. Do you really think you could persuade even three members of the Council to truly agree on what was *right* or *wrong*? It is far simpler and far wiser to consider only what is necessary."

Bitter experience has taught me that you don't engage with intellectually superior wankers who make long speeches about moral relativism. Normally when somebody starts talking like this, my first instinct is to punch them in the head, but that wasn't an option here because he could probably kill me with his brain.

"Sebastian," chuckled Acton, "if I thought you believed half of what you said, I'd stake you myself."

"My dear Acton, if I believed half of what I said, I most assuredly would not say it."

I seriously considered drowning myself in the soup.

The meal dragged on, but eventually Thierry served the last course and the party began to drift into armchairs and corners. I excused myself and pegged it upstairs to find my cigarettes. I could smoke all night if I had to. As I was leaving my room, I heard voices coming down from the spiral staircase that led to Patrick's emo-loft. Out of sheer force of habit, I stopped to listen.

"—doing here?" That sounded like Sofia.

And then a voice I didn't recognise, low and cracked, probably female. "I am here for you, child."

I'd left my knives in my room. I thought it was a bit rude to carry concealed weapons at a dinner party, particularly weapons designed specifically to kill the hosts.

I very quickly went through my options. If I went back for my daggers, I could miss something important. But if I didn't, and I suddenly needed them, there wouldn't be time. I erred on the side of armed. I grabbed my gold, because it was probably a vampire up there, and sanctified steel in case it wasn't.

I came back in on: "No, child, something far more precious."

Oh, that wasn't good.

"You're creeping me out! Leave me alone!"

"When did the dreams begin?"

"I'll scream."

Okay, that was my cue.

I rushed up the stairs, which is harder than you might think when you've got a knife in each hand. It's a real trip hazard. I burst into Patrick's room and found Sybil standing there like the Woman In Black except, y'know, in white.

She turned and smiled. Nine times out of ten, when a vampire smiles at you it's a threat. The snake draped round her shoulders lifted its head and hissed at me. I don't think it liked me either. Then, without a word, she drifted past me and down the stairs.

Sofia looked like she was having a worse evening than I was. "What are you doing here?" she asked, with a slight tremor in her voice.

"I was just passing. I thought you might be in danger."

"You were spying on me!"

Oh, for fuck's sake. Well, I had sort of been spying on her. But it was the good kind of spying. Holy shit, I was turning into Patrick. "I'm sorry, are you all right? Do you know what she wanted?"

"Just leave me alone!" Sofia picked up Patrick's miniature replica of *The Thinker* and brandished it. "I don't want any of this."

"Look, whatever is going on, I can help you."

"Patrick said you'd say that. You're just trying to get between us."

It occurred to me that sheathing the knives might be a good start. I disarmed and put my hands in the air. "Okay, okay, I'm going now."

I got out of there. If I'd learned two things over the last ten years, they were a) you can't help people who don't want to be helped, and b) trying to help people who don't want to be helped is kind of a dick move.

I really needed that cigarette.

"Patrick," I said, when I passed him on my way out, "your girlfriend's upstairs."

He glared at me. "It is no business of yours where she is."

I gave him the *whatever* gesture and went outside for a fag. I nipped round the corner out of the way, slumped against a wall, and lit up in peace. I only smoke when I'm tense or miserable which, in theory, would be a great way of cutting down, but it turns out I'm tense or miserable a lot of the time. I gave up completely when I was with Eve and almost completely since I've been with Julian. But this was a special occasion. I would have grabbed any excuse to get away from, well, basically everyone there, and Elise had abandoned me to go and stop Hugh Shawcross eating his girlfriend. She can be so selfish sometimes.

I took another drag of my cigarette. The night air smelled of nicotine and solitude. The great thing about antisocial habits is they mean you don't have to be social.

"Miss Kane." It was the Prince of Wands.

Bugger.

I wanted to tell him that, whatever he was selling, I didn't want any, but circumstantial evidence suggested he might be on my side on this one, and I'd already pissed off one Council member tonight. "Something I can help you with?"

"On the contrary, Miss Kane, I believe there is a matter with which I can help you."

I dropped my cigarette and stomped it out. "That's mighty neighbourly of you, Mr. Douglas."

"Please, call me Sebastian."

There was no way I was telling him to call me Kate. I thought about telling him I was fine on my own, but I've learned from long experience that when a vampire says they're going to help you, what they mean is they're going to do something whether you like it or not, and they want you to be grateful for it.

"All right, Sebastian," I said wearily, "how are you going to help me?"

He smiled his cat-got-the-cream smile. "There are eight voting members of the Council present. I have known some of them for centuries. You need five of them to support you if you are to avoid execution."

I wasn't liking those odds. "So what are you offering?"

"Support. I have my own reasons for wanting to see you acquitted."

"And there's me thinking you were doing this out of the goodness of your heart."

He flicked imaginary dust off his pristine, white sleeve. "Come, come, Miss Kane, such cynicism in one so young."

"I'm thirty-three." As soon as I'd spoken, I realised to him I must have sounded like a child proudly telling an adult that they were seven and three-quarters.

"Precisely. But, no, you are quite right. In my world, there are no allies, Miss Kane, except of convenience."

I sighed. "Just get to the point."

"You need five votes to live. You have mine and Acton's, and I believe I can persuade Thomas to see reason."

"The Prince of Coins hates me."

"My dear, everybody hates everybody. If that were ever a barrier to cooperation, the Council would not function. Thomas can be made to see where his interests lie."

"Okay, that means I need two more. Assuming you can deliver."

"I shall do my best. And, even though I say so myself, my best is really rather impressive."

Anyone who talked like that was blatantly evil.

The Prince of Wands was smiling at me once more. "Not evil, Miss Kane, merely practical."

Oh fuck, he could read minds.

His smile became a smirk. "I'm afraid so."

"Ha-bloody-ha."

"Unfortunately," he went on, "of the remaining Council members, there are only two that might be biddable. Sybil is insane and not, I think, best pleased with you. Halfdan is a capricious meddler who cannot be trusted. And Kemsit respects no will but her own."

That just left Diego and al-Rashid. I somehow couldn't imagine either of them leaping to my defence.

"Al-Rashid is a conservative. The Council has never executed a mortal before, and I doubt he will want them to do it now. If you present your case to him, he will likely listen."

This conversation was making me really regret throwing my cigarette away. "And Diego? He didn't seem the compromising sort."

"He is not. He is quite ruthless in pursuit of his goals. But your execution is not his goal. I believe you'll be able to deal with him."

"Uh, what is his goal?" I asked.

"I have no idea, but if you speak to him, you will find out."

"So, you just expect me to walk into his house and say 'Hi, what's the master plan?'"

His lip curled. "Do not be petulant. I expect you to come to the house of Aeglica Thrice-Risen at sundown tomorrow. I will ensure the Emperor and Death are willing to receive you."

It all sounded too good to be true, which probably meant it was. But since I had no way of knowing what the Prince of Wands wanted out of this whole situation, I was at real risk of getting in a *but I know that he knows that I know he knows* loop. It was probably a trap, but they were already going to execute me. How much worse could it get?

"Your caution is wise, Miss Kane, but I am glad you see sense." He turned and made a beckoning gesture. "Come, Hephaistion."

Hephaistion appeared apparently from nowhere, bearing his master's hat and cane. And, with that, the Prince of Wands sauntered into the night.

Poncy fuck.

"I heard that," he said.

CHAPTER SIX

NEWS & REGRETS

now fell softly on the Dream of a city. I was lost in a maze of stairs and concrete cells, walking on black feathers and silver ice. Shadows crept across walls and pressed against windows. I followed the darkness as it deepened.

In the distance, I could just make out the snow-crowned skeletons of trees.

I came to a low wall. The darkness spilled over the top like smoke. On the other side, clustered graves, half-buried beneath feathers, snow, and tangled ivy. I pulled myself up and dropped down onto a bed of broken twigs and thorns. The darkness here was so thick I could feel it heavy against my skin. It pulled at my hair and snatched the warmth from my lips. I could see nothing but graves and trees and too-bright snow.

I tried to move. I couldn't. It was like a weight pressing down on my chest.

I tried to breathe. I couldn't. Shadows gathered at the corners of my eyes.

I couldn't move. I couldn't breathe.

All around me was the beating of wings.

I woke exhausted, aching, and breathless.

Fuck.

I groped for my mobile phone and checked the time.

Twenty past six.

Fuck.

I fell back against the pillows. It was too early to get up, too late to go back to sleep.

Fuck.

I had no idea what that was all about, and if it was up to me, I wouldn't be finding out anytime soon. I should probably ask Nimue what happens if you die in a dream. I had a feeling I wasn't going to like the answer.

I lay there staring at the ceiling, feeling generally pissed off that this was time I could be spending asleep. On the bright side, at least I was allowed to leave.

So I left.

The part of me that was still seventeen and well brought up didn't like the idea of sneaking out without saying good-bye and thank you, but Acton was probably already at his practice, and the rest of the family were going to be sleeping until midafternoon at the earliest. I made do with a post-it stuck on the piano. It said, "Thanks— KK."

For the first time since I'd met her, I was in the office before Elise. I felt almost virtuous. I'd already put on the coffee and checked the answering machine, and was running through my emails when Elise arrived at eight thirty on the dot. Elise's unfailing punctuality would have made me feel bad, except, since she doesn't sleep, I kind of think she's cheating.

"Good morning, Miss Kane. I am happy to report that Miss Katz was not murdered in the night by her vampire boyfriend."

"Fantastic. Good work, team. We'll probably keep an eye on that for the foreseeable."

"I enjoy being on stakeout," observed Elise. "I believe I am good at it."

She was. But, of course, she didn't need to eat, go to the loo, or blink if she didn't want to. Once again, cheating. I was going to say *yes, you are*, but Elise found praise confusing. Telling her she did her job well was like telling her the sky was blue.

"We really need to find this guy," I said instead. "And we can't just sit around waiting for him to nom one of his friends. I'm going to talk to the nurse who let him go, see if I can find out anything useful. It's a bit of a long shot, but we're not really in a position to be picky."

"And what would you like me to do, Miss Kane?"

"Hit the news. See if you find anything that looks like a vampire attack. There's not many newly turned vampires running around. If Mr. Shawcross has been feeding at all, he'll probably have left a trail."

Patrick would have been really useful right about now, assuming he still had his police contacts, which he might not have now that he'd gone back undercover as a whiny seventeen-year-old. Not that irritating teenager was a role he had much trouble getting into. The

Prince of Wands probably had another man in the police, but I had no idea who, and I didn't want to get any closer to Sebastian Douglas than I had to.

I heard that, purred a voice in my head I was ninety percent certain was my imagination.

I finished clearing out my emails. It was mostly spam and admin, a voice mail from Dad and some photos from my stepmum Jenny, and a message from Lucy Archer I didn't want to read. Lucy was a forensic accountant and the widow of my late partner. I'd got her to do some work for me a few months back, but apart from that, we hadn't spoken for nearly a year. It's hard to know what to say to someone when you got their husband killed.

The email said, *I need to talk to you. Call me.*

I deleted it and left for the Whittington.

When I arrived, the hospital was in chaos, and when I did finally track down the nurse, I didn't get much out of him. He was pretty busy, but it seemed like he genuinely couldn't remember what had happened. That told me a bit, but not very much. Most vampires can fuck with your head one way or another. Still, at least now I had an idea of the type of head fucking—I was looking for a bloodline that dealt in memory loss. If it had been Aeglica's, he'd have remembered being terrified; if it had been Julian's, he'd have remembered . . . um, yeah.

Unfortunately, I'm not expert in this stuff, and vampire bloodlines aren't templates. You inherit stuff from the vampire who turned you, but basically it's like a human family. A lot of stuff in common, a lot of stuff not. As clues went, *look for something mysterious* was pretty close to being useless, but a lead's a lead.

I said a polite good-bye to Tony the nurse, remembering Rhona's warnings about harassing her staff. On my way to the exit I saw another body being wheeled out of Nightingale ward. My every instinct was telling me there was something shady going on there, but it probably wasn't going to help me find Hugh Shawcross, and getting in the way of public sector professionals in the middle of a crisis is just kind of shitty. Especially when you've got nothing to go on except curiosity and paranoia. But Nightingale was the respiratory unit, and the early stages of vampirism basically look like TB. So if they had an epidemic on their hands, there was a good chance it would turn into an epidemic of bloodthirsty undead killing machines. Unfortunately, even if I was right, there was nothing I could do about it short of breaking in and hammering a stake through the chest of every patient, which is the kind of thing that loses your PI licence.

My jaunt to Highgate had taken up most of the morning, and I grabbed a Ginsters peppered steak slice from the nearest corner shop. Okay, so it wasn't the healthiest lifestyle choice, but six months ago I'd have been pouring lunch out of a bottle. Julian was a crazy-making, narcissistic haemovore but it turned out she was weirdly good for me. Although she'd fed me a lot of puddings, which I was probably going to pay for when I hit forty.

Back in the office, I touched base with Elise.

"Miss Kane," she said, glancing up from her computer. "I have had some difficulty narrowing the search parameters."

I threw myself into my chair and grabbed a packet of pickled onion crisps out of my desk drawer. "What parameters have you been using?"

"Unprovoked violent attacks with heavy blood loss."

"When you say unprovoked?"

"I ruled out muggings, robberies, and gang-related incidents."

"How many have you got?"

"Twelve so far, all in the last week, all reported in local newspapers."

She spun her screen to show me a spreadsheet of incidents, times, locations, and references. I munched on my crisps as I made my way down the list. There'd been a body found mostly drained on Hackney Marsh, someone flipping out on a bus in Muswell Hill (that was uncomfortably close to home), somebody else going berserk on the platform at Archway, a patient savaging one of the nurses at the Highgate Mental Health Centre, a ten-year-old kid left for dead in Upper Holloway, and variations on a similar theme in Kentish Town, Friern Barnet, Golders Green, Cricklewood, Neasden, Camden Town, and East Finchley.

Either Hugh had been a very busy boy, or there was something else seriously wrong.

Normally the princes kept a very tight lid on this sort of thing, but Aeglica was dead and Julian was distracted with the trial, and as a result, the other two were kind of busy. Of course, for all I knew, it could have been a perfectly natural sequence of unexplained public freak-outs with no supernatural influence whatsoever, but from where I was standing, it looked a lot like somebody was raising a vampire army. If they were, it was way above my pay grade and technically not my problem. Then again, I didn't think Tash would be very happy if I let her brother get used as cannon fodder in a shadowy undead power struggle.

I told myself I should probably let the Council know as soon as possible, but I had a nagging suspicion that if I did, they'd launch a purge, and that would make Hugh's chances even worse than they already were. It's ironic, since they're supposed to be immortal, but vampires are kind of like small businesses: half of them go down within their first year.

Elise and I were in the middle of thrashing out what we were going to do next when my phone rang. I picked up without thinking. "Kane and Archer, Kane speaking."

"Kate."

Shit, it was Lucy. It was so much harder to avoid people when they were actively trying to contact you. "I was just going to call you," I lied.

"I've been trying to get hold of you for more than a fortnight."

"Sorry, I've been busy." Uncharacteristically, this was actually true.

"I've got some bad news. You might want to be sitting down for this."

"Hit me."

"There was a jailbreak last month. She's out."

Lucy didn't have to tell me who *she* was. She was Corin Black. Of the women I'd broken up with last year, Eve had messed with my head the most, but Corin had murdered more of my friends, which put her right at the top of my *people never to see again* list. She was fragile, beautiful, and manipulative as fuck. It hadn't taken me and Archer long to work out she was no good, but somehow, it hadn't seemed to matter.

She'd got us tangled up in this god-awful clusterfuck over this plaster bust of Napoleon that every collector, crook, and conjurer in London seemed to want a piece of. Archer had come off worse: she'd stuck a bullet through his lung in an effort to fit-up some rival con man who'd been hard on her tail. Me, she'd just taken for a ride, and I'd liked the view so much, I'd damn near let her get away with it. She was five feet four inches of trouble wrapped in a little black dress. And she was loose in my city.

"Kate, are you okay?"

"I'm fine," I said. "Thanks." And hung up.

"Has something happened, Miss Kane?" Elise's voice seemed to be coming from a thousand miles away.

"I'm going out for a bit."

"That is not what I asked, Miss Kane."

"I'm fine. Something's come up. I've got some things to think about." In the pub. With a drink. On my own.

I grabbed my hat and my coat and made for the door.

"Miss Kane," Elise called after me. "Kate."

I left. I almost headed for the Coach and Horses round the corner, but I used to go there with Archer so I couldn't face it right now. Besides, Elise would know to look for me there. I circled Holborn a while looking for somewhere to go and finally wound up at the bottom of Shaftesbury Avenue in a place called the Bloomsbury. It was the sort of pub that called itself a tavern, all leaded glass and cask ales. Archer would have loved it if he hadn't been dead.

This was the last thing I needed right now. I was dating a vampire, on trial for murder, looking for the missing brother of a girl I'd pulled in the Candy Bar, and having weird dreams about haunted graveyards. Sending Corin down was the one uncomplicatedly right thing I'd done in as long as I could remember, and it turned out it didn't mean shit. I should have just carried on fucking her. Then at least I'd have got something out of the deal.

I ordered another drink.

All right, get it together, Kane. You're a detective. Fucking well detect.

I ordered another drink.

Corin was a thief and a con artist and pretty near the top of her game, but she wasn't a wizard. If she was out, it was because someone had got her out, and that probably meant they wanted something and they wanted her to get it. If I found the something, I'd find her, but the kinds of things Corin usually stole didn't make it into the papers, unless you count the *Weekly World News*.

I ordered another drink and called Patrick.

It rang for a while and then went dead.

I tried again, and he finally picked up. "Thank fuck. Look, I need you. It's really important."

"Why won't you leave us alone?" cried Sofia. "It's over. You have to move on."

"Crap, no, I mean I need Patrick's police contacts to help me find someone."

She'd already hung up.

Fuck fuck.

I ordered another drink.

Later, as the sun was setting, I realised I was supposed to be meeting two members of the Council to cut some kind of dodgy backroom deal that might save my life. It was pretty much the last thing I wanted to be doing right now, but breathing was a habit I wasn't ready to kick yet. I had one for the road and called a taxi. Navigating the Tube during rush hour is bad enough when you're sober.

When I crawled out of the cab at Aeglica's old house, I was met by Hephaistion. I guess having arranged the whole thing, the Prince of Wands couldn't be bothered to show up in person.

"It is unwise to keep your betters waiting," he said, as he led me inside.

I fumbled out my phone. Oh yeah, I was late.

"The Seat of Death waits for you through there." Hephaistion indicated a set of double doors, probably leading to another of Aeglica's disused function rooms. "And you will find the Seat of the Emperor upstairs."

Maybe I was too drunk for this. "Sorry, who are they?"

"Father Diego and al-Rashid respectively. If you will permit me, it is also unwise to approach the Council intoxicated."

"Thanks for the advice, but there's not much I can do about it now, unless there's a really heavy-duty coffee machine around here somewhere."

"Sebastian will not be happy if this goes badly."

"I think I'm going to be pretty fucking narked myself. Come on, then. Show me Death."

Hephaistion took me through the double doors into an abandoned drawing room. Whatever had covered the floor had long since rotted away, leaving bare boards to match the panelling on the walls. The usual assortment of cobwebs and tattered drapes hung from the ceiling. There were a few bits and pieces of furniture, all of them covered in dust sheets. Diego de Flores was reclining in a wingback chair, watching me over steepled fingers. Hephaistion faded away discreetly.

"You're late," said Death.

"Something came up."

"You're also drunk."

"Something came up."

"It is no matter." He leaned forwards in his chair. "We can help each other, Miss Kane."

At least he got straight to the point. "What do you want?"

"Julian Saint-Germain."

Oh, this wasn't good. "What do you mean?" I asked.

"I do not care what happens to you, but Julian Saint-Germain is a traitor, a harlot, and an apostate. Somebody must pay for the death of Aeglica Thrice-Risen, and I would rather it was her."

I leaned heavily against the wall. In my current state, it was a miracle I didn't miss. "I'd rather it wasn't."

"She neglected her duty and allowed herself to be captured. She took a mortal lover who was a known consort of the Witch Queen of London. Her actions and her negligence led directly to the death of the Prince of Swords. Make no mistake, there is a good chance she will fall with or without you."

"Then why am I here?"

"I prefer certainty, as should you."

"I'm not going to sell out my girlfriend."

"Commendable." He tapped the tips of his fingers together thoughtfully. "I doubt she would show such loyalty in your place."

He might even have been right, but I'd had enough of getting people killed. "Not going to happen."

"Then we are done. You seem an honourable woman, Miss Kane. You are wasted on the likes of Julian of Colchester."

I felt like I should leap to Julian's defence, but I couldn't really think of anything. She wasn't exactly bending over backwards to get me out of this, and she talked like I was supposed to feel grateful she hadn't completely screwed me over.

"Maybe I am," I said. "But I've always enjoyed being wasted."

That had sounded way better in my head.

I left.

I guess this meant I'd officially lost Diego's vote. I wasn't seeing so straight right now, but I could definitely read the writing on the wall. The only way I was getting out of this was if I fed someone else to the Council. As the man once said, I'm no good at being noble, but there were some lines I just didn't want to cross. If your partner gets killed, you do something about it, you don't fuck other women unless your girlfriend's okay with it, and you definitely don't sell people out to crazy vampires. Because the truth is, it isn't even hard. It's the most natural thing in the world to kill a man who's trying to kill you, to cheat on someone who loves you, and to do whatever it takes to save your own scrawny neck.

It looked like me and politics went about as well as Baileys and orange juice.

I went upstairs to see who al-Rashid wanted to buy.

He was in the room where I'd gone to find Aeglica three months ago, shortly before I'd killed him. There was still an enormous picture of a naked historical chick on the wall. Al-Rashid was sitting underneath it, tapping away on an iPad.

"Good evening, Miss Kane." He glanced up. "It's a fascinating picture, isn't it?"

"It's a portrait of the most beautiful woman in Venice painted by a great master." At least that's what I'd been told.

"And what do you think it tells us about the late Prince of Swords?"

I really didn't know where this was going. "He said he admired her."

Al-Rashid was silent a moment. "You liked him, didn't you?"

"He was a thousand-year-old bulletproof psychopath."

"That's not an answer."

I shrugged. "That's all the answer you're getting. This is the point where you tell me you can help me."

He put his iPad down on a dusty side table and watched me steadily. "This is the point where you tell me why I should."

I thought very hard about what to say next. I had no idea how vampire titles worked but they called this guy the Emperor, so that had to mean something. This was make-or-break time.

I took a deep breath.

"Y'know what," I said. "Fuck it."

He didn't blink. He didn't even raise an eyebrow. "Miss Kane?"

"Look, don't take this the wrong way, but I know basically nothing about you except that however you got where you are, it wasn't by being nice to people like me. I've had a really long, really shitty day, and if there's anything you want from me, I know I'll regret giving it to you. So, seriously, thanks but no thanks, I'll take my chances."

"You're playing a dangerous game, Miss Kane."

"I know, and I fold. I quit. Deal me out. I'm done."

I walked out of there with what was left of my dignity.

And then I ran like fuck.

CHAPTER SEVEN
FIGHTING & FUCKING

I stopped at a corner on the outskirts of Holland Park and tried to light a cigarette, but my hands were shaking too much. Then I flagged down a cab and told the driver to take me to Brewer Street. It was still early and the Velvet wouldn't be open but I wasn't going there for the clubbing.

The front door was locked, so I sloped into the side alley and made for the fire doors. They technically should have been closed, but nightclub floor staff aren't exactly sticklers for health and safety. Sure enough, someone had propped them open with a crate of Beck's, and I slipped inside.

A guy I didn't recognise was lining up martini glasses in the mirrored hollows behind the bar.

"Oi," he said. "We're closed."

Ashriel, the reformed incubus who acted as Julian's enforcer, house manager, and general go-to guy, appeared in a shimmer of sex and damnation. "It's all right." The effortless seduction of his voice snuck up on me like a well-mixed Sazerac. "It's the boss's girl."

Well, I suppose it was better than the boss's pet mortal.

"I prefer 'the boss's fuck-muffin.'" I was glaring more than I'd meant to.

Ashriel rolled his eyes. "Oh, you're that Kate tonight."

"Where's Julian?"

"Office."

I pushed past him and headed up the stairs behind the bar.

"Nice to see you too," he called after me.

Julian's office was behind an unassuming door which read *Julian Saint-Germain – Manager*. It did not read *Julian Saint-Germain – Motherfucking Vampire Prince*, but it would have if she thought she could get away with it. As it was, she'd just settled on installing an actual honest-to-God throne in there. There were usually a couple of admin staff hanging around, but they'd gone home for the evening.

I went in without knocking.

She was standing in front of the window with a phone cradled against her ear. London was a smear of glitter and shadow, the rooftops of Soho rising from the gloom like battlements. Framed by the wooden ceiling beams and dressed in a frock coat of midnight-blue velvet, she looked like a cursed prince in a fairy tale.

Her head turned slightly in my direction as I came in.

"—lie to me, Sebastian," she was saying. "I know full well what goes on in my domain."

I snatched the phone out of her hand.

"She's busy," I said into it. Then I hung up and threw it into a corner of the room. It made the sort of noise you don't want electronic equipment to make.

Julian blinked. "Well, that was rude."

"You'd have stopped me if you wanted to."

"You know I like it when you get all mean and reckless." She smiled up at me, but there was a wariness in it, and her eyes were cold.

I grabbed her by the wrists and forced them behind her back. "How will you like me when I'm dead?"

"Now, now sweeting. I heard about your little meeting with Diego."

"What was I supposed to do? You hung me out to dry."

Julian bared her teeth. "You have no idea, do you?"

"How would I? You don't trust me, and I've barely seen you."

"You killed a Prince of England and didn't tell me." She was silent a moment. "I'm doing what I can, Kate, but I have to be careful."

"Oh yes, we can't have this reflecting badly on the Prince of Cups, can we?"

Suddenly my hands were empty and Julian was sitting on the throne, one booted foot crossed over the other and her chin resting in her palm. "You're coming perilously close to boring me."

"Y'know what," I said, "fuck you as well."

I turned to leave. As I was reaching for the door handle, Julian appeared in front of me. "Going somewhere, sweeting?"

"Get out of my way."

"Not until you tell me what you said to Diego."

"What do you think I said to Diego?" I shoved her back against the door and kissed her hard. She tasted of wine and rose leaves and betrayal. Her tongue was velvet soft, and her teeth were cold and sharp.

"That's not an answer." Julian yanked her head away.

I was fucked if I was going to stand there and beg her to trust me. "Yes, it is."

"How very Judas of you."

I caught her by the throat and pulled her into another kiss. She didn't resist, but she didn't yield either. I thrust my tongue between her lips, and she made a sound of mingled pleasure and anger, then bit me. My mouth filled with the bittersweet tang of blood, and a wild, artificial ecstasy rolled over me. Then we were kissing in earnest, still struggling but falling into each other at the same time.

For a second, I let myself forget that I'd thrown away my best chance of survival to protect her, and that she wouldn't believe me and probably wouldn't care. Right now, like a junkie going back for another fix, she was all I wanted. She was fragile and eternal in my arms, furious and gorgeous, and as messed up as I was.

"I know what you're trying to do." Julian's hands closed round my forearms, tight enough to bruise.

"I'm trying to fuck you," I said.

"You're trying to distract me."

"So walk away, tell me to stop."

"I should." She leaned into me and ran petal soft kisses down the line of my neck. "I really should. But I can't."

"Then don't."

I picked her up and she wound her legs round my waist. She weighed practically nothing, and I could feel the heat gathering under her clothes. She reached up and plucked off my hat.

"Be careful with that," I said. "It's the only one I've got."

She flung it into the corner where it landed on top of her phone. I guess she was still a bit annoyed about that.

I considered my options. Desk. Throne. Floor. Wall. To be honest, it was all good. I crossed the room and dropped her onto the throne. She made a surprised noise and then sprawled out like a cat on a cushion. I leaned over and took another kiss, smearing blood and bright pleasure. Julian's fingers twisted in my hair, holding me close.

My mouth seemed to cling to her skin as I tried to shed more clothes. I felt if I stopped touching her, she'd slip away like cigarette smoke.

I struggled to push the frock coat off her shoulders, but we wound up in a hopeless tangle. Out of nowhere, Julian giggled, and the sound trickled over me like champagne. I caught her shirt by the frills and tore it open to reveal white skin and a tantalising cobweb of black lace.

"You're costing me a fortune in shirts," sighed Julian.

"Then get better shirts. Or worse breasts."

I licked and nibbled my way down her cleavage and followed the crisscross of lace and skin, the texture shifting from rough to smooth under my tongue. Julian sighed and arched up under me. Her grip on my hair tightened until the sting made me gasp, and she pulled her hands away and clamped them to the arms of the throne. I pinned her wrists and straddled her lap, kissing her again until she was writhing beneath me and moaning into my mouth.

"Don't think this means I've forgiven you," she said, when I came up for air. "I take betrayal very personally, sweeting."

"I don't need your forgiveness."

I slid onto the floor and let go of her wrists to tug off her boots.

"You look good on your knees." Julian glinted a grin at me.

"Shut up." I began drawing down her ridiculously tight trousers.

"If you're angry, Kate, this is a funny way of showing it."

"It's the only way I know to get your attention."

I threw her legs over my shoulders, trapped her hands again, and bit her on the side of her thigh. Whatever witty comeback Julian had ready was lost in a sharp cry. I held her against her own throne as I teased my way up to her cunt. She was as sweet as summer, and hot desire surged through me. I might only have a couple of days left to live, but at least I was making the most of them. It briefly crossed my mind that my priorities were kind of screwed up. But then Julian's thighs tightened round me in a sort of embrace, and I stopped worrying. Stopped thinking. Stopped anything but fucking her.

"Kate," she murmured. "My damned infuriating, irresistible Kate."

I could have pushed her off the edge quicker if I'd used my fingers but I made her wait for it. I kept her on the brink until she was gasping and begging and clawing chunks out of the arms of the throne.

"Please, Kate," she said at last.

And I let her come. She threw back her head, made a sound of unadulterated bliss, and flooded me with her pleasure. The next thing I knew, I was flat on my back with Julian crouched over me, eyes wild, fangs bared. She shoved a hand down my trousers and a couple of fingers into me. I shuddered under her, and then she bit me, and there was nothing but the darkest, most beautiful, most impossible ecstasy.

When I opened my eyes, I was cradled in Julian's arms as we half lay, half sat tangled on the throne.

"Do you really think I sold you out?" I mumbled into her neck.

"Right now, sweeting, I don't care."

"Diego said that he wanted you, not me, and if I played ball he'd keep me safe. But I told him to fuck off. Al-Rashid as well."

There was a bit of a pause.

"That, my dear one, was very sweet but very stupid."

"You were just freaking out because I talked to the guy, and now you're calling me an idiot for not working with him."

"To use your delightfully modern idiom, then I was freaking out for myself." She kissed the edge of my brow gently. "Now I'm freaking out for you. I'm a vampire prince. It is necessary to demand loyalty, but it is foolish to expect it."

"Couldn't you have told me that before I screwed myself?"

She twined her fingers through the white streak that had become a permanent feature of my hairline. "I'd forgotten about your ridiculous fondness for self-sacrifice." She was looking at me rather strangely. "It's terribly endearing but not terribly helpful. I'm glad you didn't try to sell me to Diego. But at least if you had, I would have known what to do about it. I mean, I'd probably have had to kill you, but at least I wouldn't have had to worry."

I wrapped my arms around her and pulled her closer. "You'd have had to get in a queue."

"Sadly, sweeting, although I am an Englishwoman born, I have never mastered the fine art of queuing." She snuggled into me. "Besides, I think you overestimate the Council's lust for blood. Before, that is, you told two of its most influential members to fuck off. The awful truth is that you simply aren't that important. Most of the Council don't care if you live or die. They only care what they can get out of you. You're lucky not many of them know about faeries or they'd find you far more interesting."

We kissed awhile, softly and sweetly. "Well, it doesn't matter now, does it?"

Julian licked the blood from the corners of my lips. "Their case is still sketchy, and if Sebastian can be trusted, then you have at least one powerful advocate. I know it seems like I haven't been much help, but I have enemies on the Council, and I didn't want them to think they could hurt me by hurting you. I've had to depend on Sebastian."

"Couldn't you find anybody less blatantly evil?"

"There are times, sweeting, when only blatantly evil will do. Sebastian is untrustworthy and unpredictable but strangely reliable."

All the talk of my impending death was really starting to lose its charm. I twisted round and kissed her again. "I don't want to think about this anymore."

"Let me take your mind off it." Julian tangled her legs up with mine.

"Tell me a story. It's been a while since the last instalment of Tales of the Pudding Nun."

"That wasn't quite what I meant."

"Some of us aren't immortal sex monsters and need five minutes to catch our breath."

She grinned at me. "Why don't *you* tell *me* a story?"

"You want me to do *what*?" It was probably a bit of an overreaction. It wasn't as if she'd asked me to dress like a chinchilla and flog her with a copy of the *Financial Times*.

"It's your turn." She gave me the big eyes. "Come on, you've led an eventful life. You must have hundreds of stories."

I thought for a while.

"Well, there was this one case," I said, doubtfully.

Julian nestled in. "This is fun."

"This guy hired me and Archer to check out this house he'd just bought because the family there had gone like mad or something. So we went, and we couldn't find anything."

Julian blinked. "Is that it?"

"No, wait, it gets better. So we heard these noises upstairs, and we checked the upstairs bedroom, and then Archer got thrown out the window by a bed."

"You went up against an evil bed? Verily, it is the stuff of legend."

"Wait for it." I gave her a little squeeze. "So we left the house and looked the place up in the public records office. And it turns out the guy who built the place back in like eighteen somethingy-something had arranged to be buried in the basement."

"That's just weird."

"So we went back to the house, chopped down the false wall in the basement, fought a zombie wizard, and case closed."

Julian blinked again. "Is *that* it?"

"Oh, there was a bit with a floating dagger as well."

"I don't think a floating dagger is going to save this story, sweeting."

"I've still got it somewhere."

"I'm very fond of you, Kate," said Julian gently, "but that was the worst story I've ever heard."

I pulled away a bit and gave her a look. "Archer used to tell it all the time. He used to say it was a classic."

"Try again, darling. I want to hear about you, not some dead prick in a cellar."

"Why don't I tell you about the time I met this really demanding vampire prince."

Julian gave me the big blue eyes again and scrambled back into my lap.

"Fine," I sighed. "What if I tell you about my hilarious near-death experiences in high school?"

"Oh yes," she said excitedly. "I love stories about high school girls in trouble. Did you have a uniform?"

"No, I went to a comprehensive and then a sixth form college."

She gazed up at me, hope gleaming in her eyes. "Can you pretend you had a uniform? With kneesocks?"

"No. There were no kneesocks. Ever."

Julian pouted.

I ignored her. "So, anyway, once upon a time, there was a girl called Katharine who had purple eyes and long dark hair and a vampire boyfriend who, for the sake of the story, we will call Schmatrick. They were in wuv. Katharine and Schmatrick were in their final year of sixth form. Katharine was failing all her exams because she was spending all her time with Schmatrick. And Schmatrick was failing all his exams because he was spending all his time dumping Katharine for her own good or trying to kill himself because of the terrible darkness in his soul."

"These characters sound strangely familiar." Julian's hand moved idly up my arm and across my shoulder. Her touch was surprisingly tender.

"It was two weeks before their college leavers' ball. Schmatrick didn't want to take Katharine because he didn't want her to expect a life he couldn't give her. But Katharine had bought a dress anyway just in case. It was white with silver trim and made her feel like a faery princess, which ironically she didn't know she was. Schmatrick had run away to London and hadn't explained why, but one day Katharine woke up to find a ball ticket on her pillow, with a spray of red flowers resting on top of it."

"How romantic."

"Tell me about it. Katharine was thrilled. Over the next two weeks she woke up to find more letters and more flowers. The last note said that Schmatrick would send a car for Katharine on the night of the leavers' ball, and sure enough, when the night came, the car arrived. And dressed up like an idiot with red flowers in her hair, Katharine got in."

"I've got a bad feeling about this." Julian's hand gathered the warmth from my skin and passed it back to me.

"So did Katharine when she realised she was trapped in a car full of vampires dressed like evil Jedi. They took her to this great big scary house in Northumberland with honest-to-God stone dragons outside."

Julian twisted around and gave me a puzzled look. "Trismegistus Hall?"

"I don't know; I was busy being kidnapped. I didn't stop for a guidebook."

"I'm pretty sure I've been there. That's Henry Percy's estate."

Great. Trust Julian to be on first name terms with the guy who'd tried to murder me when I was seventeen. "Friend of yours, is he?"

"More of an acquaintance. What did he want with you?"

"Oh, the usual stuff. Drain my blood, suck out all my power, generally ritually sacrifice me."

"Does that happen to you a lot?"

"Quite a lot, actually. So, anyway, they chained me to the ceiling in this basement and this satanic-looking guy with a beard and a mullet comes in, puts on this white robe and this golden mask and cuts my arms open. Then they stuck this big golden bowl under me and poured this little bottle of shiny magic shit into it. And then he starts chanting in like Greek or Latin or something."

Julian leaned in and hugged me. "You poor thing. What happened next?"

"Patrick rescued me. Like he always did. It was the one advantage of going out with him."

"Does this story have a happy ending anytime soon? Or an ending of any kind, for that matter?"

I shrugged. "Well, it's my life, so not really. Unless you want to count 'grew up, became a PI, got executed by vampires.'"

"You won't be executed. Probably."

"I don't like staking my life on probablies."

"None of us do, sweeting. That's why we tell our girlfriends when we murder vampire princes." She stretched, yawned, and then slipped off the throne. She slithered into her trousers, tucked in the tatters of her shirt and sauntered across the room to retrieve the pieces of her phone. She picked up my hat and frisbeed it across to me.

"That's marching orders is it?" I said.

"You're welcome to come play with the kittens."

This was Julian's pet name for her legion of excitable lesbian groupies. There was some kind of psychic vampire sex mojo going on with them that I didn't really understand. She drew power from them somehow and, in return, they got well ... y'know ... off.

"I'm more of a dog person."

"Oh yes, how is Miss Vane-Tempest?"

Tara Vane-Tempest was the Alpha wolf of the local werewolf pack. We'd met about three months ago while I was looking into the murder of her cousin, and she'd made a pretty serious attempt to get into my pants. This had not made Julian happy.

She'd kept in touch in a Christian Grey kind of way, sending me expensive gifts, inviting me to swanky parties, and showing up when I wasn't expecting it with champagne and handcuffs, impatiently prowling the line between sexy and creepy. So far I'd been having so much fun turning her down that I'd barely even been tempted. Now I thought about it, I hadn't heard from her in a couple of weeks. Maybe I'd protested too much.

Oh, and I was in a relationship.

"Fine," I said warily. I'd never seen Julian's jealous side and she'd told me I didn't want to.

She arched a brow at me. "You know what they say about lying down with dogs."

"I'm not lying down with anybody besides you and the occasional cup of Bovril."

"See you keep it that way, sweeting."

CHAPTER EIGHT

HIPPOS & HEROES

I got off the Tube at East Finchley, texted Elise to say I was on my way, and headed down Fortis Green towards home. It was a bit after nine, dark in a suburby well-lit way and bloody cold for the time of year. Fuck the Bovril. This was Drambuie weather. I turned up the collar of my coat and hurried on, past green hedges, wheelie bins, and those cosy bay-windowed Victorian terraces that are worth a bomb.

I was about halfway home when I started to get a *too quiet* feeling and I realised the house across the road had its front door hanging off the hinges. The smart thing to do in this kind of situation is to sit tight, call the police, and do your best to be a useful witness.

I crossed the road and went to investigate.

The door hadn't just been pushed open, it was snapped in two. The little semicircle of glass panels had been smashed to smithereens, littering the front step and the hallway. Not a normal forced entry. There were several lights on inside, but I couldn't hear anything except the murmur of a television or a radio.

Here lies Kate Kane. Should have minded her own business. Beloved daughter. Sorely missed.

I slipped the sanctified steel knife out of its sheath and inched forwards, pressing myself flat to the wall.

The stairway was lined with family pictures, photographs of adorable children in various flavours of school uniform. I wish people wouldn't do that. It's like they say to each other *well, darling, if we get horribly killed, at least the person who finds us will feel really bad about it.*

But who knows. Perhaps they were all fine. Maybe they'd just had an attack of really aggressive woodworm.

I eased open the first door I came to and peered into an empty living room. The TV was on, playing the looping music of a video game pause screen. The controller on its wire was sitting in the middle of the floor. Out of sheer force of habit, I looked up. Nothing horrible dropped on me from the ceiling.

Well, that was good.

I edged back out of the living room and moved across to the opposite door. All I could see through the bubbled glass was a lot of red. Either they had terrible taste in interior design or their taste in interior design was no longer a problem.

Knife ready, I got back as far as I could and slid the door open.

The wreckage of a charming suburban family dinner and a charming suburban family lay scattered around the room. Among the blood, the bodies, and the carnage, four ragged, unhealthy-looking people lolled like overfed cats. They were all wearing hospital pyjamas and stared at me with cold, inhuman eyes, but on each one, I could see jarring reminders of their previous lives. Three of them wore wedding rings, one of them had a crucifix hanging round her neck, and one of them had the remains of a cast on his arm, covered in messages, cartoons, and pictures of dicks.

So, vampire army it is, then.

Well, fuck.

Fledgling vampires are really unpredictable. The transformation affects everyone differently. Some people wind up really sick and out of it, and even worse off than when they were human. Others get a shit-tonne of strength, speed, and anger straight off the bat. Vampires usually nurse their progeny through the change very carefully so that stuff like this doesn't happen. I normally wouldn't have a chance in hell against four vampires, not without using more of my mother's power than I could safely come back from. But, if I was lucky, these guys would be sluggish from feeding, and they looked pretty fucked anyway.

I ducked out of the doorway and grabbed my gold knife as well. I didn't want them to surround me, but I didn't want to get backed into a corner either. Basically, I was getting out of there. If everything went well, I'd get away. If it didn't, at least I'd be fighting them on open ground.

They unfolded with an eerie, disjointed grace and started gliding slowly towards me. Four legs or two, living or undead, predators all work the same; don't run, that just makes them chase you. Back away slowly, get something between you and them, and get ready to hit them when they come in. I retreated over the ruins of the front door, crunching on bits of glass and trying not to trip on the shattered wood. At least here only two of them could come for me at once.

Two of them came for me at once.

They were half-lost in an animalistic frenzy and seemed pretty committed to ripping my face off. I let them run onto my knives. I got one in the neck with the gold blade, and it went down, screaming and hissing. I tried to pull back, but it twisted the knife out of my hand as it fell. I was one for one, but I'd lost the only weapon that could really hurt them. The second one was already on me, and I buried my steel dagger hilt-deep in its chest. It didn't even slow down, and we tumbled backwards through the door.

I landed on my back with a vampire straddling my chest. I caught the flash of its fangs in the moonlight as it snapped its head around to bite me. I tucked my chin in and nutted it. There was a crunch of cartilage and a spray of blood, but I didn't have long to feel smug about it because it yanked my head back and came in for round two. I couldn't see much with my face full of vampire, but I had a horrible feeling its mates were about to join the party.

It was at times like this that I really appreciated having the option to draw on an ancient wellspring of psychotic faery magic. I reached out to my mother in the Deepwild. She was crouched on top of something helpless, all white teeth and hunger. The air was thick with the sour tang of blood and fear. There was part of me that kind of liked it. Power coursed through me, and I was just reaching up to bat the thing away, when it suddenly shot into the air, arms and legs flailing like an out-of-control puppet.

I rolled to my feet. My senses were hunter-sharp, which is how I saw the dark figure crouched on the roof. It smelled of steel and sulphur and something familiar I couldn't quite place.

The last two vampires came through the door, moving fast. I was ready for them, but so was the thing on the roof. It raised an arm. A dart sliced through the air. And one of the creatures collapsed on the driveway. Another swift movement. A second dart. And the last vampire was down.

The part of me that was my mother was not pleased to have the lost the kill or the territory. The part of me that was Kate was pleased to be alive but well aware that mysterious ninja assassins aren't fond of witnesses. I stayed back and stayed wary.

The figure rappelled off the roof and came towards me.

The instinct to rip its heart out was just about controllable.

She was wearing some kind of armoured, black-on-black body suit, all gauntlets and gadgets. Her long dark hair was flowing down her back and she was talking into a microphone that was so flash I couldn't see it.

"Situation contained. Minimum three bodies. Proceed."

As she came closer, the dark glasses snapped back from her eyes and folded into her headset.

"Hi, Kate," said Eve.

I forced down my mother's power and struggled back to myself. "What the fuck do you think you're doing?"

A black van had pulled up a couple of doors down, and teams of people in black fatigues were fanning out down the street and bundling up the bodies.

"Wow." Eve flicked back her hair. "I save your life and all I get is this lousy T-shirt."

"I had it covered."

"From underneath?"

"I know what I'm doing."

"And so do I."

That was the sort of thing people said right before they died horribly. "You do *not* know what you're doing. Look at you. You look like fucking Batman." Eve seemed momentarily pleased. "That's not a compliment," I clarified. Eve actually pouted. "This isn't a fucking video game. You'll get yourself killed." I gestured at the interchangeable minions who were cutting down the vampire who was still dangling from a satellite dish, strangely docile. "You'll get these people killed."

Eve pointed at the ruins of the nice suburban family home. "People are already getting killed. At least I'm doing something about it."

I should have seen this coming. "So this is it? This is your Master Plan? Dress up like a tosser and shoot vampires?"

For a second, she seemed genuinely wounded. Eve had wanted a costume like this for as long as I'd known her, and if she'd been going to a fancy dress party instead of hunting actual bloodthirsty monsters, I'd have been able to admit she looked pretty good in it.

"Well, we can't all be born with superpowers," she snapped.

"You know what, I'll fucking trade you. You can have the crazy mother and the predatory hunger you can barely control. I'll have the dotcom billions and the flashy toys."

Eve folded her arms. "Oh yes, because you are so tormented and bear a burden so terrible that no one else can understand. You told me about all this supernatural shit. What did you think I was going to do? Ignore it and hope I didn't wind up an after-dinner snack or a pawn in a game that nobody would let me play?"

I was breathing way too hard for someone just having a conversation. "I told you to keep you safe, not so you could turn London into a giant first-person shooter."

"Jesus Christ, Kate, will you listen to yourself? It's not your job to keep me safe and—" She stopped and put her fingers to her ear. "Acknowledged. Wrap it up, we're moving out. There's been another hit in Golders Green."

"What? What's going on? How are you tracking this?"

She was already walking away from me. Again. "I told you, Kate, I know what I'm doing, and in case you haven't noticed, this city is going to shit."

The clean-up crew were stuffing things into evidence bags and piling back into the van.

"Hey, that's mine," I yelled, as one of them pulled my golden dagger out of a vampire corpse and transferred it into a ziplock.

"Let her have it, Steve," said Eve. "She sulks if she doesn't have something pointy to play with."

Steve handed me the dagger, and I stuck it back in its sheath. Those things aren't cheap.

Once the van was loaded and all her people were inside, Eve swung herself into the back and shut the doors behind her. She sped off into the night, leaving me behind on the kerb. Which was kind of the story of my life.

So I went home.

Elise was still staking out Hugh's girlfriend so the flat was cold, dark, and empty. I'd got used to living alone since Eve had finished with me, but I'd kind of got used to Elise as well, so it was weird not having her around. I poured myself a drink, slumped onto the sofa, and watched *Downton Abbey* on ITV Catch-up. I had no idea what was going on. There was a war and a stately home and Maggie Smith. My lifestyle isn't really set up for following TV shows, but Dad and Jenny were really into it, and I thought it'd give us something to talk about when I went back for Christmas.

All in all, it had been a bit of a shitty day.

I'd just been rescued from an army of slavering vampires by one ex-girlfriend, after discovering that another ex-girlfriend had broken out of prison. I'd damn near sacrificed my life to protect my current girlfriend, only to find out she didn't want me to and that it probably wouldn't work anyway. I'd say it had been a mistake getting out of bed, but I'd also nearly died in my sleep. While investigating some weird magic dream shit for yet another ex-girlfriend.

There was a moral here somewhere, but I couldn't quite put my finger on it.

I had another drink. I was very tempted to go to bed and call it a day, but I wasn't totally convinced I'd wake up again. This probably needed sorting out. Now.

I knew a couple of ways to reach Nimue, but most of them involved leaving the house, which I wasn't really in the mood to do. If I wanted to stay on my sofa, I'd have to rely on one of her lieutenants to get me in contact. I picked up my phone and dialled the number of a call centre in Hackney. I let the automated voice finish talking and spoke into the hold music: "I need to speak to the Guardian of the Watchtower of the East."

There was a click.

"Evenin'," said the Guardian of the Watchtower of the East. "What can I do you for?"

"I need to talk to Nimue. I'm worried if I go to sleep I might die."

"Aww, that's rough, babe."

"Tell me about it."

"I'll see what I can do."

The line went dead.

I guess that was that. I hung up and put the TV back on. Nim doesn't like to be rushed, but she's never let me down when I've needed her. Soon, it began to rain. I lay back on my sofa, closed my eyes, and listened to the droplets thudding softly on the window panes.

A little while later, there was a knock on the door. The buzzer hadn't gone, so it was either Nimue or a very polite assassin. I took a knife just in case and slipped on the security chain before I opened the door.

Nim was standing outside in jeans and a hoodie, completely dry. She looked at the chain and then at the knife. "Um, hi?"

"It's been that kind of day."

I disarmed myself and let her inside.

"Mind if I put the kettle on?" she asked.

"Knock yourself out."

She went into the kitchen and started getting the tea things together. "Wow, I can actually find things in here. What have you done with the real Kate Kane?"

"Don't blame me, blame Elise."

"You've even taken the saucepans out the overhead cupboard."

"Not you as well."

Nim handed me a mug of tea. I took a sip, and it was just how I like it, strong and sweet. If you added psychotic and emotionally unavailable to that, it would also cover my taste in women. We went into the living room.

Nimue slipped off her trainers and curled onto the end of the sofa. "So, what's going on?"

I plonked myself down on the other end and stared miserably into my tea. "Corin's out, there are a bunch of vampires who want to execute me, there's an undead army rampaging around North London, Eve's involved somehow. It's all gone to shit."

Nim scooted across the space between us and put a comforting arm around my shoulder. "That sucks."

"Yes. Yes, it does."

We sat in silence for a bit.

"I spoke with the Council last month," said Nim finally. "They thought I had a hand in the death of the Prince of Swords. They only asked me about Maeve. I kept you out of it."

"I shouldn't have got you into it."

"I'm the Witch Queen of London, I'm in it up to my neck anyway. If I'd known they'd come after you, I'd have put you under my protection."

"I can look after myself."

She didn't push it. She never had. "So," she said instead, "tell me about the dreams?"

"I followed the darkness to a graveyard, and when I went in, it was like something was crushing me. I couldn't move and I couldn't breathe." I paused. "And this is where you say, 'It's okay, you can't get hurt in a dream.'"

Nim said nothing.

"Well, fuck."

"Sorry, Kate."

"Right."

There was another long silence. Nim felt so warm resting against me. So, well, human.

"So what happens now?" I asked. "I like you and I care about you, and I know we made a deal, but I'm not mad keen on choking to death in my sleep because you sent me after something I don't understand."

Nim drew away and sat cross-legged on the sofa facing me. "I'm sorry, I should have prepared you better, but I didn't know what we were dealing with, either."

"But you know now, right?"

"I can't be sure, but I've got some ideas." She tucked her hands into her sleeves. "It's probably a vampire, probably an old one, probably the same one that's causing all the attacks. Unless it's just a gigantic coincidence or a deliberate trick."

"That makes sense of a lot of things, but isn't it a problem for the Council?"

"It's the Council's problem, and it's my problem, and those two problems are different." This was one of those moments it was hard to remember that Nimue was one of the most powerful beings in London. Curled up on my sofa, she just looked like a girl I used to date. "It's a problem for the Council," she continued, "because it's a threat to their power and the stability of their society. It's a problem for me because people are dying in my city." But now, when I met her eyes, I saw the shimmering reflection of streetlights and rivers and towers. "I don't want to put you in danger, but you're one person and you can make a difference to dozens or hundreds."

Here lies Kate Kane. She made a difference to dozens. Beloved daughter. Sorely missed.

"I'm not very comforted by that," I said.

"Neither am I."

I gave her a look. "But you'd do it anyway?"

"I have to."

It seemed I couldn't turn around these days without somebody trying to sacrifice me for one thing or another. I guess it was going to be one of those weeks. At least Nim would feel bad about it. Probably. I sighed. "I don't have a choice, do I?"

"You always have a choice, but there'll always be a price. Though you may not be the one to pay it."

I really hated it when Nim got her gnomic on. "Just try not to get me killed, okay?"

Her hand closed lightly over mine for a moment. "I promise I'll protect you however I can for as long as I can."

"Uh, thanks," I said awkwardly. That could have meant everything or nothing, and knowing Nim, it probably meant both. "So, how's this going to work?"

"Tonight, we go to the Dream together."

"When you say together..."

"It'll help if I'm close to you physically."

"I bet you say that to all the girls."

She laughed. "I'm sure you can manage to keep your hands off me."

"It's not that." Meeting my ex-girlfriend in my dreams most nights already felt uncomfortably like cheating. Snuggling up to her as well was less like *unforeseen consequence of a supernatural bargain* and more like *taking the piss*. On the other hand, I really, really didn't want to choke to death in my sleep. "Look, is this a long-term thing? I'm not wild about needing a babysitter, plus it'll be really hard to explain to Julian."

Nim looked away, picking at the frayed bits at the bottom of her jeans. "I can't be sure, but if you can take me to where you were before,

I should be able to handle it from there. You shouldn't have to come back."

"What about you? I have no idea what that was, but it was pretty fucking nasty."

"I've been Queen of London for six years. This is what I do."

"Do you think you'll be able to kill it?"

"No." She glanced up. "But I can learn about it. And the more I know, the better I can fight it. The Dream is the city, and if we find its heart in the Dream, then we find its heart in the world."

"And then what?"

She folded her hands in her lap, and my crappy energy-saving lightbulb suddenly flared bright. "And then we can cut it out."

"I notice we're back to *we*."

"I gave you that sword for a reason, Kate."

"I thought you gave it to me so I wouldn't get killed."

Nim smiled. "Honestly, have you ever read a book? You don't give someone an enchanted sword to keep them safe. It's a double-edged blade."

I stared at her. "Did you give me a cursed sword?"

"It's not really 'cursed.'" There was something in her voice that suggested air quotes. "The sword goes where it's needed. And those who wield it will find use for it."

"Couldn't you have told me that earlier?"

"Would it have made a difference?"

I sighed. No, of course it wouldn't. "Come on then," I said, "let's do this."

In a desperate attempt to convince myself I wasn't having an affair, I put on my least sexy pair of pyjamas. They had hippos on them. Nim took off her hoodie, her socks, and her belt, and climbed into bed beside me.

This wasn't awkward. Not even a little bit.

"So... Come here often?"

"Now and then," whispered Nim. "But not lately."

I closed my eyes. We lay there in confused silence for a while. There's nothing like knowing you're supposed to be hunting a killer shadow monster in your dreams to stop you nodding off. Also I don't generally sleep on my back in hippo pyjamas trying not to touch the person I'm sleeping with.

"Did you say Corin was out?" asked Nim.

I made an affirming grunt in the gloom.

She slipped her hand into mine. "Are you okay?"

"Of course I'm not fucking okay."

There was a long silence.

"We can do this another night."

I gave her hand a squeeze. "No, facing unknown terror in unspeakable darkness is just what I need to take my mind off it."

"I can look for her," she offered, "if you want?"

"She's probably left London by now."

"If she's here, I'll find her."

I glared pointlessly at the ceiling. I couldn't believe I was doing this again. "I can't believe I'm doing this again."

I felt Nim shift slightly beside me. "The best stories are told more than once."

"Yeah, but when they redo things they're always shit. Look at *The Italian Job*."

Nim laughed. "Great. My entire life is a tacky remake."

I rolled over without thinking about it, and the next thing I knew, I was pressed against Nim's back, an arm thrown lightly across her waist. She was warm and soft and very human. Her hair smelled like the city after rain.

CHAPTER NINE
LOCKES & DOORS

I stood with Nimue in my arms at the foot of a hill in the Dream of a city. Snow and black feathers were falling softly through the darkness. I took Nimue by the hand and led her towards the maze of stairs and towers. Her fingers curled round mine, warm in the cold and the silence.

We came to a set of wrought iron gates crowned in shadows. Beyond them were the ghosts of trees and gravestones. I turned aside to follow the wall, looking for the place where I'd crossed the night before. Nimue's hand on my shoulder made me stop.

"This is Highgate Cemetery." Her breath misted silver. "It is a place of the dead and the dead have power here."

Nimue approached the gates and raised a hand. They swung slowly open, the chains that bound them slipping to the ground. Darkness flooded over us, and I couldn't breathe. A weight on my chest. Shadows in the corners of my eyes. Everywhere the sound of wings.

Then Nimue cupped my face between her palms and pressed her lips to mine. I tasted her breath, spring mornings and winter nights, the glitter of streetlights on puddles and the city's pale grey dawn.

"You okay?"

I checked. Still alive. "Guess so."

"What do you feel?" she asked.

"Cold and unthrilled."

"No, seriously."

"I'm feeling pretty seriously unthrilled. I just nearly died. Again."

"I won't let you die. I need you to find its heart."

"And it has to be me because . . . ?"

"Because it's who you are."

I sighed and shut my eyes. The darkness pressed sleek and heavy against me. I tasted blood and rust and quiet. A tarnished crown and the weight of many centuries. A soft and terrible anger. And a longing worn stale.

I opened my eyes. I realised I was shaking. "This way."

We went through the gates into Highgate Cemetery. We stumbled down narrow, overgrown paths, ankle-deep in flurried snow and feathers, between the twisted branches of bare trees, and over two centuries of the city's dead. We passed half-buried headstones, weathered granite and gleaming marble, crumbling obelisks, and sculpted angels.

The darkness deepened around us as I followed the trail uphill. Whatever I was tracking, I knew it now. I knew its taste and its scent, the shape of its power.

Everything, basically, except what it actually was.

And then the air was thick with wings. Great black birds, swooping from the trees, surrounding us with a flurry of beaks and claws. I fended them off as best I could while trying to shield my eyes but, tragically, I'd left my flamethrower in my other suit.

Beside me, I saw Nim step forwards. I felt a sudden sense of calm. And the birds melted into a silver mist that swirled away into the night.

We came at last to a straight road crusted with snow and lined by ornate Victorian grave markers. Ahead lay a strange octagonal building in red granite, its verdigris doors secured with a rusted chain. The stairs were ice slick as I climbed.

Something made me turn.

A woman was watching. She was tall and pale, raven haired and red lipped, and swathed in a mantle of black feathers. She raised her arms and her cloak unfurled into dark, iridescent wings.

Nim stepped in front of me, and I was falling.

I woke with a start. My phone said 5:15 a.m.

Well, fuck.

Nim lay beside me, shifting in a troubled sleep. Part of me thought I should wake her up, but the rest of me thought that it would be a spectacularly bad idea.

I rolled over, pulled up the duvet, and failed to go back to sleep.

When I finally gave up and got up at seven, Nim was still unconscious. I could hear Elise moving around in the kitchen, so I went to check in.

"Good morning, Miss Kane. I have never seen your sleeping attire before."

"I don't usually wear any, but Nim stayed over."

"Forgive me, but is 'stay over' a euphemism with which I am not familiar?"

I slumped against the fridge. "It can be, but right now it's a euphemism for 'she came to protect me from spooky shit that wanted to kill me in my dreams, and now she's passed out in my bed, and I'm not sure she's waking up anytime soon.'"

"I take it she will not want coffee, then?"

"I have no idea. She might be up in five minutes; she might be trapped like that for a year and a day."

"Do you wish me to remain with her, Miss Kane, in case she has need of something?"

"Would you? I've got a lot on my plate just now."

"May I assist you with that?"

I poured myself a coffee and grabbed a banana, and we went into the sitting room. I opened my mouth to try and explain, and then realised I had no idea where to begin. "Basically, Elise, this is one of *those* cases. It's like when you bend down to pick a bit of hair out the plughole, and it yanks up more hair after it, and so you keep pulling and pulling, and you start thinking 'Shit, how much of this stuff is there?' And eventually your whole drain is clogged, and you've spent sixty quid on sink and plughole unblocker, and all you've got to show for it is twenty handfuls of goopy crap."

Elise tilted her head slightly. "I fear that analogy may have run away with you."

"I just mean everything is connected to everything else. We were hired for a simple missing persons, and now I'm on trial for my life, hunting a vampire army, with my psychotic ex on the loose, and the Witch Queen of London passed out in my bed."

"For future reference, Miss Kane, I understand that the more common idiom is 'to open a can of worms.'"

I took a bite of my banana. I still do not like bananas. "Who the fuck keeps worms in cans?"

"Fishermen?"

"Look, we're getting off topic. Remember those dreams I've been having? Well, it turns out there's something big and nasty in Highgate Cemetery. Nim thinks it's a vampire, probably an old one.

All the vampire attacks have been centred on Highgate, and Hugh disappeared from a hospital two streets away. Either it's the biggest fucking coincidence in the universe, or Hugh was conscripted into a vampire army masterminded by this scary chick in Highgate Cemetery."

"Scary chick, Miss Kane?"

"I saw her in my dream. Tall, dark, and feathery. I think Nim's still fighting her in there. But, right now, finding Hugh is more important. If things kick off, I have basically zero chance of getting him back alive . . . well . . . undead. And then there's Eve. And then there's Corin."

"Is Miss Locke another of the worms?"

"Kinda." I crammed down the rest of the banana and washed away the taste with a gulp of coffee. "She's hunting vampires. As a fucking hobby. For all I know, she's got Hugh staked in a lab somewhere. Hell, for all I know, she could have unleashed the scary ancient vampire lady we really need a better name for."

Elise thought about it for a moment. "Perhaps we could call her Susan, Miss Kane."

"We're not calling her Susan. She did not look like a Susan."

"Bob?"

"She definitely didn't look like a Bob."

"Subject Alpha? Codename Sepulchre?"

"Look—" I gestured emphatically with my coffee cup, spilling some of it on the table. "Let's just stick with Scary Ancient Vampire Lady."

"As you wish. I shall continue to call her Susan in private."

"What I can't work out," I continued, "is where to go from here. I've got a weird feeling Corin's tied up in it somewhere as well. Someone must have busted her out for a reason, and right now, Susan is the only game in town."

"Would you like me to look more deeply into Susan, Miss Kane?"

"No, this is vampire stuff. They're secretive fuckers. The only way I'll learn is to ask someone with a really long memory, which means the Multitude or a really old vampire."

"Do you wish me to speak to Father Carew?"

"No, it's cool. No offence, but last time I spoke to the voice of the Multitude I wound up with you, and I don't have another spare room."

"Then how should we proceed, Miss Kane?"

"You're on Nim Watch. Ring me straightaway if there's any change. I don't know what I can do to help, but I do kind of give a fuck so . . . y'know." I finished what was left of my coffee and stood up. "I should probably check in with Eve first. I'm not spending the next two days looking for someone only to find out that my ex had him all along. Then, I'll probably visit Highgate just in case I can sneak into the tomb in full daylight and give Susan a good staking. After that, we're back to making it up as we go."

"Should I watch Miss Katz again tonight?"

"It can't hurt, but I'm starting to think that's a bust. If he was going back to her, he'd have gone back by now. Weirdly, that game thing you told me about might be a better bet. Fledgling vampires can sometimes snap back into old routines, so if he was used to being in the same place every week, there's a good chance he'd go back there."

"I have Mr. Warlock's number. He was most determined to give it to me. I shall forward his contact details."

Day planned, I went for a shower and got dressed. Nim was still sleeping. I smoothed back her tangled hair and kissed her forehead in a totally not-affair-having way.

"Don't fucking die."

I grabbed a second banana and set out for Locke Enterprises.

Eve's dotcom billions had bought her a sparkling dildo of a building just off the Old Street Roundabout. It didn't really have a reception, just a kind of casual foyer full of nerds sitting on beanbags, MacBooks perched on their laps. Everything from the urban art on the walls to the eclectic, hipster furniture screamed trendy, don't-give-a-fuck nonchalance, the kind of dynamic, thrown-together look you only get if you pay culture consultants millions to micromanage.

I got halfway towards the industrial espresso machine and the jellybean dispenser before a foetus with a smartphone bounced up. He was wearing distressed jeans, a blazer, and a scarf, all of which combined to make me want to punch him.

"Hi," he said, "it's totally cool to just, like, walk in off the street, but if there's anything you need, just give me a yell."

I stopped walking. "Are you the receptionist?"

"Well, what is a 'receptionist' really?" asked the foetus, managing to make sarcastic air quotes without dropping his phone.

"It's someone whose job it is to talk to people who just walk in off the street."

He pulled a face. "You're not really an out-of-the-box person, are you?"

"I'm here to see Eve."

"Very cool, but she's brainstorming with some guys right now."

I sighed. "Do you mean she's in a meeting? And if you say, 'Well, what is a meeting?' I will smack you."

"Dude. Uncool."

"Just tell me where she is."

"Okay, okay, she's in the Blue Room on twenty-seventh. I'll let her know you're on your way." He started tapping into his smartphone.

"You don't even know who I am."

"I'm putting 'scary woman in fedora.' I figure she'll either want to see you or call security."

That pretty much summed it up. I thought it was about sixty-forty in favour of security. I went looking for a lift and found a glass capsule that shuttled me up the outside of the building fast enough to make me wish I hadn't had that second banana. I lurched out on the twenty-seventh floor and wandered between open-plan work spaces and staff recreation areas until I found the Blue Room.

It's main distinguishing feature, right, was that was it was blue. It had probably been designed to make you feel like you were inside the sky, so the walls and ceiling were painted in this swirling mix of blue and grey. The carpet was cloud white and pet-rabbit fluffy. There was one central table and a lot of bits of furniture that I would only call "chairs" because people seemed to be sitting on them.

Eve was cross-legged in the middle of the table with an iPad in her hand and a couple of shiny, silver laptops open in front of her. She was barefoot, and wearing khaki combats and a tight brown T-shirt with #heyladies written on it. Apart from the vampire hunting and the phallic office block, money hadn't changed her at all.

"Okay, guys," she said, when she saw me in the doorway. "I have to take this. Go kick it about a bit and come back in, say, ten, and tell me what you've got."

Everybody packed up their tech and trooped out, several of them shooting a last, adoring look at Eve as they left.

She swivelled round on the table to face directly at me. "Have you come to shout at me some more?"

Now she wasn't wearing a superhero costume, I could see the telltale crescent of an old vampire bite on her neck, and there were parallel lines that looked like claw marks on her arm.

"I'm not going to shout at you." Calm, Kate, be calm. "But I would like to know how you got those."

I crossed the room and circled my thumb over the scars on her neck. Eve caught my wrist but didn't push me away.

"Vampire. Killed a bunch of people in Galway. I tracked it down and took it out, but it gave me something to remember it by. The other was just something random and greebly. We took it apart in the lab, but we didn't find anything."

"I thought you said you knew what you were doing."

"I do. I know it's dangerous, but somebody's got to do it. And besides," she grinned suddenly, "chicks dig scars."

She had a point. Obviously I was concerned about her safety, but at the same time, they did look pretty hot. They gave her this Xena: Warrior Princess vibe.

I realised I hadn't stopped stroking her neck.

I stuffed my hand in my pocket. Bad hand. No biscuit.

"Look," I said quickly, "I'm tracking down this missing person. One of your interns, Hugh Shawcross? I think he's been turned into a vampire. Do you know what's happened to him, and have you got him locked up in some freaky white room deep underground?"

"Don't be silly, that's a shopping mall."

"We dated for five years. There's no way you'd build a place like this and not have a secret base underneath it. You probably have big vats of chemicals and walkways with no handrails and some kind of nuclear reactor controlled by one very small switch."

"Kate, I have almost none of those things." She didn't exactly wink at me, but she said it in a very winky way. "All the walkways are fully health and safety compliant, I don't have any vats of chemicals, and the nuclear reactor has multiple fail-safes."

"So you do have a secret underground base."

Eve smiled wickedly. "You know the rules. I don't have to tell you anything until I've got you tied up in a terribly slow-moving death trap."

I found myself smiling back at her. "I'm game if you are. Menace away."

"Mmm, sadly the shark pit's closed for cleaning, and the giant lasers won't be installed until Thursday."

I suddenly remembered why I was there. Also. Girlfriend. "Look, seriously, Eve, one of your interns is missing. It's my job to find him, so can you please throw me a bone here?"

She shrugged. "Last thing I heard, he was off with a broken leg."

I gave her a look.

"I promise that's all I know. I didn't have him killed for stealing files, and he wasn't a part of a secret vampire/human hybrid super-soldier programme. He was doing some image analysis work for me."

"What, specifically?"

She sighed. "You're really not going to let this go, are you, Kate?"

"You should know I'm not really a letting-things-go kind of person."

There was a slight pause. "With one notable exception."

Oooh zing. I glared at her. "Do you really want to have this conversation again?"

She seemed to be seriously considering it, but then she shook her head. "No. Sorry. Okay, here's the deal. I'm working on software that lets you identify vampires from CCTV footage. Biometrics, autonomic movements, stuff like that. Hugh was a small part of the project and didn't know what he was working on. I didn't know he'd been turned into a vampire, and I haven't picked him up on my patrols."

The door opened, and a skinny nerd-boy with a goatee stuck his head inside. "Good to go, boss?"

Eve nodded. "We're done here."

I guess we were done here.

"Thanks for your time," I said awkwardly.

"It been good seeing you again."

I wasn't sure if she was being ironic. Then again, I never had been. "Yeah."

I left.

I really didn't know if that had gone well. I'd got the information I needed, and I was pretty sure she wasn't bullshitting me, but I had no idea where I stood Eve-wise. It was nice she didn't seem to absolutely hate me, but I wasn't ready to be a supporting character in her personal superhero movie. Featuring Kate Kane as the washed-up PI who says things like *But that's impossible, nobody's ever done that before!* On the other hand, seeing her again had been... I don't know. Good? Sweet? Weird? Like going back to a house you don't live in anymore. It would be so easy to...

Probably best I stick with the *avoid her at all costs* strategy that's worked so well for the past year and a bit.

I ticked Eve off the list and pulled out my phone to check the time. I probably wouldn't get to Highgate until noon, which is exactly what you want when you're poking around the lair of something ancient, immortal, and very likely to kill you. I got on the Tube at Bank and off again at Archway. It was a bit subdued post-murder. Passengers were eyeing each other warily and keeping their distance the way they did after the bombings in 2005. I was pretty sure that most vampires wouldn't be out at this time of day, but my fellow travellers had no way of knowing that.

It took me a while to get out of the station because of the extra security, and there was a sad little floral tribute outside. I stood and stared at it for a bit. I don't know why people insist on strapping flowers to railings and piling them up outside Tube stations, but I guess when somebody dies in such a random, pointless way doing something they do every day, it seems wrong for the place where it happened to just sit there like it doesn't matter.

Last night I'd walked into a house full of corpses, but somehow, this shook me up a lot more.

I guess Nim had been right. This wasn't just a Council problem.

I strode off up the hill. Annoyingly there was no entrance to the cemetery on the east side so I cut through Waterlow Park. It was pretty quiet, but there were a couple of kids feeding the ducks on the pond. I made it to the cemetery and dropped my suggested three-quid donation into the box. A helpful man in a green puffer jacket came over to let me know that the tomb of Karl Marx was just up the road to my left. I guess I looked like a communist or something.

Apart from the snow and the feathers and the choking oily darkness, the cemetery was exactly like it had been in my dreams. There were four or five large marble tombs right by the entrance, so this was probably going to be a quick visit. One of them was set slightly apart and built of red stone. Yep, a really short visit.

I collared Puffer Jacket and asked who was buried there. I wasn't expecting him to say *Ah, well, that's the cursed tomb of Countess Marianna von Bloodlust*, but I thought it might be useful anyway.

"That's Davison Dalziel, Lord Dalziel of Wooler. He was an MP, a baron, and he introduced the motorcab to London in 1907."

Huh. "When did he die?"

"1928."

That didn't make a lot of sense. There was no way that whatever was raising vampires all over North London was less than a hundred years old. I thanked the guy and went for a closer look.

This was a serious mausoleum, the kind that said *I'm dead and I want you to notice*: big, heavy doors with honest-to-God lions sculpted into them and a thick iron chain rusted almost solid, with a padlock to match.

No, wait. A padlock that didn't match.

I'm not a locksmith or a metallurgist or someone from the *Antiques Roadshow*, but while the chain looked like it had been there for the best part of a century, the lock didn't. It was old and rusty but not eighty-four years old and rusty.

I put on some gloves and did what we in the business call *poking at it*. The rust was worn away at the catch, which suggested it had been opened and closed very recently. I snapped a couple of pictures with my phone and went back to harass the man in the puffer jacket.

"Just out of curiosity," I asked, "has it ever been opened?"

He gave me a funny look.

"I'm writing a book," I lied.

"Not as long as I've been here."

Hmmm. So we were dealing with an ancient vampire operating out of a tomb from less than a hundred years ago that had been opened quite recently—from the outside—by somebody who had bothered to replace the lock. None of that made any sense at all. But there was no way I was going to try and break in at half past twelve and ten feet from the guy whose job it is to stop people trying to break into these things.

So, in an effort to get my three quid's worth, I went and checked out Karl Marx. You kind of have to respect a man who's buried under a giant statue of his own face.

CHAPTER TEN

WITCHES & WARLOCKS

I was racking up mysteries faster than I was solving them, and none of them were bringing me any closer to finding Hugh. I left the cemetery, headed down the hill, and stopped at a pub for lunch. While I was waiting for my burger and my potato wedges to arrive, I pulled out my phone and checked my messages. Elise had sent me a couple of texts. There was no news about Nim, but she had sent me Warlock's number. I rang it.

"Hello?" said a wary voice.

"Is that Warlock?"

"Who's asking?"

Oh right, he was one of *those*. "Kate Kane of Kane and Archer. You've already spoken to my colleague."

"Greek chick? Dresses like a librarian? Doesn't call you back?"

"That's her. We're still looking for Hugh Shawcross. She tells me you used to have a weekly meeting with him."

There was a pause. I think I pissed him off.

"It's not a meeting; it's a collaborative storytelling game."

I really wasn't sure what to say to that. So I ignored it. "It's a long shot, but I think he might show up. Do you mind if I come by in case he does?"

There was another moment of silence. Then, with poorly suppressed glee: "No, that'd be fine. I'll text you a link to the quick-start rules."

Rules? "Um ... I—"

"So, yeah, we normally start about seven, but if you could come round about five, so we can roll up a character and do the prelude?"

This wasn't quite what I had in mind, but if it got my foot in the door ... whatever.

"Sure," I said. "Cool. Where is it?"

He gave me his on-campus address, and I hung up just as they brought out my burger. I ate it quickly while mulling over the case—or rather the cases. I'd done all I could about Hugh for now, which just left Corin on the loose, and the thing in the graveyard. I wasn't sure if the two were connected, but where Corin's concerned, I don't believe in coincidences. But, at the moment, there was nothing I could do about her either. Which just left whatever was going on in Highgate Cemetery.

The problem was I needed detailed information about probably quite obscure vampire history, and right now, most vampires were too busy trying to execute me. I could have gone to Julian, but things were complicated there as well, and she'd hinted that it was safer for both of us if we kept our distance until the trial was over. That left me with people who knew about vampires, and there weren't many of those. As I'd said to Elise, I could have gone to the Multitude, but information from a giant rat gestalt tends to be pretty patchy.

I finished off my wedges, left the salad, and thought about calling it a day. Then I realised I should just go to Ashriel. I was so used to him being the guy who stood outside the Velvet in a tight shirt and occasionally got shot by nuns that I'd completely overlooked the fact that he was also about ten thousand years old and had known Julian for pretty much her entire unlife. And the Council had probably forgotten that too. Of course, the last time I'd seen him, I'd been kind of a dick, so I owed him an apology anyway.

I hate apologising.

I sent him a text to let him know I was going to swing by and made for Brewer Street. Just like last time, it was locked up at the front, so I slipped round the back. This time the barman just waved. Friday was Cabaret Baudelaire, and from the music, the glitter, and the air of suppressed panic, it looked like the boylesque troupe were in the middle of rehearsals. There appeared to be some trauma related to a broken hula hoop.

With a clatter of heels, Kauri came dashing from the wings. He was wearing a sparkly gold minidress, platform boots, and an outrageous purple wig. Behind him was a muscular, heavily tattooed man dressed in nothing but eye shadow and a cock tassel.

"Ash, honey," Kauri shouted. "We've got a prop crisis." And then, seeing me, he froze. "Oh shit, Kate."

"It's fine," I told him. "I understand."

"That creepy Spanish fuck got right in my head."

"Really, it's okay. There was nothing you could have done."

"I know, it's just—"

"Look," interrupted Cock Tassel, "sorry to piss on your pity parade, but can we focus on my hoop please."

Before Kauri could answer, Ashriel appeared in the stairwell. "What's wrong now?"

"Luke's broken a hoop and the spares are still in the lockup."

Ashriel sighed. "Give it here, ladies."

Luke handed him the loosely flopping remains of a sparkly hula hoop. "Caught it on a stiletto."

Ashriel held the broken ends between two fingers, which began to glow with a sickly green fire. Very carefully he melted the plastic and teased the two sides together. When he was done, he raised the hoop to his lips and blew on it. "You do know I once marched on the gates of Heaven under the banner of the Morning Star."

"Yes, but now," said Kauri, taking the hula hoop in one fabulously glittering hand, "you're in show business."

There was a long silence.

Ashriel groaned. "This is Hell, nor am I out of it."

"Love you too, honey." Kauri blew him a kiss. He patted Luke lightly on his exquisitely sculpted buttocks. "Back to work, Miss Thing."

They disappeared into the wings.

Ashriel cast a cool look in my direction. "She's not here."

"Actually, I was looking for you." I stared at the floor and shuffled my feet. Did I mention, I hate apologising?

"I take it you want something?"

"Uh . . . yes, kinda. But I really was going to say sorry first."

"Go on, then." The corners of his mouth twitched like he was trying not to smile.

"Oh, you utter dick. Fine. I'm sorry I was slightly rude to you the last time I was here."

He raised an eyebrow. "Just a tip: apologies sound better if you don't preface them with 'Oh, you utter dick.'"

"Interesting idea. I'll try it one of these years."

"Come on, then, take a seat by the bar, tell me what you want, and I'll fix you a Sloe Comfortable Screw Up Against the Wall."

I slipped onto a barstool. "I didn't think you did that sort of thing anymore."

Ashriel was sloshing alcohol into a highball glass. "Ha-ha, mock the celibate sex demon who's giving you a free drink."

"Good point, well made."

He pushed a pinkish-orange cocktail across the bar towards me, and I took a swig. "That's pretty comfortable."

"I could throw in a kiss if you like."

"I'm good, thanks." I sipped at the drink and tried to think of way to pump him for information without sounding like a total jerk. "So I actually wanted to pick your brains about vampire history."

"Not really my speciality, Kate."

"You've been working with Julian for half a millennium."

He frowned at me. "If you want to know something about Julian, you'll have to ask her yourself."

"Shocked as she'd be to hear it, this isn't about her. Do you know what's buried in Highgate Cemetery?"

There was a thoughtful pause. "Karl Marx?"

"Better breasts, less beard."

There was another pause, more confused this time. "What are you talking about?"

"There's some kind of scary vampire chick loose in Highgate. I think she's building an army."

"And you know this, how?"

"Spate of attacks across North London, unexplained outbreak of being-turned-into-a-vampire-itis in a hospital two streets away, and I, um . . ." I took another drink because there was no way this was going to sound good. ". . . sort of saw her in a dream."

"I was with you right up to 'dream.'"

"You're pretty sceptical for a reformed demon who works in a vampire nightclub."

"It's not the dream, it's you." He leaned his elbows on the bar and gave me a smouldering look. I don't think the smoulder was intentional, but there are some things you just can't turn off. "No offence, Kate, but you're not exactly a visionary."

He had a point. "I was with Nim, okay? We were in Highgate. Crows, darkness, crazy woman with wings. I know what I saw."

"Are you sure?"

I glared. "No, when I said 'I know what I saw,' I meant 'I'm not certain what I saw, please question me further.'"

"This is bad," said Ashriel, finally.

"I'd got that far on my own. Details, pretty-boy."

"You haven't given me much to go on—" He leaned closer. "—but crows, dreams, shadows, and scary woman with wings sounds a lot like the Morrígan."

"Oh shit." I paused. "Wait. Who's the Morrígan?"

Ashriel ran his hands through his silky honey-blond hair. "Fuck-ancient vampire queen. Ruled the entire British Isles for thousands of years. The Council took her out sometime in the seventeenth century as part of their whole pan-European No Gods, No Masters thing. They sealed her up in a crypt on Magpie Lane. If it is her, I have no idea how she got to Highgate or why she's awake."

"Well, she probably doesn't want to start a knitting circle. It seems like her current plans are something along the lines of 'Kill Everything.'"

Ashriel poured himself some Southern Comfort and knocked it back. "I have to find Julian. She needs to know about this."

"Is there any way we can keep the Council out of this? I'm trying to find this kid who's tangled up in the whole mess. And if the vampires get their purge on, he's basically had it."

"Kate, this is really fucking serious. Towards the end of her reign, the Morrígan was, to use the technical term, completely batshit insane. There was a time in the sixteen sixties when she was killing ten thousand people a month, and that's just the mortals. She was the queen of plagues and corpses and carrion. Death was her servant and darkness her crown. In case you're not getting this, she was bad fucking news."

I was getting it. "So how did they take her out the first time?"

"Sebastian."

"Oh, I should have fucking guessed. What did he do? Kill her with smugness?"

Ashriel abandoned his glass and took a slug straight from the bottle. "He was one of her progeny, and in the end, the only one she trusted. He betrayed her to the Council, but I don't know the details."

My phone bleeped. It was a text from Elise, telling me Nim was awake.

"I've got to get home," I said. "Something's come up."

He nodded. "See you, Kate."

"Thanks for the . . . screw."

"Anytime."

On the Tube heading home, I ticked off one mystery only to realise that I hadn't so much solved it as replaced it with another, slightly different mystery. I had a name for Susan but I still didn't know what she was doing in Highgate, how she'd got there, or what she wanted. And I still hadn't found Hugh.

I got off at East Finchley and was slogging down Murdered Family Street, trying not to look at the police tape or think about the corpses, the brush with death, or my ex, when I heard a roar from behind me and a familiar-looking Fat Boy started kerb-crawling me. I stopped walking, and Michelle, Guardian of the Watchtower of the South, flipped up her visor. It was hard to see under the leather, the tattoos, and the motorcycle helmet, but she was looking better than she had the last time we'd met. Then again, that wasn't difficult, because the last time we'd met, my girlfriend had tried to suck the life out of her.

"Need a ride?"

"Haven't got a helmet." When it comes to jumping onto things with strange women, I try to be safety conscious. Oh, who am I kidding?

"Got a spare." She jerked a thumb at one of the saddlebags. I rummaged and found a spare helmet pressed against two bottles of vodka, a compact but still highly illegal handgun, and a really scary amount of lighter fluid.

"You just have that to pick up chicks, don't you?" I said.

"Worked, didn't it?"

I jammed the helmet on my head and climbed up behind her.

"Hold on tight."

I put my arms around her, and we thundered off up Fortis Green. It wasn't a long journey, but it was a happy reminder of my early twenties, after I'd chucked Patrick and discovered the twin joys of hot women and heavy machinery.

We pulled up outside the flat, and I hopped off.

"I take it you're here for Nim?" I asked, as Michelle dismounted as well.

"Yep."

"Don't say a lot, do you?"

"Nope."

I should have seen that coming.

Inside the flat, Nim was awake and sharing a large pepperoni pizza with a man in a bright orange *Transport for London* jacket. Michelle grabbed herself a slice and sat down without saying anything.

"Hi, Kate." Nim waved at me. She looked basically okay for someone who'd been unconscious for the best part of a day. "Sorry to turn your flat into a war room. I don't think you've met Jacob."

"Hey," he said laconically.

By a process of elimination, Jacob must be the Guardian of the Watchtower of the West. He was a portly South Asian man with salt-and-pepper hair and a greying goatee.

"Hey," I said back.

Nim grinned. "Wow, with you three here I won't be able to get a word in edgeways."

Michelle gave her sovereign the finger.

The Witch Queen of London returned the gesture.

"Anyway." Nim turned back to me. "Do you want some pizza?"

"I always want pizza. Are you all right?"

"Tired, but fine."

"Oh, come on, how can you be tired. You've been in bed all day."

She smiled at me. "Yes, Kate, I've been slacking off fighting an undead shadow queen."

"We have taken to calling her Susan," offered Elise, coming in with a half-full washing-up bowl. "I am afraid this was the only suitable receptacle I could find unless you wish to reconvene in the bathroom."

"That looks fine," Nim replied. "Just pop it on the coffee table. Michelle, can you get the TV?"

I put my hand in the air. "Hey, can we just remember whose flat we're in here?"

"Sorry Kate. Kate, do you mind if Michelle puts the TV on?"

"Sure."

Michelle stretched out an arm and slapped the on switch. The screen filled up with static and a cacophony of babbling voices burst out of the speakers. Then utter silence. And, finally, a figure appeared on the screen. It was a skinny woman in a pink one-piece, with her white-blonde hair scraped back in a high ponytail.

"Ahwight, babes?" she said, cheerfully. And then, "Oh 'ello, Kate, it's nice to see you in person."

This had to be Rachel. "I wouldn't call this in person. You're kind of on my TV."

"Wha'eva."

Nim dragged the washing bowl over and passed her hand across the surface of the water. "The Witch Queen of London seeks communion with the Guardian of the Watchtower of the North."

After a moment a small brown face appeared in the surface of the water, and said, "Hello, Auntie Nim."

Nimue smiled into the bowl. "Hello, Phoebe. Can you get your daddy for me?"

"He's busy doing The Rit-u-al of Ward-ing Con-flu-ence and telling Mummy to come straight home after work."

A second voice, garbled like it was underwater, drifted into the room: "Phoebe, what have I told you about playing with the scrying pool?"

"Don't do it."

"We have three rules in this house, what are they?"

"Don't bother Mummy when she's working, no pudding unless you've eaten all your vegetables, even the sprouts, and do not meddle with forces beyond your com-pre-hension."

The second voice said something I didn't catch, but the tone sounded parent-y.

A little hand appeared in the water and splashed back and forth. "Good-bye, Auntie Nim," said Phoebe. "Daddy says I have to get out the scrying pool now. Good-bye, Auntie Michelle. Good-bye, Auntie Rachel. Good-bye, Uncle Jacob. Good-bye, strange lady I haven't met before."

Her face disappeared and was replaced by Gabriel's. He was looking pretty stressed. "How bad is it, Nim? Do I need to get my kids out?"

"It's not good," she told him, "but your wards should hold for a couple of days at least."

Michelle leaned forwards with a creak of leather. "I'll send some people round. We're already patrolling the area. Rach, text Tarquin and Yseult. They're nearby."

Rachel didn't move. She didn't even appear to have a mobile phone. "Done."

"All right, guys," began Nim. "I, Nimue, hereby convene this meeting of the Circle to discuss the unknown enemy that rises in the north of our kingdom."

"If it's any help," I offered, "I know who it is."

There was a long silence.

"Yes," said Nim in a *Why didn't you mention this earlier?* voice. "Yes, that would be helpful, Kate."

"She's called the Morrígan. Ancient vampire queen. Slaughtered a fuck-tonne of people back in sixteen-blahdiblah. If we don't stop her, she'll kill everything."

"Great." Michelle grabbed another slice of pizza. "So no pressure then."

"How ancient?" asked Jacob.

"I'm not sure, but I think, like, copper-tools-and-deer-skins ancient."

"Hate to say it—" Michelle's hand strayed to her neck where Julian had savaged her. "—but, if you're right, there's no way we're taking her in a straight fight." She gave me a look I couldn't read. "Your girlfriend was bad enough."

I opened my mouth to say something but realised there was absolutely nothing I could say. It wasn't like I could apologise for Julian, and she had kind of killed a bunch of people. Worse still, it hadn't really put me off her.

"It doesn't have to be a straight fight," said Nimue. "Jacob, this is your thing."

He ran a hand thoughtfully through his beard. "With a very old vampire, its biggest weakness is its bloodline. They sink a lot of their power into it, and it brings a lot of power back, but it's a way in."

"Sorry to butt in." Rachel's voice crackled out my speakers. "But the police band says some sort of riot around Chalk Farm."

Michelle glanced towards the TV. "Send Branwyn's gang down."

"Done."

"And ask them to bring me back some blood, if they can," added Jacob.

Rachel made a huggy sort of gesture through the TV. "Aw, you are a sick puppy, Jake."

"It's just blood. We've all got it."

"Fine. Done."

Michelle pulled herself to her feet. "This is fucked. We need action."

"We're taking action." Nim spoke softly, but the room fell silent around her. "I'm pushing her back in the Dream. She still thinks this is her land, and it isn't. It's mine, and I'll fight for it. You two keep doing what you're doing. Save as many lives as you can, and try not to start too many fires. Gabriel, what's your advice?"

The water in the washing-up bowl rippled. "I worry that we are fighting the wrong battle. There's something else here, but I can't see through the shadows."

"Great," said Michelle. "A seer who can't see."

"Michelle, I have been seer to the Court of London since you were six years old. If I cannot see, it is because someone has taken the trouble to blind me, and that means something."

"Are you telling me there's something even bigger and even nastier out there?" I asked. "Well, fuck."

"Not bigger or nastier, but probably more subtle and more careful."

Nimue began tidying up the empty pizza boxes. "Unfortunately, even if it is a distraction, it's a distraction that's killing people. Jacob, if we get you the blood, what can you do?"

"There's a ritual that drains the strength of a vampire. With time, and for a price, I can make it affect a whole bloodline and a whole city."

I waited for someone to ask the obvious question, and they didn't. So I did. "When you say price . . . ?"

He shrugged. "You don't mess around with life and death for free."

"What do you need?" asked Nimue.

"The blood of seven vampires from that line, the dirt from seven graves from where she rested, the ash from seven woods from seven trees, usual necromancy stuff. Then I need to anoint seven places around London without getting killed by vampires and come back to King's Cross to finish the ritual. Is there any pizza left?" Michelle shoved the last pizza box over. "Problem is, soon as I start, any vampire in the bloodline who knows the first thing about magic will know something's happening, and then we won't have much time."

This sounded pretty damn hard-core. I knew magic could do some serious shit, but this was something else. "And this will really affect every vampire descended from the Morrígan?"

"If it works." He calmly finished his pizza slice. "I've never done anything on this scale before."

"What will happen to them?"

"It will drain the energy that sustains them. The weak ones will just die. For good this time. The others, I don't know."

I looked around at the mages, waiting for a reaction. I didn't get one. "Isn't this a bit of a nuclear option? You're talking about killing hundreds of people here."

"They're not people," said Michelle. "They're vampires."

"And a lot more will die if we don't," added Nimue. "The city can't sustain an army of vampires. The Council will destroy them if we don't."

Shit. This whole clusterfuck had just got way clusterier and fuckier.

"You should know," I told them, "that the Prince of Wands is one of the Morrígan's kids. He won't sit around quietly and let you suck his life force out."

Rachel made a "talk to the hand" gesture. "Babe, I don't even know who that is."

"One of the vampire Council," explained Nim. "Unfortunately, we'll have to take that chance."

"Look," I interrupted, "I've been hired to find some guy, and I think he's one of them too. He's a twenty-something software designer. I'm not mad keen on you making him collateral damage."

"Kate, if you're right, he's already dead," said Nim gently. "I'm really sorry, but it wasn't us who brought him into this."

"And if you can get him out the city before the ritual," added Jacob, "he won't be affected."

"For the record, I still think this is a really bad idea."

"Got a better one?" asked Michelle.

I didn't.

Nimue came over and perched on the arm of my chair. "This is a bad situation, Kate, and a lot of people are going to get hurt before it's through. We have to do what we can. We're going to do this, and I'm going to ask you to help."

I gave her a look. "I'm quite busy at the moment. I've got this guy to find, and I'm on trial for my life, and my psycho ex is out of prison."

"We had a bargain."

Yes. Yes, we did. I sighed. "Fine, what do you want me for? Decoy, bait, human shield?"

"I need you to protect Jacob while he performs the ritual."

"The ritual I think is a really bad idea?"

"Yes."

"It's fine," interrupted Michelle, "I'll do it."

"No, you will not." Nim glanced over. "You have other duties."

I gave up. "All right, all right. Text me when you're ready, and I'll show up with the Sword of Getting Me into Trouble and a book for the Tube."

"Then that is all," said Nim. "I thank you for your counsel. You are free to depart."

"I live here," I pointed out.

"I don't." Michelle headed for the door. "Anyone want a lift?"

Jacob got up without saying a word and followed her from the room.

"See ya, babes." Rachel vanished, and my television flicked onto an episode of *Have I Got News for You*.

"Good-bye," said Gabriel, and the surface of the washing bowl went still and clear.

That just left me, Nim, Elise, and the last slice of pizza.

"That was most interesting," observed Elise. "I enjoy watching interactions. I have now attended both a dinner party and a convocation of mages."

Nim smiled mischievously. "If you ask Kate nicely, she might take you clubbing."

"Or she might not," I replied, firmly.

"Whatever you think best, Miss Kane. Now, if you will excuse me, I need to go and ensure that Miss Katz is not exsanguinated by her vampire lover."

"Have a good stakeout."

And now there was just me, Nim, and the pizza, and it wasn't at all awkward.

She touched my shoulder lightly. "I should go as well."

I wanted to ask her to stay, which meant I really shouldn't. I tried to pretend I was just worried about her, but having Nim around yesterday had been . . . nice. I mean, right up to the point where we confronted a scary uber-vampire in the middle of a graveyard.

"See you in my dreams," I said, instead.

"Not tonight. You need the rest."

"You're not going to get killed, are you?"

"No. I'm stronger in the Dream."

"Well, just, like, dream-yell if you need me."

She reached out and brushed her fingertips across my cheek. She was so warm. "Thank you, Kate. I know I've asked a lot of you."

"S'okay."

I curled my hand lightly around her wrist. Her pulse beat beneath the skin, strong and fragile at the same time. You're probably not in a very good place when you think a pulse is an unusual quality in a woman.

After she left, I settled down for another fun-packed Friday evening drinking alone.

CHAPTER ELEVEN

FRIENDS & LOVERS

took Saturday off, which in practice meant waking up at ten with a god-awful hangover that didn't clear until noon. Elise was on the street playing with her remote control helicopter, but she'd tidied the flat, taken out the pizza boxes, and left me a pot of coffee and a banana. Sometimes living with Elise felt a bit like living with your mum, although if Jenny had looked like Elise, I'd have grown up even more messed up than I already am.

I'm not very good at relaxation, so I stuck the TV on and wondered if it was too early to start drinking. Warlock had, as promised, sent me the demo rules for the game he was going to be running that evening. Since I'm a professional, I tried to do my homework. The cover art—which, embarrassingly, looked a little bit like Julian on a bad day—did not fill me with confidence, and about three minutes into the introductory chapter, which opened with the line *your requiem begins here*, I decided I'd rather be drunk.

I was just getting on with that when the buzzer went. Elise didn't normally forget her keys, which meant it was probably someone trying to kill me. I picked up the handset on the intercom.

"Hello?"

"We have to talk," said a voice I didn't recognise.

"Make an appointment. I'm in the book. And on the internet."

"I'm not going away until you talk to me."

"Fine." I hung up.

It buzzed again two seconds later and kept buzzing until I answered.

"Who the hell are you," I demanded, "and what do you want?"

"I want you to stop hurting Patrick."

Oh fuck, it was her, wasn't it? "Oh fuck, it's you, isn't it?"

"I know you hate me, Kate, but don't take it out on Patrick. He's done nothing to you."

I had no idea what she was talking about. I sighed. "You'd better come up."

Half a minute later, I let Sofia into my flat. She looked around as if to say *You live like this?* What with the bottle on the table and the Saturday afternoon TV, I'd say I wasn't doing myself justice, but truthfully I probably was. Sofia just sort of stood in the middle of the room, hands tucked into the pockets of her jeans with her thumbs peeking over the edges.

"What are you doing here?" I asked.

She stared at me with the defiance you can only have when you're seventeen. "You got what you wanted."

For a moment, I had no idea what she meant, and then I thought back fifteen years and I knew perfectly. "Patrick's left you, hasn't he?"

"Wasn't that the plan? Isn't that why you had those men attack us?"

I took a deep breath. I was going to have one more go at this, even though I knew it wasn't going to make a difference. "I know you won't believe me, because I wouldn't have believed me when I was your age, but I have no desire to steal your boyfriend. We broke up more than ten years ago, I thought he was a dick then and I think he's a dick now."

She looked at me with quivering sincerity. "Patrick said you'd try to turn me against him."

There was a pause.

"You do know I'm gay, right?"

There was an even longer pause.

"If you're gay, why did you go out with Patrick?"

I couldn't believe I was thirty-three and having to give a coming out speech to my vampire ex-boyfriend's seventeen-year-old girlfriend. "Sometimes that's just how it works. Seriously, Google it."

She bit her lip. "You're just trying to confuse me."

"Honestly, I don't give a fuck about you. You're never going to trust me. I'm not going to try and be your friend. I would love it if I could stop you making the same mistakes I made, but since that has never worked in the entire history of the universe, I'll settle for an end to the bullshit."

She gave me a look of mingled pity and disgust. I remembered looking at Patrick's sire exactly the same way. "Why do you swear so much?"

"Because it's big and clever and all the cool kids do it. Now tell me who attacked you."

"Vampires. Patrick protected me, but they stabbed him."

Great. Another mystery. I would have assumed it was just the Morrigan's vampire army, but from what I'd seen, they weren't armed and they'd been too rabid to think about anything except biting and tearing.

"Nothing to do with me," I said. "If I wanted to stab Patrick, I'd do it myself."

Come to think of it, I already had.

Her hands curled into fists in her pockets. "I know you want to kill me."

"Jesus fuck. Not this again. No. I don't. I can't be bothered."

"I've *seen* you."

Okay, this was getting interesting. Either she was completely crazy or there was something else going on. "Seen me how?"

"I have a dream. Every night. The vampires who attacked us take me to a big old house with dragons outside it. I'm supposed to do something, but I don't know what it is. I see you, and I see a man in a golden mask."

"Look, this has nothing to do with— Hang on, did you say a golden mask?"

She nodded. "Yes, with the rays of the sun around it."

Well, fuck. What was it with Patrick and supernaturally gifted teenagers? I guess we all have our types, but this was getting ridiculous. "This is a bit of a funny question, but has anyone sent you any red flowers, lately?"

"No."

"Okay, this is really important. If you get any, you are in real danger. Call me, call Patrick, call somebody. I don't know you, and I don't care who you sleep with or what you do, but I don't want you to get sacrificed by a psycho vampire cult."

"Wow, thanks a million," she said, in her best sarcastic teenager voice.

"Wait here." I went into my bedroom and grabbed my gold dagger from the bedside table. I half expected Sofia to bolt, but she was still there when I got back, although the knife probably freaked her out. "Has Patrick told you how to kill a vampire yet?" I asked.

She shook her head.

"Okay, so they can basically come back from anything, even fire and decapitation if they're strong enough. Piercing the heart will paralyse, but it won't kill, and anything will do, it doesn't have to be wood. Their only real weakness is gold."

I slipped the blade from its sheath.

"Keep it hidden because you'll only get one shot. Vampires aren't used to pain, especially the old ones who've forgotten what it feels like, and they back off really fast if you cut them with gold. It doesn't hold an edge well, so you're going to have to stab hard and put your weight behind it, but it might just save your life."

Sofia stared at me with real fear. "You're mad."

I get that a lot. "Just take the fucking dagger. There's clearly vampires after you and they're stronger than you and faster than you. You need to be able to protect yourself."

"Patrick will protect me."

The annoying thing was, he probably would, but that wasn't the point. "Hasn't Patrick dumped you?" It was a cheap shot, but I took it anyway.

"He'd come back if I was in real danger."

This could get very bad, very quickly. When I was eighteen, I'd thrown myself off a cliff in an effort to get Patrick to come back to me. Sadly, it had worked. "You're in his world, now you have to survive in it."

Sofia glared at me, and then, hesitantly, took the dagger out of my hand and stuffed it into her shoulder bag. She left without saying another word.

After she'd gone, I realised there was an army of crazed vampires running around the streets, and I'd just given away my only golden dagger.

Ah well, what was the worst that could happen?

Oh yes, I could get ripped apart outside my flat by baby vampires.

I was supposed to be at Brunel in about three hours, which had seriously cut into my getting hammered time. I watched half of this Saturday afternoon movie where Sean Connery plays a dragon, but I had to leave before I found out how they were going to take down the evil prince. Elise could have recorded it for me, but I didn't know how to work the machine.

Warlock lived in this weird trendy block of brightly coloured flats on the Brunel campus. I'd never gone to university but I'd seen a lot of halls of residence when I was in my early twenties and working my way around London's ample supply of bicurious undergraduates, and this was significantly less skanky than I remembered. But, then again, he was a postgrad.

Warlock himself turned out to be a lanky, straggly-haired nerd-boy dressed in various shades of faded black. He opened the door, raised a hand in a halfhearted greeting, and went back inside without saying a word. I saw a long leather coat and a fedora dumped in a corner. He did, at least, have a separate sitting area—if you counted a single two-seater sofa and a desk with an enormous computer on it as a sitting area.

"Nice hat." Warlock threw himself down in a leather swivel chair. "Put your stuff anywhere."

I took off my coat and hat and laid them on the floor in the absence of any free surfaces, and then plonked myself on the sofa.

"So did you get a look at the quick start?" He was straight to business.

"Uh . . . I sort of skimmed it."

"Don't worry, it can be quite complicated, but I'll talk you through it."

He leaned down beside his desk and pulled up two hardback books from a teetering stack of similar-looking hardback books. "'Kay, so, you can either have a look at the vampire book and decide what Clan you want to be, or you can just decide what you were like as a mortal and I'll decide who Embraced you."

"I'll go with the second one." I'd done this stuff with Eve back when I'd sat in on her D&D games, and I'd found it easier to let other people make the decisions for me. Besides, Warlock looked like the kind of guy who enjoyed explaining things to women.

"'Kay, so, it's set in, like, London in the real world, except all the things you think are just stories, like vampires and werewolves and fairies and things, are actually real."

He was clearly waiting for a reaction. "Wow," I said, "that sounds... awesome."

"Yeah, it's kind of a metaphor for the very real darkness of, like, the everyday world."

"Can I be a gnome?"

"Oh, right." He looked at me with obvious pity. "You played D&D."

"Just a couple of times with my ex."

"Well, this'll probably be quite different to your boyfriend's game."

I let that one go. I didn't want to give this guy any ideas, and he seemed the sort who'd get way more interested if he found out I was a lesbian. "Can I be a demon-hunting nun who likes pudding?"

"I like nun, but you've got to remember that most mundanes don't really know about the supernatural, so it probably wouldn't be realistic for you to be part of an organisation that hunts demons. Also it'd be quite hard for you to identify with. I mean, it's really important in this game that you play an ordinary person who is kind of cast into this"—air quotes happened—"'World of Darkness.' The pudding thing is like your personal role-playing choice."

"I'll just play a nun then."

From here, it got all technical. I spent the next twenty minutes scribbling little black dots on some kind of glossy four-page document that looked like a passport application. I wound up with a nun called Sister Julia, after Warlock vetoed the name Julian as unrealistic. Then he led me through a short introductory scene in which my feisty young nun was abducted from her cloister by what I think was supposed to be a hot lesbian seductress, but since Warlock really isn't my type, it didn't come across very well. Five minutes into his loving description of the combined agony and ecstasy of my transformation into a vampire, we were interrupted by a knock at the door.

Warlock disappeared and came back accompanied by a pretty, floppy-haired goth and a short man with a ginger goatee. He introduced them as Cody and Robb, and they both tried to squeeze themselves onto the sofa, so I moved onto the floor.

The moment my arse hit the ground, Cody the Spindly Goth shot up and offered me his seat.

"Really, I'm fine," I insisted. "I prefer to sit on the floor. It's better for my back."

This was a lie, but I thought it was a good idea to keep reminding these people I was about ten years older than they were.

"So this is Kate." Warlock reclaimed his swivel chair of power. "She's sitting in on the game until Hugh comes back. She might bring her friend Elise a bit later."

"Cool," said Robb.

"She's playing Sister Julia, a Daeva vampire who's just been embraced by Miranda Devreaux, who you'll remember as the Lancea Sanctum inquisitor who hired you guys to steal the Eye of Horus from the British Museum two Stories back."

Then the game began. It turned out that they were in the middle of a mission to negotiate with someone about something to do with harbouring a fugitive. But they had to be yanked back to the prince's court so he could tell them they had to work with my character for the rest of the job because politics. In that respect, it was quite realistic.

Around half eight we ordered pizza and sat around chatting about our actual lives. Cody turned out to be an undergrad doing English lit, and Robb, who was older than he looked, had some kind of sysadmin job at the university.

"'Kay," mumbled Warlock, through a mouthful of Pepperoni Passion, "we'd just got to the bit where you guys are breaking into the Carthian stronghold underneath Canary Wharf. Suddenly three guards with SMGs step out into the corridor in front of you and are, like, FREEZE."

There was a knock on the door.

"Hang on, guys." Warlock stood up. "Take the time to work out what you're going to do."

Robb and Cody immediately began flipping through enormously thick rule books and discussing the merits of charging versus grappling versus complicated vampire powers.

Warlock's voice drifted in from the doorway. "Dude, you're really late, we've eaten all the pizza."

Oh shit. I was on my feet, dice and bits of paper scattering off my lap.

Warlock sauntered into the room. "We've just had Nick follow the party around not doing much—"

At that moment, Hugh Shawcross came round the corner, leapt on Warlock's back, and sank his fangs into his neck.

It's dangerous to draw on my mother's power when there's civilians around in case I eat them or something, but I really didn't have a choice. My senses sharpened, and everything slowed as the Deepwild flowed through me. I rushed forwards, ripped Hugh away from his victim, and threw him heavily against the wall, cracking the slightly shoddy plasterwork. Warlock crumpled to the ground.

Hugh recovered instantly, twisted round with the same boneless agility I'd seen in the other vampires two nights ago, and sprang at me. This was a bit awkward because I didn't want to just carve him to pieces, but getting a clear shot at the heart was fifty-fifty at best. As he came in, I caught him by the throat and slammed him down over the sofa, which, thankfully, Robb and Cody had urgently vacated. As he struggled underneath me, I realised I now didn't have a free hand to draw my knife.

"Okay." I stretched out my right arm behind me. "I have a dagger strapped to my wrist. Please draw it and hand it to me, so I can stake this guy."

"Uh . . ." said Robb, ". . . that's our mate."

All my instincts were screaming at me to just rip his head off, kill everybody else, and eat their hearts.

I flapped my hand in what I hoped was a reassuring manner. "I know this is a lot to process. Vampires are real, Hugh's one of them, and if I let him go, he'll kill you all."

"No fucking way," gasped Cody.

"We can discuss this later, but right now I really need something long and pointy. It won't kill him."

Robb edged over, tentatively slipped the knife from its sheath and handed it to me. I pinned Hugh's legs under mine, forced his head back, and rammed the steel blade through his heart. He went still.

I got up shakily, pushing my mother's power back to Faerie. We gathered round Warlock, who was slowly stirring on the floor. His neck was bleeding quite badly, but it didn't look fatal.

"Someone get a first aid kit."

Robb hurried off in search of one.

"'Kay guys," slurred Warlock, sitting up, "you've just got to the bit where you're breaking into the..." He put a hand to his neck and then stared at the blood on his fingers. "What the fuck?" Then he looked at the blood on the carpet. "Holy shit, my security deposit." Then he looked at the body on the sofa. "Holy shit, is that Hugh?"

"Sooooo..." Cody looked pretty spaced out. "Turns out vampires are real."

"Huh," said Warlock.

Robb came back with a slightly crappy green first aid box, and I cleaned up Warlock's wound as best I could.

"What's going on? When did all this happen? I can't remember."

"It's a vampire bite," I explained. "Some bloodlines will do that to you."

Robb sat down heavily on the floor. "This is messed up."

"I've got to admit," mused Cody, "I always kind of thought something like this might happen one day. Like you get home and find your parents splattered all over their front room and you're like shit, the Prelude's over."

"Give me two ticks." I rang Elise, told her I'd found Hugh, and asked her to bring the car to Brunel. Then I turned back to the group. "Look. The most sensible thing you can do right now is walk away from this. Weird shit exists, sure, but it's not going to make any difference to your lives unless you go looking for it, and then it'll probably murder your face off."

There was a long silence.

"What about Hugh?" asked Robb.

"I'm going to try to help him, but I don't think he'll be back to games night anytime soon." I dragged my card case out my inside pocket. "Take my card and call me if you get into trouble or if you're about to get yourself into trouble."

"You're not coming back next week, then?" Cody looked disappointed.

"It's been... something, but this really isn't my scene."

I glanced at Hugh, who was lying on the sofa doing his best impression of a corpse.

"So..." I asked. "Got any bin liners?

CHAPTER TWELVE
RESCUES & CALLS

Forty minutes later, Elise and I were driving across London with a paralysed vampire stuffed in the boot of my Corsa.

"Congratulations on the successful resolution of the Shawcross case, Miss Kane," said Elise. "But I fear the young gentleman is in no condition to be returned to his sister."

She was right. If we gave him back to Tash in this condition, he'd rip her to pieces. Fuck, I was going to have to give her the Vampires Are Real talk as well. "Take a left here, we're going to Hackney."

"For what reason?" asked Elise, swinging the car round.

"We're bringing him to the Knights. Acton and Thierry love to take in stray maniacs."

"Do you think they will be able to help him?"

"I think so. When they found Patrick, he was a blood-crazed psycho killer, and look at him now."

Elise said nothing.

"Okay, so maybe he's not the best example, but he hasn't murdered anyone recently. That I know of."

Elise smiled but kept her eyes on the road. "I believe that is what they call damning with faint praise, Miss Kane."

"Actually, it kind of isn't. A hell of a lot of young vampires have to be put down like mad dogs, particularly if they're abandoned or brought up by somebody who's just balls-out evil."

"If I may ask, what did happen to Patrick?"

"Fuck, where to begin." I leaned back in my seat and pulled my hat down. "He was this lord's son in like the mid-nineteenth century. He was engaged to this chick called Katya, but he kept seeing these ghostly figures everywhere he went. His parents did some seriously nasty shit to him, trying to break him of it. He wound up in Bedlam in the end. Then Katya got him out. Turned out she'd been a vampire the whole time. They spent the next fifty years fucking and slaughtering people. He once told me he still sees the ghosts of everyone he's ever killed."

Elise put a hand to her mouth. It looked like she'd been practicing emoting again. "Oh how terrible, that poor boy."

"Yeah, I'd feel sorry for him if he wasn't such a complete dick."

We arrived at the Knights' some time before midnight. Good job they were vampires, or this would be really antisocial. I left Elise in the car, with instructions to get out of there if anyone tried to look in the boot, and went and rang the doorbell.

Endymion eventually deigned to answer the door. He was wearing a purple silk kimono.

"Oh, Katharine," he said wearily, "do come in."

"Can you open the garage and get Acton? I've got someone staked in the boot."

He drifted inside without further comment. "Father," I heard him call out, "Katharine has brought a corpse to dinner."

And then the garage door began to slide silently upwards.

Elise manoeuvred the car inside, and we manhandled Hugh into the house. We weren't sure where to put him so we laid him out on top of the grand piano. Endymion sat down and began picking out the opening bars of the *Funeral March*. After a moment or two, Acton came hurrying down the stairs.

"Katharine." He looked worried. "Whatever is the matter?"

"With me, nothing. With this guy, he broke his leg, got turned into a vampire, was inducted into the Morrígan's secret army, went crazy with bloodlust, and now he's staked on your piano."

Acton leant over Hugh and gently opened his eyes. Then he pulled his lips back and checked his teeth. "I think he'll be all right." He paused. "Wait a moment. Whose army?"

"The Morrígan's."

His head jerked up. "Do you know what you're saying, Katharine? The Morrígan is dead."

"Well, she got over it. I'm hoping Hugh can tell us more if you can stop him trying to kill us all."

Acton nodded. "Pull the knife out."

I pulled the knife out.

Hugh snapped upright, all burning eyes and bared fangs. Acton caught his hand and held it. "It's all right," he murmured. "Everything's all right."

An immense serenity settled over the room like a heavy blanket. I probably shouldn't have yelled at Eve the other day. I probably shouldn't have spent the night with Nim either. Maybe I should have trusted Julian and told her about Aeglica. Who I probably shouldn't have killed in the first place. I definitely shouldn't have got my partner killed. Or fucked the woman who killed him. God, I hadn't phoned my parents for ages either. They were probably worried sick.

Hugh slumped forwards on the piano and started weeping uncontrollably.

Well, this was embarrassing.

But I should have been thinking about him, not about me. I should be more open to other people's feelings.

Wait, wait, no I shouldn't. Something was just fucking with my head. I looked at Acton, who had put a fatherly arm around Hugh's shoulders and was whispering soothingly in his ear.

Great. Fucking vampire mind control. I glanced at Elise, but she seemed unaffected.

So I went out front and smoked a cigarette to clear my head. The rush of nicotine washed away the guilt, and I resolved to kick the first puppy I saw. I gave it a couple of minutes for Acton to finish whatever creepy psychic shit he was doing to Hugh and then headed back inside.

Hugh was huddled on the sofa, with a mug of fresh blood, and Acton was sitting in a chair opposite, looking all *here if you need me*. Endymion appeared to have got bored and fucked off.

"He okay to talk?" I asked Acton.

"Hugh," said Acton, "are you okay to talk?"

His hands tightened on the mug, and he nodded.

I got down to business. "Okay, first thing's first. You *are* Hugh Shawcross, right?" It would be just my fucking luck to have rescued a completely different fledgling vampire nerd called Hugh. Besides, Rule Eleven: always double-check the obvious.

He nodded again.

"What do you remember?"

"I broke my leg. There was this woman at the hospital. She was beautiful, and she was there, and then she wasn't. Then I was ill, and they moved me, and she was still there. There were ravens watching me, perched on the end of my bed. I tried to tell them. Then I got worse. Then my leg was better. And she was calling me, so I left. I had to find something."

"What were you looking for?"

"Something that was stolen. I don't know what it was. But I have to find it. She wants me to find it."

"You don't have to do anything you don't want to do," said Acton, with gentle authority.

Hugh sagged and took a sip of blood. "I think I hurt people. I think I hurt my friend."

"Oh, Warlock's fine," I told him. "I got to you before you could do any real damage."

He looked at me with wide, bloodshot eyes. "Wait. Who are you?"

"My name's Kate Kane, I'm a private investigator. Your sister hired me to find you."

"Tash." His hands tightened around his mug. "I can't see Tash like this."

"No, you really can't."

His eyes filled up with tears again and I looked at the floor and waited for him to stop crying.

"It gets easier," said Acton.

"But what if I kill someone? What if I've already killed people?"

Endymion appeared briefly in the doorway in a shimmer of purple. "We've all killed people, darling," he purred. "One gets over it." And then he fucked off again.

"Not helpful, Dimmy," Acton called after him.

Hugh shuddered and took another sip of blood.

"What's past is past," Acton went on. "But I can teach you to control yourself now. You need never hurt anyone again, if you don't want to."

"Why would I want to?"

Acton gazed at him serenely. "Some feel that violence is sometimes justified, in the right cause, or for the right person."

This was edging outside my comfort zone. Hearing these two have a heart-to-heart about power, violence, and the ethics of being a vampire made me a little bit worried about how cavalier Julian was about all this stuff. I kept telling myself I knew what she was, and what I was getting myself into, but maybe I didn't. On the other hand, she was amazingly good in bed.

"Look, before you get started on the Twelve Step Programme, can I ask some more questions about the deadly vampire army that's set to destroy London?"

"What army?" asked Hugh.

"The woman you saw has been turning people all over North London. There must be hundreds of you by now."

"I don't know anything. Sometimes I'll go somewhere or I'll do something, and I won't know why I've done it, but I'll know it's what she wants."

Well, that had been less useful than I'd hoped.

A long shudder passed through Hugh's body. "What's going to happen to me now?"

"You can stay here for as long as you need," said Acton.

I leaned over and whispered in Acton's ear, "Um, about that. Can I have a quick word?"

He nodded, and we nipped into the study, leaving Hugh with Elise.

"I probably shouldn't be telling you this," I told him, "but the Court are planning something big. They're going to try and wipe out the Morrígan's entire bloodline. All of them in London at least. Can you take Hugh out of the city until it's over?"

"Of course, Katharine. Thierry will take him to the house in Durham."

"Thanks." I stared blankly at the bookcases. "Um, this is a bit of a funny question, but is Patrick in?"

"He's upstairs. I think he's having a hard time of it at the moment."

"Yeah, he's split up with his girlfriend."

"I'm sure he's doing what he thinks is best for her."

Sure he was. When you were dating Patrick, he only did what he thought was best for you. Although, towards the end of our relationship, I'd begun to suspect he just did what he wanted and then decided it was best for you afterwards.

"Is it all right if I go up and see him?"

Acton patted me paternally on the shoulder. "Our home is your home, Katharine."

I left Hugh to be looked after by Acton and Thierry and told Elise I'd be right back. Then I climbed up the spiral staircase to Patrick's emo-loft. Hard-core cello music—I mean, not Metallica on Four Cellos hard-core, like actual classical music hard-core—was filling the air with sad. He was probably lying on his bed reading *Wuthering Heights*.

I emerged into his room to find him huddled against a wall with his head in his hands. A copy of *Swann's Way* was lying discarded on the floor.

"Wow," I said. "Is this what you did all those times you dumped me?"

Patrick looked up at me with red-rimmed, tear-stained eyes. "Come to gloat, have you, Katharine?"

"No, Patrick, it's nothing like that—"

"I'm not taking you back, Katharine. I still love Sofia. It kills me to be apart from her, but I can see now she does not belong in my world, and she never can, and she never will."

Why was there never a stake around when you needed one? "Sofia seems like she's a smart girl. I'm sure she knows what she's getting herself into."

"No! How can she know?" He leapt to his feet and started storming about the room. "How can someone so beautiful, so innocent, know the kind of darkness I walk in night after night, the danger, the constant, constant temptation?"

I got out of his way. "I think she's in danger right now."

"I know!" He put an actual wrist to his actual forehead. "That's why I had to leave her."

"Patrick, I know this might be hard to understand, but I think she's in danger for reasons that have nothing to do with you."

That shut him up for all of three seconds. And then he turned to me with a look of cold hatred. "It won't work, Katharine. You know if I go back to her I can only destroy her, but that's exactly what you want. I won't be a pawn in your jealous mind games."

Sigh. "I swear I'm going to slap you if you don't snap out of this. The people who tried to kill me fifteen years ago are going to try to kill your girlfriend. I don't know who they are, or what they're doing, or why they're doing it, but unless you want Sofia to wind up eight pints of blood lighter, you need to go back to her right now."

"Get out," he roared. "You've done enough damage."

I got out.

Elise was waiting for me downstairs. Hugh was still shaking on the sofa, and Thierry was sitting next to him, holding his hand, and talking to him softly while Acton hovered supportively nearby.

I beckoned to Elise. "Let's hit the road."

"Thank you for having me," said Elise to the Knights. "It has been a very pleasant evening."

Thierry glanced up "You are always welcome, Elise. I am just sorry we did not have time to extend our full hospitality."

"You are too kind."

Realising this could take a while, I dragged Elise out the door, which was harder than it looked, what with her being made of solid marble. We piled back into the car and headed for home.

"Have we have achieved case closed, Miss Kane?"

"Pretty much. Now, I just have to work out what to say to Tash. Something slightly more tactful than 'Your brother's been recruited into the army of an indestructible vampire queen.'"

"Perhaps you could say he has gone to stay with a very nice family in the north of England."

"That just sounds like I'm having him put down. I might as well just say he's gone to live on a big farm somewhere in the country."

"You could suggest he has contracted a rare blood disorder and has gone away for treatment."

"And one of the symptoms of this rare blood disorder is death?"

"Giving all credit to Miss Shawcross, I consider it unlikely that she will think to check her brother's pulse when she next meets him."

"Yes, but he can't eat any more. What's he going to do at Christmas dinner? Claim he's become a nothingatarian?"

"I believe you are overthinking this."

I gave a look which was sadly wasted because she was being all responsible and paying attention to the oncoming traffic. "You're the one coming up with the elaborate cover stories. My plan was just to say, 'Hey babe, vampires are real and they got your brother.'"

"I'm sure you know best, Miss Kane."

In any case, I was going to wait until morning. They say giving people bad news never gets any easier, but it gets way harder after midnight. We got in at about two, and I made myself a cup of Bovril to keep me warm in place of a girlfriend who was actually there. I was just climbing into bed with it when my phone rang. Unknown number.

I sighed. What now? I picked up. "Kane."

"Hello, sweeting. I was just thinking about you."

I sat up so quickly I nearly spilled my Bovril. In the background, I could hear the raucous sounds of a typical Saturday night at the Velvet.

"That'd mean a lot more if I didn't know you were covered in half-naked lesbians right now."

"It's just you and me, I promise."

"I like the sound of that."

There was a longish pause.

"I miss you, Kate," Julian said, at last.

That was news to me.

"This"—she sounded a little sulky—"is where you say you miss me too."

"Oh, yeah, right, sorry, long day."

"You are a terrible girlfriend."

"So are you."

"We're made to be together, sweeting. Nobody else would have us."

I felt myself smiling. "Speak for yourself. I'm a fucking catch."

"And I, my dear, am a motherfucking vampire prince."

I put down my Bovril and snuggled under the covers, holding the phone close to my ear. "So, is this the point where I'm supposed to ask you what you're wearing?"

"Why don't you try and see where it takes us?"

I sighed. "It's one of those fucking awful frilly shirts, isn't it?"

"You do know the purpose of this conversation is not for you to criticise my sartorial preferences?"

"Sorry, I've always been crap at this sort of thing."

Julian's voice turned silky. "What sort of thing is that, dear heart?"

"Sorry, I thought we were having phone sex."

"Technically, Kate, I think we're currently failing to have phone sex."

"Oh come on." I fluffed up my pillows and got comfy. "Do people ever really get off on that sort of thing?"

"I've been alive for over eight hundred years and in my experience, the answer to the question 'Do people ever really get off on that sort of thing?' is invariably yes."

It was a nice idea but . . . "Look, I'm kind of a hands-on girl."

"Well," Julian purred down the line at me, "why don't you put your hands on, girl?"

I gagged. "I cannot believe you just said that."

"I thought it was about your level." Julian laughed.

"Fuck you."

"Would that you could."

"Is this supposed to be getting me hot?"

The mirth vanished from Julian's voice, and she wrapped around me like velvet chains. "You don't like the thought of fucking me, Kate?"

I tasted wine and rose leaves, so rich and sweet that, for a moment, I couldn't breathe. A shiver of awareness ran through my whole body as though I was waiting to be touched. Distantly, I wondered if I ought to be freaking the fuck out, but right now, it felt pretty damn good.

"I like the thought of you fucking me," Julian murmured. "I'm thinking about it now. I'm on my hands and knees. Would you like that, Kate? Me, on my hands and knees, and you're holding me down."

I felt a brush of silk at the edges of my fingers and my hand closed around empty air. But I could imagine she was there, just as she said, her body a pattern of silver and shadow, trembling against me. I could breathe again but words weren't happening. "Ngh."

"You pull me back by the hair. It hurts, but I like it, and I know you like it too. You like hurting me, Kate, just a little. You twist my head around and kiss me, and it stings like your hand in my hair."

I felt the ghost of a touch against my lips. My back arched against a fall of empty air, and I slithered down my pillows. The tips of Julian's fangs pricked my tongue, and I gasped. I put a hand to my mouth and saw a smear of blood on my fingertips.

"And then you fuck me. Your fingers deep inside me." She gave a long sigh of pleasure that swirled over my body like a scattering of petals. It felt weird as hell, but I spread my legs and Julian's voice slipped over me and into me. "You hold me down and make me take it. And I want it."

"God," I gasped, "I wish you were here."

"So I do. I want you to fuck me. I want to taste you. I want to make you come."

"That, uhh, that'd be nice."

"Touch yourself, Kate."

And I did, without even thinking about it.

"Taste yourself, Kate."

And I did, without even thinking about it.

"Do you want me?"

I was drowning in her. Sex and power and wine and rose leaves.

"Yes, fuck, yes."

"Touch yourself and think of me touching you. My mouth on your cunt, my fingers inside you, your blood on my lips. How much I want you. How much I want you to come. I want to hear you. I want to hear you gasp. I want to hear my name."

I gasped.

"I want to hear my name, I want to hear my name while you come. Touch yourself, make yourself come, and say my name."

I was slick with wanting her. I could taste blood. My fingers moved as she commanded.

"Now, Kate. I want to hear my name."

By then, it was only the word I could manage.

CHAPTER THIRTEEN
DUST & ASHES

The next day I slept late and woke up happy. Then I remembered that I had to tell Tash the Teetotal Lesbian that I'd found her brother but couldn't bring him back yet because Reasons.

I had a shower and found Elise in the kitchen with a frying pan.

"Miss Kane," she cried. "I have discovered something remarkable." She picked up an egg with one hand and cracked it open. "You see, this fluid is entirely colourless but with the application of a little heat..." She tipped it into the pan and pointed excitedly. "It is transformed by alchemical processes into a wholly different substance."

"And it's good with salt and pepper too."

"That is not all, Miss Kane. I have learned that if you separate the colourless part from the yellow and whisk it vigorously with sugar until it is light and frothy, then the application of heat transforms it into another substance again."

There was something strange happening to my oven. Oh yes, it was on. And inside, a tray of meringues was cooking merrily.

It says something about my life that fried eggs and meringues was not the weirdest breakfast I'd ever had. To be honest, it probably wasn't even in the top ten. I left Elise in the kitchen, heating eggs in increasingly unusual ways, and went to ring Tash.

I told her I'd made some progress and could she swing by the office to talk about it. I think I probably panicked the hell out of her, but I reassured her that her brother wasn't dead, which was only technically a lie. She told me to give her a couple of hours. If I left immediately, it would give me time to finish up the paperwork. I left immediately. And I was just finishing up the paperwork when Tash knocked on the door of my office.

"It's open."

She was looking better than the last time I'd seen her. It wouldn't have been hard because she'd been, basically, a wreck. She still didn't have the *I will try and bonk you in a doorway* vibe I remembered from the Candy Bar, but she seemed to have got to that all important *probably going to be okay* stage in the process.

"You said you had something?" She hurried inside and sat down. "Oh, hi, by the way."

"Hi. So. Look." I tried to find a way to express the fact I had some good news and some bad news that wasn't *I've got some good news and some bad news*. "I've got some good news and some bad news."

An *oh fuck* expression spread across Tash's face. "What's the bad news?"

"Hugh got involved with some really bad people and can't come home right now. But," I added quickly, "he's fine. He's staying with some friends of mine. They're looking after him."

"What sort of bad people?"

Don't say vampires. Don't say vampires. "The less you know the better."

"I want to know. I'm not a child. Is it drugs?"

"Something like that."

Her nose wrinkled. "Hugh was a drug dealer?"

"Not in so many words." This wasn't going well.

"What, was he running a meth lab?"

"God, no. Look, he got mixed up in something that wasn't his fault, but it involves some really scary people. He's out of it now, but he's going to have to lie low for a bit."

She was silent a moment. "Can I see him?"

"Um, not just yet."

Tash stood up and moved restlessly round my office. "So, what you're saying is Hugh was into something really bad that isn't drugs, but you can't tell me what it is, or who's involved, or where he is, or what's going on?"

"The important thing here is that Hugh's all right, he's safe, and he's with friends."

"You keep telling me that, but why can't I talk to him? For all I know, he's dead in a ditch, and you're just making this up to make me feel better."

She had a point. I could have given the Vampires Are Real talk, but since I had no way to prove it, I'd just have sounded crazy. The other option was to get Hugh on the phone but that was risky. I had no idea what his mental state was like. I also didn't have much choice.

"Hang on a sec," I said. "I can try ringing him, but be aware he's been through a lot."

Tash nodded and sat back down.

I fished Thierry's number out my contacts list and dialled it. He answered in a couple of rings.

"Katharine, *chérie*."

"Can Hugh talk? I've got his sister here. She's worried about him."

"One moment."

Over the line I caught the vague sounds of someone hurrying to a telephone call, Thierry warning Hugh not to mention the V-word, and then Hugh's voice: "Um, hello?"

Since he'd opened with *hello* and not *I vant to drink your blahd*, I decided he was probably safe to talk to his sister for a couple of minutes at least. I handed over the receiver. I would have given them some privacy but I needed to be on hand in case Hugh flipped out. Tash didn't seem to say much, but there wasn't a lot she could say: I now believe you aren't dead, I hope the mysterious whatever-it-is keeping you wherever you are ceases to apply at some point in the near future.

She hung up, looking an odd mix of shaken and reassured.

"Okay?" I asked.

She nodded.

"Look, I know this isn't exactly what you were hoping for, but as far as I'm concerned, this is kind of it."

She nodded again. "How much do I . . . ?"

"Don't worry about that for now. I'll invoice you when Hugh comes home." It wasn't exactly industry standard billing practice, but it probably only added up to a couple of days work, and I'd felt a bit of a shithead asking Tash to dip into her student loan before she'd actually got her brother back. Besides, she probably had one more really awkward conversation in her future.

She left a few minutes later, and I left a few minutes after that. I'd at least sorted out the case that had got this whole thing started. That just left the psycho vampire queen and the woman who murdered my partner. The Morrígan was for bigger fish than me to deal with, which meant I was probably going to wind up chasing Corin Black in circles. Again. When I got home, I called Elise into the front room to talk shop.

"Miss Kane," she told me. "I was about to start making a soufflé."

"Elise, you don't eat, why have you suddenly started cooking?"

"I find it fascinating. You take raw ingredients and fashion them into something that is quite other than what they were. It is a process to which I can relate."

"You're a model fucking housemate, you know that?"

"I do not like to think of myself as a model, Miss Kane."

I winced. "Sorry, I just meant you're like really good. You cook, you clean, you don't make noise, and you don't use the bathroom."

"I am happy to be living with you." She smiled at me. "I am gratified to have a friend."

I panicked. "Uh, can we talk about work for a minute?"

"Of course, Miss Kane."

"The Shawcross case is closed and so, until we get another job, I'd like your help with something personal."

She gave me a look she had clearly been practicing. "I have told you before, I am not carved that way."

"Oh, very funny. I'm looking for this woman called Corin Black. She was serving a mandatory life sentence for blowing away my partner, but someone busted her out."

"Why would anyone do such a thing?"

I sprawled out on the sofa and propped my feet on the arm. "Probably because they wanted her to nick something. She's a high-end art thief, specialising in occult shit. She's smart, she's manipulative, and I sometimes think she's got a guardian fucking angel. She'll be pretty much impossible to catch, but we're going to try."

"Where would you like me to begin?"

Elise very slowly put both hands on her hips.

I stared at her. "What are you doing?"

"I have noticed that some people find it disconcerting if I stand still for too long. I am experimenting with a variety of poses."

"Okay. Um. Carry on. So, Patrick's police contacts would be really useful right now, but for the first time in fifteen years, he's not talking to me. So we're going to have to do it the old-fashioned way."

"Am I looking at newspaper archives again, Miss Kane?"

"'Fraid so."

Elise brought a hand to rest on her chin. I was pretty sure this was more disconcerting, but I didn't have the heart to tell her. "What should I be looking for?" she asked.

"You're looking either for weirdos who've had weird stuff stolen or break-ins where it doesn't seem like anything of value is missing."

"I will see what I can do."

"Start Monday, obviously. This is your day off. Go back to your eggs."

I pissed away the rest of the day doing basically nothing. Given the choice, I'd have preferred to spend my time having red-hot vampire sex with my girlfriend, but since that wasn't an option, just being able to chill the fuck out for a few hours was a welcome change.

I'd just taken the soufflé into the living room so I could eat it in front of *Downton Abbey* when the buzzer went. Knowing my luck, it would be Patrick or Sofia or Thierry telling me Hugh had escaped.

I picked up the handset. "What is it?"

"Katharine Kane, by the authority of the Council you are commanded to face judgement for the murder of Aeglica Thrice-Risen, Prince of Swords."

Well, fuck.

Last time Caradoc and his goons had come for me, we'd been in the middle of a Tube station, so I'd been pretty sure they wouldn't just rip my head off, but this time there was nothing to stop them kicking down the door and eating me. Years of putting up with Patrick had taught me that vampires don't need an invitation to get into your house. I knew I should have got those wards fixed.

"I'll be right down." I hung up and called to Elise in the kitchen. "I'm being arrested by vampires again. Don't wait up."

"Do you require any assistance, Miss Kane?"

"Can you record *Downton* for me? And if I don't come back, you know the drill. Keep my stuff, tell my parents, leave my name on the door."

"Am I permitted to change it to Kane (deceased) & Archer (deceased)?"

I pulled my coat on and grabbed my hat. "Good to know you've got my back, Elise."

"Always, Miss Kane."

There wasn't much point in going armed because I wouldn't stand a chance if we got into a fight, and they'd probably take my weapons off me anyway. I briefly considered bringing the Sword of Killing Everything but I thought they might take that the wrong way.

I went downstairs and let Caradoc's minions bundle me into a black sedan. There was no banter. Caradoc didn't even bother to gloat. They just drove me from my front door to Aeglica's mansion. The Council were assembled in the upstairs room where I'd told al-Rashid to fuck off. They'd taken down the enormous picture of the naked chick. Shame. It would have felt strangely appropriate.

Here lies Kate Kane. Executed by vampires underneath a portrait of a hot woman. Beloved daughter. Sorely missed.

Aeglica's ceremonial sword was still there, though. I guess that did set the proper tone.

The Council, the princes, Halfdan, Mercy, and Caradoc were seated around a large table they'd had dragged up from one of the other rooms. Kemsit was sitting cross-legged in the middle of it, looking much as she had last time, like a kid who'd run away from home and become evil.

"This Council," she said, "is convened to pass judgement on the mortal Katharine Kane, Princess of the Deepwild, Knight of the Witchcourt of London, who is accused of the murder of Aeglica Thrice-Risen, Fenwalker, Shadowdweller, Oathbreaker, Kinkiller, Manslayer, Exile, Hero, who in England was called the Prince of Swords."

I glanced at Julian, trying to work out how fucked I was, but her expression was unreadable. It didn't look like she cared whether I lived or died.

"I call upon Mercy to give the case for execution."

Mercy rose and pushed back her veil with taloned fingers. Her skirts rustled as she glided to the centre of the room. She looked at me with pure black eyes, just long enough to let me know that this was personal, and then began to speak.

"Aeglica Thrice-Risen was a loyal servant of this Council. Since the fall of the Morrígan, he fulfilled the duties of the Prince of Swords, standing between our kind and our enemies. For three and a half centuries, he fought and bled for us. He was slain by this mortal, of whose true allegiances we know nothing. The safety of our people depends on the strength of this Council, and it would be folly to allow this travesty to go unanswered. A message must be sent to those who would defy us, to those who would destroy us, and to those who would subvert this Council to their own ends."

Shit. I was kind of outclassed here. My whole case had been *it was an accident M'lud*, and right now, I wasn't sure even I'd acquit me.

After Mercy had returned to her seat, Kemsit asked if anyone wanted to speak on my behalf.

There was a resounding silence from Julian.

Then Acton stood. "If it please the Council, I have known the accused for half her life and have always found her to be a person of honesty, integrity, and compassion. Although there is no doubt that she killed Aeglica Thrice-Risen, I do not believe that she intentionally murdered him, and I trust that her actions were for the greater good of this Council and this city."

Kemsit, who had been listening attentively with one hand on a pair of brass scales, looked up. "Does anyone wish to make reply?"

Caradoc shot to his feet. "This is a farce. This mortal slew my master, and we sit here debating the merits of punishing her for it. There is right, and there is wrong; there is strength, and there is weakness. To let the murder of a prince go unpunished makes fools and cowards of us all."

The Prince of Wands glanced at Kemsit and then spoke up. "While I am not certain that Sir Caradoc's tone is appropriate for this chamber, I believe he raises a valid concern."

Great. The fucker had sold me out.

"It seems to me that this is a matter not of justice but of vengeance. The accused most certainly killed the Prince of Swords, and his progeny are within their rights to take revenge, but it would set a dangerous precedent to hold a mortal accountable to Council law. Those who are bound by the law are also protected by it. If we try Miss Kane for murder, then we must try every vampire hunter that rams a stake through the heart of a fledging. I can speak only for myself, but if a mortal crosses me, I would rather simply kill them."

Diego leaned across the table, fingers steepled, and after getting the nod from Kemsit, spoke. "Ordinarily, I would concur, but this situation is more complex. The accused is not merely a mortal, but a mortal who is known to act on the behalf of the Prince of Cups. The question is, therefore, not whether our law applies to mortals, but how it applies to those who work through mortals."

Julian raised a hand. "By which argument, it is not Kate who should be on trial. I sincerely hope that you are not trying to turn these proceedings into, if you'll pardon the phrase, a witch hunt."

"Perhaps," said Kemsit, "we should hear from the accused. If she acted on your orders, then she has no case to answer." Her gaze fell on me, heavy as stone. "Katharine Kane, what have you to say in your defence?"

I glanced uncertainly between Diego and Julian. If I was going to sell Julian out, now was the time to do it. She'd probably be okay anyway. I mean, she'd survived for eight hundred years. How much damage could I do? Then, again, she'd probably dump me, and possibly kill me as well. Oh, yeah, also it would have been wrong.

"The death of Aeglica Thrice-Risen was an accident," I said. "I didn't intend to kill him, and for what it's worth, I'm sorry he's dead. Julian didn't order me to do anything."

"Has all been said that must be said?" asked Kemsit. The room was silent. "Then the Council passes judgement. I shall call on each of you in turn to declare the accused guilty or innocent of the crime laid against her. I remind those here gathered that should the votes be balanced, mine shall be the deciding voice. I say now that I find the accused guilty. She slew the Prince of Swords, and there is an end to it."

Well, fuck.

One by one, Kemsit indicated the members of the Council, starting with the princes.

The Prince of Wands smirked. "Innocent. A mortal is neither bound nor protected by the laws of our kind."

"Innocent." The Prince of Coins looked sourly at his colleague. It seemed like Sebastian came through on that one.

Halfdan stopped lounging and sat upright. "Guilty. Nothing personal, Miss Kane, but Sebastian seems to want you alive, and that worries me."

"Guilty," snapped Diego. "If she acted alone, then she bears the guilt alone."

Acton cleared his throat politely. "Innocent. I believe intent is as important as action, and I believe Katharine's intentions were honourable."

Sybil said nothing.

"You wish to abstain?" asked Kemsit.

Sybil nodded.

That just left al-Rashid. The guy I'd told to fuck off. Well, this was going to be interesting.

"Innocent." He gave the faintest trace of a smile. "Mercy is a virtue."

From where I was sitting, Mercy was looking pretty pissed off.

On the other hand, against all the odds, I seemed to be alive.

"Katharine Kane," said Kemsit, "you have been acquitted of the charges laid against you."

I wasn't sure if I was supposed to say anything. Was I supposed to thank them for just barely voting not to rip my head off? On the other hand, if I said something they didn't like, they might just decide to kill me anyway.

Luckily, at that point, the window exploded. And an actual swarm of ragged feral vampires came crawling down the walls.

The one time you leave the house unarmed . . .

The next thing I knew, Julian had slammed me into a corner and was standing in front of me like a cobra ready to strike. The room had descended into bloody chaos except for a still point in the dead centre where Kemsit sat unmoving on the table.

Caradoc and al-Rashid had both leapt onto the windowsill and were stemming the tide pretty damn effectively. The Prince of Wands had fucked off and was standing behind the door, not drawing attention to himself. I guess he didn't want to get blood on his nice white suit.

Mercy was tearing people apart with a ferocity I wouldn't have expected from someone dressed like Mary Poppins. The Prince of Coins had pulled a gun and was picking off anybody who made it through the front line. Acton just stood there, looking concerned and sorrowful, and nobody seemed to want to attack him. Halfdan seemed to have vanished.

One of the vampires sprang onto the table and tried to bite Kemsit in the neck. It crumbled to dust as it touched her. She didn't even blink.

On the other side of the room, Sybil had backed one of the attackers against the wall and was holding it mesmerised as her snake slowly coiled round its body. Diego had something pinned to the table and seemed to be snapping its fingers, one by one.

A couple of them came for me, but Julian just bamfed between them and clawed their throats out. It didn't kill them, but it made them back the hell off.

Suddenly, a couple of fledglings broke free from the melee and rushed to the back of the room. The Prince of Coins levelled his pistol and calmly shot one of them in the head, but the other grabbed Aeglica's sword and bolted for the door.

Caradoc sprang down from the windowsill. "Stop the thief," he yelled.

The Prince of Wands extended one languid hand and pushed the door closed. Caradoc came up behind the vampire, wrested the sword from her hand, swung it round in an arc, and split her in two from shoulder to hip.

Mercy wheeled round in a flurry of black taffeta and gore. "Caradoc, that weapon is not yet yours to wield."

It was nice to know that not even a bloodbath could get in the way of the incessant vampire bickering.

And then the room was full of ravens. And standing in the middle of them was the Morrígan. Just like when I'd seen her in the Dream, she was tall and pale with a kind of terrifying beauty like a sheer drop off a cliff. Somehow, it was worse in person. I felt I should be on my knees. I looked round and realised that half the Council already were.

"You have something that belongs to me," she said. Her voice was darkness and dead things. She turned slowly in a swirl of feathers and shadows until she faced Caradoc.

To give the guy his due, he was still standing. "We defeated you once, Dread Queen. We will do so again."

The Morrígan laughed. I've heard a lot of creepy laughs in my time, and that was going straight in at number three. "Then step forth, Sir Knight, and strike true."

She spread her arms wide, stirring the wings folded at her back, and a raven swooped down and landed on her wrist.

There was no way this was going to end well.

Caradoc charged, bringing Aeglica's sword round and cutting savagely down into the Morrígan's neck. There was nothing there but feathers. And then her hand erupted through his chest and lifted him off the ground. He just hung there for a moment, not moving, the sword slipping from his grip. One of the Morrígan's birds landed on her palm and began tearing at Caradoc's face.

I didn't like the guy, but that was pretty grim.

At last, she lowered her arm and shook him onto the floor in a shower of blood and ick. He lay there, twitching, his face a terrible ruin and what my A-level biology told me was probably vitreous humour streaking down his cheeks like tears.

The Morrígan bent to pick up the fallen sword.

"That is enough." Kemsit still hadn't moved. "You were found wanting. Your time is over."

"The treaty is broken. I am here to claim what is mine."

"Nothing here is yours."

The Morrígan twisted something out of the hilt of Aeglica's sword. Then Kemsit was standing in front of her, one frail, girlish hand wrapped around the Morrígan's wrist. Where she touched, the skin began to crack, greyish flakes falling away between her fingers. With a series of heavy, almost comical thumps, the Morrígan's birds began to fall from the air.

I could feel the hand closing round my heart again, and I had to struggle to breathe.

The Morrígan lashed out and laid Kemsit's face open to the bone. Slowly, the blackened edges of the wound began to knit together.

Kemsit didn't move, but the desiccation kept creeping up the Morrígan's arm. Slowly her fingers uncurled, and something dropped to the floor with a *plink*.

"I will rain death on this city." And she vanished into darkness.

There was a very long silence.

Thomas Pryce, the Prince of Coins, tucked his gun away and stepped forwards. "It seems we are at war, and we have no war leader. I therefore propose the following course of action. Al-Rashid, I would ask you to take charge of the defence of the city until a new Prince of Swords can be appointed."

Sir Caradoc clawed himself painfully into a seat. He was healing but slowly. "You will not," he rasped, "hand this country to an infidel."

"I concur," said Diego.

Pryce shrugged. "Infidel, papist, it's all the same to me."

While they were quarrelling over a five-hundred-year-old religious dispute, I picked up the thing the Morrígan had dropped. It was a shard of pottery, about three inches long. I had no idea what it was, so I pocketed it for later. Yes, a millennia-ancient vampire queen was looking for it and might want it back, but hey, a clue was a clue.

Things had quieted down again and al-Rashid was agreeing to protect London from the Morrígan and her army of disposable undead psychopaths.

The Prince of Coins turned to Halfdan, who had reappeared as mysteriously as he'd vanished. "I take it we can count on your support."

He flashed a wide, oddly charming grin. "Actually, I was thinking I'd sit this one out. I hate to be mercenary, but I'm really not sure what's in it for me."

"We gave you the North!" growled Caradoc, turning his slowly healing face towards the Regent.

"Yes, you did, and I've still got it whether I help you or not."

The Prince of Wands stepped out of the shadows. "I'm sure you don't need me to remind you, brother, that our former mistress is not forgiving."

"That was the problem with the Morrígan. She always took everything so seriously."

"We also," continued Pryce, "need to send word to the Scots and Irish princes, and the Lords of Wales."

"The Morrígan had followers in Ireland," said Julian.

"All the more reason to tell them." The Prince of Wands pushed aside the body of a fledgling and reclaimed his seat at the table. "If they know that we know that she has returned, then they will not be tempted to conspire against us out of the false belief that we do not know. Of course, they may already know, but at present, we have no way to know what they know. If we tell them, we will know what they know, and all we will not know is how long they have known it."

"You must be getting to me, Sebastian," drawled Julian, "because that almost made sense."

The meeting looked like it was going to drag on for a bit, and since they'd apparently forgotten I was there, I went for a cigarette. Outside, the moonlight washed over a wasteland. Aeglica's overgrown garden had withered away. The weeds on the driveway were dust, the grass brittle skeletons. The rose bower where I'd seen him playing chess with Mercy was a ruin of bare thorns.

I've smoked in worse places.

CHAPTER FOURTEEN
VAMPIRES & CHAMPAGNE

After the trial, the slaughter, and the death of an innocent garden, Julian took me back to one of her many shag pads to celebrate what I suppose was technically a victory. I was, after all, still alive, and I hadn't sold anyone out to stay that way.

"Ah, that sink brings back memories," said Julian, as the automatic light came on in the kitchen.

"It brings back memories of being attacked by a killer tentacle monster."

"Oh, you always focus on the negative."

She pulled open the fridge, which was stocked entirely with champagne and little boxes of expensive chocolates.

"How many girls are you planning to bring back here?" I asked.

"As many as you want, sweeting."

"Just pour me something."

Julian grabbed a bottle and popped the cork. "Darling, this is Krug 1988." Her expression turned dreamy. "A fine year by all accounts. An ineffable penetrating flavour, with remarkable depth and sophistication."

"Do you want me to drink this or have sex with it?"

Julian grinned, teeth glimmering. "Why choose?"

I caught her up and kissed her. Wine and rose leaves and freedom, and the taste of Julian's laughter, sweet in my mouth. I'd almost forgotten what it was like, just being with her, without shadows, betrayals, and my imminent execution hanging over us. Yes, she was still a vampire prince and I'd never be her number one priority, but right now, I couldn't seem to remember why that bothered me. She made me feel good, like being drunk without the comedown, and I needed that. She pressed into me, curling round me like a snake. Her body was cold and fragile, but the arm she slipped round my waist was impossibly strong. And we kissed and kissed forever, the way you only kiss someone when you thought you'd never do it again. We kissed until I couldn't breathe and Julian was whimpering against my lips.

We broke apart, still standing close, Julian's cheek resting against mine. I could feel the flutter of her eyelashes.

"I'm glad I didn't lose you," she whispered.

I'd been beginning to wonder. She hadn't exactly moved heaven and earth to save my arse. But she'd spoken up for me at the trial. At the last possible fucking minute, but she had spoken up.

"I'm not that easy to get rid of."

"You won't be here forever."

Here lies Kate Kane, died peacefully in her sleep aged 94. Beloved daughter. Sorely missed.

"I think I've got a few years in me yet. And if you keep up the 'woe is me, I'm immortal' stuff, I'll crack this bottle over your head."

"I know, and I'm so lucky to have you, but I can't not think about it."

"So you're celebrating my unexpected survival by mooping about my inevitable death?"

Julian gave me a little squeeze. "You're right, I'm being silly. I just realised how close I came to..."

She trailed away, and I didn't fancy asking her to finish the sentence. Close to losing me? Close to sacrificing me? Close to killing me herself?

This was turning into one hell of a celebration.

I snatched the bottle out of her hand and took a swig. Bubbles burst over my tongue like they were all going yay. This really wasn't a drink for drowning your sorrows, but fuck it, I shouldn't have had any sorrows. I was alive and in an expensive flat with my hot vampire girlfriend. It wouldn't last forever, but what does?

"Are you drinking my vintage Krug like it's a bottle of Beck's?" asked Julian.

"Yeah, I am. Do you want to make something of it?"

"You're a complete barbarian."

"I'm barely getting started. Now cut the emo and do what you're good at."

Julian pulled away mischievously. "I've been around for eight hundred years, sweeting, I'm good at a lot of things. I can open an oyster, illuminate a manuscript, extemporise a mean sonnet, and fly a biplane."

"I was kind of hoping you wanted to fuck."

"You modern girls have no appreciation for poetry."

I seized her by the cravat and pulled her into another kiss, and then we tumbled onto the kitchen floor in a tangle of limbs and velvet. I just about managed to stop the champagne spilling everywhere. I put the bottle down and started tearing at Julian's clothes. She'd gone military for the Council, all epaulettes, gold piping, and thigh boots.

"Y'know," I said, "for a sex vampire, you are fucking murder to get undressed."

"Anticipation is the quintessence of erotica."

"Oh, shut up." I poured the champagne over her mostly naked body.

Julian shrieked and wriggled. "I can't tell if this is a waste of perfectly good champagne."

"I think it's a perfect use of good champagne."

I pinned her down and kissed her again, wine trickling between our lips, light and golden, mingled with the deep, dark taste of the vampire prince of pleasure.

Julian sighed. Her eyes were so very blue in this light. "I'm inclined to agree." She tipped her head back, to expose the graceful, vulnerable curve of her throat. I followed the rivulets down her neck, and she shuddered, skin flooding warm beneath my mouth.

I was starting to feel a little light-headed, but I hadn't drunk nearly enough for it to be the champagne. There were probably things I should have been worrying about, but they could all go fuck themselves. I felt like one of the bubbles that had gathered on Julian's skin. I drifted across the surface of her body, showering her in light, fleeting kisses, fizzing with lazy desire, and thinking of nothing, living for a moment in Julian, and Julian alone.

I picked up the bottle and spilled more champagne over her torso, letting it run over the planes of her body and pool in the hollows of her hips and collarbone. She was beautiful, gleaming like a nymph in a waterfall. A waterfall that cost two hundred quid a bottle.

"This is fun," she said, happily.

She arched, catlike, and the liquid gathered, swirled and rushed about in little sparkling streams, breaking into tributaries that arrowed interestingly southwards. I bent my head and pursued them with my tongue, chasing the taste of sex and celebration.

I drank champagne from Julian, and I couldn't imagine a better way to serve it. It glistened on her breasts, gathered in her navel, and left spirals across her ribs as she writhed under me, her hands gliding over my shoulders.

Then my hat fell off and flopped over her face. Julian burst out laughing, batted it away, and wrapped her legs round me. "Maybe you should take your coat off as well. Go crazy."

"Can't. Busy."

I took another drink from the bottle and kissed her in a flurry of bubbles, licking the champagne from her lips.

"Can you actually taste that?" I asked, coming up for air.

"No, but I can taste you."

"Do I have an ineffable penetrating flavour, with remarkable depth and sophistication?"

"In your own way."

"What do you mean 'in my own way'? Is that no? Am I a can of Budweiser?"

Julian reached up a hand and ran her fingertips over my cheek. "No, Kate. It's complicated and hard to describe. You taste of desire and regret and passion and recrimination and hope and loss and power. It's strongest in your blood, but I can catch a trace of it on your lips and on your skin."

"I have no idea what to say to that."

Julian twined her arms around my neck, pulled me down, and kissed me. Her teeth grazed my tongue, blood, pleasure, and champagne mingling wildly in my mouth, until everything was bubbles and darkness. I shuddered against her, my hands clutching at her hips, my mouth on her mouth, my thoughts slipping away, falling with her into ecstasy, bright and gold and black.

Later, Julian peeled me out of my sticky seriously-in-need-of-dry-cleaning suit and carried me through to the bedroom where—as I'd discovered the last time I was here—she'd inexplicably had a bath installed. At least it wasn't full of monster guts anymore. She lowered me into a cloud of bubbles and steam and climbed in after me.

"I feel like such a lesbian stereotype," I said, sleepily.

Julian wriggled between my legs and rested her head against my shoulder. "Sweeting, I've been taking baths with my lovers for the past six hundred years. I think I can safely say I was doing it before it was fashionable."

"You'll be asking me to move in next."

"I got through that phase in the seventeenth century. You know how it is, you try to take things too far too fast, and you end up in a midnight duel to the death on the roof of the Bastille."

"Did you win?"

"Well, it was sort of a draw. It usually is when you're both immortal."

"Bad breakup?"

"You could say that."

I drifted for a while, feeling warm and shagged out. I had dozens of tiny red bite marks running up my arms like I was a really cack-handed heroin addict.

"So, what happens now?" I asked.

"I thought we might wash the champagne off, head to bed, have sex five or six more times, and then you'll probably need to sleep."

"I meant with the Morrígan and the army and everything."

"Oh, that." Julian twisted round to glower playfully at me. "I was hoping we could take a night off."

"Sorry, I just got thinking about it."

"You're in a bath with me naked between your legs and you're thinking about another woman. I'm almost insulted."

I skated my hands across her slick, bubble-dusted skin. "I'm thinking about an insane vampire queen who lives in a graveyard with a bunch of ravens and apparently killed thirty thousand people in the sixteen sixties. I don't think she really counts as another woman."

"Really? I'd have thought she was just your type."

"Are you seriously asking me if I would hit that?"

"I would." Julian shrugged. "Those cold, piercing eyes. The wild hair. The talons. To say nothing of the wings."

"I can't believe we're having this conversation."

"You can always judge a person by how many of their enemies you want to sleep with."

"Classy."

Julian grinned and began soaping me down, paying what I thought was an unnecessary amount of attention to certain regions.

"But actually," I went on, pulling Julian's head back out of the water, "what is going on? I kind of need to know."

"You know," she sighed, "a lot of women would be overjoyed to have a girlfriend who doesn't need to breathe."

"Sorry, I'm just worried."

"You don't have to worry. The Council has it under control."

"Is this the sort of under control where she bursts in through the window and has people's eyes pecked out."

"Caradoc will be fine." Julian waved a hand dismissively, splashing soapy water all over the bedroom floor. "We heal fast."

"Yes, but me and thirty thousand other people don't."

"Al-Rashid knows what he's doing, and we'll soon have elected a new Prince of Swords. We took her down before, and we can do it again."

I caught her before she could dive back under. "How did you take her down before? Ashriel told me that Sebastian sold her out somehow."

Julian really didn't look like she wanted to talk about this, but she seemed to have accepted I wasn't letting it go. "He spied for us. The Morrigan would have flayed him alive if she'd suspected, and by that time, she was completely unpredictable. Towards the end, she was killing everyone close to her. As far as we know, there were only two survivors, Sebastian and Halfdan the Shaper. It was a really bad time."

"I don't get it. Did she just wake up one morning and decide to go batshit crazy?"

"She's old, Kate. Very old. The world she lives in is so different from the world she was born in, she can understand nothing except power and death. It happens to all of us if we survive long enough." She swivelled round and slipped lower in the water as if she was cold.

I kissed the tip of her shoulder. "You're doing okay."

"I think so. But the problem is I won't know when I'm not." She shook herself, droplets flying off her hair. "Anyway, Sebastian told us who her followers were, who could be trusted and who couldn't. He helped Thomas Pryce broker the deal with the Shaper that gave us the North. And he gave us the only thing that had power over her."

"What's that and can we get it again?"

She traced her fingers idly over my knee. "It was a clay beaker about three-feet tall. History isn't really my speciality, sweeting, but according to Sebastian, the Morrígan's people buried their dead with these jars full of, well, I have no idea. Bits of their lives, I assume. It was her last link to the world she came from, but it was broken when she rose as a vampire. Somehow, Sebastian put it back together piece by piece. It must have taken him centuries."

"What? He managed to build something that had been buried, smashed, and lost five thousand years ago?"

"When Sebastian sets his mind to something, he does it. And he is a magician."

"Yeah, but to go to all that effort just to take somebody down."

"We all need a hobby, darling. And for a lot of us, it's revenge."

"So what happened next?" I asked.

"We destroyed her armies and her followers, which just left her, but she'd lived so long, she couldn't be killed. Even by gold. Even in sunlight. But when she learned we had the beaker, she surrendered. It was remarkably peaceful, actually. I think, by that stage, she was tired of fighting, tired of everything really. We kept four pieces of the pot as security and sealed her up underneath a priory on Magpie Lane. We had to move her to Highgate Cemetery in the nineteen hundreds when they rediscovered the crypts."

"But why has she woken up now?"

Julian shrugged again. "She always had the power, but I don't think she wanted to. I think she was sort of ready to die, or get as close to it as she could manage." Aeglica had said something like that before he died. "So, what, she just slept it off?"

"I don't know. It doesn't matter."

"It does matter. She tried to take something out of Aeglica's sword. That was one of the fragments, wasn't it?"

"Probably. Aeglica always did like to keep things close."

"Something must have changed. You've had these things for four hundred years. She wouldn't just decide to come after them now."

"Nothing can have changed." Julian shifted impatiently against me. "She's been locked up in a tomb."

"Someone broke into the tomb. I went to investigate for Nimue, and the lock had been changed."

Julian's glanced back at me. "That's impossible. The Morrígan wouldn't tolerate trespassers. She was asleep, not dead."

"It might be impossible, but it's the only thing that makes sense. Someone went into the tomb, and now the Morrígan is up, awake, and angry. I think someone stole her beaker, and now she's trying to get it back, starting with the bits she knows you have."

"I'm sorry to repeat myself, Kate, but that's impossible." Her fingers dug a little into my leg. "She's five thousand years old. You can't just sneak up on her and take her stuff. It would take extremely powerful magic and an extremely talented thief."

Huh.

"Look," I said slowly, "I'm not promising anything, and I might be completely wrong on this, but I know the tomb was broken into, and I think I know who did it. I don't know how or why but, if I can find her and I can get this thing back, will that help?"

Julian slow-blinked at me. "Yes, Kate, if you can give us the Morrígan's one weakness, that will help us fight her. But, as much as I respect what you do, I'm not going to pin all my hopes on a hunch."

"No, that's fine. But, at least, it's making sense now."

"Right, good. Now where were we?" She twisted round again and vanished below the waterline.

I dragged her up. "You know, the mages have a plan as well, right?"

"I have never known anyone fight so hard to stop me from going down on them." She sighed. "Yes, I know the mages have a plan. Acton told us at the meeting. Sebastian is going to get out of town, and the Witch Queen can do what she likes. We'll be more than happy to let her do our job for us, but again, I'm not pinning my hopes on a ragtag group of mortals with spell books. Now, is there anything else you want to ask, discuss, or talk about?"

"I'm done."

"Are you absolutely certain?"

"Yes, I'm certain."

"And you're sure you want this oral sex? You wouldn't prefer to discuss ancient history, formulate disaster survival plans, or watch paint dry?"

"No, I'm good."

Julian kissed me with damp lips and slithered down my body back into the water.

CHAPTER FIFTEEN

TRAINS & TUPPERWARE

Julian whispered good-bye just before dawn and was gone in a swirl of smoke and shadows. I rolled over to her side of the bed, claimed all the duvet, and went back to sleep. I woke up again at nine. Technically I didn't have a boss to complain about me being late for work, but I do sometimes pretend to be a professional. And I'm a bit old to get away with fucking all night and sleeping 'til two. I texted Elise to tell her I'd be late in again and went to use Julian's hard-core power shower. Then I remembered I'd trashed my clothes.

I dripped into the kitchen, salvaged my trousers and my pants from the soggy mess on the floor, and clambered into them. I'd have to go to work smelling of stale booze and sex, but it wouldn't be the first time. My shirt and jacket were past saving, so I raided Julian's wardrobe. It turns out borrowing your girlfriend's clothes is really difficult if she's half your size and dresses like Adam Ant. I managed to squeeze myself into one of her ridiculous ruffly shirts, bunching the sleeves up so I didn't look like a kid who was outgrowing her school uniform. I couldn't find any jackets to fit and had to settle on something heavy and brocade-y that might have been a dressing gown.

And so, disguised as a complete bell end, I grabbed a box of chocolates, put my hat back on, and went to work. I just hoped I wouldn't get any walk-ins. I rocked up at about eleven to find Elise diligently compiling newspaper reports.

"Good morning, Miss Kane," she said. "Did you have a pleasant evening?"

One of the unsettling things about Elise is that her face only moves when she wants it to, so you don't get the usual visual clues. Most people can't help smirking if you show up looking like the world's most confused drag king. Elise didn't even twitch. "Got put on trial, got in a fight, got laid. I had a blast."

"I hope you were not harmed."

"Julian doesn't like it that rough."

"I was, of course, referring to the fight, but I see you have wilfully misinterpreted me for comic effect. I am quite entertained."

I poured myself a coffee and slumped behind my desk. "How's it going?"

"I believe I have uncovered some promising leads."

"Hit me."

Elise tapped a few commands into her keyboard. "There was a break-in at Christie's, a Professor Fox at All Souls College reported several items missing from his personal collection, and there was a recent robbery at a gallery on Brick Lane, but the nature of the theft has yet to be disclosed."

"Okay, when did these things happen?"

"The twelfth, nineteenth, and twenty-fifth of November, respectively."

"Can you find out when Corin got out?"

"The tenth, Miss Kane. I had already taken the liberty."

I went to look at one of Elise's beautifully constructed and cross-referenced spreadsheets. "Okay, scratch Christie's. She doesn't usually go for big targets, and not even Corin could pull off a job like that two days after getting out of prison. So that leaves the gallery and the professor. Is there any more you can tell me?"

Elise flicked up a web browser with several open tabs. "The gallery is owned by a woman who goes by the name of Isis Fortuna."

"Which means she's either a mage or a hipster or a hipster mage."

"I bow to your superior experience. The other gentleman is a professor of anthropology with a large collection of mystical and religious artefacts. He has reported the theft of a candle in the shape of a human hand dating from the seventeenth century and an ornately decorated skull dating from the fourteenth."

"This candle," I asked, "it wasn't a left hand, was it?"

"I am afraid that information was not made available to me."

I went and flopped back down behind my desk. "Well, fuck. If Corin's managed to nick a Hand of Glory, she could be basically anywhere."

"I am sorry, Miss Kane, that term is unfamiliar to me."

"It's a magic doodad that makes you invisible or puts people to sleep or opens locks or something. They're really useful for getting places you shouldn't. They've gone pretty rare since we stopped hanging people. Probably wouldn't get you past an ancient killer vampire queen though."

"Do you have any theories about the skull?"

"That could be anything. A malicious, familiar spirit, an ancient death curse, a really macabre potpourri holder."

"Those unfortunately seemed the only likely candidates."

"Come on then." I drained my coffee and unflopped. "We've got some legwork to do."

"Are we going to kick arse and take names, Miss Kane?"

"I was thinking we'd maybe just ask them some questions. Politely."

"That would also be appropriate."

We hopped on the Tube and headed straight for Liverpool Street. I don't normally come to this part of town, because I don't often find myself needing vintage clothing, vinyl LPs, or bespoke Italian office furniture.

"This seems a most vibrant area, Miss Kane," said Elise, as we wove through a thin-ish crowd of quirkily dressed shoppers, past walls covered in the respectable sort of graffiti, and places with self-consciously meta names like This Shop Rocks, Pictures on Walls, and Beyond Retro.

"Yeah, it's been tarted up a bit since the Ripper murders."

"Which murders?"

I sometimes forgot that Elise was less than a year old and there was quite a lot of stuff she just plain didn't know. Her creator had built her for a very specific purpose, so he'd prioritised handjobs and personal grooming, and skimped a bit on general knowledge. "Five dead prostitutes in the eighteen eighties. Never solved. Source of a million conspiracy theories. Archer was kind of into the case. He liked the mystery of it, but I always found it a bit skeevy."

"Perhaps I shall Google it."

"Oh, Eve had this massive comic about it if you're interested."

"I believe the preferred term is graphic novel. My creator was quite insistent upon it."

We found the place nestled between yet another vintage shop called Yet Another Vintage Shop and a restaurant that appeared to be named "?". Isis Fortuna turned out to be a gallery/hair salon. The window displayed a mixture of arty pictures of crows in flight and photographs of models with outrageous hairstyles.

Elise sighed. "Sometimes I think I would like to have my hair cut."

"Well, why don't you?"

"Sadly, my hair, like the rest of me, is impervious to physical damage."

Her hair was long, dark, and slightly wavy, the sort of hair I'd have been really jealous of when I was about twelve. It didn't look or feel like it was made of stone. "Uh, it's nice the way it is."

"Perhaps it could be styled. That had not occurred to me previously."

We went inside. The door had one of those old-fashioned bells that jingle when you open them. The place was all exposed brickwork, overpriced art, hair dressing stations, and sofas. A young man with very thick glasses and an immaculate quiff got up from where he was perched on the arm of one of the sofas. "Hi, welcome to Isis Fortuna. Are you here for the static art or the hair art?"

He didn't seem bothered by my outfit, which either meant he was a consummate professional or just had no taste.

"I'm here about the break-in."

He gave me a bit of a wary look. "The police have already been."

"I'm a private investigator. I'm looking for someone. I think they might have been responsible. Can I talk to the owner?"

After a moment, he nodded. "Give me a moment, and I'll see if she's available."

He disappeared into a back room, leaving us with the static art.

I took the opportunity to have a quick snoop, but there wasn't much worth snooping at. If Isis Fortuna was a mage, she was either relatively weak or powerful enough to hide it really well.

Elise had gone to look at the static art. "This is most interesting, Miss Kane. The eclectic juxtaposition of disparate elements and styles creates a very satisfying effect."

I stared blankly. "I'll take your word for it."

"Perhaps we should purchase some for the flat? I am very fond of the instructional poster on the subject of surviving a zombie apocalypse, but I feel it lacks emotional resonance."

It had quite a lot of emotional resonance for me. Eve had bought it as a souvenir after our third anniversary. "Hey, I like that poster."

"As you wish."

There was a short silence while we looked around the salon-slash-gallery.

"Miss Kane," said Elise. "Do you believe this bare shelf is an ironic comment on the quintessential emptiness of human endeavour, or do you believe something as been, as we say in the detective business, nicked?"

I went over and had what we in the detective business call a look. There was a small shelf with a slightly faded card bluetacked to the wall. *Not for sale.*

"I'm not going to rule out the possibility it's some kind of arty joke, but it definitely looks like something was kept here, probably something not very valuable or else it would have been under glass or, at the very least, fixed to the shelf."

"I am no expert, Miss Kane, but it seems contrary to the principles of thievery to take the one thing in the building that has no monetary value."

"So either we were wrong and there was nothing on the shelf to begin with, or Miss Fortuna didn't know what she had." I ran a finger across the shelf to see if there was a convenient layer of dust with a telltale gap in a helpfully recognisable shape. There wasn't.

Then I heard the faint rustle of a beaded curtain, and Isis Fortuna herself swept into the room. She was the kind of girl I would have gone for about eight years ago. She had a haphazard punky look, long green hair, shaved on one side and braided on the other. Her exposed ear was a cutlery drawer of piercings, and a peacock feather hung from the other. She was wearing a studded leather jacket over a fishnet vest, through which her neon-orange bra was clearly visible.

"You can tell Nimue to go fuck herself," she said.

So definitely a mage then.

I held up my hands. "Whoa. Easy tiger. I'm here strictly on my own time."

"The hell you are. You work for the Witch Queen and everyone knows it."

"I work for myself." I had technically sworn an oath of fealty to Nimue, but that didn't mean I was on anyone's leash. "I'm here about the robbery."

She folded her arms, her weight resting on one hip. "Fuck off."

"Wow, I thought hairdressers were supposed to be good with people."

"I'm good with customers, not thugs who bust into my place and try to strong-arm me."

I really wasn't in the mood for this. "Is that what you think I'm doing here?"

"Well, isn't it?"

"If I was, you'd know."

"I believe there has been a miscommunication." Elise stepped neatly forwards. "Miss Kane and I are not here on Court business. We are looking for someone, and we believe she may have been responsible for the break-in at your establishment."

"And who the fuck are you?" snarled Isis.

"My name is Elise. I am Miss Kane's assistant."

She gave Elise a long look. "You're one of Russell's girls, aren't you?"

There was a slight pause. Elise had gone very, very still. "I was unaware that there were others."

"Oh, there are others. Believe me."

"Look," I interrupted, "she's right. I'm not here for Nimue. I'm tracking a fugitive, and I think we can help each other. Also the sooner you talk to me, the sooner I'll get out of your, um, hair."

There was a brief silence.

Isis Fortuna shifted to a slightly less *fuck you* pose. "All right. The break-in wasn't a big deal. Whoever it was, they just took some crappy old statue."

"A crappy old statue of what?"

"Napoleon. I thought it had a kind of kitsch edge that really set off the rest of the collection, but it can't have been worth more than twenty quid." She jerked her thumb in the direction of the empty shelf. "I stuck it over there."

Well, fuck. It was a crappy statue of Napoleon that had got Archer killed last year. I spent weeks chasing this piece of tat that was supposed to have a thingamy of tremendous magical power stashed inside it, bodies racking up around me the whole time. Then it turns out that everyone's nuts, my client's a murderer, and the damn thing's a fake with nothing in it.

"Where did you get it?" I asked.

"Friend of mine skipped town last year and left me a box of stuff."

"This friend got a name?"

"Syme."

That figured. Syme was the guy that Corin had hired Archer and me to keep an eye on. He was dead, but there was no point telling Isis that. He must have ditched the real statue before he got whacked.

I pulled out my phone which had exactly one picture of Corin on it. She was glancing over her shoulder as if she expected someone to step out of the shadows and pull a gun on her. "Have you seen this woman?"

Isis glanced at the picture for a second. "I think someone like that came in last month, but I couldn't say for sure it was her."

That sounded like Corin all right. When she wanted to be, she was the only thing you thought about. But when she didn't, she was a fucking ghost.

"Are you going to tell me what this is about?" asked Isis.

I gave her the short version. "She killed my partner. She might have killed your friend as well."

Isis looked unconvinced. "Why did she want a bust of a dead French dictator?"

"I'll tell you if I ever work it out."

"Honestly, I'm not sure I care. If two people have already been killed over it, I don't want it. Oh, and you know I don't really want you to tell the Witch Queen to fuck off, right?"

"Fine by me. I'm not a messenger service, anyway."

"Before we leave," said Elise suddenly, "would it be possible for me to arrange an appointment with you? My hair cannot be cut, but I am quite interested in having it styled."

"Talk to Janus. He'll sort something out."

While Elise and the boy with the quiff scheduled an appointment, I went outside for a smoke and a think. It looked like Corin had finally got whatever it was she'd been looking for a year ago. I didn't know Corin nearly as well as I once thought I did, but I was ninety-nine percent certain she wasn't a mage herself. Which meant she was either working for someone, she was going to sell the thing on, or she was going to use it as leverage. There'd been a lot of real heavy hitters involved last time round, and she could have been in bed with any one of them. That might even have been why they busted her out of jail, but then that wouldn't explain why she woke up the Morrígan. If she even did.

Part of me figured that if Corin had done this job, it was unlikely she'd done the one in Oxford as well. But the part of me that had dealt with her before said that I couldn't rule it out. Either way, it looked like me and Elise were taking a road trip. And by *road trip* I meant a two-hour drive up the M40.

I was just stamping out my cigarette when my phone rang. Unknown number. Sometimes I don't know why I even bother having caller ID. "Kane."

Rachel's voice crackled over the line. "Got a message for you, babe."

There was a moment of static, and then Jacob spoke: "Tonight. King's Cross. Six."

Then the line went dead.

Great. Because I didn't have enough to worry about. I've been involved in a few necromantic rituals in my life, and if there's one thing I've learned, it's that they never ever go to plan. But a deal was a deal, and in an absolute best-case scenario, there was a very slim chance that this would solve all of my problems.

Oh, who was I kidding?

As soon as Elise was done, we hopped the Tube back to the office, and Elise drove me home so I could change my clothes and pick up the Sword of Killing Everything. Since I still had a couple of hours to kill, I looked up Marcus Fox on the Oxford University website and gave him a ring. He seemed quite happy to talk to me and quite keen to get his stuff back, so I told him I'd swing by tomorrow afternoon. Assuming

I hadn't had my soul sucked out through my nose in a magical ritual gone horribly wrong.

Then I had to get to King's Cross in the middle of the rush hour, which was almost as bad. I fought my way off the train and found Jacob waiting for me on the platform.

"Let's go," he said.

I nodded.

It didn't look like we were in for an evening of scintillating conversation.

We squeezed onto the Northern line and headed south, basically forever. Jacob had his eyes closed for most of the journey. I was pretty sure he was doing some weird mage stuff. About three-quarters of an hour later, the train terminated at Morden and we got out. As soon as the last stragglers left the platform, Jacob fished around in the Tesco's bag he'd been carrying and pulled out a Tupperware container filled with slightly reddish goop.

"Should I ask?"

"Blood and ashes."

He did his thing, and I did mine. Mine involved standing there with a sword in a bin liner waiting for something to try and kill us. Nothing did.

"They'll know now," he said. "Be ready."

We got on the next train northbound and rode all the way to High Barnet. At least we got a seat this time. We arrived, rinsed, and repeated. I stood against a pillar trying to look casual, while Jacob wandered around the platform, muttering and anointing shit.

Then it was back on the Tube to King's Cross, onto the Metropolitan line and out to Uxbridge. At this time of night, everyone was either at home or still in the pub so the trains were nearly empty. Without the noise of the crowd, the carriages were silent except for the metal heartbeat of the lines and the occasional rustle of an abandoned newspaper. Even at the best of times, other Tube travellers tend to look suspicious as all hell, but when you're actively expecting to be attacked by vampires, they properly freak you out. I caught myself glaring at a pair of drunk seventeen-year-olds who were half-asleep on top of each other. And then a guy with a long coat got on, and it was all I could do to stop myself running him through on principle.

We made it to Uxbridge at about ten. All the lights on the train slowly faded away, and it lay there beside the platform like a discarded snakeskin. Jacob got on with the ritual while I paced up and down impatiently. I'm not cut out to be a bodyguard.

We swapped platforms and took the Piccadilly line to Acton Town, where we switched to District and stayed put until Upminster. We hit chucking out time hard, and the Tube filled up with chattering theatregoers, drinkers committed enough to stay 'til closing but not enough to go clubbing afterwards, and nice middle-class teenagers with generous curfews they didn't dare break.

I let myself relax just a little. A smart vampire wouldn't attack in the middle of a crowd, and a crazy frenzied one wouldn't be able to blend in. We repeated the whole shebang at Upminster. By now, I was almost hoping something would come for us. At least it'd give me something to do.

Here lies Kate Kane. Killed by irony. Beloved daughter. Sorely missed.

Then it was back on the train, back to Acton Town and back onto the Piccadilly line, this time bound for Heathrow.

By the time we got there, everything had shut down except us. The train rushed through silent, empty stations. And when we reached our destination, it just waited for us to finish.

"Are we nearly there yet?" I asked, as we got back on the Tube and started rattling back the way we'd come.

"Shh."

I hadn't even brought any boiled sweets.

We changed to the Circle line at South Kensington and then to the DLR at Tower Hill. Trains were waiting for us on the platforms. It was a bit of a relief to get on the DLR. We were out of the tunnels, so I had something to look at that wasn't cables and black walls. The city glittered gold behind us, and I remembered standing with Nim in the Dream. We used to do things like this all the time, back when we were together. Suddenly I missed it. Then I realised I hadn't dreamed about her for a couple of nights. And I missed that too.

It was nearly two in the morning by the time we were done at Woolwich Arsenal and heading back to King's Cross. As we pulled into the station, the automated voice echoed eerily through the carriage: "This is King's Cross St. Pancras. This train terminates here."

I guess that meant we were done.

We got out and Jacob led me up the frozen escalator to the ticket offices and the barriers. "Now for the hard bit."

I stifled a yawn. "Couldn't we have done the hard bit six hours ago?"

Jacob knelt down and began scrawling an actual pentagram on the ground with the stuff in his Tupperware box.

And that was when the vampires attacked.

There were three of them, all dressed in slightly old-fashioned, charcoal-grey suits. If psycho vampire enforcers had a uniform, that would be it. I'd been expecting a pack of frenzied Morrigan mooks half-crazed with bloodlust, but these guys were clearly pros, and I had no idea who they were or where they'd come from. They came in slowly, covering all the exits and I realised I was thoroughly flanked. I'd been ready to be outnumbered, not outmanoeuvred.

I tried to buy some time by engaging them in witty banter.

"Who the fuck are you?"

"Old friends, Miss Kane," replied one of them.

I stared. She was an icy blonde in glasses, with her hair scraped into an aggressive knot. She looked a bit familiar, but I couldn't think from where. I was pretty certain we weren't friends.

I heard the tap-tap of posh shoes on tiles and a fourth vampire walked calmly in from the street. He wore a navy pinstriped suit under an ankle-length wool coat. He appeared to be in his late forties, with a mane of wavy, brown hair, an actual wizard goatee, and a smug predatory look.

His name was Henry Percy, and the fucker had kidnapped me before.

"My, my," he purred. "How you've grown. It seems like only yesterday your oh-so-zealous lover was carrying you away in his arms."

I groped for a suitable comeback. "What the shit are you doing here?"

He gave me a tigerish smile. "Your friend is attempting to annihilate my bloodline. I t-take that rather personally."

"Why didn't you just get out of town?"

"You are interfering in matters that do not concern you."

"Actually, I'm pretty fucking concerned. Last time we met, you tried to sacrifice me, and I still have no idea why."

"Tragically, you will never f-find out." He waved a hand dismissively. "Kill them."

Two of the vampires swooped towards us. I summoned my mother's power. It came easily, and I felt it rush through me like a river in flood. I caught the scent of the Deepwild. I brought my sword up, still in the bin liner, and rammed it through one of my attackers. I just had time to see the look of surprise on his face before he withered to dust in front of me.

My mother laughed.

"Interesting," said Henry Percy.

It had given the blonde pause for thought, so I spun round to see if Jacob had been eaten yet. The other vampire had carried him all the way across the station and pinned him against the wall.

I smelled fresh blood, but it hadn't ripped his throat out yet, which meant he was probably protecting himself somehow.

I started running, pulling the tatters of the bin liner off my sword as I went. Blue fire exploded at my feet and licked up my legs. I was probably going to feel that when the faery magic wore off.

Being a Tube station, there was virtually no cover, so I threw myself down behind the ticket barriers. Another fireball whoomphed into the metal.

Like the man said: interesting.

After a second or two, I poked my head up. The blonde was standing in the middle of the empty station with pale blue flames coiling round her fingers and gathering in the palm of her hands. I was pretty sure that was cheating.

A tongue of fire lashed out towards me, and I quickly ducked. I know how to deal with vampires. I know how to deal with wizards. But vampire wizards are just taking the piss. I was going to have to rush her, but even at faery speed, I'd still get a fireball in the face. And then have to fight a vampire.

Out of the corner of my eye, I saw Jacob come forward. The vampire he'd been struggling with was lying rigid on the floor, dead or at least out of it. The blonde spun on her heels and sprayed blue fire in his general direction. He raised a hand. The flames billowed around him, and he kept walking.

I reckoned it would take the vampire about two seconds to realise the pyrotechnics weren't cutting it. I vaulted over the barrier and charged. What happened next was a blur even with my mother's senses. I caught a flash of blue heading towards my face, and I felt rather than saw a rush of motion as Henry Percy shot past me. But I didn't really have time to worry about that because the blonde was all up in my grill. That, and my hair was on fire.

She tried to pull away so she could carry on pelting me. But I caught her by the arm and brought my sword level with her chest. Her other hand flared blue and slashed at my face. So I stabbed her. She slumped to her knees and withered to dust.

I wasn't so great myself. My face was bleeding badly, and even with my mother's power, I felt weak. I dragged myself round, just in time to see Henry Percy sink his fangs into Jacob's neck.

I'd been right. I made a shitty bodyguard.

Jacob had his eyes closed. He looked pretty together for someone having his blood sucked out. He reached up and brushed his fingers over the vampire's face, leaving a trail of blood and ashes. Percy hissed, hurled Jacob to the ground, and leapt away like a cat from a garden sprinkler.

Well, this had been a clusterfuck. I had no idea if we were winning or not but I readied my sword, mustered what was left of my strength and attacked.

I hadn't exactly been waiting for this for fifteen years, but I was damn well going to make it count.

As soon as I got close, something heavy and invisible knocked me flying. I crashed into the far wall of the station and dropped, winded, to the floor.

Great. Now I was fighting a fucking Jedi.

Henry Percy sauntered over, heels clicking, coat swishing. Whatever Jacob had done had really messed up his face. The skin was greying and peeling across one cheek, and his left eye was covered by a milky film.

I pushed myself to my feet and thrust my blade towards him. I felt of wave of pressure hit me from the side, and I went down again, my weapon clattering onto the ground.

He stared down at me. "It has been a p-pleasure meeting you again, Miss Kane." Then he bent and picked up the sword. "I think I should take this for your own safety. Children should not be p-permitted to run around with sharp objects."

"Fuck you, Percy."

He arched a brow. "A raconteur as well. I b-bid you good evening, Miss Kane."

And with that, the patronising bastard fucked off.

The last of my mother's power faded, and I was suddenly very aware that I was bruised and bleeding on the floor of King's Cross Station at half past two in the morning. Very, very slowly, I hauled myself upright.

In the ruins of his pentagram, Jacob stirred and sat up.

"That could gone have better," I said.

"Yes."

"Sorry."

He shook his head. "I wasn't expecting a sorcerer." He was quiet a moment. "They seemed to know you."

"It's a long story. Can we finish the ritual?"

"A mage isn't much use against a vampire who's tasted their blood." He pushed himself to his feet. Apart from the wound on his neck, he looked basically okay.

"I thought he was going to kill you."

"He knew what he was doing. If he'd killed me, I'd have death-cursed him to shit."

"What do we do now?"

He shrugged. "Do you need a lift home?"

CHAPTER SIXTEEN
ANGELS & DEMONS

now was slanting silver outside the windows of an empty train. The dark folded thick around us. Nimue sat by my side, looking out at the Dream of the city. She was tired. She was resting her head on my shoulder, her curls spilling down my arm.

"It didn't work," I said.

"I know."

"I couldn't stop them. He took the sword."

Nimue slipped her hand into mine. She was cold. "It will find you again."

"How's Jacob?"

"Angry with himself but unharmed. His power is rooted in the dead. If he hadn't been focused on the ritual, the vampires would have been no threat."

"I should have stopped them."

"You've never faced corpsefire before. It weakened you. If you were fully human, you'd be dead."

There was a long silence. I was tired too. I leaned into Nimue. The snow swirled, mixed with feathers.

"Jacob said they knew you."

"Remember those guys who kidnapped me when I was seventeen? It was them. They're led by this psycho wizard vampire called Henry Percy. He said he'd come to stop us wiping out his bloodline, but I don't know. He could've just left town. It's just . . . I don't know. It doesn't add up but I can't think right now."

"You're asleep, Kate."

"It's bugging me."

"Think about it in the morning. Rest now." Her lips brushed against my cheek, softer than the snow.

"What's next?" I asked.

"I'll keep fighting her here. And I'm sending word to other courts. It makes me look weak, but this is bigger than London."

"The vampires are mucking in, now that they've stopped trying to chop my head off."

"If tonight's anything to go by, it seems like they're not all on board."

The darkness began to deepen, and the train came silently to a halt.

"This is your stop, Kate."

I woke to the smell of fresh coffee and my own singed hair. Honestly, I felt pretty shitty. I lurched into the bathroom to catalogue the damage. Three long cuts ran down my cheek, part burn, part claw mark. Ow. I cleaned them up and showered the smoke out my hair, dressed, and staggered into the kitchen for my caffeine fix and the obligatory banana.

I explained my new exciting injuries to Elise, and then we piled into the car, swung by the office to pick up the Corin file, and set off for Oxford. I pulled my hat over my face hoping to sneak another hour's kip on the road, but Elise put paid to that when she cranked up the volume, popped out my trusty Leonard Cohen CD, and replaced it with some kind of German thrash metal.

I pulled my hat down even further, but it was no use.

"Elise," I groaned. "What the shit is this?"

"This, Miss Kane, is 'Sehnsucht,' the opening track of Rammstein's 1997 album of the same name. The album is probably most famous for the fifth track, 'Du Hast,' the title of which is a play on the homophones *hasst*, meaning hate, and *hast*, meaning have."

"And you think this is appropriate music for half nine in the morning, why?"

"I find the rhythms soothing. I would also remind you that the last time we were on an extended car journey you made me listen to 'Diamonds in the Mine' three times in a row."

"It's a classic."

"It is an old man screaming into a microphone about the inefficiencies of the New York postal service."

Mercifully, after an hour, Elise let me change the CD. I thought about putting on *Songs of Love and Hate* just to spite her but decided that would be childish. I stuck on some Tom Waits and fell asleep.

Elise woke me up a little while later.

"Miss Kane," she said, "these roads appear to be laid out most illogically. I attempted to take the shortest and most expeditious route to our destination only to find that I was not permitted to turn in the direction I intended. I have been driving in circles for some time now."

We blundered around for another thirty minutes, trying to navigate the one-way system and find a damn parking space. We eventually ditched the car near a boathouse and headed a few streets south to where Professor Fox lived. He had one of those big, gold, historical-looking houses tucked away on a leafy crescent north of the city centre. Time was, it would have been the poshest thing I'd ever seen, but since coming to London, I've been hanging out with millionaire vampires and werewolf aristocrats. Hell, Eve could have bought this place thirty times over and not even noticed. Still, it was a bit of a step-up from my two-bedroom flat on Muswell Hill.

I climbed the steps and rang the doorbell. It was opened by a silver-haired man in a velvet smoking jacket. He had a slightly weather-beaten look and pale blue eyes glittering behind silver-rimmed spectacles. Basically, he was the kind of professor I'd have had a crush on at university. If I'd been straight. And if I'd gone to university.

"Miss Kane, I presume?" he said. "And Miss Archer?"

"Archer's dead, this is Elise."

"I'm terribly sorry. Would like to come inside?"

He led the way into a tastefully furnished living room, all wingback chairs and shelves full of those old, leather-bound books that I'm pretty sure nobody actually reads.

"Tea? Coffee? It's a little early for anything stronger."

I went for coffee, and he disappeared into another room, returning a few minutes later carrying a tray. He settled himself into a chair and carefully laid out a cafetière, two cups, a jug of cream, a bowl of those rough-cut sugar cubes you get in fancy cafés, and a plate of those little Italian biscuit things.

"So," I said. "Break-in."

"Gracious me, how direct."

"It's my job."

"No, no, I find it quite refreshing. I've been moving primarily in academic circles these past thirty years, where circumlocution is an art form."

"Can you tell me more about the things they took?"

He crossed one leg over the other and leaned back with the air of a man about to blow my tiny mind. "That very much depends on you, Miss Kane. Tell me, do you consider yourself open to unusual ideas?"

I bet he said that to all the girls. "Try me."

"You know, of course, that I am a collector, and I assume you know what it is that I collect."

Yep, he was one of those. I wanted to say *you collect magical doodads that you probably don't understand anywhere near as well as you think you do*, but I didn't think that would go down well.

"Cultural artefacts?" I offered with my best *oh please educate me* look.

"That is one way to describe it, but they are so much more than that. My collection houses items of real power."

"What kind of real power?" I asked dutifully.

He poured cream into his coffee and took a sip. When he felt he'd built the tension enough, he looked me in the eyes and said, "The supernatural, Miss Kane."

There was a silence, and I realised that was my cue to be shocked. "Wow," I replied, with as much sincerity as I could manage.

"It is a little hard to encompass at first."

I bet he said that to all the girls as well. "So what was taken?"

"A Hand of Glory and a demon's skull. The Hand of Glory is a candle fashioned from the left hand of a hanged criminal. While it burns, its owner will not be seen by those he does not wish to see him."

"And the demon skull?"

"An interesting historical curio. It was seized after the dissolution of the Templars in 1312."

"Does it do anything?"

"Not every item in my collection has an obvious function, but that does not diminish their individual value." He patronised me over the top of his glasses. "I must say, you are a very practically minded woman, Miss Kane. Most people express far greater incredulity when I discuss these matters with them."

"The way I see it, stuff you don't believe in can still kill you." I produced a printout of Corin's picture from her file. "Have you seen this woman?"

He looked sheepish.

"I'll take that as a yes."

"She told me she needed to use my telephone..."

"And, let me guess, one thing led to another?"

He actually blushed. Corin had that effect on people.

"And this was a couple of days before your stuff went missing?"

He nodded. "I did mention it to the police, but so far, they haven't found her. She told me her name was Jenny."

"Can I see where you keep your collection?"

"That didn't end well for me last time," he said, with a half smile.

"You wouldn't have let me in if you hadn't checked my credentials."

"Very true, Miss Kane. Step this way."

Professor Fox's collection was housed in a large, humidity-controlled cellar, protected by an alarm, a reinforced door, and a numeric keypad. It would have put off most casual thieves, but Corin was far from casual. The artefacts themselves were stored in oak-fronted, glass-panelled display cases like you get in museums. Again, most of them were locked. Again, it wouldn't have stopped Corin. I wasn't that deep into the occult black market, but I was pretty sure a lot of this shit was worth serious money. If Corin had gone straight for the skull and the Hand of Glory, she must have needed them for something specific. It would have really helped to know what the skull was for. And if anyone would know what you could do with a demon skull it would be a demon.

We said our good-byes to the professor and I asked him to email me some pictures of the missing items. The moment I got back to London, I called Ashriel, and he agreed to drop by the office that afternoon. Elise and I had a pub lunch, or rather I had a pub lunch and Elise watched me eat and talked excitedly about all the new things she'd done in the last couple of days.

Back at the office, I hauled Archer's whiteboard out of the broom cupboard. He'd have been really proud of me if he hadn't been dead. I drew up a timeline. Corin had got out on the tenth of November, had broken into Professor Fox's collection on the nineteenth and hit Isis Fortuna on the twenty-fifth. She'd been a busy girl. Today was December twelfth, which meant she could be anywhere. Hell, she might not even be in this world.

I took a step back and looked at the board. It wasn't really a timeline so much as three dates in a sort of row with nothing much to connect them up. If I could find somewhere she'd been in the last day or so, I could track her scent, but her movements were too random for that.

This was starting to look depressingly like square one.

Okay, Kate, think about this. What do you know about this woman?

She's always on the run. She's a compulsive liar. She's capable of murder. She's really good in bed (probably not helpful). She's working with someone or for someone, who'd helped her get out of prison, but she values her independence and probably won't want to stick with them. Which means she's probably going to screw them over, which means she's going to have to find someone else to hide behind, because that's what she does. Last time it was me. So she'll be working in cash, and she'll need large amounts of it quickly. So she'll need a fence, one that specialises in magical bling. There couldn't be too many of those in London, at least ones who knew what they were doing.

"Miss Kane," said Elise, coming to the back office, "there is a well-configured gentleman to see you."

"A what?"

"A tall gentleman, with pleasingly symmetrical features, and what I am given to understand constitute 'bedroom eyes.'"

"That'll be Ashriel. I didn't think he'd be your type."

"I am not certain I have a type, Miss Kane. I was merely making an observation."

Ashriel had poured himself into the same chair he'd sat in on his first visit three months ago.

"Do you require anything?" asked Elise, following me into the room.

Ashriel's eyes flicked curiously in her direction and stayed there.

"Mr. Ashriel, do you require anything?"

"Um," said Ashriel. Then he seemed to pull himself together. "No, thank you."

Elise nodded and disappeared into the kitchenette.

"Ground control to Major Ashriel?" I waved at him.

His attention snapped back to me, honeyed whiskey and whispered secrets and good old-fashioned down-and-dirty fucking. "What do you need, Kate?"

"What could I do with your skull?"

"Ideally, you could leave it exactly where it is."

I printed out the catalogue photo Professor Fox had sent me. "Okay, but what if I made it into something like this?"

Ashriel gave a low whistle. "Where the hell did you find one of these, and no pun intended."

"Long story. I'm looking for someone who nicked one."

"It's a soul box. You can, y'know, put souls in it."

"Why would you want to do that?"

"A couple of reasons. You can put someone else's soul in it, and then you've got someone else's soul to do what you like with. Or you can put your own soul in it, to keep it safe for a bit."

"Safe from what?"

"Demons, for a start. If you, say, wanted to shag an incubus..." He waggled his eyebrows at me. "... or a succubus in your case, you could put your soul in the box and you'd be more or less safe. Wouldn't be much fun for the demon though, and to be honest, you're better off having a wank."

"Thanks for that. Good to know. Anything else?"

He thought about it for a moment. "It could be useful if you had to go up against a serious mage or a powerful vampire. Vampire bites wouldn't affect you, apart from the blood loss, and they couldn't read your mind or sense your presence. And most ritual magic would slip off as well."

"So, hang on." I stared at the picture. "What's the downside here? Because it sounds like I should get me one of these."

"Kate, take it from someone who knows, you've got a soul for a reason. You kind of need it. Plus demons don't die, so if you leave your soul in there for too long, it'll get eaten. I've seen it happen. And then the demon gets your body. That never ends well."

"Let me get this straight. If someone put their soul in this box, they could, purely hypothetically, sneak up on an ancient sleeping vampire and it wouldn't sense them?"

He shrugged. "Guess so."

Once again, I was grateful that, as a paranormal detective, I didn't need evidence that would stand up in court. *Well, M'lud, the accused was hired by persons unknown to steal an ancient ceramic pot in order to wake up the former vampire queen of the British Isles. How, M'lud? We don't know, but we think she stuck her soul in a box and used a candle made out of a dead man's hand.*

I couldn't prove any of it, but I was pretty damn certain that was how it had gone down.

If I could figure out why, I'd be laughing. Or, more likely, dying.

I slid the printouts into the Corin file. "Okay, next question. If I'd stolen one of these and used it and wasn't going to use it again, who would I sell it to and how much would I get for it?"

"These babies are fantastically rare. To make one, you have a decapitate a demon, stop its body getting sucked back into hell, and be up to your elbows in some serious infernal magic. You can't put a cash value on it because the people who want this sort of thing aren't types to deal in money."

They never are. "Do you know if one's popped up recently?"

Ashriel shook his head. "I'm not as tuned in to that stuff as I used to be."

"Well, can you point me at anyone who is?"

There was a brief pause.

"I could," he said slowly, "but I don't think it's a good idea. I know you can handle yourself, but I'm not going to send you off to chat with demons."

"I've met demons before."

"You've met the kind of demons who get caught. The ones who stick around are either like me or, uh, not like me. They've been around for a long time, which means they're very powerful, they only want one thing, and they know to get it."

"I'll be careful."

"No you won't. Kate." He gazed at me across the desk. I got hit by a wave of his blood sugar sex magic, and it suddenly occurred to me he probably had a hard time getting people to take him seriously. "I don't have many friends, but I think you're one of them. And friends don't send friends to get their souls sucked out."

"Uhh, thanks. If you had a soul I wouldn't want it to get sucked out either. Not that you do. So, um, forget it. Look, I really need to find this thing, and if this is the only way, I'm going to do it."

He was still staring at me. I think he was genuinely worried. "There's no way I can talk you out of this, is there?"

"Basically, nope."

"Fine, but can I at least come with you? If it comes to a fight, we're probably both dead, but we usually don't attack our own kind."

"Honour amongst thieves, huh?"

He looked away. "We fought a war together. We lost, but it still counts for something."

As usual, I couldn't think of anything comforting to say, so I changed the subject. "Do we have to go a crossroads at midnight or something?"

"Not exactly. Have you heard of the Angel of St. Paul's?"

"Vaguely." There were rumours floating around of an old man who sat outside St. Paul's Cathedral and could make wishes come true, but those kind of stories are two a penny, particularly in my line of work.

Ashriel rose gracefully. "Come on, we're going to see him. I'll give you a lift."

I'd learned to my cost that Ashriel drove a green Mini Roadster that wasn't really compatible with my legs. "Honestly," I said, "I fancy the walk."

St. Paul's was about half an hour from my office, and we set off together.

"So," he said, in his best casual voice, "when did you get the new assistant?"

"I made a deal with the Multitude to find the King of the Court of Love."

He grinned. "And the deal was you got an extraordinarily beautiful young woman to help with your filing? That's not exactly a Faustian bargain, is it?"

"You know, I honestly think it just likes to help people."

"Help people? It's an enormous sentient rat gestalt."

"Yeah, but that doesn't mean it's got to be a dick."

There was a short, awkward silence.

"So," he asked, still using his casual voice, "what's her story?"

"This might sound a bit weird, but she's an animated statue."

"That doesn't sound weird at all."

"I really need to get more mortal friends. So, yeah, a wizard made her, didn't like her, threw her out."

"Didn't like her?" He sounded incredulous.

I shrugged. "Be careful what you wish for, I guess."

"She seems . . . nice."

"She did say you were well configured."

"She said I was what?" He slanted a wary glance at me. "Is that good?"

"I have no idea. Elise has her own way of thinking about things."

I see a lot less of St. Paul's than you might think. The movies want you to believe that you can see the Cathedral and Big Ben from basically every window in London, but actually, I hardly ever had a reason to come down here. In fact, thinking about it, I might have only ever seen it on TV.

It looked smaller in real life. These things always do.

There was a steady trickle of tourists going in and a scattering of people sitting on the steps, talking and eating sandwiches. Slightly apart from the crowd, in the lee of one of the pillars, a man sat feeding the pigeons from a crumpled bag of breadcrumbs. He looked to be about fifty or sixty, which meant my streak of *men in their late fifties who were really beings of unspeakable power and evil* continued unbroken.

"Is that what passes for subtle among your people?"

The demon's head came up, and he looked straight at me with pale silver-blue eyes.

"Nice start, Kate," said Ashriel. "We should go over, but don't sit down."

"Hadn't planned on it."

We climbed the steps. The Angel of St. Paul's raised his hand to shield his eyes from the sun and squinted up at us. "Come and sit down."

"I'm good, thanks."

"Feed the birds?" He held out his little bag.

There are two schools of thought about the pigeons in London. One is that they're a charming feature of the landscape of the capital.

The other is that they're basically rats with wings. I was squarely in the rats camp. "No, thanks."

He smiled in a way that reminded me of my granddad. "What is it that you want?"

I was just about to say *I want to talk to you* when Ashriel cut in. "We don't want anything. I'm going to ask you some questions. The lady here is going to listen."

"It's been a long time, Ashriel." He frowned slightly. "You look like shit."

"I'm not the one in the mac and the flat cap."

The Angel of St. Paul's smiled again. This time, he did not remind me of my granddad at all. "Fine words from a vampire's lapdog."

Ashriel smiled back. The sort of smile that was all teeth and no warmth. "And there was me wondering why we don't have these little talks more often. Have you heard anything about a soul box?"

"Why would you want to find one of those?"

"I didn't say I wanted to find it. I'm just asking if you've seen one."

"Perhaps, perhaps not." His eyes glinted like light skittering across diamonds. "Why don't you let the lady speak for herself?"

I had my sanctified steel dagger strapped to my right arm, and I seriously considered pulling it on him. But even if I survived the fight, I didn't fancy getting done for knifing an old man in the street. "I'm fine."

"I'm not here to play games," said Ashriel, with a touch of impatience. "I thought you might know something. I thought if you did you might tell me. Apparently you're not going to."

There was a moment of silence. A strange warmth touched the Angel's ice-bright eyes. "I would help you, Ashriel, for old time's sake, but I'm afraid that would involve breaking a promise."

"Then I guess we're done."

"Don't be a stranger." He glanced at me. "And if there's ever anything you desire, you know where I am."

"Well, that could have gone worse," said Ashriel, as we walked away.

"True, we didn't get killed. But we got no useful information whatsoever."

"That's not strictly true. I think the Angel would have told me where the box was if he could. Since he didn't, he probably has a deal with someone involved."

Huh. "I'm not sure that really helps."

"Probably not, but it's always better to know these things."

We pressed on through the meandering late-afternoon crowds.

"Is there a Plan B?" I asked.

"We're going to a bookshop."

"What, and say, 'Hi, do you have anything on ancient mythical demon boxes?'"

"We're looking for someone."

"Are they going to be any more helpful?"

"It's worth a shot."

About half an hour later, we found ourselves at Foyles on Charing Cross Road. It did not exactly look like a hive of demonic activity.

I gave Ashriel a sceptical look. "What kind of demon hangs out in a bookshop anyway?"

"A dangerous one. Be careful."

"Is there anything I shouldn't say or do?"

"Don't sleep with her."

"We're going to see a succubus who works in a bookshop?"

"Gethsemane isn't exactly a succubus."

Inside, it was basically a book temple. The truth is, I've never really been a big reader. Patrick lent me his copy of *Wuthering Heights* once, but I couldn't really get into it. Sometimes he'd try to talk to me about the book, and I'd just agree with everything he said. I don't think he ever worked out I hadn't read it.

We wandered up and down the aisles and went up and down the escalators, which I would have found exciting when I was about four.

"What are we looking for?" I asked, eventually.

"I'll know when I see it . . . Wait. There."

I followed his gaze. We were in that kind of weird crossover section between fantasy, horror, and romance, where it's all books with swirly writing and flowers on the cover, and half of them have the word *night* in the title. A strikingly handsome man wearing the world's most nonthreatening jumper had just caught the eye of the young woman who'd been browsing there.

He gave her a self-deprecating smile. "Hi," he said, in a voice of sex and chocolate that reminded me of Ashriel's but about a hundred times more potent. "Sorry to interrupt, but you seem to know a lot more about this than I do."

She gave him a wary but interested look. If she was thinking it was too good to be true, she was right.

"I'm looking for something for my goddaughter, Isobel. I know she really likes this writer called Lauren Kate, but I think she's read all her books, so I was wondering if you could point me at something similar."

The mark guided him over to one of the shelves, and they began talking together in low voices. After a couple of minutes his laughter rang out, sweet as honey. The woman gazed at him, entranced, and when she reached to take a book down from the shelf, he reached up too and his hand brushed hers.

And I felt it from across the room.

There was no way I letting an incubus drag some poor woman off on the first floor of Foyles. I checked my knife was ready to go. It was, but if I couldn't get away with stabbing someone outside St. Paul's, I really couldn't get away with it in a crowded bookstore at four in the afternoon.

There was only one thing for it.

"Kate, don't—" called Ashriel, behind me.

"Darling, there you are," I cried, as I rushed across the floor towards them. I grabbed the incubus in an enthusiastic embrace. "Oh, and you've found a book for Isobel. You're so clever."

The woman's hazy eyes cleared. "Um, sorry." She backed away quickly. "I should leave you guys to it. I hope your goddaughter likes the book."

Her footsteps clattered on the wooden floor as she retreated in obvious embarrassment.

The demon turned in my arms, sliding his hands around my waist. His body shifted against me, hard planes and muscle fading into softly curving flesh. "Congratulations," she murmured, "you have my attention."

She looked a little bit like Eve, a little bit like Julian, and a little bit like every girl I've ever wanted to sleep with but not quite managed to.

Her eyes were gold like Ashriel's, but warmer and deeper, pulling me in like a bottle of bad whiskey.

Note to self: never cockblock a sex demon.

Her hand cupped my cheek, turning my lips up to hers. Sex and promises and forevers came rolling off her like scent. I think she was about to kiss me, and I didn't care. I wanted her to.

I wanted her to take me away.

She could have me.

She could do anything to me.

It would kill me, but I'd beg her for it.

"Gethsemane." *Ashriel?* I had a feeling that was good, but I couldn't remember why.

I leaned up impatiently and curled my fingers into her upper arms, frantic for her touch.

She sighed, and it rippled over my skin like silk. "I hope this is something interesting, Ashriel, otherwise I'm having your pet for dinner."

And even though I protested, she stepped away.

Suddenly I remembered who I was, and what I was doing, and my all-important don't fuck demons rule. I went for my knife and Ashriel's hand closed over mine.

"Don't do that either," he whispered. "You've fucked this up enough already."

I really wanted to pull the knife anyway, but I figured there was no way that could end well, so I stood down.

Gethsemane watched me, looking tauntingly hot, and smirking. "What's this about?"

"I was wondering," said Ashriel, "if you'd heard anything about a soul box showing up on the market."

"I'm not precisely in the mood to help you right now. I'd been after that one for weeks."

"I don't suppose 'sorry' will cut it?"

"*You* don't have anything to apologise for."

Two pairs of golden eyes looked at me expectantly.

"I'm sorry I stopped you from sucking an innocent woman's soul out of her body?"

Gethsemane curled her lip. "Don't be passive-aggressive, darling, it doesn't suit you."

She was right. I preferred just plain aggressive.

"Look," I growled. "You fuck with me, and I'll fuck with you right back, and I fuck harder than you think."

Okay, that had sounded better in my head.

She tossed her hair over her shoulder. "Careful, you're almost starting to sound like fun."

"I promise you, it will not be fun. I don't like demons, and I don't like people who fuck with my head, which means I *really* don't like you. Tell us what we need to know, and if you're really, really lucky and I'm feeling really, really generous, I won't hunt you down and kick you back to hell."

"Or—" Gethsemane ran the tip of her tongue over her teeth. "—I could just kill you now as I originally intended."

"Can't we just talk about this?" tried Ashriel.

"Nothing personal, darling."

Her power hit me again, but I was ready for it this time. I reached out to the Deepwild and the dark places. My mouth flooded with the taste of blood. I smelled damp earth and broken stone. I let the hunt take over.

There were weaker creatures in the paper tomb, but my quarry was a thing of sulphur and shadow. The knife was in my hand. I sprang. We were pressed against a wall of wood. My knife was at her throat, blood black on the blade.

I scented fear, sweet and seductive.

A voice from behind. "Okay, Kate, you've made your point."

And I remembered I was not here for this.

Slowly, I let it slip away. The strength and the hunger and my mother's kingdom.

"If you wanted it rough," she gasped, "you only had to ask."

I shoved the knife hastily back into its sheath. If anyone had noticed and called the cops, I'd be looking at actual jail time for that little stunt. "Do we have a deal?"

"You mean, I tell you what you want to know, and you don't kill me?"

"Yep."

She flicked out a fingertip and ran it across my jaw. "You know, I could almost like you, changeling."

"You're not my type."

"Oh, but I am."

"Cut the banter and the shape-shifting bullshit. Are you going to help us or not?"

"Fine, since you ask so nicely."

I stepped clear, and her body flickered, flowing into a new form. He was tall and slender, snow-drop pale with a cascade of silver-blond hair and delicate, androgynous features. He shook his head irritably. "Better?"

"Whatever. Now tell us about the soul box."

"I heard someone pawned one to the Merchant of Dreams a couple of weeks ago. I went along to see if there was anyone interesting in it, but it was empty."

"There. Was that so difficult?"

He gave a long-suffering sigh. "Can you please go away now? You're cramping my style."

"Um, thank you," added Ashriel.

Gethsemane gave him a look. "Think nothing of it. I do so love meeting new people."

He sauntered away, hips swaying, hair wafting behind him.

CHAPTER SEVENTEEN
SHADOWS & DREAMS

Everyone in my line of work knew about the Merchant of Dreams, the mysterious proprietor of the pawnbrokers on Seven Dials where you could buy or sell basically anything. Old jewellery, memories, years of your life, magic-enchanted demon skulls. I'd never been. I don't go in much for retail therapy. I headed down there the next morning, leaving Elise to take care of the office.

The shop front was that very specific colour of faded green you only ever see on dingy antique stores. If there'd ever been a sign, it was so worn I couldn't read it. Only the traditional brass balls hanging over the door told you what you were walking into. Even though the shop was open, there was still a metal grille padlocked over the windows. I peered through the grill at a selection of obscure and dusty artefacts, each accompanied by a neatly handwritten ticket.

Well, there was no point standing outside like an idiot. I pushed open the door and went in.

A narrow aisle led through a labyrinth of teetering merchandise to a glass-fronted cabinet at the back of the shop. Standing behind it was the Merchant of Dreams.

They were small, slight, and angular, dressed in faded black velvet. As I got closer, I realised they were younger than I expected, with tousled just-fucked hair, sharp cheekbones, and thin smiling lips. They watched me through eerie, heterochromatic eyes, one ink-black, one ice-blue.

I was going to go out on a limb and say faery-blooded. "You the Merchant of Dreams?"

"Some people have called me that." They had a light voice, feminine but slightly husky, with an accent that could have been from anywhere.

"My name's Kate Kane. I'm a private investigator. I'm looking for a soul box."

"You have expensive tastes."

I was getting really sick of people being gnomic at me. "Do you have one?"

"I do."

"Can I see it?"

They smiled. "Nothing is free, my dear."

"You want me to pay you to look at it?"

"I am the Merchant of Dreams. Everything is for sale and nothing is free."

I sighed. "What do you want?"

"The price is in the paying, not the sum."

"So, you don't take credit card then?"

"Oh no." They pointed at the card machine that nestled next to the till. "We accept all major credit cards and traveller's cheques."

"Fine. Whatever. How much?"

"The price is in the paying, not the sum."

"Oh, for fuck's sake." I dragged a tenner out of my wallet and threw it onto the counter. "Will that do?"

They picked it up with long, agile fingers and rang the amount into an old-fashioned cash register. When that was done, they reached under the counter and produced an ornately carved skull, its eye sockets stoppered with smoked glass. I guess one ornately carved skull looks a lot like another, but I checked it against the catalogue photo and they seemed to match. "Who brought this in?"

The Merchant of Dreams smiled at me again. "Nothing is free, my dear."

I gave them another tenner.

"A young woman who was running away from something." They shrugged. "About five foot four, dark hair, big eyes, and a fragile look."

Yep, that sounded like Corin. "Did she hock anything else?"

I was out of notes. I fished a two pound coin out of the depths of my wallet and slid it across the counter.

"A plaster bust of Napoleon, but that's not for sale yet."

I sighed and slapped the last of my change on the counter. "What's the deal with the bust and what did she trade it for?"

"The bust contains a phial of the Tears of Hypnos, and she pawned it for the sum of one penny."

That didn't sound like Corin. She never gave away anything for less than more than it was worth which meant all she wanted was a safe place to put it. She could have stuck it in a locker or a deposit box, but both of those would have been traceable, and nobody stole from the Merchant of Dreams.

"What the hell are the Tears of Hypnos?"

They just smiled at me.

Shit. "Look, I'm out of cash."

"The price is in the paying, not the sum."

I patted down my pockets and found a tatty old ballpoint pen in my inside pocket. I hesitated for a moment because giving personal items to a faery is a really bad idea. Honestly, I'd probably stolen this from a hotel, and it didn't look like I'd chewed or got blood on it. I slid it over.

The Merchant of Dreams picked it up and turned it curiously between their long fingers. "The stuff that dreams are made of."

"That doesn't help."

"Nevertheless, it is the answer to your question."

This was getting me nowhere. I looked at the skull. It was basically my last link to Corin and as close as I was going to get. If I was right, she'd stashed her soul in it before she went tomb raiding. On a hunch, I picked up and sniffed it.

The Merchant of Dreams arched a quizzical eyebrow.

I could definitely sense something. It wasn't really a scent, more an impression, masked by a trace of sulphur. I'd been using my mother's powers a lot recently. I got the sense she didn't mind and that worried me. If I carried on like this, I'd be skinning tourists in Regent's Park and waking up in strange places with blood on my lips. Still, a half-faery paranormal PI has to do what a half-faery paranormal PI has to do.

I reached out. The Deepwild was waiting for me. I focused on Corin and tried to imagine her standing where I was standing, the skull cupped in her pale, restless hands, looking up at the Merchant of Dreams with those *save me* eyes of hers.

And then I caught the scent, intense around the skull—sex and fear and Chanel No. 5.

I put down the skull and followed the trail.

I didn't get very far.

It stopped in front of an old oak wardrobe at the back of the shop. I dragged open the door. A trace of Corin lingered on the old fur coats hanging inside.

Then nothing but the sharp, clean smell of snow.

Well, fuck.

I drew my senses back in and stomped over to the counter.

"Is there, by any chance, a gateway to another world in that wardrobe?"

The Merchant of Dreams grinned. Their teeth looked a little sharp.

"I'm going to take that as yes." I sighed. "Okay, I'm going to run a scenario past you. This woman comes into your shop. She's got an armload of magical tat to unload and urgent need for cash and a quick way out of town. There's scary people following her, so it can't be anything too ordinary or too obvious, but it just so happens that you've got your very own otherworld stashed at the back of the shop."

"And what if she did?"

"Then I'd say we have a deal to make."

"Music to my ears, dear."

"Send me to where you sent her."

"That won't be easy. Not for someone like you."

"Why, have they got a no smoking policy?"

"No, but my patron has a 'No killing me and annexing my realm into the Deepwild' policy."

Guess I'd been right about the eyes. And it was sounding like Corin had got herself a first-class ticket through Faerie. "It was just that one time."

"A Faerie realm here, a Faerie realm there, sooner or later, it all adds up to real money."

"Look, can you do it or not?"

"Of course," said the Merchant of Dreams, twiddling their fingers like a bad stage magician, "but nothing is free."

"Yeah, I got that memo. What do you want?"

They thought for a moment, head cocked to one side. "This is a special service and requires a special payment."

"I bet you say that to all the girls."

They ignored me. "I require a single feather."

"But not just any feather, right?"

"A feather plucked from the wing of the mad queen of the vampires."

"Oh, I must have left it in my other pants."

"Not to worry, dear. Consider it a loan, one you will have thirty days to repay."

"And if I can't pay?"

The light left their eyes. "Then you go to debtor's prison."

Okay, so my choices were: let Corin escape (again) or cut a deal with a crazy changeling pawnbroker, which would mean I'd have to either get up close and personal with the Morrígan or find myself trapped in some god-awful faery dungeon for all eternity. The smart thing to do was quit while I was ahead, but I wasn't really ahead and I've never been a quitter. "Guess I'm in."

"Then we have a deal."

I felt something at the edges of my senses, like when you see lightning out of the corner of your eye. Ah, faery magic. Great. No backing out now then.

"Just one moment." The Merchant of Dreams slipped out from behind the counter, flipped the *Open* sign to *Closed*, and locked the door. They opened the wardrobe, lifted out one of the coats, and put it on. It came down almost all the way to their ankles. "Step this way, dear."

I followed. First came the ice water rush of walking between worlds, and then it got very, very cold and very, very dark. We were standing in a snowbound forest, thick with shadows. Through the distance, I could just make out the jagged spires of a white palace nestled between two hills.

"Where the fuck are we?"

"I don't usually give freebies, dear, but since you've paid for the tour, I'll tell you. This is the realm of my patron, the King of Shadows, the Queen of Winter."

I knew more about Faerie than most people, what with my mother and everything, but it's not like I'd ever studied it. "Who are they then?"

"One and the same."

Oh, right. That was another thing about faeries, they were basically whoever they wanted to be, even if that meant they were two people.

We trudged along in silence. My feet crunched on the snow. The sky was dead black, scarred with grey clouds. Here and there, lanterns hung from the trees, casting yellowish light and eerie shadows.

"Last time I was in a forest like this," I said, "I wound up in a fight with a unicorn."

The Merchant of Dreams nodded. "Ah yes, the Realm of the Pale Stag. We share a border." As they spoke, the breath coiled silver from their lips and disappeared into the darkness.

That was it for my haunted forest anecdotes. "So you're a changeling, huh?"

"Yes."

"Aren't you worried you'll lose yourself?"

"Not all those who wander are lost."

I gave them a look. "Don't quote Tolkien at me. I had enough of that with my ex."

"Then, no, I do not worry. I have always found my way back."

We walked on a while.

"You're really into this stuff, aren't you?" I asked.

They folded their arms across their body like they were suddenly feeling the cold. "I found Faerie kinder than the workhouse."

"The workhouse? How old are you?"

"As old as my tongue, a little older than my teeth."

"Is that a perk, then?"

"One of many, dear." Their smile gleamed through the shadows. "I am the Merchant of Dreams. Everything is for sale and nothing is free and I always get my share."

"Do you have, y'know, an actual name?"

"Yes."

"And are you going to, say, tell it to me?"

They were silent. Guess that was a no, then.

Perhaps it was my imagination, but the forest seemed to be getting creepier. A low wind was moaning through the trees, and I kept thinking it was calling to me. Branches clutched at me like fingers of the drowned. Sometimes I'd glimpse faces in the knots in the wood. They didn't look happy.

"Nice place you've got here."

The Merchant of Dreams had their gaze on the dim horizon. "Debtor's prison," they said flatly.

Right. Better see about getting that feather.

We walked on for I don't know how long. I was glad to have a guide because there was no way I'd have been able to find my way around this place on my own. Haunted forests aren't big on landmarks, and I'm not big on haunted forests. Under normal circumstances, I'd have worried that this was a gigantic setup, but if I knew anything about faery magic, the Merchant of Dreams couldn't go back on a bargain.

"There." They pointed.

I looked and saw nothing but more forest.

"Between those two trees."

Between those trees was still more forest, but since this was Faerie, that meant absolutely nothing.

"What's on the other side?" I asked.

"What you bargained for."

I decided to chance it. "And what did Corin bargain for? Since I paid for the tour."

They thought about it for a moment. "That seems fair. She traded the soul box for twenty thousand pounds, an unregistered Walther police pistol, and safe passage through my patron's realm to a place where she would find someone who would protect her."

"Thanks."

"This was a trade, not a favour."

There didn't seem much I could say to that. I had a murderer to catch, and I wasn't about to stand around in a haunted forest debating social conventions with a magic pawnbroker. I headed for the gap between the trees.

"Oh, and Kate?"

I stopped. "What?"

"Sheyne."

"What?"

"My name."

I was pretty sure that hadn't been a trade. "Thanks."

The Merchant of Dreams nodded and walked away into the darkness.

I pressed on through the trees until I felt cold wash over me. The good news was that I was probably out of Faerie. The bad news was I could be basically anywhere. I appeared to be in a very slightly different spooky haunted wood. Over the past six months, I'd dealt with a faery shit lord, demons from Hell, and bloodthirsty vampire armies, but the countryside really freaked me out. I'd never been a Girl Guide; I've never gone camping. I had a hard enough time finding my way around parks, let alone some strange forest fuck knows where. I pulled out my phone in the hope of finding myself on GPS, but there was no reception.

Well, fuck.

If it came down to rainwater and berries, I was killing myself.

I suppose if things got really bad, I could call on my mother's instincts but, knowing my luck, I'd probably go feral and spend the next six years living in a forest, stealing picnic baskets. Besides, the more you use that kind of thing, the easier it is to keep using it. It's basically like drinking. By the time you should be stopping, you've forgotten it's an option.

I tried to look on the bright side. Assuming I was still in England, then this place couldn't be that big. It was probably only a few miles across, so if I just picked a direction and kept walking, I'd get to a road eventually. Of course, I wasn't sure how that was supposed to get me to Corin, but mystical faery bargains have a way of working out.

I set off vaguely forwardish.

On the whole, things could have been worse. The real world was about a million times safer than Faerie, and I was pretty sure I was still in England, which meant I wasn't about to get attacked by a bear or a pack of...

I heard wolves howling in the distance.

Okay, either I wasn't in England at all, or this was werewolf territory. That wasn't as bad as it sounded. Most werewolves are very reasonable people, as long as you don't blunder onto their land without announcing yourself. Oh, wait. But, if I was lucky, I'd be at Safernoc, and I'd be able to tell them that their Alpha wouldn't want me dead until she'd had a chance to bang me.

If this was woofle country, then I'd be better off heading towards the blood-curling howls than away from them. For a start, if you run away from them, they'll just hunt you harder. Plus, werewolf land tends to have a lot of other greebly shit living on it.

I caught a flash of white through the trees.

Before I had time to worry about it, half a tonne of pissed off unicorn thundered out of the forest towards me.

I threw myself sideways onto the frost-cracked earth. The bastard just missed me, and I was on my feet before it could turn around. I've tangled with unicorns before and they're nasty fuckers.

It swung itself round to face me and stared at me with its dead black eyes. There was something faintly familiar about its air of horsey malevolence, and it was looking at me like this was personal.

"Oh shit," I said. "Not you again."

It lowered its head and pawed the ground.

"Look, we can do this the easy way or the hard way."

It snorted, steam rising from flaring nostrils.

"I'm a motherfucking faery princess. Show me some respect."

To my surprise, it did. It was staring like it hated me, but it knelt passively on the ground and lowered its horn.

"This better not be a trick. I can still send you to the magic glue factory."

I edged my way cautiously round to its side, and when it didn't try to impale me, I swung my leg over its back. Werewolves plus a unicorn with a grudge meant that this was definitely Safernoc. Corin's bargain for passage through Faerie to a place where she would meet somebody who would protect her was suddenly making a lot of sense. Fond as I was of Tara, she was exactly the kind of person that Corin could get her hooks into. Somebody aggressive, horny, and overprotective.

My unicorn rose grudgingly to its feet. "Okay," I told it. "Take me to the big house."

And off we went.

Safernoc Hall rose out of the darkness like something from a really cheesy horror movie, all black towers and flying buttresses. I ditched the unicorn in the car park, knowing full well it would fuck off the moment my back was turned, and headed for the entrance. I knocked and the door was answered by someone straight out of *Downton Abbey*.

"I need to see Tara."

The butler stared down his nose at me, which took some doing because I was about three inches taller than him. "Miss Vane-Tempest is not receiving visitors."

"My name's Kate Kane. She'll see me."

"No, madam, she will not."

"Look, it's important."

"It always is, madam." And the fucker closed the door in my face.

Right. Plan B. I skirted round the side of the building, looking for something I could climb up or crack open. At the back, I squinted up and saw a light coming from an open window. It was four floors up, but there was a proper Romeo and Juliet balcony complete with climbing ivy, and it was as good as I was going to get. I swung myself up.

Here lies Kate Kane. Splatted on the flagstones while breaking into a Gothic mansion looking for a werewolf and a con artist. Beloved daughter. Sorely missed.

I was never an outdoorsy kid, but I've climbed into a few windows in my time, not always for professional reasons. It was tough going, but I didn't let go, and I didn't look down.

I scrambled over the edge of the balcony and pressed myself flat to the wall, so I wouldn't be stupidly visible from inside. When I got my breath back, I peeked round the corner. Even though the window was open, the curtains were mostly drawn and waving around in the wind, which made it hard to see anything. I slipped in behind the curtain and took another look.

Well, I guess I'd found Tara.

And Corin.

They were kind of busy.

And I was standing upwind of a werewolf.

Tara's head snapped round, her eyes a feral amber.

I waved. At this stage, I didn't know what else to do.

Corin made a girly noise, slithered out from under Tara, and wrapped herself in the covers. Tara snarled, rose from the sheets like a really pissed off Venus, and stalked towards me. She was naked except for a gold leather corset-harness and the obvious attachment. It should have been too absurd to be intimidating, but this was Tara Vane-Tempest, model, It Girl, and Alpha werewolf, and she looked as if she was about to blow my house down.

"What the hell are you doing here?"

"It's kind of a long story, but I'm after her." I pointed at Corin who was huddled up against the headboard looking terrified and innocent. She was probably working out the angles.

"And what made you look in my bedroom?" demanded Tara.

"Like I said, long story."

I realised I was sort of screwed here. Okay, bad choice of words. Tara was exactly what Corin was always looking for. And I was guessing Corin was just Tara's type, in a predator/prey kind of way, with those big doe eyes and that neck you could snap with one hand. There was no way I was going to be able to convince Tara that Corin was a low-down, lying, cheating, swindling, murdering femme fatale, at least not with her sitting right there looking all *save me, save me*. Right now there was a good chance Tara would fling me off the balcony.

"Basically," I said, a bit desperately, "there's this vampire queen tearing the shit out of London. I thought Corin might have seen something important."

I didn't think it was possible, but Corin's eyes went even wider.

Tara just looked even more pissed off. "I might have known you were tangled up in this, Kate Kane." She leaned in, pressed her face against my neck and inhaled. The golden waves of her hair tumbled between us. She was kind of sweaty and very naked, all soft breasts and muscular thighs, and a generous dildo poking into my hip. I'd forgotten quite how little sense of personal space Tara had. "You smell of shadows and dreams. And dead things."

I pulled back. "Look, clearly this was a mistake, you've got your thing going on. I'll come back later."

She grabbed both my wrists and yanked me into the room so hard, I fell over. She slammed the windows shut, undid the harness and tossed it aside. "You've got a lot of explaining to do." She shrugged into one of her trademark silk dressing gowns that concealed absolutely nothing. "The pack moves on the Morrígan in the morning. You will tell us everything you know."

"Shit." I rubbed my wrists. "Not you guys as well. This is already a giant clusterfuck. Do us all a favour and stay out of it."

Tara leapt across the room and pinned me to the ground. She crouched over me, the ends of her hair and the loose silk of her dressing gown brushing lightly against my body. She put her lips to my ear, her breath a rush of heat, and whispered: "I've told you before not to tell me my business. You will come before the pack, and you will tell us what you know."

I had three choices. Talk my way out, fight my way out, or sex my way out. Last time, sexing my way out hadn't gone so well. "If that's what you want, fine."

She sprang to her feet and, after a moment, I risked sitting up. She reached out and pulled on the bell rope, and a couple of minutes later, there was a knock on the door and a servant entered.

"Take this woman to the large dining room. And if she tries to run, give the call and we will hunt her down."

"Very good, my lady."

I'd already crossed Tara enough for one lifetime, so I went quietly. I wasn't exactly thrilled about being taken to the dining room. It was a bit too *all the better to eat you with*.

CHAPTER EIGHTEEN

WOLVES & LAMBS

I was shown into a vast chamber, all hardwood and chandeliers. The walls were lined with family portraits, most of them showing intense, athletic-looking women with wolves at their feet. I spotted Tara's picture straightaway because it was closest to the door. She was standing in full hunting pinks, incredibly tight trousers, and incredibly shiny boots, an arm resting against the neck of one of those impossibly white horses you only get in paintings. A vast golden wolf sprawled at her feet. I was pretty sure that was her as well. The next one along showed a dazzling young woman in a sea-green ball gown standing against the open windows to a formal garden. A silver-grey wolf sat primly by her side, staring out of the portrait with a cold ferocity. I was just thinking how much I'd like to hit that—the girl, I mean, not the wolf—when I realised they were both probably the Dowager, the terrifying old woman who had been overtly hostile to me every time we'd met.

"Ah, Miss Kane," came a plummy voice from the bottom end of the table. "Do come in. The others will be along presently."

I hadn't seen Jumbo, the Vane-Tempest PR man, since he'd helpfully pointed me in the direction of a soul-sucking stag monster at his cousin's funeral. "Hi."

"How nice to see you again," he purred. "I'm so glad you weren't devoured."

"That makes two of us."

I walked the mile and half down the dining table to take the chair next to him. Jumbo was a fat, balding man, currently clutching a cocktail in one hand and a cigar in the other. He was one of those harmless-looking people who totally aren't.

"If you'd care for a snifter, I believe they're still serving drinks in the library."

It was a nice idea, but there was no way I was going against Tara's orders, especially if it meant walking into a room full of werewolves who weren't expecting me. There are some things even I won't do for a free drink. "I'm good."

"I must say," he went on, "Tara brought you in at rather short notice."

"Really short."

"You have an air of displeasure, Miss Kane. I hope you are not here under duress."

I sighed. "It's a long story."

"The best ones always are. I presume you have something to tell us about the situation in London."

I might have known Jumbo had his finger in that pie as well. "Looks like."

"I would not wish to partner you at bridge, Miss Kane."

"It'd be a good call. I've never played."

"That much is obvious. You have no talent for communication."

"Ooh, burn."

He popped the olive out of his drink and into his mouth. "Now, now, Miss Kane, it was an observation, not an insult. I understand that you are a woman of action."

"Damn straight. But, since you're not, do you want to tell me what's going on here and how you know about the Morrígan? Did Corin say something?"

"Please, Miss Kane, credit us with some ability to discharge our sacred birthright. There has been, shall we say, an explosion of vampire activity in the capital, but I suspect, given your associations, you know at least as much about that as we do. We've been investigating the matter for some time. And, remember, start from the outside and work in."

I was about to ask what the hell he meant when the doors opened and a throng of chattering toffs spilled into the room. All of them were dressed up to the nines and most of them were carrying martini glasses. I'd first run into the Vane-Tempests during all the crap three months ago and I recognised a few of them from the funeral. There was the Dowager Marchioness of Safernoc, a bundle of octogenarian hostility in a green velvet evening dress. When we last met, she'd made it pretty clear she hated me and possibly all humans. She was escorted her by grandson, Henry, who seemed to be the only one of the family who wasn't a complete arsehole. I vaguely remembered two of the others from when I'd gate-crashed a polo game. Tara had called them Tuffie and Smudge, but I wasn't sure which was which.

"You're probably in somebody's chair," said Jumbo, and I jumped up quickly. We'd had a dog when I was growing up, and it used to get pretty shirty when the cat tried to sit in its basket.

I stood there like a lemon waiting for everyone to take their place. Eventually there were only two seats left, the big one at the head of the table and one to the left of it, opposite Henry and next to either Tuffie or Smudge.

The last time I tried to sit in a vacant seat, it'd been part of a mystical circle and it hadn't gone well.

"Is this me?" I asked Tuffie or Smudge.

"Yah."

I sat down.

There were more knives on the table in front of me than I had taped to the bottom of my desk. Not to mention the weird bits of silverware that looked like they'd come from an operating theatre.

I was just getting settled when everybody stood up again and Tara swept into the room. She was wearing another one of her impossible dresses. This one was basically a gold sheath, split to the hip. At least she'd dressed for dinner.

She lowered herself into her chair, which meant the rest of us could sit down as well. Conversation resumed. And just like that, I was stuck at another dinner party. If anything, it was worse than the last. Tara was pointedly ignoring me. Note to self: never cockblock demons *or* werewolves.

Henry made a few attempts to talk, but Tara cut him off every time. And Tuffie or Smudge was too busy talking werewolf shop with whoever was sitting on her other side. At least the Dowager was at the other end of the table, but I could feel her glare from here.

I had to sit through six courses of this. When the starter or the entrée or appetiser or whatever you call it was served, Jumbo's weird comment suddenly made sense, and I think I used all the right cutlery. The food was probably really nice but I wasn't in the mood to appreciate it. I tried to pick up on the conversation around me so I'd have some idea what the hell was going on, but there were too many people talking at once, and I couldn't filter out all the polo and fashion show stuff from the hard-core wolf politics.

Finally, they brought the coffee round, and Tara got to her feet. I was all set to jump up as well, but nobody else moved so I stayed put.

"Brothers, sisters, friends," she announced. "Tonight we are fortunate that Miss Katharine Kane has come to bring us news from London."

Everybody stared at me, and I stared at Tara with my best *what the fuck* face on.

"Stand up," she whispered.

I stood up. I hate public speaking. You're usually told that if you're nervous you should imagine the audience naked, but I'd already seen Tara naked and she was no less intimidating. Also, she was clearly doing this to freak me out, and I wasn't about to give her the satisfaction.

"Look," I said, "it'd be really helpful if you told me what you want to get out of this."

There was no way I was spilling my guts to a bunch of strangers. I didn't know what they already knew, and I had no idea what they'd do with what I told them.

"Tell us what the vampires are doing."

"You know the Council's in town?"

From halfway up the table, a dark-haired woman in her early forties leaned forwards.

Tara glanced her way. "Julia?"

"Which members?" she asked.

This was the kind of information that could get people killed, but I figured they were old enough to take care of themselves, and I gambled on the idea that a half-dozen powerful vampires might encourage the werewolves to back off. I listed the names of the Council in rough order of scariness. Julia retrieved from beside her chair a book so hefty it was probably a tome and started leafing through it.

"So—" She paused about a third of the way in. "—that's the Emperor, the High Priestess, Justice, Death, Temperance."

Tara braced herself with both hands on the table. The whole conquering general vibe nearly stopped me noticing her breasts. "Where does that leave us?"

"Justice will represent the greatest threat. The records date her back to the first dynasty. If she comes into direct conflict with the Morrígan, there could be disastrous consequences."

I thought back to Aeglica's garden. If that was what happened when Kemsit and the Morrígan squared off for two seconds, I didn't like to think where it would end if they really got into it.

Tara's attention flicked back to me. "Why has this happened now?"

Well, Tara. The murderous con woman you're currently fucking woke her up.

"I don't know all the details," I hedged, "but I'm pretty sure someone woke her up. I'm pretty sure it was Corin. And I'm pretty sure someone bust Corin out of jail so she could do it. But I don't who or why or what the hell they hoped to get out of it."

Tara's eyes flashed. "If you're playing me, Kate Kane."

"Did I hear that correctly?" came the Dowager's diamond-sharp tones from the other end of the table. "Are you currently bedding the mortal who woke the vampire queen?"

Tara's lips curled back and she snarled.

The Dowager just smiled.

"May I ask," enquired Jumbo, easing himself into the conversation and nodding in my direction, "if you know what the Morrígan's plans might be?"

Again, I was pretty sure that information wouldn't get anyone killed. Tara might have been a dick, but there was a part of me that weirdly respected her. Or wanted to do her. One of the two. "She's looking for something, and she's building an army to get it."

"This is not to be borne," snapped the Dowager. "The vampires have been flouting the Compact for five years, and we have done nothing about it. And see where it has led."

"The Compact was with the Council, not the Morrígan," said Julia softly.

"They must know what she is doing, and if they do not, they are weak and must be replaced. If they fail to keep their house in order, we shall do it for them."

Tara came to her full height, which was pretty damn full, especially in those heels. "It is no longer your place to say what this pack does or does not do." For a moment, things seemed to be going my way. "But I cannot let the vampires spawn unchecked."

Or maybe not.

Jumbo looked up lazily from his coffee. "It would be inadvisable to antagonise the Council."

"Does the Council rule here, or do you?" demanded the Dowager, glaring at Tara.

The last thing we needed was a pack of werewolves rampaging around London. It'd be just about okay in a mass murdering sort of way if they stuck to the Morrígan's minions, but I was pretty sure their intel wasn't that good. I've seen werewolves on a cull before. They think they've got a sacred right to control the populations of other supernatural species, and they don't really discriminate. If they hit London, they'd probably kill anything that smelled like a corpse.

"Tara," I tried. "Think about this."

I realised too late it was the last thing I should have said. Tara hates taking orders, especially from me, especially in front of her family. She gave me a furious look. Some days you just shouldn't get out of bed. Then she turned back to her family. "We hunt at dawn."

Well, fuck.

I had to warn Julian.

The party broke up for brandy and cigars, and I took the opportunity to slip away. I ducked into one of Safernoc's endless supply of posh person rooms and pulled out my phone. The reception was terrible so I stood by the window and hoped. Since I knew dialling Julian's personal number would be a waste of time, I decided to ring the Velvet. I'd barely opened my contacts list when Tara's hand closed hard over my wrist, and she yanked away my phone. She dropped it onto the floor and drove one of her six-inch heels through the screen. I lose more handsets that way. Okay, that's not really true.

"I'm sorry, but I can't let you do that."

I glared at her. "You could have just said."

"I'm still very angry with you, Kate Kane."

I couldn't tell if that was a threat or a come-on. "Look—" I held my hands up in that surrendery gesture she seemed to like. "—it's not too late. You can stop this."

"We have a duty."

"What, to ride into London and slaughter everyone?"

"To protect the land and its people. I will not stop this, and neither will you."

I didn't like where this was going. I didn't have my silver dagger on me, and I couldn't have taken Tara even if I had.

Here lies Kate Kane. Eaten by a lingerie model and not in a good way. Beloved daughter. Sorely missed.

But all Tara did was drag me off. When people are manhandling you, you've basically got two choices: fight them or go with it, otherwise you just look like an idiot. I'd already ruled out fighting, so I went with it.

She whisked me through the corridors of Safernoc, down a flight of honest-to-God stone steps, and into an actual motherfucking dungeon.

"You've got to be kidding me."

She gazed at me with a mixture of frustration and affection. "I don't trust you."

She had a point.

She pulled me into a cell and snapped a pair of manacles onto my wrists. And we weren't talking Ann Summers fluffy handcuffs here. We were talking good old-fashioned cold iron as thick as your thumb.

"Can't we talk about this?" I asked.

"I'll be back for you, Kate Kane, when it's done."

"Just so you know, I'll be pretty bloody angry."

She leaned in close, her hair tickling my neck. "I'll make it up to you."

"You really fucking won't." I twisted away from her, and she backed off.

"Well, what am I supposed to think? You don't answer my calls, you return all my gifts, and then you walk into my bedroom when I'm fucking another woman."

"What? And you took that as an invitation to lock me up in your authentic medieval dungeon and then do me?"

"I've seen the way you look at me, Kate Kane."

I tried to fold my arms and realised I couldn't. "And how's that?"

"Like you're not sure if you want to stab me or fuck me."

"Right now, I'm leaning towards stab."

Tara laughed.

I didn't. "You don't get to laugh. You're locking me up."

"All's fair in love and war, Kate Kane."

With that, she left in a swirl of gold and locked the door behind her. I gave my bonds an experimental yank, hoping they'd be old and rusted through. They weren't. Clearly, the Vane-Tempests were the hot pick for this year's Ideal Dungeon exhibition. I tried to call on my mother's strength, but I got nothing. I knew iron chains could hold faeries, and it looked like they could hold me too. Since I couldn't brute force my way out, I gave the setup a once-over in case there was an obvious weakness or a convenient spare key. I was manacled on a long chain that ran through a thick iron ring bolted to the floor. I was basically fucked.

The last time I'd been in a mess like this, Elise had bailed me out, but there was no way she'd be able to track me through a faery realm to Oxfordshire. She was good, but she wasn't that good. I should have texted her, but I'd forgotten what it was like to work with a partner, and once again, Corin had put me off my game.

I sighed and plonked myself down on the floor. They'd have to feed me eventually. Maybe I could knock someone out and steal their uniform or whatever. Of course, I'd still be chained up.

There was nothing for it but to wait. Being imprisoned is a real bummer, and since Tara had smashed my phone, I couldn't even play *Angry Birds*.

Time passed. Then some more time passed. Then some more time passed.

Her lies Kate Kane. Died of boredom. Beloved daughter. Sorely missed.

I lay down on the floor and closed my eyes. Sleeping would pass a good few hours, and if I was really lucky I'd be able to get through to Nim in my dreams.

"Kate?"

Wow, that'd worked quicker than I expected. Then I realised it wasn't in my head, it was outside the door.

"Kate?"

Now I was paying attention, I recognised Corin. She was the only person I've met in real life with a transatlantic accent, and I'd know that breathless, broken voice anywhere. She always sounded like she was either terrified or having an orgasm. No wonder she and Tara got on so well. Talking to Corin is like that movie that Eve made me watch where the guy stops the computer blowing up the world by playing noughts and crosses with it. The only winning move is not to play.

"Fuck off, Corin."

"I know you're angry with me Kate," she whispered.

"You murdered my partner. Angry is kind of an understatement."

"I know what I did was wrong, but I was lost then, so lost and so afraid."

"No, lost and afraid is what happens when you let go of your mum's hand in a supermarket. What you did is shoot a man in the chest."

I caught a glimpse of Corin's face pressed against the grill in the door. Her lovely eyes had already begun to glisten with tears. I turned my back on her.

"I know you must hate me," she continued. "I know you have no reason to be kind to me, but Tara is in such a fearful temper that I really must know what you told her about me."

Okay, Kate. Think about this.

I wanted to say, *I told her you were a lying, murdering scam artist*, but the fact was I hadn't, and Corin had something I needed. The problem was going to be getting it out of her without letting her get inside my head.

I swung round to face her. She was watching me through the bars, wide-eyed and stricken.

"I told her what I'd worked out."

Corin said nothing but stifled a sob.

"I know someone broke you out of jail. I know you robbed Marcus Fox and Isis Fortuna, and I know what you took. I know the deal you made with the Merchant of Dreams. And I know you woke up the Morrigan."

"Oh, Kate," she whimpered, "I had no choice. They'd have . . . they'd have killed me."

A tiny, irrational, and faintly horny part of me wondered why anyone would want to hurt this poor, innocent girl.

"Look, Corin," I said. "I really need to know who hired you."

"I can't . . . I . . . you don't know what they'll do to me."

"I'll protect you." Oh shit. She'd got me again.

"You're so good to me, Kate. I know I don't deserve it."

"Tell me who hired you."

"Not now. I . . . I . . . the old woman, she doesn't trust me." I'll bet she didn't. "Perhaps tomorrow, when we can be alone."

She vanished from the window and slipped away as quietly as she'd come. And that was when I realised I'd given her everything she wanted and she'd given me fuck all.

CHAPTER NINTEEN
KISSING & TELLING

She didn't come back tomorrow. I was only visited by a couple of servants who brought me food and the other necessities of being stuck in a prison. Yet again, I was depressed to realise that this wasn't the least dignified situation I'd ever been in.

I spent another day bored out of my skull. It wasn't even as if I had a case to think about. Until Corin told me who hired her, I'd done as much as I could. At least they brought me some blankets.

I'd resigned myself to another night on a cold dungeon floor when I heard Corin's voice.

"I'm so sorry," she whispered. "I came as soon as I was able."

Given I'd assumed she was leaving me to rot, I was actually pretty grateful she was there at all. "It's fine."

"We have to leave. I'm so terribly afraid of what will happen if the wolves return, and they find us, or they hear that I've been speaking to you."

"You can get me out of here?"

"I can try. I'm not strong like you, Kate, but I do what I can."

Almost immediately, there was a soft click, the door eased slowly open, and Corin slipped into my cell. Her eyes glistened. "Oh Kate, it's so hard to see you like this."

"Unchain me and you won't have to."

She knelt down beside me, trembling slightly, but the moment she started to work on the lock, her hands were rock steady. Within seconds, I was free. She was good, I had to give her that. Too good, that was the problem.

"You will keep me safe, won't you, Kate?"

"Yes." Oh shit. I kept doing that. "Right, how do we get out of here?"

Corin reached into a tatty canvas satchel and pulled out the Hand of Glory she'd nicked from Professor Fox.

Instinctively I took the Zippo out of my jacket pocket, leaned forwards, and lit the candle. Corin's delicate face flared gold in the sudden light.

"We must go," she said. "Quickly."

We crept through Safernoc Hall, the pale light of the Hand of Glory keeping us hidden, and out to the courtyard where the various members of the Vane-Tempest family had left their fleet of terrifyingly expensive vehicles.

"How's your hot-wiring?"

Corin gave me a look of wounded innocence. "Oh Kate, I wouldn't begin to know how to do such a thing."

I knew she was lying, but I went with it anyway.

She reached into her bag again, and this time brought out a set of car keys. "I know I shouldn't have. But I could see no other way."

She led me over to a gold TVR Chimaera, which I was pretty sure had to be Tara's. I'd have felt bad about stealing her car if I hadn't just spent the last day pissing in a bucket. As it was, she was going to be very lucky if I didn't drive it into a lake when I was done with it.

Corin meekly handed me the keys, blew out the Hand of Glory, and shrank into the passenger seat.

I hopped in beside her and put the pedal to the metal, and a few minutes later, we were cruising at high speed through Safernoc Forest. I thought I saw a unicorn glaring at me through the trees, but it was probably my imagination.

"Okay," I said. "Spill."

There was a long silence and, finally, Corin spilled. "You mustn't be angry with me, I don't know who they are, only what they asked me to do."

"You must have spoken to someone."

"I . . . I . . . I have no idea who she was. She was a vampire, I think. She came to visit me in prison. I thought she was a lawyer at first. I hardly saw anyone when I was there except lawyers and wardens. I was so very alone."

I was not going to feel bad for Corin. I was not going to feel bad for Corin. I was not going to feel bad for Corin. "So what did this vampire lawyer lady look like?"

"Very pale and very cold. I remember that she wore glasses and had blonde hair, pulled back."

I was pretty sure I'd killed someone who looked like that. "How did they get you out?"

"I don't really know. She told the guards to let me out and they did."

"Is there anything else you remember? Anything at all?"

"Oh. There is one thing. The night before they came for me, I had a red flower on my pillow."

Well, that sorted out the who. But it still left a big, steaming pile of why. I'd met Henry Percy all of twice, and he'd been trying to kill me both times. I had no idea what he wanted or why he thought waking up the Morrígan was the way to get it, and honestly I didn't care. I just needed to stop him.

"So what happened to the pot?"

"I left it in a storage locker in Kentish Town and left the key in a dead drop in Hyde Park."

Okay, that was a bit more to go on. Now, if I was a smug beardy vampire wizard and I'd stolen a sodding great pot from a deranged vampire queen, what would I do with it? The sensible thing would be to put it in a vault somewhere. Or maybe not. Even if you had a very good reason to wake the Morrígan, she was dangerous and unpredictable; you'd want to keep the thing that controlled her nearby. The more I thought about it, and from what I'd seen of Percy, he was the kind of guy who'd have it in his front room with a bunch of flowers in it. Like hiding a letter in a letter rack.

I needed a rest and a shower, but before that, I needed a plan. The pack had more than a day's head start on me. There was no point trying to warn the Council because if they hadn't noticed a full-scale werewolf attack by now, they were beyond help. So, I made for the Velvet. Julian was probably fine, but I'd feel way better knowing she hadn't been eaten.

We arrived at Brewer Street at about seven in the morning according to the clock on the dashboard. It was also telling me it was Sunday, which meant I'd lost a whole day in Faerie. Of course, I was expecting the club to be closed, but there was usually someone around, since neither Julian nor Ashriel actually needed to sleep. But when we arrived, I found the shutters down and a sign on the door saying it was closed for refurbishment until further notice. Things must have been more serious than I thought, and I needed to find someone who could tell me what the hell was going on.

I jumped back in the car and spent the next couple of hours on a whistle-stop tour of common vampire haunts. Aeglica's old house was completely deserted. I even tried PCM Capital, the Prince of Coins' financial fortress, and that was in complete lockdown. They were apparently closed for business, but I could just about see the shapes of armed men lurking behind the windows.

It was official: the vampires had gone to ground.

So I went home, left Corin sitting on my sofa looking small, and phoned the office on my landline. I knew I still had one of those for a reason.

"Miss Kane, I have been worried."

"Sorry, I've been in a faery closet and a werewolf dungeon."

"Business or pleasure?"

"Business. What did I miss?"

"I believe the situation has escalated considerably. There have been several more violent incidents since you left, and I am now seeing reports of savage dog attacks. I assume this is in some way linked to your incarceration."

"The werewolves have stuck their noses in. I think they've decided to clean up the city."

"There have been several high-profile altercations between the various factions which the newspapers are describing as a sudden upsurge in gang-related violence. I believe the situation has, as they say, gone to shit in a shoebox."

"Has anyone tried to reach me?"

"No, Miss Kane."

I sighed. Everything I'd done for the last couple of weeks was beginning to look a lot like a waste of time. Even if Henry Percy was behind it all and even if I could find him and even if he had the thing the Morrígan was looking for, that didn't mean I could get it off him or get it to her or do any of that while the entire supernatural population of the Southeast was at each other's throats.

It was like that film with the planes in the war. I couldn't do anything about the mess until I could get through to someone on the Council, but I couldn't get through to the Council because everything was such a mess.

When in doubt, do the job in front of you.

"Elise," I said. "I need you to find out everything you can about a vampire wizard named Henry Percy. He's a smug git, so I think he's probably one of the ones who hides in plain sight. He's got a house in Northumberland called Trismegistus Hall, but I need to know where he stays in London."

"Certainly, Miss Kane. And may I enquire about your activities?"

I hadn't thought that far ahead.

"I was kind of going to have a shower."

"And after that? I do not mean to be presumptuous, but the events of the last two days have reminded me that it is prudent that we keep one another informed of our whereabouts."

"Yeah, I'm sorry about that. Things happened kind of fast, and I wasn't thinking."

"I understand. But, given your track record, we should plan better for kidnappings."

"It's only been twice."

"In the last three months, Miss Kane. I feel that is on the high side of average. And, if you'll permit me, you have not answered my question."

I thought for a moment. Whatever was going down, Tara would probably be at the centre of it, but I had no way of finding her, and if I didn't, she'd probably get herself killed. I needed backup, but there wasn't any.

Unless... "I'm going to see my ex."

"Could you narrow it down a little, Miss Kane?"

"I'm going to see Eve."

I hung up and went to wash off two days of dungeon living. I should probably have been a bit less aggressive about telling Eve to get out of my world because I was going to look pretty silly going back there now and asking for her help. But she did say she was working on a way to track vampires, so maybe she could do werewolves as well.

I was scrubbing the ming out my hair when there was a timid knock on the bathroom door.

"Uh, I'm kind of in the shower," I called out.

And, of course, Corin crept in anyway.

"Um, I'm in the shower."

"I'm so sorry, Kate. It's just you've been so kind to me, and I . . . I haven't thanked you as I should."

I'd been thanked by Corin before. It would be a really bad idea to go there again. "You don't have to thank me."

"I know, but I want to." Her fingers gently drew aside the shower curtain. A spray of water droplets glistened on her neck and turned interesting bits of her blouse transparent.

"Look, I'm seeing someone."

"I'm so sorry, I shouldn't have. I'm just so very alone." She perched on the side of the bath, looking distraught and slightly damp. The water gathered on her hair and left silver trails across her collarbones. "Oh, Kate, what's to become of me?"

She was playing me, and I knew she was playing me, but that never stopped it working. I touched one of her slender, trembling shoulders. "I'll make sure you're safe."

Her hand came up to cover mine. "I know you will. I don't deserve you, really I don't."

I had to get rid of her. I had to get rid of her right now.

Corin swung round and stepped gracefully into the shower. "I understand," she whispered, looking all wet and vulnerable, "if you don't want me in that way anymore."

I just knew she was going to press herself against me, and she'd be slender and silky and yielding in all the right places, so I grabbed her by the wrists. It didn't help. She made a little noise, somewhere between a whimper and a sigh, and tilted her face up to mine. Droplets of water shimmered on her parting lips.

I accidentally kissed her.

Well, fuck.

It felt so wrong, it felt so right; I kissed an untrustworthy, manipulative, pathologically deceitful murderess, and I liked it.

I jerked back. "Get the hell out."

There was no way I was doing this again. It was ending, and it was ending now.

She gazed at me with those big innocent eyes. "Kate, I-I'm so sorry . . ."

I clambered out of the shower, dragging Corin behind me. She struggled just enough for it to kind of turn me on. You had to hand it to her, she was good at what she did. I pulled her dripping down the hall and into the living room, holding her by one wrist as I rang the police from my landline. It was seeing more use in the last couple of weeks than it had in the last year.

"Kate," she whimpered, "don't."

"I'm not playing this game again. You helped me out and I'm grateful, but you still killed my partner and you're going down for it."

She wriggled helplessly. "If you send me back there, I'll die."

A voice at the other end of the line asked me what service I required. "Police."

Corin twisted out of my grip and dived behind my sofa. When she stood up again, she had her bag over her shoulder and a pistol pointed at my heart. "Please don't do that." Her voice was trembling, but her hands weren't.

I very carefully hung up the phone. "Guess I should have searched that bag, huh?"

"I'm sorry, Kate. I don't want to hurt anybody. I . . . I never wanted to hurt anybody."

"You're pointing a gun at me. You can drop the act."

She looked genuinely confused and slightly hurt. "I don't know what you mean. I care about you. I'll always care about. I just can't go back to that terrible place. Don't try to come after me."

She circled round to the door and backed out of the room. I heard my front door open and close. Chasing after her naked sounded like a good way to get shot and look stupid, so I called the cops again. I was just telling them that a dangerous criminal was leaving my flat when an engine revved outside. I ran to the window, phone in hand, just in time to see Tara's car speeding away.

That hadn't gone great, and it had come this close to going really, really badly. Putting aside the fact that I could have been shot, there were no two ways about it: I was a shitty girlfriend. All it took was a pretty face, two days in a dungeon, a daring escape, and an experienced seductress in a see-through blouse, and I was anybody's.

I'd have to do something special for Julian to make up for it.

Like maybe stopping a crazy vampire from eating her city. That, or flowers.

I squelched back to the bathroom, towelled myself off, and put on a clean suit. I rang Eve from the landline. Fortunately, her number was still on speed dial.

"Kate?"

I took a deep breath. "I need your help."

Eve may have been an overambitious workaholic who had to be the smartest person in the room, but at least she wasn't a gloater. "What's up?"

"You said you could track vampires."

"I said I was working on a way to track vampires."

"Look, it's too complicated to explain over the phone, but everything's going to hell. I think I can fix it, but I need your resources."

"You always think you can fix it."

"We're still here, aren't we?"

"Just about. Kaykay, I'll clear my schedule, but I want in on the action."

"The action is probably going to be an enormous clusterfuck bloodbath between every vampire in London and every werewolf in the Southeast."

"Then I definitely want in."

I wanted to give her the *this isn't a game* speech again, but it hadn't gone down well the last time, and since I'd just asked for help, I didn't have a leg to stand on.

"On my way."

CHAPTER TWENTY
BREAKING & ENTERING

I swung by the office to check in properly with Elise and grab the spare mobile and the car. Efficient as ever, she'd dug up the London address of Henry Percy. He'd made her job easy by living completely openly under his original name and, indeed, opening his house to the public as a tourist attraction for six months of the year. Thank God for cocky vampires.

An hour later, I was standing with Eve in a bright white elevator hurtling down into her actual-I-shit-you-not top secret underground lair.

"You told me you didn't have one of these."

Eve grinned. "Yes, but you knew I was lying."

We went through yet another retinal scanner and stepped out into a vast gleaming mezzanine, like a shopping mall for science, full of busy-looking people in lab coats or fatigues or, occasionally, both. I'd been expecting something basically like this, but I wasn't quite prepared for the scale of it. I knew Eve had been successful, but I didn't know she'd been full-on Zuckerberg.

"What the fuck?"

"Oh, come on. You've got to admit, this is pretty fricking awesome."

"What do you do with all this stuff?"

She bounced a bit. "Science."

"Is any of this actually legal?"

"I'm not stupid. There's an understanding. Legally, this is just a large private security firm."

At that moment, there was a friendly chime and a soft voice announced, "Response team to psionics, response team to psionics." This was followed by a scramble of activity.

"Uh, is that bad?" I asked.

"It's all perfectly routine, Kate. This way."

I followed Eve through a set of swishy doors into supervillain central. It was a circular room right at the heart of the facility. The walls were a shifting montage of images and data, and the only item of furniture was, well, I guess you could call it a chair: an elliptical steel shell on a swivelling base, with a high-backed leather seat and buttons on the arm rests. Eve hopped into it with more glee than dignity. I just stood there.

"Welcome to Project Daedalus."

"Eve, you are fucking nuts."

"Yet still the most normal person you've dated this century."

She had a point.

"Look," I said. "I need to track a werewolf. Actually, I need to track a lot of werewolves."

"The system isn't set up for that. It's still a prototype. I've got people on the ground though, and there have been a lot of wild dog attacks in the past couple of days."

"I need to find Tara Vane-Tempest."

Eve blinked. "The lingerie model? What do you think I am, Gossip Girl? Have you tried Twitter?"

"She's an Alpha werewolf, and I need to stop her before she gets a lot of people killed."

"Seriously?" Eve typed frantically into one of the keyboards embedded in the armrests of her chair. "That explains a lot."

"Can you help or not?"

A map of London flickered across the walls. "I can plot a trajectory based on incident reports. It'll show us where they've been, and might be able to predict where they're going. I can cross-reference that with vampire movements, but it'll take a while to recalibrate, and we'll have to wait until sundown for a better read on the vampires."

"Great. Call me when you've got something."

There was a long silence.

"I don't work for you, Kate. I'll help you, but I want to know what's going on."

I sighed and told her everything. It felt weird to be talking to Eve about this stuff again. When we first got together, we talked about everything when we weren't fucking or when Eve wasn't trying to get me to play D&D. And then she got successful, which meant she got busy, which meant I got busy, which meant she got busier, which meant I got pissed off, and the talking was the first thing to go.

Eve raised an eyebrow. "That's a lot of carnage for a vase."

"When all you've got is a ravening vampire army, every problem starts to look like a lack of wanton slaughter."

"And you really think if we give the Morrígan this . . . what . . . item of home furnishing, she'll go away again?"

I shrugged. "Old vampires don't think like the rest of us. And it's basically all I've got right now."

"Cool, where do we start?"

"We don't start anywhere. You stay here and get me Tara. I'll handle the rest."

She literally double facepalmed. "You know, for about ten seconds, I thought you weren't going to be a dick about this. You're in my office, asking for my help, using my resources. You don't get to say what our next move is."

And there was me thinking we'd never be fighting about money again, but this wasn't the time for a domestic. Besides, if Eve wanted to get herself killed, it wasn't my problem. Not anymore.

"Okay, if you want to tag along while I break into the house of an insane vampire wizard, then be my guest."

"I'm not tagging along, Kate. I'm coming with you. Now give me ten minutes to suit up."

"I am not going out in broad daylight with you dressed as Batman."

"I'll wear a coat. It'll be fine."

It was not fine. Eve pressed a button and the seat descended through the floor. I put my head in my hands, and when she emerged, she was wearing the same suit of body armour I'd seen her in a few nights ago, except this time, she'd topped it off with a floor-length, black leather trench coat. It did look pretty hot. It did not look inconspicuous.

Ignoring my protests, she led me out of the office and down again to an even more underground car park, where she had a flotilla of nondescript black vehicles. A squad of five identically dressed minions was waiting by a large-ish van.

"They are not coming with us. This is a quick B&E job, not the Normandy Landings."

"They're just backup, Kate; we don't know what we're getting into."

It was just typical of Eve to muscle into my operation with her fancy ideas like thinking ahead and not getting horribly killed. I shut up, hopped in the van, and we headed off.

"So what's the plan?" asked Eve.

"Get in, get the thing, get out."

"That's the plan? That's your plan?"

I shrugged.

Eve sighed, hit a button, and a screen flipped up on the dashboard.

"Right, where did you say this place was?"

"It's called Syon Park. It's near Kew Gardens or something."

"We're breaking into a stately home?"

"Yeah, I've been doing that a lot lately."

A couple of satellite images flashed up on screen, alongside a friendly-looking website welcoming visitors to Syon Park.

"Kaykay, looks like the park's open, but the house is closed. I think our best bet might be walking in the front door."

I gave her a look. "That's the plan? That's your plan?"

"Well, you didn't give me much to go on. It looks like there's a garden centre next to the stable block. We might be able to get in through there."

"You're not dressed like someone about to buy a ficus."

"No, but I'm dressed like someone who can kick your ass if you don't shut up about my wardrobe."

I shut up about her wardrobe.

"You know," she went on, "if this place is open to the public, they'll probably have CCTV. I can try to do something about it, but it'll take a while."

"I'm slightly more worried about giant tentacle monsters. Nobody's going to be watching the footage live, and I don't think Henry Percy is going to try and prosecute us for stealing his magic pot."

"Why not? I thought vampires were all about playing the system."

"Not if they've basically declared war on their entire government."

"Cool."

I peered out the van's tinted windows to see if we were nearly there yet. We were threading through bad traffic on the Chiswick High Street, past tatty off licences and dodgy pubs. It didn't look like the kind of place you'd stick your giant wizard palace. We pulled up in the car park of a Majestic Wine Warehouse, and Eve and I jumped out. Eve buttoned up her coat and turned up the collar. On the one hand, it meant you couldn't see most of her armour. On the other hand, it made her look like Inspector Gadget. If he was hot. And a girl.

It was still a couple of hours before sunset, so hopefully Percy was keeping a low profile if he was around at all. But it did mean that we were basically breaking into his house under cover of daylight.

"Oh, we are so fucked," I muttered.

"We'll be fine. What's the worst that can happen?"

"We'll be captured and slowly tortured to death by a crazy vampire wizard."

"It won't come to that."

"What are you going to do? Call in an airstrike?"

Eve said nothing.

We nipped over the zebra crossing and turned left down a long, walled alley where a series of cheerful blue arrows pointed the way to the Snakes and Ladders playground, Syon House, and the garden centre. The dome of an enormous glass conservatory loomed on the horizon like a lost boob. We strolled into the garden centre, doing our level best to look casual. It was the Monday before Christmas and the place was doing a pretty good trade in poinsettias and fir trees. We browsed for a bit in an effort to blend in, just two everyday lesbians doing their last-minute Christmas shopping at a stately home in Brentford.

We wandered out into the aquatics and general nonsense section, where you could buy bits of decorative wood and massive chunks of quartz. I stared at a lump of green stone. "Who'd pay for four hundred quid for a rock?"

"It's a fountain topper, Kate. It's not that expensive."

"Sorry, clearly things have changed since the last time I was having a fountain installed in my two-bedroom flat."

"Look, this is a posh-people shop. They're going to sell posh-people things. Try not to take it personally."

"I'm just saying rocks are, like, free. You can pick them up off the ground."

Eve jammed her hands into her pockets. "I can't believe I missed this crap."

I opened my mouth to tell her that some of us had been raised to know the value of money, but then I realised I missed it too. It's not like Eve had been rich when we started dating, but she'd always been the sort of person who bought expensive cheese from Covent Garden when you can get perfectly good cheddar for two quid from the supermarket.

We stared at the overpriced rock for a while like it was some kind of metaphor for our relationship. Heavy and green and with a hole through the middle. It wasn't a very good metaphor.

"Back door," whispered Eve, "four o'clock."

I glanced wildly around.

"Over there." She pointed over her shoulder.

Between the restaurant and the pointless fish shop, there was a blue gate leading to the gardens and the conservatory. It was locked with a numeric keypad. We could probably have climbed over it but we'd have looked bloody obvious trying. I sauntered over there and took a closer look at it. Fortunately, it was cold enough that not many people were sitting outside and only the most dedicated rock fanciers were poking around this part of the shop.

It was a fairly simple lock, mechanical not electronic. I guess Percy didn't worry too much about mortals breaking in to nick his shit, which meant he probably had something really nasty waiting inside. I couldn't see any subtle way to bypass the lock, short of trying every possible combination or ripping the damn thing off. Yes, he'd figure out how we got in, but hopefully he'd be too busy fleeing the Council to care.

Eve came over and nudged me out of the way. "I've got this." An eyepiece snapped into place, blue lines crisscrossing over the surface as she stared at the lock. She tapped in a code, turned the handle, and pulled the door open. I slipped inside as quickly and quietly as I could manage, and Eve darted through behind me.

"Neat trick."

"It's a surface-analysis package. Measures minute variations in the wear of the metal. You can work out which buttons are pressed most often. The codes for those kinds of locks don't have to be in order."

Huh.

We skirted the edge of the conservatory. Up close, it was even more ridiculous. This guy had a room for his plants that was bigger than my parents' house. In the middle of the garden was a fountain with a statue of a flying dude, and just beyond that, a pair of wrought iron gates, also locked, this time properly, in a key-requiring way. I could probably have picked it with enough time and the right kit, but right now I had neither and it was easier to go over. I scrambled up, doing my best not to impale myself on the spikes at the top, and finally dropped down the other side. Eve pulled back her sleeve, and a grappling hook shot out from her wrist.

"Oh, you've got to be kidding me."

She grinned and whipped neatly over the gate.

We were in another little walled alley, which led to the main building. Syon House looked like a child's drawing of a castle, big and square, with crenellations and turrets, all done in thick gold stone. I guess this *was* the sort of place where you'd build a crazy wizard palace.

The front was way too exposed, so we were going to have to go in round the side. A long run of lowish outbuildings led to an extension that was bolted onto the north wall. Probably the servants' quarters. If we would get onto the roof of that, then we could dash across to the main house. The whole thing was raised so the ground floor was actually about ten feet up, and the windows looked period appropriate which meant they'd probably pop open fairly easily.

"How much weight can that hook take?" I asked, peering up.

"About sixty kilonewtons."

I sighed. "And what's that in real money?"

"About six tonnes."

"Think you can get us there?"

"Hell to the yeah."

Eve put her arm around my waist and pulled me against her body, which was pretty solid right now but still felt familiar. I reminded myself that this was a business hug.

"Hold tight."

She fired off her grapple again. It hooked onto the battlements at the end of the stable block, and whisked us into the air. The last time I'd flown about in someone's arms, Julian had been carrying me across London. This was way shorter, but I guess I'd got a taste for it. I was a bit breathless when we landed on the roof of the extension.

"Um, you can let go now."

Eve pulled away.

"Um, that window over there looks like a good bet."

Eve was busily snapping bits of her tech back into place.

"I'll just go deal with that, shall I?"

I nipped over the roof, moving as lightly as I could because I had no idea how much weight it would take. As I'd thought, the window was old and not very secure, and it only took a moment's work with one of my daggers to pop the catch and slide it open. I slithered inside and put my foot straight through a glass display case.

"Shit."

Eve stuck her head through after me. "Smooth, Kate, smooth."

I landed in the hall and cleared the worst of the glass out of the way as Eve slipped gracefully through the window. It turned out I'd stood on a bronze cast of some kind of fruit, which wasn't quite what I'd been expecting in the lair of an evil mastermind.

"What is that even doing there?" I asked.

"It's celebrating the fruiting of the first mangosteen to be cultivated in the British Isles."

"How the hell do you know that?"

Eve's eyepiece snapped out of the way, and she grinned. "Google image search."

"What the fuck is a mangosteen?"

"A tropical evergreen tree believed to have originated in the Sunda Islands and the Moluccas of Indonesia."

"You just looked that up on Wikipedia, didn't you?"

"Yep. And my Facebook status is currently 'Infiltrating Syon House.'"

"You're joking, right?"

"Course I am. I'd never use Facebook."

We were standing in a fairly narrow corridor with lots of heavy oak panelling that I thought was probably wainscoting. The walls were lined with portraits of serious-looking historical people. I figured it was probably best to avoid the front of the house, in case there was anything big and slobbery there, or, you know, a security guard, so we headed off the other way, passing a really elaborate family tree and a cabinet full of fans.

Eve stopped to take a look at the tree. "Hang on a second. You said this guy's name was Percy, didn't you?"

"Yeah? So?"

"What, you mean, he's an actual Percy? One of the was-in-Shakespeare Percys?"

"I don't know. Maybe?"

"Did you not even watch *The Hollow Crown*?"

I remembered seeing it advertised on telly, and I'd thought at the time it was the sort of thing that Eve would have made me watch if we'd still been together. "I was distracted when it came out because my girlfriend had left me and my partner had just been murdered."

"Well, that was a conversation killer. But, seriously, Kate, this guy is descended from fucking Charlemagne."

This was kind of a feature of my relationship with Eve. She'd say a thing and expect it to mean something to me, and it wouldn't, and then I'd feel like an idiot. "And that matters why?"

Eve shrugged. "Charlemagne was the dude. The guy invented paladins and, like, Europe."

"Is this going to help me find a magic pot?"

"Holy Zarquon's singing fish, have you no intellectual curiosity?"

We pressed deeper into the house, past a bunch of posh staterooms, and through the kind of dining room where you'd hold intimate gatherings for you and thirty of your closest friends. Finally, we came out into an enormous, book-lined gallery that seemed to run the whole length of the building. It was pretty bloody bling, with gold candlesticks on every available surface and vast mirrors between the bookshelves.

Eve went straight for the shelves.

"Pots, not books."

She'd dragged down a slim, leather-bound volume and was eagerly flipping through it. "I'm looking for clues."

"So, what, you're going to read everything in the library?"

"Kate, I'm pretty sure this is an original John Dee."

And there was that *you should know what this means* feeling again.

"Look," she went on, "if we can get some idea what he's up to, we'll be a whole lot less likely to get killed."

"Yes, but the longer we stand around in his house, the *more* likely we are to get killed."

Eve shrugged and stuffed the book into her inside pocket. Normally, I feel quite strongly that you shouldn't nick things on investigations, but this guy had tried to kill me twice and had stolen my sword, so he could kind of go fuck himself.

I dragged Eve out of the library, through the far door, and we came out into a room entirely decked out in blood-red silk. He might as well have just scrawled *I am a vampire* over the walls. By my reckoning, we'd walked more than halfway round the ground floor of the house and found nothing remotely pot-shaped. The whole building had been pretty low on hiding places. There'd been lots of little nooks and alcoves, but they'd either been empty or full of statues. I was getting a nasty feeling there was going to be a hidden safe behind one of the portraits or something, and we didn't really have time to pull up every carpet and look behind every picture.

I gave the room the once-over, checking under the sofas and in the fireplace. There was a silk folding screen in the far corner. It was far too obvious as a hiding place, but I checked behind it anyway, just because it was there. Nothing.

I was just going to tell Eve we should move on and try the next room when I noticed there was a very slight mismatch in the hang of the wall coverings.

An actual fucking secret door. I should have known.

CHAPTER TWENTY-ONE
BLOOD & GLASS

I approached it really bloody carefully. It was probably rigged to explode or turn me into a chicken or something. I let my senses sharpen, and I ran my fingers gently over the wall, trying to feel the shape of any enchantments. There was something cold and sharp and brittle. I followed the trail out and away from the door. Razor threads spiderwebbed across the room and spiralled towards the huge antique mirror above the fireplace.

Well, fuck. I fucking hate mirror monsters.

"Okay." I sighed. "I'm going to open this door, and something nasty is going to come out the mirror and try to kill us."

Eve stripped her coat off, dumped it on a chair, and started adjusting the tech strapped to her forearms. "You couldn't be a tad more specific?"

"Not really; could be anything. Big cloud of poisonous shadow. Image of your worst fears. Flowy liquid metal thing. Straight up army of demons."

"And we fight any or all of those things how?"

"We work it out when they show up."

"Sometimes I am genuinely amazed you're still alive. Look, why don't I go back to the library and see if I can find something on mirrors?"

"Take too long." I crossed the room and yanked open the door.

"Oh, you—"

There was a snapping sound like breaking ice, and the mirror shattered, shards of glass sheeting down onto the carpet and into the fireplace.

I went for my knives.

The scattered fragments of the mirror sprang up like a marionette, taking the shape of a distorted, many-legged spider thing. It lunged straight for Eve, making the kind of eerie, high-pitched noise you get when you run your finger around a wineglass. The creature lashed out with two of its limbs, gouging deep scars into Eve's body armour.

I rushed it, realising at the last second that my knives were practically useless. They skidded across what I suppose was its body, scoring nothing but a few shallow scratches and a nails-on-chalkboard shriek for my trouble.

Eve, who'd only given up on one thing in her entire life, smacked her gauntlet into it, sending cracks across its surface. She'd been doing tae kwon do since she was about ten, but I was pretty sure she had no experience fighting giant mirror spider beasts, and one swipe of its legs could take her head clean off.

I dropped my knives and looked for something I could use as a weapon. The far side of the room was lined with hefty marble tables, topped with fancy mosaics. I dashed over, reaching for my mother's strength, and shouted a hasty warning. Eve jumped clear as I grabbed a table and hurled it at the monster.

There was an explosion of glass and dust and stone, and then silence.

Eve rolled to her feet, panting a bit. "Wow, that's some serious property damage. Hulk smash."

The table had knocked a huge chunk out of the fireplace and been none too kind to the carpet.

I was trying to think of a witty comeback when I was interrupted by a crackle of shifting glass. The shards sprang back together, creating four smaller copies of the spider thing I'd just fucking killed.

I should have guessed that had been too easy.

Eve brought up her guard. "Oh shit, ads."

I grabbed the nearest chair and walloped one of them as it came skittering towards me. It stayed down for all of two seconds before its broken pieces reassembled. Great, now there were eight of them and I was running out of furniture.

They were about the size of large cats now, and moved about as quickly. Two of them jumped on me, jagged glass pincers shredding my clothes and ripping into my skin. I was bleeding, like, a lot. I tried to pull them off but only managed to slice up my hands as well. Oh, this was not good.

There was a crunch as Eve grabbed one of the spiders and threw it against a wall, shattering it into yet more pieces that turned into yet more spiders. She rushed over and yanked the little fuckers off me in a shower of blood. Well, at least I was taking the carpet down with me.

Eve was clinging to the struggling creatures as a glinting tide of tiny mirror monsters started to crawl up her legs.

We needed a plan.

"Run," I yelled and did.

There was a tinkling of glass from behind me as Eve shook off her attackers, and we bolted through the secret door, slamming it behind us with a crunch. I heard a scrabbling against the wood as the spiders tried to tear their way through.

Eve bolted the door, but it was only a matter of time.

It looked like we'd found Percy's study. It would have been quite cosy if it weren't for the complete lack of any other exits. And the swarm of deadly glass monsters lurking outside.

There was a three-foot earthenware pot just sitting on the desk like it was taking the piss. From the looks of it, it had been broken into about eight hundred bits and carefully pieced back together. Guess this was the MacGuffin, then. No sign of my sword, though, which was a bugger because it would have been really handy right now.

"Kate, you're a mess."

I was about to say I was fine, but there was blood seeping through the ruin of my clothes. There was enough residue of my mother's power still sloshing through me that I didn't really feel much pain, but I was probably going to fall over in a bit. I tried not to think about it. "Okay, we've found what we came for. Now we just need to get it the hell out of here."

"How about we deal with your extensive blood loss first?"

"Well, sorry, but I came out without my field surgery kit."

Eve sighed, dropped to one knee, and unbuckled something from her calf.

"That's a field surgery kit, isn't it?"

"Shut up and drop your trousers."

"Wow, it's just like we're dating again."

I backed up against Percy's desk and unbuckled my belt. It really wasn't the time to be worrying about the quality of my pants, but I kind of couldn't help it.

Eve pressed between my thighs in a thoroughly nonsexual way and started poking around. "You know, one of these is about two inches from your femoral artery."

I stared at the fancy moulding on the ceiling. "I love it when you talk dirty."

There was a cracking from the doorway.

"I haven't got time to stitch this up now. I'll get the worst of the glass out and whack some bandages on it."

"I'd really like to be able to put my trousers back on."

"Give me a minute."

It was slightly less than a minute and I was back to fully dressed, or as close to fully dressed as I could get with everything in tatters. That just left the giant pot, the killer monsters, and getting out without getting arrested.

Something pointy thrust its way through the door, filling the room with a chorus of high-pitched shrieks.

"Uh, any ideas?" I asked.

"Build a time machine, go back six hours, tell ourselves not to do this."

"Thanks, that's really helpful."

"Well—" Eve folded her arms. "—what's *your* plan?"

"I was thinking maybe we could get ripped apart by tiny killer mirror monsters."

Eve slumped into Percy's upholstered desk chair and swung it onto its back legs.

I glared at her. "You're carrying a million bits of kit. Haven't you got anything to help with this?"

"I must have left my tiny unkillable-glass-spider killing device at home. I don't even know what they are."

"My best guess, based on my years of hands-on experience, is that they're some kind of tiny unkillable glass spider."

Another shard pierced the door.

"I'm really glad," snapped Eve, "that an unhelpful wisecrack is the last thing I'm going to hear before I die."

"No, the last thing you're going to hear is that awful whining noise."

The chair rocked forwards with a thump as Eve sat bolt upright. "Kate, you're a fucking genius."

"Am I? Oh good."

"Okay, maybe I'm a fucking genius. Give me your phone."

I fished the spare mobile out my pocket and handed it over. Eve whipped a set of watchmaker's screwdrivers out of yet another belt pouch and flipped off the back panel. "What are you doing?"

"Feedback loop."

"Thanks. But what are you doing?"

"I can explain this to you, or I can save our arses."

Suddenly, the microphone on my phone started emitting the same terrible noise as the creatures outside. I was pretty sure I wouldn't be keeping it as a ringtone. Eve dashed across the room and bunged my phone through one of the cracks in the door. The screaming got louder, and then louder again, and then even louder, at which point I stuck my fingers in my ears. I could still hear it, and it was getting to the point that I could feel my teeth vibrate. I wasn't sure what Eve's plan had been. Maybe it was to make things so uncomfortable that getting torn to shreds would seem like a welcome relief.

Then either I went deaf or everything went quiet.

I think I said, "What happened?" but the ringing in my ears was so bad I couldn't really tell. Eve tried to explain but I could barely follow her technobabble at the best of times. "What?"

My hearing was coming back slowly. Enough to hear the impatience in Eve's voice. "*Star Trek* analogy version: it's like an opera singer breaking a glass."

I eased the door open carefully and peered into the room. The floor was covered in a shimmer of glass dust and the remains of my spare phone. I lose more handsets that way...

I let out a breath I didn't even know I'd been holding. The immediate danger was over, but there was no way Percy hadn't noticed his wards going down. Somehow, I had to get out of the study, through the house, and across the grounds, without being spotted, while carrying the giant vase that every vampire in London, including a five-thousand-year-old death queen, was looking for.

I went to grab the thing and noticed just in time that it was sitting in a magic circle. A magic circle drawn in blood. I knew jack-shit about the occult, so I had no idea what that meant, but it couldn't have been good. I gave it a sniff—mercury and old paper, wealth and secrets. Not just blood, but Henry Percy's blood.

I glanced up at Eve. "I'm going to grab this pot. And then something bad is going to happen."

"For fuck's sake. Didn't you learn anything the last time?"

"We're alive, aren't we?"

"Kate, I'm serious. Why don't we go back to the library and see if we can find out about this circle and how to . . . what's the word . . . defuse it?"

"Percy has to know we're here by now. He'll be sending people. We need to get this and get out."

Eve activated her headset. "Cover the grounds, expect hostiles. Send the chopper, I need evac."

"What happened to subtle?"

"Well, if he already knows we're here, there's no point. Besides, sneak your way in, fight your way out. There's a reason it's a classic."

While we waited to be rescued, I bust open the desk and started rifling.

Eve folded her arms. "Oh, now there's time to loot."

"I need to know what this bastard's up to. If you want to be Giles, be my guest, but the second the chopper gets here, I'm grabbing the pot and we're leaving."

"I'm way hotter than Giles."

I found a stash of letters in the bottom drawer, but I didn't really have time to read them properly. Even so, it wouldn't have helped. They were all Greek to me. Half of them literally.

"Found it." Eve plonked a book down on the desk and pointed at a picture of a mystical circle.

"Great. What's it do?"

"I don't know; it's all in Latin. Let me scan it and run it through a— Hold on." She put a hand to her ear. "Vampires incoming." Then she spoke back into the headset: "Do not engage. Repeat, do not engage. We're moving out."

There was nothing for it. I grabbed the pot. It didn't fall apart. I didn't die. So that was good.

Eve swept up the book, and we hightailed it back into the red room and towards the front of the house. We skidded across a marble-floored antechamber ringed with golden statues of Greek gods and then into a vast, echoing entrance hall decorated with a similar theme of naked dudes and more money than taste. I glanced through one of the windows only to see a small group of vampires gliding over the front lawn. Shit, I'd dropped my knives. But, given I was carrying an enormous pot, it wasn't like I was in much of a state of fight them anyway.

"Courtyard this way." Eve kicked open a door on the opposite side of the room, and I chased after her as quickly as I could with the crockery.

It was one of those fountain and hedges arrangements, remarkably low on cover unless we wanted to hide in the pond. I stared up at the dark, chopperless sky.

"Two minutes," whispered Eve.

I put down my pot and got ready to punch a vampire in the teeth. I heard the front door open. I could tell Percy's goons meant business because I didn't hear their footsteps in the hall.

Eve fired her grappling hook at a statue of a lion that someone had plonked on the roof for no reason, and shot upwards. Guess I was on bait duty.

I ducked in beside the door, waited for the first vampire to come through and coldcocked him in the mouth. It didn't stop him, of course, just broke his jaw and wrecked his day. As he came snarling to his feet, one of Eve's darts struck in him in the neck, and he went down again. One day, I'd have to ask what was in those things.

Since a body lying right there was a bit of a giveaway, I dragged him across the courtyard and dumped him in the pond.

Blades whirred overhead and a black helicopter came into view over the battlements. It belatedly occurred to me that I had no idea how I was going to get myself, Eve, and a bloody great pot into a helicopter.

It seemed like the rest of the vampires had figured out where we were. Eve took one out with another dart and then rappelled down the side of the building to join me.

A rope ladder thwooshed into the middle of the courtyard. I bundled the pot under one arm and caught the ladder. Eve dropped another vampire and grabbed on beside me.

"Go, go, go," she yelled.

There was a jerk, and I nearly dropped the pot as the helicopter pulled us into the sky. Then there was another jerk as they started winding the ladder up. I couldn't hear anything or say anything, and the rush of wind had blown off my fucking hat, but I was damn glad I was getting out of there.

Then a bright blue fireball exploded just above me. The chopper rocked and the ladder burst into flame.

We were already high enough up that letting go wasn't an option, but it wasn't like I could climb a burning rope with one hand either.

I was just weighing up my options, and then I didn't have any.

The ladder snapped.

I barely had time to realise I was falling before Eve wrapped herself around me and we shuddered to a bone-jolting midair stop.

Thank fuck for that grappling hook. I was never taking the piss out of her Batman suit again.

I wound both arms around the pot and tried not to think about the very thin cord that was holding both of us tethered to I don't know what a good hundred feet above Brentford.

I didn't want to look up, and I didn't want to look down, but I could see flickers of blue flame shooting past us, so I just shut my eyes and hoped it'd sort itself out.

We went whizzing upwards, and then I felt hands dragging me into the relative safety of the helicopter.

I decided it was probably okay to open my eyes.

We were in a smallish cabin with benches along the sides. I crawled onto one and wedged the pot in beside me, next to a couple of dudes in black. Eve was crouched on the floor, talking rapidly into her headset as she scanned the books we'd nicked.

"Any joy?" I asked.

"Not sure, it's some kind of warding ritual, but magic isn't really my thing."

"Warding against what?"

"No clue. I think it says something about concealment here. Probably something to do with the blood. If we knew whose it was, we might be able to work out what it was for."

"Uh, I'm pretty sure it was his own."

"Okay, that's really weird. Why would you want to keep yourself away from something you stole and were keeping in your house?"

I thought back to Jacob. He'd said that vampires could be targeted through their bloodlines, which was how the Kill Everything Ritual was supposed to work. The Kill Everything Ritual that Henry Percy had gone out of his way to stop.

Because he'd raised the Morrígan.

And he was descended from the Morrígan.

Which meant that that the circle wouldn't just keep him away from the pot, it would stop the Morrígan hunting it down as well.

In fact, that was probably why she hadn't found it already.

Oh, fuck.

I twisted round, looked out of the window, and saw a flock of ravens, black against the city lights below.

CHAPTER TWENTY-TWO
METAL & FEATHERS

A taloned hand burst through the floor.

Eve stared at it for a moment and then signalled her minions to take firing positions.

"Eve, trust me, this is way above their pay grade."

"Stuck in a helicopter. Can't really sit this one out. And if we're going down, we're all going down fighting."

With a groaning of metal, a large chunk of the chopper gave way, offering us a charming view of the empty sky, the distant city, and the enraged vampire queen flying directly below us.

I leaned over the gap. "We've got your pot. We just want to talk."

The Morrígan's hand shot out, grabbed me by the throat, and hauled me through the hole in the floor. My stomach lurched as I realised that my own neck was the only thing between me and the world's least successful skydive.

Darts whistled past me and sank into the Morrígan's flesh. She didn't notice.

I kicked my feet pointlessly against empty air and wrapped both arms around the wrist that held me.

"I will take what is mine." The Morrígan's voice cut through the thunder of the helicopter and the shrieking of the ravens. "Then I will kill you all and lay waste to this city."

I had to admit, I wasn't exactly negotiating from a position of strength. What was my counteroffer going to be? Let me go and I won't bruise your thumb with my windpipe?

Times like these, a girl really needed her mum.

The Morrígan's hand tightened around my throat, her claws beginning to gouge into my skin.

I closed my eyes and opened myself to the Deepwild. Blood and the power of dark places rushed over me. On the topmost branch of the tallest tree in our kingdom, my mother perched and waited, still as stone and moss.

I lashed out at the Morrígan with my mother's strength. It wasn't enough. There was a dull red fire behind my eyes.

I struggled, but I needed more. I needed everything.

My mother smiled.

In the other place, my daughter is dying, and she gives herself to me at last.

I open my eyes in that far world of steel and stone.

My body is not to my liking. Too small, too weak, too mortal.

I change it.

The corpse queen looks and sees me for my true self. She bares her fangs and pulls me to her. I feel her teeth in my neck as I drive my fingers through her unliving flesh and wind them in her entrails.

I laugh with the joy of it.

The corpse queen rips at my neck and laps at my blood. I draw out a handful of viscera and cast it free on the wind. I bury my hands in her feathers and tear the wings from her back in a spray of blood and shadow.

We fall together, clawing at each other in an ecstasy of hunger, and crash to earth upon tamed grass and enslaved trees.

The corpse queen scatters in shadows and feathers and mist. I turn my face to the wind and seek the scent of fresh prey.

A human creature lowers herself from the sky machine that follows us.

She speaks. "What the fuck?"

I turn and look at her. "Run."

"Kate, what's going on?"

"You will run, and I will catch you, and when I catch you, I will kill you."

"Oh fuck, you're her." *She inches slowly backwards. Perhaps she thinks I will not notice.* "Listen, Kate, I know you're in there somewhere."

"We are one and the same, child." Somewhere, my daughter screams at me. A petulant tantrum. *"Perhaps I will not kill you. You have strong bones; you would make a good hound. Or a deer perhaps, to be hunted and devoured, night after night."*

"I'm not going to run." *She steps forwards.*

"It will be quick if you run."

"Sorry, I don't negotiate with psychopaths." *She steps forwards again.*

As she comes closer, I think of ways to make her pay for her insolence. Perhaps I will peel off her skin and fashion a new sheath for my knife. While she watches. Once she is within arm's reach, I catch her by the hair and drag her to her knees. She brings up one hand and strikes at my thigh, and I feel the cold, sickening burn of iron pierce the muscle.

I roar at the outrage of it, reach down, and snap her arm. I scent pain and fear. A shadow stirs at the back of my mind. My daughter glares at me with fury in her purple eyes. The shock of iron still sears my blood. She claws at the edges of our mind, and fights for dominion over our weakening flesh.

Unattended, the human strikes me in the chest, knocking the breath from my daughter's body.

The other place no longer to my liking, I return, for the present, to the Deepwild.

"Jesus, fuck, enough already," I wheezed. "Stop punching me."

Eve stopped punching me. "Kate?"

I was kneeling on the cold grass, feeling as shit as I'd felt in a long time. "You fucking stabbed me."

"You kind of needed it."

I tried to stand up, but my body felt weird, like when you get in your car and somebody's fiddled with the driver's seat. And, if it hadn't been for Eve's sudden injection of cold iron, I'd still be a passenger. "I guess I kind of did. Thanks."

"Anytime."

I made another attempt to be functional and made it upright. My leg hurt like hell, which was nice, because it matched the rest of me. I held out a hand to help Eve up and noticed that her right arm was hanging limp at her side. I gestured awkwardly. "Was that . . . me?"

She shook her head. "It was your mother, Kate, not you."

"In my body. I could have killed you."

"But you didn't, and that's what matters. Now, do you want to stand around angsting, or do you want to save this city?"

"Where's the damn pot?"

"On its way to HQ. And we should be too."

I looked round. We were in some sort of park, with a sodding great gold statue sitting in a pointy gothic tower. "Is that the Albert Memorial?"

"Looks like." Eve flicked on her headset. "Send a car to Kensington Gardens."

Tangled in the grass were a scattering of black feathers. These were probably worth a fortune to the right sort of person, but things the right sort of person is willing to pay for are things the wrong sort of person is willing to kill for. I didn't need the aggro. I picked up one and stuck it in my inside pocket. I'd have put it in a ziplock bag, but it wouldn't fit.

Then we limped down to the road to wait for pick up.

"You know," I said, "we should probably both get to a hospital."

"There's a surgical unit back at base. They'll patch us up."

Well, at least I wasn't going to have to make up any interesting stories to explain the stab wound. Slipped while trying to scratch my arse with a kebab skewer. We were both too exhausted and stressed out for chitchat, so we just slumped there in silence until the car arrived.

Back at the Locke Cave, I had my leg stitched up, and Eve got her arm set and splinted. My mother had dealt with most of my glass cuts and other injuries, so I guess I'd handed my body to a crazy faery queen and come out vaguely ahead on the deal. Unless you count nearly killing my ex-girlfriend.

Once I'd got my lollipop and my *I was brave at the secret underground medical facility* sticker, I was given my pot and escorted back to Eve's office. She'd shed the Batman costume and was sitting in her chair, with images flickering and flying across the screens around her. Her arm was in a sling, and she had that tight, focused look she always got when she was shaken.

"You okay?"

She spun round. "Fine."

"This is me you're talking to. You don't have to be fine."

"We broke up. You don't get to play that card anymore."

"Giving a shit is not a card."

"Whatever, Kate. I need you to get that damn vase out of my building. I don't have the resources to handle another attack of that magnitude."

Part of me felt that this would be a perfect time to say I told you so, but the part of me that wasn't an arsehole kept my mouth shut. "I'll be out of your hair as soon as I've worked out what I'm going to do with the pot, and we've found Tara. Unless I can talk her down, there's going to be a whole lot of killing."

"I'm trying to track her, but they keep on the move. They're sweeping the city systematically from the centre outwards. I've isolated twenty-six confirmed incidents so far."

"Incidents of what?"

"What do you think? Werewolves eating people. Probably fledging vampires because the older, smarter ones have all gone to ground like you said."

"And what about Tara?"

"I've run face recognition on a crap-tonne of footage, and she's come up a bunch of times but never in the same place. I know where they've been, but I couldn't put you within a mile of where they're going."

Maybe within a mile would be enough. I was pretty certain I could track a pack of wolves with my mother's power, but if today was anything to go by, I wasn't at all certain that if I went to the Deepwild again, I'd ever get out. "Don't they have some kind of base?"

"There's no evidence of one. They never backtrack. My best guess is they're either staying on the streets or moving between safe houses. I could follow the money, but that's going to take time, especially because werewolf property goes back for generations, so half the records will be on paper."

"Thanks, anyway. It was always a long shot."

If nothing else, I'd probably distracted the Morrígan for long enough that she wasn't going to rip Tara's head off anytime soon. And Julian was nowhere to be seen, which meant she was probably safer than I was, especially since I was wandering around with the thing the unstoppable vampire queen was tearing the city apart to find. In a funny way, it was quite liberating. I'd spent so long juggling all this complicated, political shit that it was nice to have my problems stripped back to staying alive. Assuming I could pull that off, I could probably sort out the Morrígan, and if I was lucky, that would sort out the werewolves as well. Then maybe the Council would leave town. And then maybe I could get five minutes with my girlfriend.

"Look," said Eve. "I'll keep working on it, and if anything comes up, I'll let you know."

"You remember you dismantled my phone, right?"

"I'll get someone to give you one before you leave."

"Okay, thanks." There was an awkward silence. "And, you know, sorry about your arm and, like, everything."

"It's fine. It's just that . . ." She gave a one-shouldered shrug. "Nothing."

I didn't know what to say to that. Or maybe there were lots of things I wanted to say, and I didn't know how to say any of them. I stared at the pot instead. "Have you got any bubble wrap?"

They gave me a phone that was flashier than either of the ones I'd lost this week, helped me wrap my urn, and arranged for a car to take me wherever I needed to go. Which was a bit of a problem, because I didn't know where that was.

The only person I could think of who'd last more than ten seconds if the Morrígan came calling was Nim, but I'd lost her number and the number of Rachel's call centre with my other phone, and I didn't have time to do the ritual that would have put me in touch with her. I'd been to dinner at Gabriel's years ago, but the guy had three kids—there was no way I was dropping in unannounced with a vase full of murder. I had no idea where Jacob hung out, and it probably involved dead people or trains, but I was pretty sure I knew how to get to Michelle. There was a lesbian metal bar near Clapham Junction called the Duchess of Malfi, and last I'd checked, she was using it as her unofficial HQ.

The car dropped me off at St. John's Hill, and I casually carried my enormous bundle of crockery up the road and into a pub. It was just as dark, noisy, and full of lesbians as I remembered. It smelled of leather, sweat, and beer, and they were playing something I thought was probably Judas Priest or Megadeth, or one of the other three metal bands I'd heard of.

Michelle was at the bar, fiddling with a Zippo, and nursing a shot of whiskey. I stuck my pot on a spare stool, leaned over, and bellowed in her ear that I was looking for Nim.

Michelle shrugged. "So call her."

"Lost her number."

She gave me a look that said *you suck*, tossed back her drink, and took me outside. She dug out a battered packet of Marlboro Reds and offered me one. I wasn't sure it was the time, but I never say no to free fags. We lit up.

"What's up?"

"I've got the thing the Morrígan's looking for, and she's already come after it once."

Michelle took a drag on the cigarette and blew the smoke into the flame of her lighter, where it gathered in a hazy spiral. She whispered Nim's calling name, and then said: "Kate's got something for you. We're at the Duchess."

She snapped the lighter closed and leaned back against the wall to finish the cigarette.

I did the same. It was that or try to make conversation.

I quite liked Michelle. I thought we probably had a lot in common. Unfortunately, one of those things was being shit in social situations.

Just as I was stamping out the stub, a black cab pulled up and Nim got out. She looked like she hadn't slept properly in days, which was probably true. I kind of wanted to give her a hug and smooth the tangles from her hair, but I couldn't do that in front of Michelle. Also, girlfriend.

"What did you do, Kate?" she asked.

"Can you narrow it down a bit?"

"Something hurt the Morrígan. Something hurt her badly."

"Yeah, that was kind of my mum. I think it's probably temporary, but I've got her pot. She tried to kill me to get it back, but it didn't take."

Michelle lit up another cigarette. "How does that help us?"

"I'm fuzzy on the details, but like, blah-hundred years ago she agreed to go away in exchange for this thing, but I think the Council had to convince her she couldn't just take it from them first."

Nim reached out and took the pot. She peeled away the bubblewrap and ran her fingers gently over the cracked surface beneath.

"Um, just so you know, this thing was in a magic circle that stopped her tracking it. And now it, well, isn't."

"This is my city, Kate. If I don't want something found, it won't be found."

"I was kind of hoping you'd say that." Otherwise I'd just got us all killed. I guess I could cross *Find the thing* off my to-do list. That just left *Use the thing to defeat the Morrígan*, and I had no clue how to get from one to the other. "So, is this it? Can you beat her now?"

"I don't know. But this has power over her. I can feel it."

"Julian said it was buried with the Morrígan five thousand years ago. It's the only thing she actually wants. But I've no idea how we, y'know, use it."

She met my eyes over the rim of the pot. "I'll confront her in the Dream and tell her we have what she seeks."

"And that'll work, will it?"

"It'll help. It's a question of sovereignty. Right now, I have something she wants, and I will give it back to her if she relinquishes her claim on my city. We've been fighting each other to a standstill for a while now, and I get the sense she's lashing out because it's all she can do."

This was kind of above my pay grade. "Do you need me for anything?"

"This will go better without the interference of the Council or the wolves."

"They're not going to listen to me. We'll just have to hope they keep each other busy."

Nim gave me one of her mysterious smiles. "You have more influence than you think."

"I'll keep an eye on things, but I can't make any promises. Call me if you need anything. Shit, I've got a new mobile number."

"That won't be a problem."

"Oh, yeah, magic."

Nim carefully put the pot into the back of her taxi and climbed in after it. I waved her off. I was pretty sure I'd done the right thing, probably the only thing, but part of me was still afraid I'd just given my ex-girlfriend the box from *Kiss Me Deadly*.

"We done?" asked Michelle.

"Um, I guess so."

"Later."

She went back into the bar, and I headed for the Tube.

CHAPTER TWENTY-THREE
LIONS & WOLVES

It was close to midnight by the time I got home. Elise was sitting in the middle of the living room, building one of her model airplanes. I gave her my new number, filled her in on the situation, left her to it, and went to bed, too tired from all the breaking, entering, and being possessed to even think about making a cup of Bovril.

I really needed a rest, but I sort of hoped I'd see Nim in my dreams. I didn't.

An unfamiliar ringtone jerked me awake. It took me a few bleary moments to realise it was probably mine. I groped for it, trying not to look at the time as I answered with a grunt.

"I've got something." Eve's voice.

I grunted again.

"Wow, you really suck at this rapid-response stuff."

"I'm awake, I'm awake; what's going on?"

"I think I've got a hit on Tara."

I woke up more. "Where?"

"Heading towards Aldgate."

"Any idea what she's tracking?"

"I'm only getting one vampire in the area. At St. Botolph's."

Weird. The last time I'd been there, I'd gone to talk sewers with a giant rat gestalt. I really hoped the rats weren't taking sides in this as well because that would get really icky really quickly. "Thanks." I was about to hang up but then I thought of something. "Hang on, have you been up all night?"

"That's the magic of Penguin Mints."

"Eve, you need to rest."

"Sleep's for the weak. Besides, I'd have been raiding anyway if my arm was up to it."

"Seriously, go to bed."

She laughed and hung up.

I crawled out of the covers, dragged some clothes on, and staggered into the front room.

Elise's model plane was looking about four hours better than when I'd come in.

"Miss Kane, I cannot help but notice that you have awoken far earlier than is customary or healthy for you."

"Got to get to Aldgate. Shit's kicking off. Maybe."

"In which case, I believe I should drive the vehicle as driver fatigue is reckoned to be a contributing factor in twenty percent of road accidents."

Elise was so concerned for my health that she laid off the Rammstein so I could sleep in the car.

She woke me up when we arrived at St. Botolph's. It was pretty much as I remembered—a jarringly old-fashioned church-with-spire stuck in the middle of the financial district. Just up the road, the predawn light glittered on the Gherkin. The doors of St. Botolph's stood open. Most churches go out of their way to be welcoming, but five in the morning is pushing it even for Jesus.

We ditched the car illegally just outside and went in.

There was a bit of a party going on. Tara, Henry, and a bunch of werewolves were bunging up the nave, face-to-face with Caradoc and a couple of his goons. Caradoc was mid-grandstand, declaiming something about ancient rights and honoured bargains. I'm pretty sure some of it was even in Latin.

Edmund Carew, Voice of the Multitude, was up by the altar, looking down with that scary peaceful expression that said *I'm totally not a giant swarm of rats in a person suit*. Although the rodents teeming round his feet might have been a giveaway.

He smiled at us as we came, and Elise waved cheerfully.

Everyone else ignored us, and I wondered how best to force myself into whatever was going on so I could tell Tara to back down. Because that always worked so well. We slipped down one of the aisles, trying to get into a good position to interrupt.

Eventually Caradoc paused for I would have said breath, but vampire, so I guess it was dramatic effect.

Tara curled her lip. It wasn't quite a snarl, but it wasn't quite anything else. Her eyes glowed wolf amber in the half-lit church. "I'm losing patience, yah. What's this about?"

"Your invasion," Caradoc went on, "is justified in terms of the Compact sealed between our two peoples in the dying days of the seventeenth century. By the terms of that same Compact, I seek to end your aggression this very night."

One of Tara's stiletto heels tapped against the flagstones. "You're so still wasting my time."

"As Prince of Swords, it is my right to stand in the stead of my people and to resolve by single combat any charge laid against them."

Well, that was news. With everything that was going on, I was surprised the Council had found time to appoint him.

Tara stopped tapping, and the silence felt heavy somehow. "You're challenging me?"

Carew cleared his throat in that polite Church of England way. "By the terms of the Compact, it is not a challenge until the words are spoken." His voice was soft, but beneath it was the echoing chorus of the Multitude.

Elise leaned over to me. "He is such a nice gentleman," she whispered.

Caradoc nodded gravely. He was standing with his hands folded on the pommel of Aeglica's sword, looking a hell of a lot like a statue on a tomb and a lot better than the last time I'd seen him. "I, Sir Caradoc of Gwent, challenge you, Tara Vane-Tempest, Marchioness of Safernoc, to single combat for the right to wage war against the vampires of London."

Tara's eyes swept contemptuously over him, and she smiled, well, wolfishly. "Yah, darling. Bring it on."

"As the challenged party," came the many voices of the Multitude, "the Marchioness of Safernoc may choose the location of the duel."

"Wherever you like, pretty-boy."

I'll say this for Caradoc, he didn't rise to insults. "The car park beneath Hyde Park at dusk. It is a large place that will give vantage to neither party, and I can arrange for it to be cleared of innocents and witnesses."

Typical. Driving in London is bad enough without bloody vampires closing down the car parks. And I was sort of starting to feel I'd missed the boat here. I'd been waiting for the right moment to fix this mess and now it seemed like there was a whole new one. On the plus side, it looked like the werewolves would be going from attacking all the vampires to attacking one vampire. Which probably counted as progress.

"I accept your terms."

Caradoc bowed like he meant it and stalked out. And I guess that was my cue.

I stepped out the shadows. "Uh, hi."

Tara didn't even turn. She'd probably known I was there all along. She had a creepy habit of smelling me. "Didn't I lock you up, Kate Kane?"

"It didn't stick."

She prowled towards me across the church floor. Despite the fact she was running some kind of psycho slaughter-thon, she still looked like she was on her way to a film premiere. "I hope you're not here to tell me my business again."

"Funny story..."

She sighed and gave me a glare that was almost affectionate. "Do you never learn?"

"I found the thing the Morrígan's after, so you can call off your dogs." Shit. "I mean, like, metaphorically."

"Oh, you've taken care of it, have you?"

With hindsight, expecting Tara Vane-Tempest to turn round and say *Splendid, there's nothing left for us to do, let's all go home and have crumpets* had been a bit optimistic. "Well, kind of. I think I can get her to go back to sleep."

"And what will you do about the hundred or so fledgling vampires she unleashed onto the streets of London?"

"That's the Council's problem."

"The Council had the opportunity to contain the situation. They failed."

"You didn't give them much of a chance."

"Has it ever occurred to you, Kate Kane, that your priorities are not as they should be?" She watched me steadily. "Every day I was, as you put it, giving the Council a chance, people were dying."

Bugger. Tara had a point. But there was no way I was admitting it. "I get that, but as far as solutions go, 'kill all the vampires' is just a bit genocide-y and will probably start a war, which last time I checked, is not a good way to save lives."

"Do what you must, as will I."

"But you don't have to do this."

"A challenge has been issued. I cannot withdraw."

"So, what, you're going to fight Caradoc for your right to kill everybody?"

"I am going to fight Caradoc for the right to do my duty." She was in front of me, close enough to run her perfectly manicured fingertips through the white streak in my hair. "And, just think, Kate Kane, if I lose, all your problems will be over."

I caught her by the wrist. I wasn't sure whether I was supposed to be pushing her away or pulling her closer. "Look, I know you shacked up with the woman who murdered my partner, locked me in a dungeon, and are making my life really difficult right now, but I don't actually want you to get killed."

Her eyes gleamed. "So you do care."

"Yes, yes, our relationship has reached that very special not-actively-wishing-you-dead stage. I'll send you flowers later."

Well, I'd given it my best shot, and it had gone about as well as it always did, but at least this time, I hadn't got chained up or nearly killed.

Elise and I piled back in the car and went for home. I shuffled down in my seat, wondering if I could catch twenty minutes sleep.

"That was most interesting, Miss Kane. I have never before been privy to an incitement to ritual combat."

"Next time I'll bring popcorn."

"I confess the experience has left me uncertain as to our next course of action."

"Tell me about it."

"Am I correct in identifying that as an idiomatic interjection and not as a genuine request for further information?"

"It's six in the morning, I've had four hours sleep, idiomatic interjection is about all I'm capable of right now. Basically I think we have to wait this one out." I yawned. "Knowing vampires and werewolves and rituals, half the major players will probably turn up at this thing tomorrow."

"Will we be permitted to attend, Miss Kane?"

"I don't know about permitted, but I'm going anyway. It's probably my best chance of seeing Julian. Plus for all I know, the Morrígan is going to show up and slaughter everyone."

Elise's attention flicked my way for a moment. "Surely that is an argument in favour of, to use the colloquialism, staying out of it."

"How long have you known me, Elise?"

"A little over three months, Miss Kane."

"In that admittedly short time, have I ever stayed out of anything?"

When we got back to the flat, I confusedly ate half a banana because it felt like breakfast time, and then realised I could just go back to bed instead. I woke up after midday feeling approximately human, only to discover I had a couple of missed calls from Eve. I faffed a bit until I figured out how to use the phone, which was smarter and therefore more annoying than either of my old ones, and then rang her back.

"Hi, Kate, we've made some progress on the papers."

"Did you actually sleep last night at all?"

"Dude, do you want to hear about scary vampire rituals or my sleeping habits?"

I sighed. "Rituals, please."

"Kaykay, this is some pretty hard-core hocus-pocus bullshit. I found a really seriously annotated copy of a ritual which translates roughly as The Ascent of the Discarded Stair."

"The what?"

There was a silence.

"Well, I don't want you to panic, and obviously the translation's uncertain, but I think he's trying to become a god."

Great. Another one. I should have guessed. It's basically number three on the deranged wizard checklist: get laid, get rich, achieve unlimited cosmic power. "I wouldn't worry, Eve, people try this sort of thing all the time."

"Oh you just have to be Miss Seen It All Before, don't you?"

"I was trying to reassure you. I mean, what, did you want me to freak out and run around shouting 'We're all doomed' like that bloke in *Dad's Army*?"

"Don't piss on my first apocalypse."

"Sorry, Eve, this sort of thing usually doesn't go anywhere. There are lots of powerful things out there that don't like to share."

"So, what you're saying is that this would only have a chance of working if every major supernatural creature in England was distracted by, for example, the awakening of a psychotic vampire queen?"

Shit. "Look, we still don't need to panic. These things are really hard. You have to get all kinds of weird stuff, and if you don't do it exactly right, you blow your face off."

"He's probably been planning this for five hundred years. I think we can assume he's sussed the logistics."

"Okay, you're right, I'll put this on my list of things to worry about, right below getting my throat ripped out by the Morrígan. Have you figured out any details?"

"Basically, as far as I can tell, being a god is like being in a really, really exclusive club. You can either inherit it, like the Egyptian pharaohs, get voted in like the Roman emperors, or kill someone and steal their membership card."

"So what's Percy's plan?"

"He's going after the throne of Apollo. There's this two-part ritual, one at each solstice. In winter, which I guess is what he's doing now, he has to get the Delphic oracle to proclaim him the God of the Sun. Then in summer, he has to mix the blood of a faery lord with something called the Tears of Hypnos, and this will allow him to transubstantiate into a divine form which, well, is sort of the sun."

In the spirit of continuing not to panic, I thought about it for a moment. "Look, let's think about this rationally. Is it actually a problem if Henry Percy is the sun?"

"It'll probably transform a good chunk of England into his own personal kingdom entirely subject to his immortal will."

"Like a faery realm?" That was probably quite a big problem.

"I'm not sure, but I think it's basically the same thing. When you get right down to it, a god is just a powerful otherworldly being that people worship."

I guess I'd just figured out why Percy had tried to sacrifice me when I was seventeen, but it didn't help me much now because I still had no idea what the deal was with the oracle. "What's the deal with the oracle?" I asked. "Didn't that go out with, like, Jesus?"

"There's nothing in the books, but there's something in the letters. This chick who's writing to him apparently used to be one, and wants it back. It's something wibbly about sacred bloodlines. That's all I've got, sorry."

Well, it was better than nothing. "It's better than nothing," I said.

"You know the solstice is in two days, right?"

"If I'm not dead by then, I'll look into it."

"I'll let you know if I find anything else."

"Thanks. You've been, um, yeah." I hung up quickly.

Huh. Guess that explained some of the whys, but it didn't help much with the what-the-fuck-to-do-about-its. Part of me couldn't help thinking that trying to become a god when you were already immortal was just a little bit cheeky. Part of me felt I should have had a sense of closure. I'd spent fifteen years not knowing why Henry Percy had tried to kill me, and now I did. But quite a lot of people have tried to kill me over the years, and honestly, it'd got to the point that I'd given up worrying about their motivations. As the saying goes, haters gonna try to sacrifice you.

I was in that unsettled place where I didn't technically have anything to do, unless you counted watching everything go to shit. The sensible, grown-up thing would be to go into the office and start working on actual paying cases. I'd been saving the world pro bono for about a week, and while I'm sure it made me a better person, it didn't actually pay the bills. On the other hand, since there was even less guarantee than usual I was going to live through the next few days, making sure my electricity didn't get cut off wasn't exactly a priority.

In the end, I compromised and spent the afternoon tying up loose ends. If you're going to die, you might as well go neatly. I swung by Seven Dials and handed the feather from the Morrígan's wing over to the Merchant of Dreams. They seemed a bit surprised that I'd actually managed to get one, but they thanked me politely and didn't try to pull any faery bullshit. I was half-expecting to find out there was some kind of infuriating loophole that meant they got to lock me up in a tree forever, but apparently not.

I spent what was left of the afternoon helping Elise with the invoicing and the other bits of admin I'd got really used to having her do for me. And then we set off to Hyde Park to gate-crash a duel.

The car park was apparently *Full* which I suspected was a tangled web of lies. I drove down the ramp to the barriers, where there were a couple of Caradoc's goons waiting with *fuck off* looks on their faces.

I wound down the window. "Hi, you might remember me from that time you arrested me. Or that, um, other time you arrested me. I'm here for the fight."

"None are to be admitted."

"Oh, come on. Look, we can do this whole big thing where you try to keep me out and I sneak in the back and it's a waste of everybody's time, or you could just let me in right now."

"None are to be admitted."

"Your boss isn't big on initiative, is he?"

He glared.

Elise glanced over. "Is it time for Plan B, Miss Kane?"

"I guess so."

We sat there in silence for about twenty seconds.

"Forgive me for asking, but what is the nature of Plan B?"

"I'm hoping if we sit here for long enough, they'll get bored and let us in."

There was a blare of horns as a limo glided down the ramp and got stuck behind us.

I guess that was Plan B.

One of Caradoc's men rapped on the roof. "You will need to move."

"I can't."

"I suppose you think you've been very clever."

"I told you this'd be easier if you'd just let me in."

In the rearview mirror I saw a door open, and Henry jumped out of the limo and came to investigate.

"Ah," he said, "what's causing the holdup?"

"A mortal is trying to breach the perimeter."

I waved.

Henry peered into the car. He looked like he was trying not to laugh. "Oh, for God's sake, you pointless minion, just let her through."

"I do not take orders from dogs."

"Look, it's a very straightforward situation." And then he punched him.

The enforcer staggered back and then turned on Henry, fangs bared. It looked like the fight was starting early.

There was a polite cough from inside the car park, and Thomas Pryce stepped into the light. "Is there a problem, gentlemen?"

The mook scowled. "He attacked me."

Henry folded his arms haughtily. "Fellow was being unreasonable."

Pryce sighed and pressed the button to lift the barrier. I gunned my engine, ready to go.

"Our orders were no mortals."

"I have found that if Miss Kane wants to be somewhere, keeping her out becomes expensive."

The goons backed off, Henry got back into the limo, and I drove inside. It was kind of the poshest car park ever: all gleaming white floors and bright lights. The company that ran it probably sold it as a bespoke parking solution or something. A bunch of vampires were standing around in the middle.

I tucked my car into a corner where I was pretty sure it wouldn't get wrecked in the fight. Even so, it was probably the classiest thing that had ever happened to it.

The wolf mobile dropped Tara and the pack, before turning round and leaving. The vampires and werewolves formed themselves into a circle, kind of like when two kids used to fight in the playground at school.

Elise and I put on our best *totally meant to be here* faces and walked right over there. It was a bit of a low turnout. Julian and Thomas were the only princes who'd bothered to turn up. And, of the Council, there was only al-Rashid and Diego.

"I see you brought your cat's-paw," sneered Diego at Julian.

"If that's my girlfriend you're talking about, she's here of her own accord. As usual." There was a puff of shadows from the far side of the circle, and Julian bamfed over. "What are you doing here?" she whispered.

"Looking for you."

Julian insinuated herself between me and Elise, and took our arms like a very small Hugh Hefner. "Oh, how sweet. Did you miss me or am I just in mortal danger?"

"Little from column A, little from column B."

Our impromptu threesome slotted into the circle between Thomas Pryce and al-Rashid. Tara and Caradoc were already in the middle, quietly sizing each other up.

Then, I heard a strange scrabbling in the walls and rats came pouring out of the air vents. Their claws skittered on the floor as they rushed towards us, their bodies flowing into the shape of the skinny, floppy-haired emo kid I knew as Jack.

"'Scuse me." He squeezed his way into the circle and stood there, looking bashfully at his battered Converses.

"Ah, who the hell are you?" demanded Tuffie or Smudge.

"This one speaks for the Multitude." The many-voices echoed through the empty car park.

Tuffie or Smudge looked awkward. "Just checking. No offence, yah."

"S'alright." Jack shoved his hands into the pockets of his oversized combats. "But, like, I've got to do the fight now."

Al-Rashid muttered something about this not being the way things were done in Istanbul.

"So . . ." Jack blew his fringe out of his eyes. "You two are going to fight now, and if you win—" He nodded at Caradoc. "—like, the pack will go home and not bug you anymore. But if you win—" A nod for Tara. "—then they get to, like, kill you all or something. Only not like now. Like in a war or something."

Well, that had been less ritual-y than I'd expected.

Jack trudged off to take his place in the circle. "So like . . . one two three go."

They went.

CHAPTER TWENTY-FOUR

CONFLICTS & RESOLUTIONS

aradoc shot forwards and caught Tara by the throat before she had a chance to change. Tara jabbed the heel of her hand into his chin and raked her claws down his face. For a moment, I thought the guy was going to lose his eyes again. You'd think he'd want to invest in goggles or something.

Caradoc twisted his head away and hurled Tara through the circle and across the car park. She slammed heavily into a pillar, shifting as she fell. She landed on four paws, tearing free of the tatters of her dress.

It was probably wrong, but I found it kind of hot.

Caradoc came forwards cautiously, trying to circle her. Tara dropped her belly to the ground, watching him through gleaming amber eyes. He charged and Tara lunged forwards, sinking her teeth into his leg. There was a sort of cracking noise, like when you're jointing a chicken, and Caradoc went down.

There was a nasty struggle on the ground, all fur and blood and snarling. And then Caradoc was up, and Tara was flying across the car park again.

Right into my bloody car.

"How terribly unfortunate," said Elise. "I am certain that will not be covered by the insurance. I recall the specifications of the policy quite distinctly."

Tara crawled out of the backseat of my Corsa, scattering broken glass. I didn't like to think what she'd done to my upholstery. Caradoc edged warily past her, reached down and ripped off the fucking door.

"I do not believe that is covered by the insurance either."

"Well, sweeting," drawled Julian, "that's what you get if you park in a bad part of town."

Caradoc snapped off the top of the window frame, straightened it out into a kind of swordy shape and threw everything else aside. I guess he was a stick-to-what-you-know kind of guy. He went for Tara again, trying to impale her on his shiny new metal spike. She swerved away, and he gouged a deep wound into her flank. As he pulled his arm back for another strike, she wheeled round and sprang at him. The tip of the weapon pierced her shoulder, but he took her full weight on his chest and crashed backwards, somehow managing not to damage any more of my property.

Tara snapped at his face, forcing him to bring his hands up in self-defence. They struggled a moment, then Caradoc shoved the wolf away, sending her and his makeshift spear tumbling across the floor. He attacked at full vamp speed, a blur of claws and fangs and righteous anger.

In a rush of gold, Tara shifted back to her human form, ripped the piece of window frame from her shoulder, and plunged it straight into Caradoc's heart.

He dropped. Looking pretty surprised.

There was a long silence broken only by Tara's harsh breathing and then by a golf clap from Julian. "Well, that was efficacious."

Diego gave Julian a look that said *if I had my way, I'd be strapping you to a rack about now*.

Tuffie or Smudge hurried forwards with one of Tara's trademark wispy dressing gowns. She slipped her arms into the robe, the marks on her body already closing as I looked at them. Not that I was looking.

Jack shuffled forwards. "So, um, the challenger loses, so I, um, guess the war goes on. This is still, um, neutral ground, so don't, like, kill each other until you get outside." Then he exploded into a swarm of rats and scattered.

Tara shook out her hair. "I will give you one hour's grace, and after that, we will kill any vampire we find on the streets."

"You know," observed Thomas Pryce, "this is all needlessly wasteful."

"It is typical of your kind to negotiate when you have already been defeated."

"Miss Vane-Tempest, I cannot think of a better time to negotiate."

She swept past him. "I have nothing to say to you."

Her dramatic exit was spoiled by the white Ford transit van that came trundling down the ramp into the car park. And I'd thought my car looked out of place. It came to a halt in front of the wolves, the back doors swung open, and a kid in a blue school uniform with her hands cuffed behind her back tumbled out onto the floor.

"Philippa!" cried Tuffie or Smudge.

Mercy descended from the back of the van like a very conservatively dressed avenging angel. She rested one taloned hand on the girl's shoulder. It didn't look hard, but Philippa cringed. "Do you know how foolish it is that you send all of your children to the same two schools?"

Tara froze. "Let her go. Now."

"Or what?"

"Or we'll kill you all."

"Isn't that your plan anyway?" Mercy's fingers tightened slightly. "This is simple retribution. You exterminate us, we will exterminate you. I believe, during détente, they referred to it as mutually assured destruction."

Philippa whimpered, and Tara took a half step forwards. "This violates the Compact."

Mercy tilted her head slightly. It reminded me of Aeglica. "You are entitled to attempt to control our numbers. We are entitled to defend ourselves."

"Defend yourselves," snarled Henry, coming to Tara's side, "not abduct children."

"The law does not constrain us to fight only with weapons of your choosing. This girl is just an example. Unless my agents hear otherwise, a generation of your people will be wiped out."

Tara's whole body tensed. This wasn't the kind of situation where you made a lot of sudden movements and sudden movements were kind of her thing. "You wouldn't dare."

"You have no idea what I would or would not dare. Call off your hunt, go home, and leave our business to us."

"Let Pippa go."

"Take your cub." Mercy stepped away. Philippa scrambled to her feet and ran, teary-eyed, to where the pack was waiting. "Now, do you agree to my terms?"

"For the moment. But you've made an enemy today."

Mercy folded her clawed hands neatly in front of her. "I've tried making friends. I found it unreliable."

The wolves left about as quickly as you'd expect from people who'd just been told their kids were in mortal danger.

There was a slightly stunned silence in the car park.

"Unorthodox," murmured al-Rashid, "but effective."

Thomas Pryce smiled. It was kind of unpleasant. "Well played."

Mercy curtsied flawlessly. That was kind of unpleasant as well. Then she swept to where Caradoc was lying paralysed on the ground and yanked the bit of my car out of his chest. She put back her veil. I was pretty glad I couldn't see her expression. "I think this means you're working for me now."

He drew in a sharp breath, presumably out of habit. "You grasping, manipulative bitch."

"You grasping, manipulative bitch, Your Highness."

"I will not take orders from a whore."

"Sir Caradoc, you have known me for four hundred years. In all that time, did it not occur to you that I was never ashamed of my profession? And you will take whatever orders I will give, or I will break you."

He rose to his feet and turned to rest of the vampires. "This woman knows nothing of warfare. She cannot wear the mantle of Prince of Swords."

"Can I just point out," said Julian, "that, of the two of you, you're the one who was just lying on the floor with a stake through his heart?"

"I fought for my people."

Thomas Pryce sighed. "The job of a prince is not to fight, but to win. In case you have failed to notice, it is no longer the twelfth century, and the ability to swing a sharp piece of metal is no longer the most desirable quality in a leader."

Caradoc wheeled round and gazed plaintively at Diego. "Will you stand for this?"

"I'm sorry, but I will abide by the decision of the local princes, however shortsighted."

"If the Council has no further need of me." Caradoc bowed stiffly and left. He seemed to have got the message. Probably for the first time in his life. Or unlife. Or whatever.

The rest of the vampires left shortly afterwards, leaving me alone with Julian and Elise and the remains of my car.

Elise picked up a piece of shattered metal. "I fear the vehicle has suffered terribly."

"Yeah, it's kind of a write-off."

"Oh no, Miss Kane, I did not believe you would discard a thing so casually."

"It'll cost more to fix than to replace."

Elise turned away and I remembered, too late, that the last time she'd been to a wrecking yard she'd been, well, in it.

Shit.

I put my hand awkwardly on her shoulder. "Fine, fine, we'll keep the car."

"Really, Miss Kane?"

"Yes, really. Sorry I was insensitive."

"I believe the Automobile Association would be able to help us."

Julian crunched through the wreckage. "If you don't mind, my dears, I'd rather we didn't invite a collection of mortals to the site of a supernatural duel, entertaining though it would be to watch you explain how you wrecked your car in an empty car park and why so much of the bodywork has blood on it."

Elise very slowly folded her arms. It looked kind of awkward, and I don't think I'd ever seen her do it before. "I will not abandon the vehicle, Miss Saint-Germain."

"Oh, for pity's sake." Julian put a hand to her brow. "How about I ask Ashriel to arrange something?"

"That would be very kind of you."

Julian stalked off up the ramp, coattails streaming behind her.

"You okay to wait with the car?" I asked.

"Of course, Miss Kane. I will ensure it is well taken care of."

I set off after Julian. I guessed Mercy and al-Rashid would sort out the vampire army, and it looked like war was off the menu for now, which meant that, assuming Nim did her bit and Henry Percy didn't ascend to godhood behind my back, I was basically done. I was kind of hoping that meant I could actually spend some time with my girlfriend.

As soon as I got above ground, my phone went off.

Well, fuck. Because apparently the universe is out to cockblock me. "Kane."

Rachel's voice crackled over the line. "Nimue needs you at Highgate. We've got a situation."

Of course they had.

I hung up just as Julian pounced on me. "Oh, sweeting, I've missed you. Let's go back to my place, or your place, or any place, and fuck like the Borgias."

"Did they fuck a lot?"

"Honestly, history has somewhat exaggerated their reputation, but the sentiment stands."

"Well, that sounds great, but I kind of have to go."

Julian frowned. "What could possibly be more important than me? Kate, we haven't had sex for nearly a fortnight."

"There was kind of a war in the middle."

"War can be a powerful aphrodisiac."

"Not if your girlfriend's hiding in a basement somewhere and hasn't bothered to tell you where she is."

"Firstly, it was a very comfortable and well-appointed basement, and secondly, I tried to call you several times, but you never bothered to answer."

Shit. "Tara sort of stood on my phone."

"You really must learn to control your pets."

"Look, I have to go. It's kind of life or death."

"Isn't it always? Now, tell me what's going on."

Nim's only instruction had been to keep the vampires away from this, but this was *a* vampire, not *the* vampires, and I'd been keeping so much back from Julian it was starting to feel unpleasantly like cheating. I sighed. "Nim's got the pot, she's gone to fight the Morrígan, something's gone wrong, she needs me."

There was a long silence.

"Thank you for telling me," said Julian in her best *I'm not angry, I'm just concerned* voice.

"I need to get to Highgate, like, now."

Julian looked up at me, grinned, and swept me into her arms.

"Oh, not this not again."

"Sweeting, do you want to play hard to get, or do you want to get to Highgate?"

"You enjoy this way too much."

"I enjoy everything way too much."

She leapt into the air, taking me with her. It was kind of less romantic than last time, partially because she was moving a lot faster and partially because we were on our way to a graveyard to throw down with a crazy vampire death queen. Julian carried me over the rooftops of the weird pyramid-y housing estate I'd seen in my dream and over the wall into the Highgate Cemetery.

The moment we landed, I realised this wasn't going to be fun. My breath caught in my throat, and I felt an icy pressure slowly tightening around my heart. I panicked out of habit, but it didn't seem to be getting any worse, which meant I probably wasn't going to die. Straightaway, anyway.

It looked like the rest of the place hadn't been so lucky.

The trees were bare, the ivy withered on the graves. The ground was scattered with dead birds and dust.

Julian looked up like a meerkat. "Kemsit's here."

Oh dear.

We started to edge our way between the headstones towards the Morrígan's tomb. I had no idea where Nim was, but I really hoped she showed up soon, and I really, really hoped she had a plan.

As we approached the main path, I saw Kemsit standing in a teenagery slouch beside a blingy Victorian obelisk. She was still barefoot, still wearing the same torn jeans and faded T-shirt. A browny-gold cat with really big ears sat bolt upright at her feet.

I circled round to get a better look, just in time to see the Morrígan descending from her tomb, tattered wings trailing behind her.

A strange awareness tingled on the back of my neck. I turned and Nim was there. A few flakes of snow spiralled down from the sky and settled on her hair.

Julian glanced from Kemsit to the Morrígan to Nimue and flicked up her brow. "Nice to see you've got this so thoroughly under control, Witch Queen."

Nim shrugged. "I never said it would be easy."

"You haven't got a clue, have you?"

"Bicker later," I snapped. "Now, what's the plan? There is a plan, isn't there?"

Nim touched me lightly on the arm. "I need you to take out the creepy child vampire."

"You know she could kill me instantly right?"

"Can I just point out," said Julian pissily, "that we've just got Kate acquitted for murdering one member of the Council. Are you now proposing she walk up to another and, to put it crudely, lamp her one?"

"I'll protect her."

"Her," I interrupted, "is standing right here. And, to be fair, she's not keen on the lamping plan either."

"If these two kick off, a lot of people are going to die," said Nim. "I just need you to distract the girl while I talk to the Morrígan."

"Fine." I threw my hands in the air. "Protect me."

Nim took a step towards me and pressed her mouth against mine.

"Oh, you are fucking kidding me," cried Julian. "You're protecting her with your lips? New plan. Stop kissing my girlfriend right the fuck now. I'm dealing with this."

We broke apart, and Julian bamfed across the graveyard, putting herself between Kemsit and the Morrígan.

She put her hands on her hips. "I can see you're about to have a cataclysmic showdown. But could you possibly consider not?"

Kemsit blinked. "No."

"You are without the authority of the Council. Stand down."

"No. Now is the moment to act. I will act."

The Morrígan lifted an arm and a raven landed on her wrist. "You will try. And I will flay the skin from your body and weave your bones into my hair."

Julian spun round with a kind of *for fuck's sake* look on her face. "Will you shut up?"

Kemsit clenched her fist and Julian dropped.

Fuck.

"All right. All right." I pulled Nim close. "Get protecting."

Nim put her lips over mine in a way that was definitely nothing like kissing. I felt her breath, cool like the falling snow, and sweet with secrets.

I didn't stop to ask if it had worked. I just broke away and dashed over to Julian. She was looking pretty fucking dead. But, since she was already dead, hopefully it wouldn't take.

Kemsit took a few steps forwards, the cat twisting round her ankles. "You are not needed here. Go."

"You just re-killed my girlfriend."

"She will recover. Go."

There was a rustle of feathers as the Morrígan swept towards me from the other side. So, on the one hand, they weren't fighting each other anymore. On the other, they were fighting me.

Nimue stepped out of the mist behind the Morrígan and tapped her on the shoulder. "I would speak with you, Dread Queen."

The Morrígan turned slowly, but I didn't see what happened next because at that point Kemsit grabbed me round the throat.

Well, I wasn't killed instantly, so something must have been working right. Still, being throttled? Not so great.

"You have become an obstruction."

I wrapped one hand round her wrist and slammed the other into her elbow. She was old, she was strong, but when you got right down to it, she still had the body of a twelve-year-old. "I bet you say that to all the girls."

Kemsit pulled her arm free and placed the palm of her hand against my chest. I could feel a weight against my heart, but it carried on beating.

She frowned.

I felt kind of shitty about it, but I backhanded her across the face. She staggered and slipped and landed in an undignified heap on the ground.

There was a yowl from somewhere near my ankles, and the cat leapt at me, hissing and spitting and scrabbling its way up my chest like a really angry mountaineer.

I ripped it off and held it at arm's length while it wriggled and swiped. Not really sure what to do with it, I chucked it over my shoulder.

Kemsit was already on her feet. She looked vaguely confused. I guess she hadn't been in an actual fight for a couple of millennia.

"Look," I said. "I basically can't hurt you, and you basically can't hurt me. Shall we just call this a draw?"

"You interfere in things that do not concern you."

I jerked my thumb over my shoulder. "Actually, she's interfering, I'm just helping."

She stared past me at whatever was going on with Nim and the Morrígan. "Who is the mortal?"

"Witch Queen of London."

"Ah." She paused. The cat slunk between my legs and crawled into Kemsit's arms. "That is acceptable."

Then she turned and walked away.

Okay. I had no idea what had just happened, but it'd turned out a lot better than I'd expected.

I knelt down by Julian and opened up my wrist against her fangs. A shiver of decidedly inappropriate pleasure ran through me, but I grit my teeth and rode it out. Julian stirred slightly, so I glanced up to see what the hell was going on with Nim and the Morrígan.

They stood facing each other, a few feet apart. The air was thick was snow and feathers.

"And why," asked the Morrígan, "should I not simply tear out your eyes and feed your carcass to my birds?"

Nim tucked her hands into the pocket of her hoodie and shrugged. She looked very small and scarily mortal right now. "I don't know. Why don't you?"

The Morrígan swept forwards in a swirl of black feathers and flashing talons. I winced, and by the time I stopped wincing, the Morrígan was on her knees at Nim's feet, snow dusting her tangled hair and ruined wings.

"What you do in the rest of these isles," said Nimue softly, "is not my concern, but I am Queen of this city."

"I was here when the city was nothing but earth, and I shall be when it is nothing but ashes."

"And then you may return and be Queen over a dead land. But while my city lives, you will sleep."

"I came only for what is mine."

The snow was falling thickly now, turning the world silver like in my dreams, and surrounding Nimue in a shifting mantle. "It will be returned to you. And you will return to your rest."

The Morrígan bowed her head. "I accept."

There was a swirl in the mist and a roar of engines in the distance. After a minute or two, Michelle and a couple of her gang walked through the gates. As she approached, wings of fire unfurled from her shoulders and flames danced between her hands, forming the shape of a sword. A tall young man with red, waist-length hair was cradling the pot in his arms.

The Morrígan rose to her feet, reached out and took the beaker. For a moment, she was utterly still in the snow, her fingers curling tenderly over its broken surface.

Then she turned, walked into the tomb, and the doors closed behind her.

Nim's hands traced a pattern in the air and the chain that had sealed the tomb coiled itself back into place. Then she knelt, took up handful of snow and blew gently across her palm. The flakes stirred and danced, shimmered silver for a moment in the air and settled over the door. It hardened swiftly into frost, which sparkled like tiny stars, and then faded away.

"Right, pub," said Michelle.

Nim dusted off her hands. "You coming, Kate?"

I helped a still-shaky Julian to her feet. "I think we're good."

The mages disappeared into the mist, leaving me alone—at last—with my vampire girlfriend. Okay, we were in a graveyard, but with the snow and everything, it was quite pretty.

"You know," she drawled, "if you keep kissing witches, we're going to have words."

"It's just the way it works."

"Oh, how terribly convenient."

This probably wasn't the best time to tell her I'd accidentally kissed Corin. Then again, the last time I'd decided it was a bad time to tell Julian something, it hadn't worked out so well.

"Um," I said.

CHAPTER TWENTY-FIVE
PATRICK & SOFIA

woke to the taste of wine and rose leaves, the smell of fresh coffee, and Julian hard at work between my legs.

It beat the hell out of an alarm clock.

Afterwards, we lay in a happy pile, and I appreciated the perks of dating the vampire prince of pleasure.

"So," I asked, "Mercy's Prince of Swords now, huh?"

Julian stretched her arms lazily over her head. "You can never just enjoy a moment, can you?"

"I like to have an idea what's going on. It stops me getting, y'know, killed."

"Well, it hasn't been formalised yet, but after last night's performance, I doubt Caradoc will have much support from the Council. He's older, but he's never been a thinker."

"Was Aeglica?"

"No, and look what happened to him."

I didn't actually like to think about what happened to Aeglica. As vampires went, he hadn't been that bad. And I really try to avoid murdering people if I can help it. "What's going to happen to the Morrígan's army?"

"They'll be dealt with quietly."

"You mean you're going to kill them all?"

She rolled onto an elbow and gazed at me lazily. "No, we're going to send them to live on a lovely farm in the country with all the blood they can drink. Yes, of course we're going to kill them."

"But they're people. You can't just slaughter them because it's convenient."

"They've been turned, abandoned, and let loose on the city. They haven't learned to control their bloodlust, and we haven't got the means to teach them. It's terribly unfortunate, sweeting, but we don't have prisons, and we don't really do rehabilitation."

"I sent this guy to Acton, and he seems to have sorted him out."

Julian shrugged. "He could probably save a few but not hundreds, and how would you decide who lives and who dies? It's the only way, sweeting." She slithered over and kissed my nose. "But it's adorable that you care."

"I'm not sure that opposing mass murder counts as a cute little foible. I might as well have just left it to the werewolves."

"That was a question of what Pryce would call demarcation."

I sighed. "Of course he would."

There was a silence.

Julian turned her big blue eyes up to mine again. "Well, since it means so much to you, I'll see what I can do. But I'm not promising."

It probably says something about the state of your love life that your girlfriend promising to try and murder slightly fewer people seems like a really sweet and romantic gesture. "Thanks. I do actually appreciate it."

"You can make it up to me later." Julian slid her leg between mine, leaving me in no doubt how exactly she was expecting me to do that.

"Um, the guy I sent off with the Knights. He's not going to be randomly executed, is he? I went to a lot of trouble to find him."

"I shouldn't worry. Acton never lets anyone interfere with his little projects."

"His sister sort of hired me to find him. I told her he was lying low because Reasons, but I don't know what happens now he's, y'know, dead but still walking around."

"Oh, it's fine, darling." She grinned. "We'll just kill everybody he's ever met or cared about."

"Ha-ha."

"Kate, we've been dealing with this sort of situation for centuries. It's up to him whether he wants to reintegrate with his family, and if he does, Sebastian's people will handle it."

"I'd assumed there'd be some kind of don't-tell-anybody-ever rule."

"We tried that, it just caused a lot of unnecessary headaches. If the survival of our species could be jeopardised by one individual telling his sister that we exist, we would have been wiped out long ago." Julian rolled over me and kissed me deeply. "As much as I'd love to stay with you all day, I should go. The Velvet's been closed too long already."

I suppose technically I had a job as well. I didn't have any work, but I still had a job.

"There's one more thing," I said, watching Julian slither interestingly into her tight leather trousers. "Can you take something to the Council for me?"

Julian stopped and gave me a look. "You mean, as well as asking for clemency for a bunch of uncontrollable blood-crazed fledglings?"

"This isn't a request, it's information. I think Henry Percy woke the Morrígan."

"Mad alchemist Henry Percy? Why would he do that?"

"I think ... um ... he wanted to distract everybody so he could become a god."

"Well, the man certainly knows how to divert attention. We'll look into it."

"And the god thing?"

"I'm not sure the Council has a policy on ascending to godhood. But if he did really wake the Morrígan, we're going to be very cross indeed."

Julian finished dressing and left a few minutes later. I had a shower, a coffee, and a banana, not necessarily in that order. Elise was just on her way out to oversee the repairs on my Corsa, so that left me with nothing to do except treat myself to a day off and a *Downton Abbey* marathon. Or I would have done, if I could work the TiVo.

I was still fiddling with one of the three new remote controls that had shown up in the front room since Elise arrived when the window burst open and Patrick barged in.

"Katharine," he rasped.

He looked like shit. His skin was pale, his cheeks were gaunt, his eyes were red. Also, his hair was a mess, but that was kind of his look.

"What the fuck?"

He leaned over me and grabbed my arms. "It's Sofia."

"Let me guess, you've dumped her again."

"If only I had." He let go of me for a moment to put a hand tragically to his forehead. "She has been taken."

"Can't you just go and get her back?"

Patrick has this creepy ability to tell where his girlfriends are every second of the day out to a radius of several hundred miles.

"Something is keeping us apart."

"And you think I can help, how?"

He pulled away and stalked up and down my very small apartment. "If you have any feelings left for me at all, you will help me."

"Patrick, I *don't* have any feelings left for you at all. Unless you count irritation and wishing you'd leave me alone."

He whirled back around and got right up in my grill. "I know I have hurt you, Katharine, but Sofia is blameless in all of this. She is innocent and pure like a white dove I—"

"Oh, will you shut up?" As much as I would have loved to tell Patrick to fuck off, it sounded like Sofia was really in trouble, and Patrick's fetishes aside, I wasn't going to let an innocent girl get hurt. She'd already told me she was having visions of people trying to kill her, although since she'd thought it was me, they probably weren't a hundred percent accurate. Unless it was one of those movie things where I go to try to save her and end up killing her with the power of irony. "Look, tell me what happened, and I'll see what I can do."

"We were at a ball at her school."

Wait. He actually took her? He must have grown as a person. I made *go on* noises.

"I was called away by the Prince of Wands because of the events in Highgate Cemetery. I was gone less than half an hour, but when I returned, she'd been taken, and I could no longer sense her."

"And you didn't see anybody?"

Patrick shook his head tormentedly.

Okay, that meant Sofia's visions were the only clues I had. It was a good job they'd been pretty familiar. "You know she had dreams, right?"

"Of course, she told me everything."

"About the people trying to kill her?"

His face froze, and he was silent. I took that as a no. I wouldn't have told him when I was her age either. "She said she dreamed of a man with a golden mask and a house with dragons outside it."

Patrick posed dramatically. "Then I know where she is."

"Yeah, yeah, so do I. I was there too, remember? Now get your car and meet me in five minutes."

"No, Katharine. You have done enough. I must do this alone."

"Patrick, don't be such a bell end. You asked for my help and you're getting it whether you want it or not."

"I'm not coming back to you, Katharine." He turned away from me and stretched out one arm in a gesture of anguished rejection. "I love Sofia now."

"I know you might not believe this, but I actually care more about the life of a seventeen-year-old girl than where you stick your dick."

Patrick disappeared through my window and a few minutes later his silver Volvo S60R pulled up outside my flat. Annoyingly, I was probably going to wind up fighting a castle full of vampires, and I'd given my gold dagger to the girl they'd already kidnapped, and I'd had my magic sword stolen by one of the vampires I was about to be fighting. Which meant we were basically going in armed only with my hand-me-down faery powers and Patrick's misplaced sense of righteousness. I mean, I suppose the sensible thing to do would have been to take a step back, ring Elise, possibly Julian, and try to get backup, but we were pushed for time, Patrick would probably have driven off without me, and I've never been a big fan of sensible anyway.

Twenty minutes into the road trip, it occurred to me that not only was I going to have to take on a castle full of vampires with my bare hands, but I was going to have to spend five hours in a car with Patrick first. I turned on the CD player and heard the tinkling strains of *Clair de* fucking *Lune*.

"Jesus, Patrick, how long can you keep listening to the same piece of music?"

"It is a very beautiful movement."

"Your whole life is a very beautiful movement."

"Thank you, Katharine."

I don't know why I even try. I got rid of Debussy and dug through Patrick's music collection. I found a home-burned mix CD labelled *For Patrick*. It had a heart over the i. I stuck it in, and "Why Does It Always Rain on Me?" whinged through the speakers. I suppose it was sort of his theme song. Why does it always rain on me? Is it because I saw ghosts, got committed to a lunatic asylum, and was transformed into a vampire by a crazy stalker chick when I was seventeen?

I went to pull my hat down over my eyes, and then remembered I'd lost the fucking thing. So I lay back and pretended I was asleep. The next track on the album was the radio edit of "Creep," which was also strangely appropriate. Alienated, obsessive, and a little bit PG-13.

I thought back to what Eve had told me about the ritual, and kicked myself for not working it out earlier. Though to be fair, I'd had a lot on my mind and going from *Patrick's new girlfriend is having funny dreams*, to *she's the last heir of a line of prophetesses dating back to the oracles and Delphi, and the crazy vampire alchemist who abducted me when I was seventeen will need her for the first part of the ritual that he needed me for the second part of* was quite a big leap. Hopefully, if I could nip this in the bud now, I'd be able to avoid an inconvenient sacrifice attempt six months down the line, assuming I was still his go-to faery princess.

The last of the light was bleeding out of the sky by the time we arrived many *Clair de Lune*s later at Trismegistus Hall.

We ditched the car as close as we dared and headed in on foot. The place was pretty much like I remembered, big old house with lots of windows, sort of turrety bits at the corners, and four stone dragon heads on the lawn.

I thought about asking Patrick if he had a plan, but he'd never been one for thinking ahead. Then again, neither had I.

"So, kick down the door, fight the baddies, get the girl?"

He nodded gravely.

We hurried towards the house, but when we were about halfway there, the ground starting shaking like that bit in *Jurassic Park*. Call me a pessimist, but I didn't think it was a good sign. At least last time, Percy'd had the good manners to keep the magical death traps inside the house.

I steadied myself, and scanned the area for what I'm sure Eve would call incoming hostiles.

There weren't any. Just me, Patrick, the house, some neat little woods, and four stone—

Oh, you have to be shitting me.

The perfectly maintained lawn ripped open and an enormous, four-headed stone dragon rose up from the mess, shaking grass and soil from its roughly carved back.

Patrick hadn't stopped and was already nearly past it. The creature's tail swung round and smacked him square in the chest, sending him flying. Ordinarily I'd have quite enjoyed it, but tonight he was my backup.

Okay, Kate, you've got no weapons, it's made of stone, its standing between you and where you want to go, and it's just taken out the hundred-and-fifty-year-old vampire.

If I was lucky, it'd be slow.

I tried to edge round the thing. It drew one of its heads back, and I saw a dim red glow build in its mouth.

Okay, so slow but fire breathing.

I rolled aside as it lobbed a bolt of searing molten rock at me.

Okay, so not fire breathing, lava breathing. I wasn't sure that was any better.

Patrick was back on his feet, and with his usual total lack of common sense, charged the dragon head on. He very nearly got a ball of magma in the face, but ducked aside at the last second.

Well. Fine. Play to his strengths.

"You keep it occupied," I shouted. "I'll think of something."

I tried to think of something.

What I really needed right now was magical backup or some kind of pneumatic hammer. And the only magical weapons nearby were in the mouths of the monster that was trying to kill me.

Fuck it, it was worth a shot.

Patrick was trying to get close, but what with the fireballs and everything, he wasn't having much luck. Truthfully, I didn't know what he thought he could do, even if he didn't get incinerated. It wasn't like he could bite it. Maybe he was going to annoy it to death.

I waited 'til all four heads were busy trying to barbecue Patrick, then I circled round and scrabbled onto its back. It was damn near vertical and swaying violently, but at least there were plenty of handholds. The instant I, um, mounted, another one of its heads whipped round and tried to bite me. I ducked as a set of massive stone jaws clamped shut in the air above me. Truthfully, I wasn't mad keen on getting any closer to them, but I sprang up and got my arms around its neck.

It shook its head like a dog coming out of a pond. I dug my fingers and knees into the stone. If it managed to throw me off, I was basically fucked. I could already feel a vibration in the rock as it readied its next blob of molten death phlegm. While I did my best impression of a spider monkey, the head I was on twisted back towards Patrick, and I felt its neck grow warm and then hot beneath me.

Calling up as much of my mother's strength as I dared, I wrenched its jaw back around and pressed myself in tight as a spew of liquid rock burst out of its mouth and spattered against one of the other heads and part of the body. The rush of heat was intense, and I was pretty sure I could smell my hair burning. Again.

The dragon gave a rough grating roar, and I threw myself to the ground and crawled the fuck away.

I glanced over my shoulder to make sure it wasn't going to shoot anything at me. Thankfully, it had gone the way of every many-headed monster I've ever seen, in real life or on TV, and started fighting itself.

"Katharine," cried Patrick. He caught me by the wrist and dragged me after him like he was saving my life. "Run."

Ah, Patrick. How I'd missed him.

By the time we'd got to the lawn and in sight of the house, the dragon was a pile of faintly glowing rubble.

Patrick tugged at my arm. "Come, we must rescue Sofia."

I twisted into his grip and broke his hold. Over the years, I've got pretty good at that.

I had a quick look at the building, trying to work out the best point of entry. Years of experience told me the wide-open front door might be a good place to start. Of course, my years of experience were also shouting *it's a trap* in that raspy voice Eve used to do.

I briefly thought about sending Patrick in first, but not only would it have been kind of a dick move, chances were they would be expecting him not me.

I approached as stealthily as you can when you're walking on gravel in full view of about thirty windows and have just fought an exploding fire monster.

Nothing killed me.

The entrance hall was decked out in the same style as Syon, all marble, bling, and naked dudes, and as soon as I stepped inside, I remembered the place. I'd been kind of busy getting kidnapped the last time, but I guess it had made more of an impression on me than I realised.

I tried really hard not to be seventeen again.

I followed mirrored corridors that were all too familiar, down a flight of twisting stone steps to Henry Percy's lavish underground sacrificing chamber.

It was almost the same as I remembered: more bling, lots of dribbly candles, and weird shit on the floor. Except this time I wasn't chained to the ceiling. Sofia knelt in the middle of a circle with seven red-robed vampires standing around, masked and chanting. On a raised platform at the far end, a man in white robes and a golden sun mask stood behind a table of magical doodads. He had an honest-to-god wand in his right hand, like he was Albus fucking Dumbledore.

Patrick shoved me out of the way and dashed forwards, shouting Sofia's name.

The man in white lifted a hand, and Patrick flew across the room and cracked into a marble pillar. In seconds, he was on his feet again, snarling.

I could have told them it takes more than throwing him bodily across the room to get Patrick to back off.

As the chanting reached a crescendo, Sofia jerked to her feet. Patrick rushed forwards, but before he could reach her, she said something in a language I didn't understand, but I assumed was some kind of ancient Greek, and a brilliant light flared from the golden mask.

If it was possible for metal to look smug, I'd have said it looked smug.

Okay, Operation Nip This in the Bud, probably a failure. I'm not an expert on mystical god rituals but bright flashes of light are usually not a good sign.

Slowly, the man in white reached down and picked up a bloodstained dagger. He turned towards Patrick and raised the blade. Oh crap, they had a sample of his blood, didn't they? That probably explained why he hadn't been able to track her. I had no idea how powerful that sort of freaky blood magic was but Patrick was not in a good way.

He sank to his knees, his face twisted in horror and anguish. "Sofia," he gasped.

"I am sorry, Patrick." The masked man's voice echoed everywhere at once, full of power and glory. "The girl has served her purpose, but there will be other mortals."

I'd been waiting for the best time to act, but having no idea what the hell was going on had made it a bit difficult. But now it looked like I was going to have to rescue both of them.

By fighting eight vampires. One of them possibly a god.

I came running down the steps hoping that raw enthusiasm and good intentions would make up for the lack of numbers, weapons, or a plan.

Before I could really do anything, Patrick suddenly broke free of the spell that had been binding him and lurched to his feet, screaming "Nooooo!" like he was in an actual fucking movie.

So, ancient blood magic? Not as powerful as Patrick's inappropriate obsessions with underage girls.

Then chaos happened.

The entire circle jumped on Patrick in a blur of red robes and got the full force of his psychotic sense of romance.

When I looked away from the bloody melee, I saw the man in white was gone, and a door, half-concealed by shadows, had opened behind his platform.

There was no fucking way I was letting him escape. At the time, I'd taken being tied up and nearly murdered as just part of being a teenager, but in retrospect, I was pretty pissed off about it.

Figuring that, for all his flaws, aggressively protecting seventeen-year-olds was what Patrick did best, I left him to take care of Sofia and pegged it after the man in white.

I ran down what was blatantly a secret passage, up a flight of stairs, and through a door which, of course, had a false bookcase on the other side. I'd come out in the library. Say this for Percy, the guy respected the classics.

"Ah, Miss Kane. I'm so glad you could join me."

Henry Percy was waiting for me in a wingback chair by the fireplace. He was wearing a pinstriped suit like when we'd met at King's Cross. I wondered where he'd stashed the robe and the mask, but I didn't wonder too long because I was distracted by the fact he had my motherfucking sword over his lap.

"Sorry I'm late, the traffic was murder."

He came gracefully to his feet. "You were much less flippant the last time you were here."

"I've grown as a person."

I was horribly aware that the last time I'd fought Percy, I'd been holding the sword, there'd been a mage backing me up, and I'd still lost. And now he was halfway to being a god as well.

He prowled around me, trailing the tip of the blade along the ground. "So, we have, at last, come full circle."

As long as he was talking, he wasn't trying to kill me, and the more time I had to come up with an ingenious escape plan. "We've not come full circle, we've just got in a fight twice."

"Ah, Miss Kane. There is so much more to this than you realise."

"Yeah, yeah, I got the becoming a god thing. I'm not impressed."

He stopped dead, that pissed off vampire stillness creeping over him. "How enterprising of you."

He raised a hand, and I was flung backwards across the room, straight into a heavy oak bookcase. Several volumes came tumbling down on top of me.

He lifted the sword and strolled casually towards me.

I grabbed the nearest book and wanged it at him. I was pretty sure he wasn't expecting that because the corner caught him on the side of his head.

He blinked and lifted a hand to his brow. I was expecting him to say something condescending, but instead, he just bared his fangs and hissed.

He lunged for me, quick but wild. I rolled out the way, and from the angry snarl behind me, I was pretty sure he'd just wrecked another one of his precious books.

If I wasn't actually going to win this fight, I could at least do as much property damage as possible.

I nipped round the next bookcase over, and shoved it as hard as I could, which was pretty fucking hard, what with the adrenaline and the remains of my mother's power still in my system. Groaning like a wounded buffalo, the case pitched and cracked and tipped a good tonne of paper, leather, and antique hardwood onto the Wizard Earl of Northumberland.

It wouldn't hold him for long, so I bent down and grabbed the most stake-shaped bit of shelf I could find.

There was a wave of telekinetic force that sent me crashing into the wall yet again, and then an explosion of book shrapnel as Henry Percy emerged from the wreckage. He shook dust from his mane and glared at me like he'd gone way past just wanting me dead.

He came forwards slowly and, with each step, made a sweeping gesture with his hand that sent another chunk of library flying right at me. There wasn't much I could do except bring my arms up and try to stop anything sharp or heavy from going through my head. It wasn't like I could outrun the room I was standing in.

At last he was looming over me, sword raised. His eyes were wild and cold. "Just f-fucking die."

He stabbed me.

From experience, I was expecting it to hurt a lot more.

There was just pressure, cold steel against my skin, and the slightest of scratches. Then the blade shattered.

Nim had told me it wouldn't draw human blood. It was kind of reassuring to know that I counted.

I reckoned I had about three seconds before Percy realised what was going on and just bit me. I snatched up one of the shards of the sword, hoped like hell it had kept some of its power, and thrust it towards his heart.

Percy's left hand came up protectively, and my weapon went through his palm.

He screamed like someone who was feeling pain for the first time in five hundred years. While he was processing that, I stood up, punching him in the jaw on the way.

He fell backwards into an undignified heap, cradling his hand. Blood ran down his arm and soaked through his expensive suit.

Another wave of force pushed me backwards. It was weaker than before, but it gave Percy time to get to his feet and start scrambling away from me.

I grabbed my bookcase stake and charged. Yet another wave of force hit me, but I just pushed through it.

This fucker was going down, and I think he realised it. He half turned, swept his one good arm in a half circle, and suddenly everything was on fire. Starting with the carpet and the piles of books. Then licking up the walls and spreading over the bookcases. Everything bursting into eerie blue flame. It wasn't hot, but I was starting to feel tired.

I filed all that away in a box marked *later* and jumped on Henry Percy as hard as I could, hammering my stake into his heart with all my body weight. He had just enough time to look really, really angry before he dropped to the floor, paralysed.

Huh. I'd expected that to feel more satisfying. I guess revenge was cool and all, but the whole trapped in a burning building thing was really taking the edge off.

I'd kind of been hoping that staking Percy would take care of that, but the fire was still there, and still spreading, and if I didn't get out of here soon, it was going to be a pretty short-lived victory.

Just then, I heard a piercing scream from the direction of the secret passage.

I looked down at Percy's impaled corpse. Rule Twelve said very clearly that just because you rammed a stake through somebody's heart and left them in the burning wreckage of their library, that was not a guarantee they were dead. On the other hand, I had nothing to decapitate him with, and I'd have felt like a prize dickhead if Sofia got eaten by vampires while I was trying to saw some bloke's head off with the edge of my Oyster card.

Also fire.

Leaving Percy on the floor and the flames raging, I ran back through the secret passage.

CHAPTER TWENTY-SIX

SERPENTS & GIFTS

I'm not usually a stop-and-take-stock-of-the-situation kind of girl, but this time I had no fucking clue what was waiting for me in the ritual chamber. So I lurked outside for a moment, trying to work out what the hell had gone wrong now. It was kind of quiet in there, which was either a good sign or a very bad sign, and I've never got anywhere betting on good.

I was just about to burst in, when someone spoke.

"Fear not child, it will all be over soon."

I'd heard that low, rasping voice before. What the fuck was Sybil doing here? Also when somebody says everything will be over soon, the last thing you want to do is give them a chance to demonstrate.

I shoved open the door and charged into the room like an idiot just as Sybil sank her teeth into Sofia's neck. I jumped over the unconscious bodies of Patrick and the half-dozen vampires he'd been fighting, grabbed Sybil by the hair and yanked her head back. The funny thing about pulling hair is that the only people who do it are six-year-old girls and hardened street fighters: in either case, it tends to work.

Sofia collapsed to the floor, bleeding and shaking. Sybil hissed and struggled against me, but while I was pretty sure she was as old as dirt, she wasn't a fighter. I was kind of low on weapons so I punched her in the head and kept on punching her in the head while I tried to come up with a better plan.

She thought of one first.

Turned out, it was *transform into a giant snake*.

I was left holding absolutely nothing and wrapped in a python. Eve had always said turning into a giant snake never helped anyone, but Sybil seemed to have it down. She tightened around me. In the last couple of weeks, I'd come to realise just how much I take breathing for granted.

I tried to remember the technique for escaping from a python. It was either smack it on the nose, run up a hill, or wait until it's nearly eaten you. Since my arms were pinned, waiting wasn't my style, and I'd forgotten to bring my hill with me, I was going to have to try something else. Sybil might not have been able to throw a punch, but she had the grab-and-squeeze thing down pat.

Here lies Kate Kane. Crushed to death by a crazy vampire prophetess in the shape of a giant snake. Beloved daughter. Sorely missed.

I was just getting those pretty red spots in front of my eyes when I heard a gentle voice saying something I still didn't understand in a language I still guessed was some kind of ancient Greek.

There was a shiny bright light coming vaguely from above me or around me or something and the terrible crushing pressure on my ribcage got a whole lot less terrible.

Sybil uncoiled herself and turned back into a crazy middle-aged hippie.

I choked for bit and struggled to my feet.

Sofia was standing in the centre of the room, surrounded by a glow like evening sunlight.

"I will return for what is mine, child." Sybil bared her teeth at Sofia, her eyes a poisonous green.

I was pretty sure we had the advantage, but since the only weapon I had right now was a glowing teenager who didn't understand her powers any better than I did, I wasn't going to push my luck.

"Look," I said, "I know you've got a raging hard-on for oracle blood but Percy's dead, this house is kind of on fire, and I'm having a really bad day, so can you please just fuck off?" She turned and drifted out like really angry smoke.

I was unbelievably glad that had worked. Plan B had been *stand around and see which of us was most flammable.*

Sofia was gradually dimming. "There's no need to swear."

"Sorry, I didn't realise this was a PG rescue mission. Now come on, let's get out of here."

I picked up Patrick, who was stirring but still out of it, and threw him over my shoulder. And we ran back upstairs, through the less on-fire bits of the house, out the front door, and across the lawn to a safe distance.

Trismegistus Hall was in a bad way. Unnatural flames were dancing behind most of its windows, and there was a weird blue shadow against the night sky like the afterimage of fireworks. We were going to have a hell of a time explaining this to the fire brigade.

I dumped Patrick on the ground and turned to see if Sofia was okay.

To my surprise, she gave a little smile. "Thanks for saving my life. And trying to warn me."

I scuffed my toe against the turf. "S'okay. And you did kinda save my arse too."

"I didn't want any of this." She twisted a finger anxiously in her hair. "Why won't everyone just leave us alone?"

"Is that an actual question that you want me to try and answer, because I think I sort of can?"

She nodded hesitantly. "What's wrong with me?"

Oh, fuck. I was nowhere near qualified for this. "First off, there's nothing wrong with you. It's just the world is bigger and more complicated than you thought it was two years ago, and you happen to have some power, or something, that other people want to use."

"But I'm just an ordinary girl. Patrick is the only special thing that's ever happened to me."

"There's no such thing as an ordinary girl."

There was a groan from the ground, and Patrick sat up. "Sofia," he emoted, "what did she do to you?"

Sofia threw herself into his arms. "She didn't hurt me. Kate saved me."

Patrick stared at me with that confused look he gets when he's trying to fit other people's behaviour into his messed-up view of the world. "Thank you, Katharine, but this changes nothing between us."

I sighed. "I can live with that. Just give me a lift home, and we'll call it square."

While Sofia and Patrick were having a tender reunion, I heard sirens in the distance and saw the flashing lights of the emergency services coming up the drive.

It looked like we'd miss our stealthy escape window, and speeding away past three fire engines and two police cars would look kind of suss.

"Patrick, you need to take care of this."

He stopped staring longingly into Sofia's eyes for half a second. "I do not have the authority. This is the Shaper's territory."

"Dude, for fuck's sake, we're standing outside a burning building full of dead bodies. If you don't do something, we're all going to jail for really quite a long time."

He failed spectacularly to do something. One of the fire engines pulled up in front of the house, and people in uniform swarmed out and got to work.

A slight figure in a dark green waistcoat swung down from the back of the truck and sauntered over. It was Halfdan the Shaper, grinning and holding a fireman's helmet under his arm.

"You do get around, don't you, Miss Kane?"

Great. I had no idea what this guy's deal was, but he'd tried to get me executed, so I didn't think we were friends. "I get that a lot."

Patrick stepped protectively in front of Sofia. At any moment I was expecting him to tell Halfdan to kill us and spare the girl.

Halfdan's bright eyes gleamed in the firelight. "No hard feelings about the trial, I hope?"

"If I took it personally when people tried to kill me, I'd be really insecure by now."

"Fantastic. Now, what the bollocking fuck is going on here?"

"Kill us if you must," said Patrick. "But spare the girl. She is innocent."

"I've spent a thousand years trying to avoid doing things I must. Which includes repeating myself. If one of you doesn't tell me what happened, I'll kill the girl just to ruin your day."

I'd forgotten how bad Patrick was at dealing with people whose minds he couldn't control. I made a *nobody needs to die here* gesture. "Okay, first of all, Sofia, Halfdan the Shaper, Halfdan the Shaper, Sofia. So can we all stop calling her 'the girl,' please."

Halfdan gave a little bow. "A pleasure to meet you, Sofia. I do hope I won't be eating you this evening."

"Here's the deal," I rushed on. "Henry Percy woke up the Morrígan to distract you all while he turned himself into a god. He captured Sofia, we came here to rescue her, there was a fight and a fire, he's probably dead in the library."

I hadn't quite had the balls to lie outright to him, but I was hoping I'd glossed over the *Sofia is magic and special and probably delicious* issue.

Halfdan peered at Sofia, grinning his too-big grin. "It's remarkable, isn't it, how many magical rituals need *perfectly ordinary* seventeen-year-old girls."

"Yeah." I shrugged. "It's completely weird."

He laughed. "Oh, you do entertain me, Miss Kane. I'll handle this from here. If you're not south of Sheffield by morning, I'll kill all three of you. Just sort of because."

He put his helmet on and strolled off to talk to the police.

Taking the hint, we headed back to Patrick's Volvo, and I crawled gratefully into the back.

They played their mix CD all the way home. When Patrick didn't need to change gears, they were holding hands.

I stretched out on the backseat, trusting Patrick's supernatural reflexes to stop us crashing into anything while I wasn't wearing a seatbelt. It was only about seven o'clock in the evening, but I'd been in three fights and taken two five-hour car journeys, so I was kind of knackered.

Sofia looked tired as well. Nearly getting killed takes it out of you. I know from experience. But she seemed to hate me less now, which I shouldn't have cared about either way, but kind of did. And the truth was, I kind of worried about her. Dating Patrick was bad enough, but discovering that you have exciting new supernatural powers and a bunch of people wanting to kill you makes it about eighty times worse. I knew that from experience as well.

I shut my eyes and took stock of the case. Not that it was a case so much as a bunch of stuff that happened. I'd stopped Percy, and I had a pretty good idea what he'd been up to. If I was really lucky, he'd be dead, but I'd be a fool to rely on it. Hopefully, the Council would be so pissed about the Morrígan, they would have him executed, but I suppose technically he was Halfdan's problem now, and I knew better than to try and second-guess really old vampires, especially when they had a reputation for being unpredictable.

There were a couple of little things that still nagged at me. I really wish I'd worked out what had happened to the golden mask, but it was probably somewhere in the wreckage. And Percy had gone down pretty easily for someone who was halfway towards being a god. But for all I knew that was how the ritual worked. I had a nasty feeling that Sofia being this glowy sun oracle thing was going to come back and bite somebody in the arse as well. Hopefully not her, but that was kind of out of my hands.

That's the thing with this business. You go in thinking it'll be about getting answers, but really, it's about getting results. Sofia was basically okay and knew a bit more about who she was. Tash was probably getting her brother back. The Morrígan was sleeping again, and her army wasn't rampaging around slaughtering people anymore. I'd cleared my name with the Council, and I'd paid my debt to the Merchant of Dreams. Corin had got away, but you can't win 'em all. I reckoned I could live with that.

I got Patrick to drop me off at the Velvet. I should probably have gone home to bed, but I hadn't really been able to have a girlfriend for the past fortnight and I wanted to see Julian.

The Velvet was back to its usually gaudy, glittering self. Ashriel was working the door in a Santa hat and, inside, Miss Parma Violet was presiding over Cabaret Baudelaire. I climbed the winding stairs to Julian's balcony and found her sprawled on the chaise longue, in full black tie and a shiny top hat. For once, she wasn't surrounded by an army of half-naked lesbians.

I leaned against one of the flaking golden pillars. "No kittens tonight?"

Julian turned my way and flicked up the brim of her hat. Her eyes gleamed very blue. "They'll be along later, but I was hoping I'd see you first."

"I'm probably not going to be very good company. I've been in a car with Patrick for ten hours."

"No wonder you look so miserable. Come and sit down, sweeting, and I'll see if I can balm your woes."

"I've never heard it called that before."

Julian lifted her legs gracefully out of the way and then plonked them back on top of me once I sat down. I idly slid a hand beneath the cuff of her trousers and stroked her bare, cold skin.

"So, dear," she purred, "how was your day?"

I told her about Patrick and Sofia and Percy and Sybil and the ritual and having to listen to *Clair de Lune* about eighty million times.

"Well," she said, when I was finally done, "apart from *Clair de Lune*, that sounds just like the sort of thing you'd enjoy."

"What, nearly being crushed to death by a giant snake?"

"You like danger, Kate. There's no point pretending otherwise." She glinted at me. "If you didn't, you'd have a different girlfriend."

I moved between her legs and caught for her wrists, holding them over her head. "You're not that dangerous."

She smiled up at me, her hands fragile under mine. "Keep telling yourself that, sweeting."

She kind of had a point. "Oh come on, you haven't tried to kill me in at least three months."

"I haven't needed to. Everyone else has been doing it for me."

"And look how well that worked out for them."

She arched her body against mine, hooking a leg around my waist. "Ah, but they don't know your weaknesses like I do."

"You have a weird line in pillow talk."

"You started it."

She kind of had a point. Again. But I was too tired to care. I let go of her hands and just kissed her, sinking into wine and rose leaves and the promise of a long, dark night. Julian wrapped herself around me and held me tight like only an ancient immortal sex monster can.

Julian's lips moved, featherlight and velvet soft, over my jaw. "I've got you a present," she whispered in my ear.

I popped the top few buttons on her starched white shirt. "Can I unwrap it now?"

"No, I mean an actual present. But you can unwrap me anytime, sweeting."

I jerked up. "Shit, I haven't got you anything at all."

"I'm an eight-hundred-year-old vampire prince with near limitless resources. I'm quite difficult to buy for." She leaned over the back of the chaise longue and fished up an extravagant hat box that looked like it had been wrapped by Rowan Atkinson in that scene in *Love Actually*.

"Uh, thanks." I sat there, cradling it in my lap and feeling awkward. "Do you want me to save this for Christmas?"

"You know how I feel about delayed gratification."

"Right."

"Besides, I assume you won't want to take me home to meet your parents."

There was a slightly too-long silence. "I'll just open it now."

To be honest, my parents probably wouldn't mind, but I couldn't really see Julian playing Trivial Pursuit or joining in our annual family tradition of ignoring the Queen's speech.

I pulled out my sanctified steel knife and cut through the ribbons.

Julian laughed. "How Alexander the Great of you."

"Oh, shut up." I suddenly remembered I was meant to be sounding grateful and pleased. I'm really bad at the whole present thing. I'm bad at giving them and bad at getting them. I kind of wish everybody would just buy their own stuff. It'd be less hassle all round.

I finally broke into the box.

I stared.

"Holy shit, how the fuck did you manage that?"

She looked just a little bit smug, but I guess she deserved to. "We sent some people to clean up Syon House, and that was lying in a pond in the middle of the courtyard, along with one of Percy's lackeys."

"Oh my God."

I reached into the box and pulled out my hat. It smelled a bit damp and it looked, if possible, even more battered than before, but it was my damn hat, and Julian had got it back for me.

I put it on.

Julian pounced on me, and we rolled off the edge of the chaise longue onto the floor. She straddled me and tugged off her jacket. Beneath her partially open shirt, I caught a glimpse of purple satin.

Then she leaned down and kissed my neck, her teeth scraping lightly over my skin, following the line of my artery.

I tipped my head back, baring my throat to her.

My hat fell off again. I didn't care.

Start at the beginning of the *Kate Kane, Paranormal Investigator* series with *Iron & Velvet*.

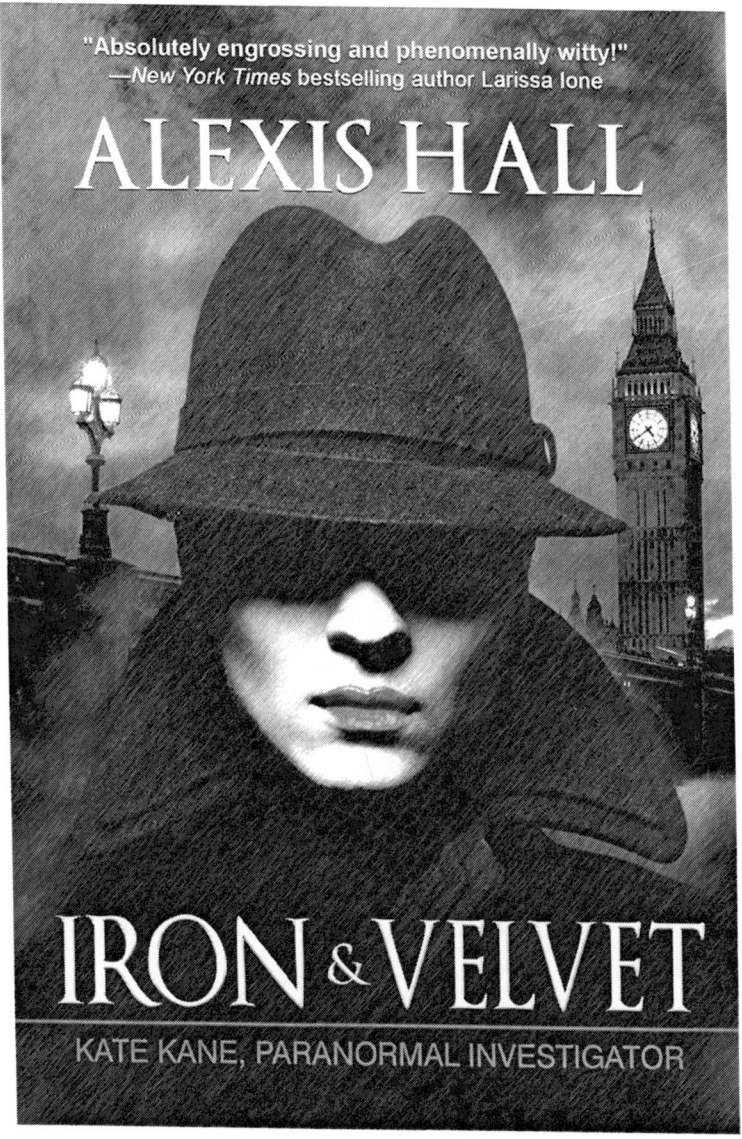

riptidepublishing.com/titles/series/kate-kane-paranormal-investigator

Dear Reader,

Thank you for reading Alexis Hall's *Shadows & Dreams*!

We know your time is precious and you have many, many entertainment options, so it means a lot that you've chosen to spend your time reading. We really hope you enjoyed it.

We'd be honored if you'd consider posting a review—good or bad—on sites like **Amazon, Barnes & Noble, Kobo, Goodreads, Twitter, Facebook, Tumblr**, and your blog or website. We'd also be honored if you told your friends and family about this book. Word of mouth is a book's lifeblood!

For more information on upcoming releases, author interviews, blog tours, contests, giveaways, and more, please sign up for our weekly, spam-free newsletter and visit us around the web:

Newsletter: tinyurl.com/RiptideSignup
Twitter: twitter.com/RiptideBooks
Facebook: facebook.com/RiptidePublishing
Goodreads: tinyurl.com/RiptideOnGoodreads
Tumblr: riptidepublishing.tumblr.com

Thank you so much for Reading the Rainbow!

RiptidePublishing.com

ACKNOWLEDGMENTS

Once again, thanks to all the usual people, particularly my partner, my wonderful editor Sarah Frantz, and my dear friend AB for trudging around Highgate Cemetery in the snow while I engaged in the haphazard tourism which, in my world, passes for research.

ALSO BY ALEXIS HALL

Spires series
Glitterland
Glitterland: Aftermath (Free download)
Waiting for the Flood
For Real
Pansies (Coming soon)

Kate Kane, Paranormal Investigator
Iron & Velvet

Sand and Ruin and Gold

Prosperity series
Prosperity
There Will Be Phlogiston
Liberty & Other Stories

Coming Soon
Looking for Group

ABOUT THE AUTHOR

Alexis Hall was born in the early 1980s and still thinks the twenty-first century is the future. To this day, he feels cheated that he lived through a fin de siècle but inexplicably failed to drink a single glass of absinthe, dance with a single courtesan, or stay in a single garret.

He did the Oxbridge thing sometime in the 2000s and failed to learn anything of substance. He has had many jobs, including ice cream maker, fortune-teller, lab technician, and professional gambler. He was fired from most of them.

He can neither cook nor sing, but he can handle a seventeenth-century smallsword, punts from the proper end, and knows how to hotwire a car.

He lives in southeast England, with no cats and no children, and fully intends to keep it that way.

Website: quicunquevult.com
Twitter: @quicunquevult
Goodreads: goodreads.com/alexishall
Newsletter: quicunquevult.com/newsletter

Enjoy more stories like *Shadows & Dreams* at RiptidePublishing.com!

Damned if You Do
ISBN: 978-1-62649-023-9

Falling Sky
ISBN: 978-1-62649-040-6

Earn Bonus Bucks!

Earn 1 Bonus Buck for each dollar you spend. Find out how at RiptidePublishing.com/news/bonus-bucks.

Win Free Ebooks for a Year!

Pre-order coming soon titles directly through our site and you'll receive one entry into a drawing to win free books for a year! Get the details at RiptidePublishing.com/contests.

CPSIA information can be obtained at www.ICGtesting.com
Printed in the USA
LVOW07s1159110916

504132LV00007B/647/P